Other titles by this author

Darcy Farthing Novels

    Currents of Vengeance

    Current Assets

    Alternate Currents

    A Current Deception

    Currents of Sin

Children's Book

    Sometimes Naughty-Always Loved:
    Mary and Her Big Cat Brain

Currents Deep and Deadly

Currents Deep and Deadly

Arleen Alleman

Copyright © 2010 by Arleen Alleman.

Library of Congress Control Number: 2010912078

Revised Edition: 2019

ISBN: Softcover 978-1-0749-7053-6

All rights reserved. No part of this book may be reproduced or transmitted in any form or by any means, electronic or mechanical, including photocopying, recording, or by any information storage and retrieval system, without permission in writing from the copyright owner.

This is a work of fiction. Names, characters, places and incidents either are the product of the author's imagination or are used fictitiously, and any resemblance to any actual persons, living or dead, events, or locales is entirely coincidental.

To Ellen Taylor
Mom, you are greatly loved and missed.

Acknowledgments

I am grateful to Dr. DiAnn Ellis, Mildred Simmons, Marilyn and Bob Tribou, and Sharon Wolff for their early reads of my manuscript. Their candid comments and encouragement were absolutely essential to completion of this project. Thanks also to Liz Jordan, a true diplomat, for her insights about U.S. consulates. A big thank you to the real-life cruise lines and their employees, who provided not only pleasurable experiences but a wealth of technical information about cruise ships and shipboard activities. That said, for this story I created a fictional cruise line and ship with some characteristics that, to my knowledge, do not exist in the real world. The history and geographical references throughout are the result of research combined with my own travel experiences in the ports of call.

I am glad you found this book. It is a new and improved edition of the first novel in a six-book series. The subsequent stories take place during a five-year period in the lives of the main characters you meet in this book. Their ordeal aboard the Sea Nymph forged lifelong bonds, and together they face more mystery, crime, and violence, as well as emotional ups and downs inherent in friendship and romance. There is also more travel to near and far destinations, and a celebration of diversity and rational thinking. I hope you enjoy all the Darcy Farthing Adventures. I welcome honest reviews posted on booksellers' Websites. Reviews are very helpful to readers and invaluable to authors. You can communicate with me anytime at www.arleenalleman.com, on Facebook, or @aallemanwrites on Twitter. Happy reading!

I'm in a cage with bars of glass,
Can't break out to save my ass.
I have the strength, but lack the will.
Those deadly splinters scare me still.

Darcy E. Farthing, 1989

Prologue

A golden girl is rowing a golden boat a hundred yards off shore where the clear turquoise shallows dip steeply to deep sapphire. Her boat is in fact painted bright yellow with a horizontal white stripe just above the waterline. The tall slender darkly tanned girl wears white shorts with an orange halter top.

If you stood on the fine white sand bathed in the purest white light looking into the summer sun on this hot January morning, she would appear as a bright spot gliding effortlessly against the tide. But the girl's movements are not without effort for she has been rowing back and forth parallel to the shore for more than an hour without resting.

She feels the intense ache in her powerful shoulders as she glides through the water creating tiny splashes along the sides of the boat where the oars rhythmically slide into the smooth sea. She experiences the tug of a familiar hypnotic state of mind as she forces herself to ignore the burning pain radiating down her arms and into her wrists.

Her long fingers encircle the oars and she adjusts her hold on the smooth patina, developed from so many sweating palms and fingers gripping and sliding over the turned oak. She glances at her feet with their long slender toes tipped in fuchsia, braced against the bench in front of her. She feels the tickle of long wavy blonde hair on her cheeks as it flutters in a breeze of her own making. *Where did these traits come from, this hair, and my eyes—especially my eyes?*

These are questions the girl has been asking about herself, but only of herself, for as long as she can remember. It would do no good and perhaps considerable harm to involve others in her queries. But often at night when she dreams of the pleasant and secret shadowy time with her beautiful blonde guardian angel and experiences the lovely feeling of belonging, she believes she almost knows the answers.

She sighs deeply, tosses her head to shake the strands of moist hair from her face, and resignedly turns toward shore as she has done on so many mornings. Perspiration trickles down her back with a welcome coolness now that the sea breeze pushes her forward. The pain is stronger now, but she shuts it out with an even stronger mind. Despite the heat, she shudders with the thought and hope that one day she might gain a better understanding of the secret dream.

Part One
Welcome Aboard

1

You can truly believe you have a handle on how your little slice of life fits into the whole pie. But just when you think pepperoni is all you'll ever need, someone dumps a bunch of onions, peppers, and mushrooms on top and a mind-blowing revelation smacks you in the mouth. My name is Darcy Farthing, and this is my slice-of-life-with-everything-on-it story.

The thing is I never expected to write a book about my own experiences. I always tried to keep personal matters private—it seemed impossible to explain some aspects of my life and somehow dishonest and confusing to speak only about carefully selected pieces of the whole me. Another reason for guarding my privacy was that I didn't seem to feel the same way about the world as most people and just couldn't believe things they believed. I was a cynic. So I just stopped talking about myself and my beliefs or lack thereof.

But it wasn't as if I needed an intervention or a self-help book. I had made an educated and well-thought out decision that gave me comfort with my outlook. The world abounds with all sorts of intriguing mysteries and perhaps sadly, they all have rational explanations—even those still beyond our understanding. I knew just because billions of people believe something doesn't make it true.

Through the millennia many widespread beliefs have been challenged and debunked. It once was common knowledge that the sun and planets rotated around the earth. Amazingly and at their own peril, for sixteen centuries, scientists—including Copernicus in 1543—proposed theories of a heliocentric solar system. Finally the scientific evidence and the invention of the telescope provided the smack needed for the masses to accept that the earth was not the all-important center of the solar system.

Despite my cynicism about common belief systems, I have to say my story describes unlikely events many would attribute to a higher power. I've come to understand that inherent spirituality and human politics for that matter are basic underpinnings of all communication and societal development, so they must influence virtually every thought and action, and must flow through the natural currents of every real-life story.

During the past year, when I realized I was going to write this book, I spent a lot of time thinking about how our lives seem to flow between events and how we can choose to ride one current or another at any given time, thereby passing up alternate currents we may not even know exist. It's as if we can lie back and float down calm waters enjoying a particular view of the world on either side, perhaps believing there is a natural order or predestination guiding us. Or we can frantically fight the rapids constantly trying to make midstream corrections because we believe we are truly masters of our own destiny.

I envision these currents flowing from second to second, from one event to the next, until they arrive at a completed life of experiences. Inevitably, because there are so many of us and only so much space and time for each of our lives to unfold, our currents intertwine with those of others, and real and complex coincidences are inevitable. I have now come to accept that small-world stories occur with startling regularity with no particular meaning, and I've also decided as much as any other variable, the way currents flow through our lives comes down to chance.

But chance or randomness can be scary, so people generally want to believe that everything happens for a reason. This apophenia, the built-in requirement to see meaning in everything, appears to be a genetically or culturally inherited trait. And so ideas abound about how everything must be connected.

Take for example synchronicity theory, first proposed in the 1920s by the Swiss psychiatrist Carl Jung, as an explanation for why meaningful events happen at the same time but are not related by cause. Jung believed that an overarching structure binds such events together and somehow incorporates the human psyche with the physical world. Synchronicity is a complicated paranormal explanation for why coincidences occur. As with spiritual theories that try to explain how individuals and their "energy" are directly tied to a cosmic plan, people want to believe these ideas are supported by scientific evidence.

But there can be no scientific basis for a construct that is outside the physical world—if such a realm exists—because its validity cannot be tested or measured. In fact, scientists are taught to overcome their apophenic tendencies in order to analyze variables and separate causal relationships—those with statistical significance—from outcomes that can be attributed to chance or coincidence.

If you think about it, trillions of events are happening in the world at the same time every moment of every day, and some are directly related while most have absolutely no connection in space or time. But somewhere along the continuum of events there have to be overlapping occurrences that will have meaning for at least one of us, but only if we are in the right place at the right time to recognize them.

For example, as you wait in line at your local Starbucks you are surprised to encounter a person from your hometown on the other side of the country. They would be there even if you decided to skip your latte that day. Or, by chance you find a potato chip with a shape that, to you, is a meaningful representation of a famous historical figure. You publicize your discovery and others agree. If I found the same chip I would simply eat it and miss the opportunity to make big bucks on eBay.

Armed with this logic, perhaps I should not be troubled by the layers of coincidence that occurred during the four weeks I describe in this book. But I am, probably because I'm only human. Many of the bizarre happenings have been resolved, but others remain mysteries. The circumstances were not only baffling and traumatic, but changed my life and the lives of others in deeply fundamental ways. I suppose that is why I decided to write about them.

I'll describe these events from my own observations and perspective. In the event I must describe other people's thoughts, actions, and histories, I trust the reader will forgive me for creatively filling my knowledge gaps with logical extrapolations, which do not change the essence of the story.

And so taking a deep breath and trying to suspend my natural inclination toward privacy, I begin in January of 2008 at a time when I believed as in many times before that finally I'd found a man who could accept my quirks and savage independence and could also be the life partner I craved. He and I were embarking on what promised to be an exciting and romantic trip of a lifetime.

2

"Please remove your cap and sunglasses, miss." I heard the cute Australian accent and looked up at the tall skinny security guy with spiky blond hair grinning down at me. He gestured down at his partner, a squatty gal photographer standing beside him, as he checked out my boarding card—and me. "Thank you, Ms. Farthing."

"Now look at this spot," the gal said, as Aussie kept grinning at me while he pointed to a round white sticker just below the lens of the boxy camera contraption. I understood that this process was creating a necessary record of each face that would be accepted on and off the ship during the cruise, but I didn't like it because I looked like crap.

"Smile, and welcome aboard," she said, obviously straining for some enthusiasm. "And have a wonderful trip."

"Gooday," said Aussie, still grinning as he handed back my passport and plastic boarding card before turning his attention to the next person in line. I was packed tightly in the midst of a bunch of strangers—except for my guy, Doc—inside the Jetway-like loading ramp winding ever higher from dock level to the ship.

Suddenly I realized I was developing an alarming queasiness with nowhere to go. The sickening feel of my unwashed, hat-dented blonde mop lying limp against my cheek was only adding to my discomfort. That was when I realized I was already having second thoughts about the hastily planned trip. *It's a little late for that,* I told myself. *Come on, Darcy, who wouldn't want to sail away to South America for four weeks on a romantic cruise?* But I had to admit the thought of spending the next month alone with Doc and captive on a floating village with nearly four thousand strangers was already giving me a tight-chest feeling. Not good at my advanced age of forty.

After the ID photo, which felt like an exceptionally bad motor vehicle department experience, I jammed the beige go with everything Liz Claiborne cap back onto my head and replaced my retro black Wayfarer sunglasses. At least no one knows me, I thought, as we continued past security toward the top of the gangway.

I have to admit at that moment I still thought Doc (that was my pet name for Dr. Jason Johnson, self-proclaimed to be the finest general practitioner in Denver) could be the sexiest guy ever, and his perpetually tousled sandy hair and gold-flecked brown bedside manner eyes were a smash combination that pretty much made me lie down and roll over for any idea he had. "What?"

"Darcy, I asked twice if you want to go straight to the buffet for lunch or directly to our cabin." What Jason really wanted to know was did I want to christen the room immediately or was food more important to me than partaking of his fare.

"Well, what do you think, Doc? I guess the cabin will be great." Shit, never mind I'm on the verge of fainting from low blood sugar because last night I pretended I wasn't hungry because you needed me to need you more than food. *Is that about the same as wanting me to need you more than life?* Then the single cup of coffee and dry bagel this morning after a rough-and-tumble night at the Holiday Inn were not helping my feeling that things were happening too quickly, and something was sorely lacking.

This was my first cruise, and Doc had assured me I would absolutely love the experience. My intuition and common sense were already telling me otherwise, but at my own peril I was ignoring these helpful traits in favor of nurturing our relationship.

I found myself pondering what I would say to another woman who admitted she was "living" for her guy in order to keep him—like my mother did. I'm not even married to Jason, for Christ's sake. Oops, I've been trying to stop using profanity, not because I think it's a sin, but because I know that swearing on a long-dead guy is pointless no matter how extraordinary he might have been. Anyway, I would probably make a rude comment and tell that woman to grow up and get some self-esteem. No guy is worth doing things you really don't want to. *Really?*

I did not arrive at this obvious insight through my inherent pragmatism, science education, or extensive and checkered dating history. Nor was it a result of my own two-year marriage, which is ancient history and a nightmare that culminated in, without a doubt, the worst act of my life . . . *let's jump off that thought train right now.*

No, this lesson was learned early in life from the pitiful Patricia Farthing. She demonstrated how easy it can be to completely deny your own reality and happiness for the sake of security even with an occasional black eye not to mention hundreds of nights of emotional torture. With all that wisdom gained at Mom Patricia's knee, I remember the first thing I promised myself was I would not be like her and marry an asshole like she did. That pretty much set the stage for breaking promises to myself.

Even as a child, I knew my home situation was not normal. I was particularly bothered by the knowledge that as far as I could tell I was the only kid with an alcoholic, abusive father and an unbelievably weak-willed mother. In fact, sad to admit, I sort of looked down on my parents or at least viewed them as people with whom I had little in common and from whom I could learn almost nothing positive. I remember daydreaming that I was adopted and about finding my real parents were beautiful, bright, loving people. Then I woke up and just knew I had to put up with Patricia and Richard for a few more years but eventually would be able to leave them behind.

As it turned out, I did leave the tattered nest right after high school thanks to a science scholarship. Since I was already living in Albuquerque, it was convenient to attend UNM. I did not want to live at home so I worked at a series of nondescript jobs in the partly refurbished Nob Hill neighborhood not far from the campus. Maybe I really was adopted, since I turned out to be above average in the smarts category. Despite some devastating personal setbacks I managed to achieve an undergraduate degree and a master's in biochemistry.

As happens fairly often when I have a few moments of inactivity or stress, my thoughts wildly digress. I was jolted back to the present by Doc's insistent nudging as he tried to move me onto the deck of the ship. To be fair, Doc and I planned this vacation together when we were celebrating our two-week anniversary. With my history of short-lived romances, somehow it made sense at the time. Now two months later I realized the fact we were still together wasn't much to brag about, but for me it was the longest run I'd had with the same guy in ten years.

So here I was on this month-long vacation, at first happy and excited about getting away from work and having a new experience. But here at the top of the gangway sandwiched between Doc in back and a very overweight and wheezing woman in front, who had apparently forgotten to pack her antiperspirant, second thoughts ran rampant. It occurred to me perhaps I hadn't fully factored in the reality of being with all these people, including Doc, 24-7 in a somewhat confined space. *I'm already feeling more captive than captivated by our vacation plans and the World of Seas Cruise Line.*

Then the discussion, dare I say mini-argument, about the type of stateroom we would book came back to me. Jason insisted all we needed was an inside cabin, which means no window much less a private outside balcony, and don't even think about a suite. He said it would be silly to spend the extra money for an ocean view when we would hardly ever be in the room. Besides, he reasoned rather paradoxically with his hand traveling the length of my naked back, the dark and cozy 160-square-foot cabin will be very romantic.

I acquiesced easily since I knew absolutely zero about cruise ships and let Doc make all the arrangements. Now after an additional six weeks to gain a more enlightened understanding of Jason, I was not so naive. I knew the conservative, sometimes downright cheap Jason, not the sexy, romantic one, made that decision.

We finally crossed the wide deck and entered through double glass doors into the *Sea Nymph*, a name that was an oxymoron if I ever heard one, since far from nymph like, it was an enormous whale of a ship. I hadn't even had a chance to look around outside before we were pushing our way through a horde of our fellow cruisers to enter through the glass doors. Most of them seemed to be just standing in the way peering goggle-eyed at the sumptuous brass, granite, and marble interior.

How does this thing stay afloat? To my eye, everything was extraordinarily heavy, ornate, and out of place in a seagoing environment. The walls were virtually papered with large framed modern art pieces and three-dimensional paper and metal sculptures of birds, kites, and stylized airplanes.

Because of my New Mexico roots and if I am honest, because I've a touch of OCD, I prefer minimalist Santa Fe-style décor, so this opulence seemed a bit oppressive. In fact, my chest felt as if it was about to cave in, and bright lights flashed at my periphery, only some of which emanated from the wild colors and patterns draped on every size and shape of human form imaginable. It was like Mardi Gras with the gaudy people clashing dramatically with their opulent surroundings.

I told myself it was probably just hunger and anxiety getting to me, but just as I thought I might actually lose consciousness, we were suddenly somehow clear of most of the crowd and standing on what appeared to be a dance floor in a more or less round room about forty feet across.

With fewer people in the way, I glanced down at my sequined strappy feet and was surprised to see beneath them was a beautiful and complicated mosaic star pattern. The floor was fashioned from at least eight different colors of natural inlayed woods. They ranged from dark mahogany or even ebony to something like red purpleheart or maybe rosewood, cherry, and green poplar, all the way to the palest white pine. It was absolutely stunning.

A bar situated at the far edge of the room was not yet open, but I could feel it beckoning to me nonetheless. The construction was fairly typical, made of light-colored wood with vertical grooves on the front and a pleasing curve that extended about twenty feet in front of a mirrored back wall. Glass shelves hanging against the mirror were well stocked with high-end liquor bottles but only half as many as there appeared to be. Out in front, nine comfortable-looking stools upholstered in a contemporary teal, brown, and mustard geometric pattern invitingly awaited patrons.

A crew member dressed in a crisp white jacket with black tie worked industriously behind the bar, and he periodically turned in our direction to complete some task. Like a classic Latin movie star, he was dark and quite handsome but not tall, and as we approached I could tell he was humming rather tunelessly as he sliced lemons. I really wanted to go over and sit on a stool to chat with him, and I pushed the limit of my monovision contacts to see his name tag. Too bad, we were too far away, and I had no legitimate reason to move closer with Doc impatiently moving toward the elevators.

As we passed by the cocktail lounge in front of the bar, I noticed little groups of teal faux suede bucket chairs arranged around spotless round marble tables. *All right, this could be any classy club on land, couldn't it?* Suddenly I was imagining the Latin bartender looking appreciatively into my big blues with a fabulous white-toothed smile as he handed me an icy cold extra dry Ketel One martini, slightly dirty with extra olives and shaken, thank you.

I was still feeling a little queasy when I happened to look up and almost fell over backward from vertigo. We were on a ship but the space defied logic by soaring up about eight stories. The balconies of upper decks surrounded this vertical space and light poured from somewhere I couldn't see from my vantage point. Real or fake—I couldn't tell which—philodendrons, caladiums, palms, bird of paradise, and other sundry plants I couldn't identify draped from the first two levels cascading down in a stunning jungle effect.

A strong sense of déjà vu washed over me, and suddenly I remembered the Marriott Marquis on Peachtree Center Avenue in Atlanta, a beautiful hotel with a similar soaring central lobby where I once spent a few days compliments of my employer, Shrinden Pharmaceuticals. That was about thirteen years ago when I began my job as a prescription drug sales representative.

The trip was memorable not only because my work was new and exciting and I had money for the first time, but because it marked the first of many short-lived affairs with physicians who were also my clients. I suddenly had a brief and unwanted flash of recall. A Middle Eastern complexion, lots of body hair, and not much else of note mercifully passed quickly . . . *Best not to dwell on old trysts now that I'm settled with Doc.*

With more than a hundred work trips under my frequent-flier belt, I still like to travel. I'm comfortable with airplanes and even the security nuisance. I guess airports are still like my second home, and I even relish the long waits in gate areas due to cancelled flights. I think this is because the delay is out of my control, and it's about the only time I have to myself to read a novel without feeling massive quantities of guilt over the fact I'm not memorizing protocols for the latest miracle drug to push on health care professionals.

I like airport bars too. After all I met Doc at Lefty's on B concourse at DIA. I had stopped for one drink while I waited for my flight to Chicago, and there he was nursing a Fat Tire and looking like a young Robert Redford in a crisp pale blue oxford shirt, perfectly fitted red tag 501s, and incongruously, Gucci loafers with (you have to be kidding) no socks. He was so cool! When we began to hit it off and exchange information, neither of us could believe we were both from the local area rather than the typical, "Oh, you're from DC and only get out this way every two months or so?" *And you're probably married anyway.*

Instead, my two-bedroom adobe-style patio home situated on a bluff overlooking Colorado Springs is an hour commute to Doc's million-dollar restored 1920s craftsman on Downing Street near Denver's upscale Washington Park. The irony occurred to me that Jason is a doctor I met in an airport rather than one who is a client Shrinden pays me to hook up with, so to speak. Somehow, this seemed all the more reason to believe he was the life partner I was looking for. In retrospect, I guess that was odd thinking for someone who did not believe in fate.

Just as I was deciding part of my present discomfort was due to this ocean-travel business being way outside my flying comfort zone, Jason slipped his arm around my shoulder. His lips brushed my ear, causing a shiver and, uh oh, was that a wave of nausea? Needless to say this was not the pleasant sensation it should have been, and his words didn't help. "Baby, it looks like we've boarded late enough so the cabin will be ready for occupancy, and we can spend the afternoon there—just you and me in paradise."

"Oh boy, Doc, what could be better?" How about the food court, the pool, the bingo parlor, a lovely deck chair in the sun, this bartender uh bar, or hanging out on the prow like Kate and Leonardo? But OK, I'd committed to the accommodations and now to a romantic—maybe there's room service—afternoon ensconced there, so off we went to find the love nest.

3

Having boarded on deck 6 we had to descend to deck 2 to find our stateroom. As we waited for the elevator behind three spry seventy-something couples, I couldn't help but notice the quaintness of their matching shirts. One his and hers set of pale blue tees was adorned with a huge picture of a beach with a purple stingray wearing only sunglasses and a big grin. He or she—thankfully it was impossible to tell—rested on a lounge chair under a cheery red-and-white striped umbrella. A huge pink hotel loomed in the background, and the unlikely scene was underscored with the words SCUBA ARUBA in large orange letters. These folks had obviously been around.

As we entered the elevator among the giggling, drunk-on-fun seniors, I tried to imagine Mom Patricia and Daddy Dick in this kind of happy, healthy, corny togetherness. Although only in their sixties, it was utterly impossible to imagine them healthy or happy much less traveling to exotic ports of call. Just then Doc gave me a rolling-eyes look that said *quaint* was not the word he would use to describe our travel companions.

When we finally arrived at deck 2 we'd lost the giddy folks to the upper levels. Just outside the elevator Doc consulted a three-dimensional Plexiglas floor plan shaped like the hull of the ship then motioned for me to follow. *Isn't deck 2 barely above the waterline and the crew's quarters? Is this steerage or third class or something?*

My sense of direction has never been that sharp, but my sinking feeling matched the level of our deck as we negotiated the maze of narrow passageways lined on both sides with stateroom doors all looking disconcertingly alike. The passages were subtly lit by soft fans of light rising from stone wall sconces spaced at twenty-foot intervals. The atmosphere was quite elegant, so why did the word *dungeon* keep looping through my mind? More unusual artwork adorned most of the walls in the spaces between doors, but how could anyone appreciate it in the close quarters and poor lighting? As I trailed along behind Doc, my ill feeling morphed into something much worse. *I'm afraid I'll never find my own way back to the light and the pleasant central area with my already-favorite bartender.*

Up ahead, I saw with relief that cruise pro Jason had found stateroom 2021. As usual I was bringing up the rear pulling my wheeled carry-on bag. Suddenly movement from the right caught my eye. I was passing what appeared to be a workroom for the crew. The door was propped open, and at a glance I could see a stainless steel sink and counter with shelves above and an ice machine to one side. Toward the back of the small space two men dressed in black—crew uniforms I assumed—stood facing away from the door conversing with their heads close together. They did not appear to notice us.

My well-honed inquisitiveness automatically slowed my step. I almost came to a stop as I fiddled with my bag, catching a sentence or two as I edged past the doorway. One man was saying in heavily accented English, "I don't know how I let myself get talked into this. It is crazy dangerous."

The other quickly answered with a lighter Spanish accent, "Just remember we are in it all the way. Think about the money. You know it can be done easily."

I had moved along the passageway out of hearing range. The short exchange was odd, and although what I'd heard was completely out of context, it was disturbing. Looking back on it I'm not sure why I didn't mention this to Jason. Instead, I proceeded to our cabin on the right side of the passageway where he was holding the door open for me having used his ID card/door key to gain entry.

4

Mick stepped down heavily from the van onto the warm pavement, took a few steps to the side, and waited patiently for his luggage to be off-loaded. "Thanks," he said, handing the driver a three-dollar tip. After hoisting a navy blue carry-on bag to his shoulder, he dragged the matching drop-side duffel toward the terminal. He was anxious about his decision, but for good or ill he was committed, having left his vehicle in Miami and taken the shuttle to the dock to board the *Sea Nymph*.

Waiting in line to enter the two-story white stucco building, his thoughts wandered back two days to when he was sitting at his center island gazing at the beautiful mica and garnet spotted granite while surfing the Internet with his morning coffee. He so enjoyed the quiet, albeit lonely, mornings in the modern kitchen of his Florida-style home.

Every now and then he glanced out the picture window in the breakfast nook where he could see a wide section of the canal and his private boat dock at the bottom of the gently sloping perfectly mown lawn. Mick didn't have a boat, not yet at least. Maybe next year he would find the enthusiasm to buy one. He stood up and craned his neck to study the water but was disappointed when he didn't see any visiting manatees. He looked back at the Web page as it finished loading, and that was when he saw the ad for last-minute cruise bookings. He made a quick and fateful decision that he would take the four-week South America excursion.

He never even entertained the idea of a cruise back when he had a life and wondered why during the happy pre-cancer days he never thought of taking a vacation like this with Beth. With that realization a cascade of grief and guilt poured over him so powerful that he grasped the edge of the counter to keep from collapsing off his stool. Even after two years he struggled every day with lasting depression due to the devastating loss of his wife of fifteen years and, just six months later, of his beloved parents in a bizarre accident. He was definitely not yet himself, and he'd done a lot of things he would never have thought possible in his search for relief from the pain and loneliness that seemed to be eating him—consuming his life, really.

Over the past two months he had thought a lot about taking the cruise, ever since he spent Thanksgiving in Las Vegas. With no family left to celebrate the holidays with, the trip to Vegas would be an impersonal distraction—at least that is what he told himself. But it turned out a little personal after all. At the Athens Olympia Hotel and Casino, he renewed acquaintance with a woman he'd known briefly but intimately a few years ago when he visited Vegas on a business trip during Beth's illness—an indiscretion that had caused him horrible aching guilt ever since.

The affair was short-lived, but he knew she was a very good person with a messed-up life, and he still thought about her now and then. On the recent trip when he went to visit her, he began to think that perhaps she could become an important part of his life again and could help diminish his emotional pain. But as it turned out she had big problems of her own—a lot of baggage and a powerful and nasty husband. Ultimately Mick decided to move on and rejected the idea of the cruise, which they had discussed.

That is, until he found this last-minute discount booking opportunity. Not that money issues were even on his radar anymore. The trip would consist of four weeks on a ship sailing from Miami around the tip of South America and ending in Valparaiso, Chile. Then a long flight back to Miami, which he didn't need to worry about either. He would essentially be alone, but that was something he was starting to get used to, and he was on a mission of sorts. *Well, what the hell, why not go for it, since I don't have much to lose anymore?*

So he'd made the necessary calls including one to his boss at the Government Accountability Office in DC to ask for an extension of his leave. The conversation with Ken Worthford, assistant comptroller general for Law and Justice, had been tense. Mick's impression was that Ken's generosity and understanding regarding his personal crisis were waning. Under Ken's management, as director of State Law Enforcement Issues, Mick led a team of twenty analysts who conducted audits and investigations of federally funded law enforcement agencies.

But over the past two years, he'd used virtually all his annual leave and quite a bit of sick leave in order to avoid the demands of his job. He was entitled to this time off of course, but that didn't get deadlines met and reports issued to the Congress.

Ken told him that too many draft reports were piling up and needed Mick's review immediately upon his return. With obvious annoyance he added, "Senator Sawyer has called several times asking where you are, but I don't recall any assignment you have right now that involves the senator, so I don't understand why he would be calling you directly."

The comment was blatantly facetious. Since GAO is essentially the investigative arm of the Congress, Mick technically worked for the members including New York senator Bill Sawyer. Yet he and Bill had been close friends since undergraduate school at Cornell where they both started out as political science majors. Of course, Bill moved on to prelaw and eventually launched his successful political career, while Mick ended up with an accounting degree and an MBA. Ken was less than ecstatic about their relationship, which he perceived as a conflict of interest, but Mick didn't really care because his few close friendships took priority over almost everything else in his life, especially now.

"It's OK, Ken. It's personal, and I'll call Bill before I leave." Ken's reaction to this was a prolonged silence ending with chilly and obviously reluctant approval for the additional month's leave, ostensibly because January was a slow month for congressional decision makers . . . as if they thought and acted with greater expediency in any other month. Mick knew this would be the last time he could beg off of work and that after this trip he would have to get back to his job full time.

After hanging up, he called Bill and caught him as he was leaving his office for the day. Hearing his friend's voice always improved Mick's mood. "Hey, buddy, Ken says you've been looking for me. What's up?"

"Hi, it's good to hear your voice. I've been a little worried. When are you coming home? Happy hours at Sam and Harry's are not the same without you."

"Well, believe it or not I'm about to leave on a four-week cruise around the tip of South America, so I won't be seeing you for a while longer." Mick waited for his friend to answer until the pause became awkward. Just as he started to add an explanation, Bill finally spoke softly and deliberately.

"Mick, what the hell are you doing? The idea of a cruise right now frankly seems nuts. I'm worried about you, and I know Ken is too. Forget the cruise and come home. You can distract yourself with work, and you do have friends here, you know."

"Yeah, I know, and I know how it sounds. Just trust me on this. It's something I want to do, and then I'll be back to work full bore . . . just one more month."

"I don't know, this isn't sounding so grounded." Bill stopped and sighed audibly. Then, "Oh, what the hell, be sure to call me as soon as you get back. I'll meet you at your condo and we can catch up. Anyway, it sounds like a very exciting trip. You know, going around Cape Horn on a ship can be a rough experience, and cold even though it's summer down there. Take a coat and have a good trip. You deserve it, buddy."

"Thanks, I'm all set, and I'm really not cracking up. I promise I'll tell you all about it when we get together. Take care. Bye."

That evening Mick cleaned his house and washed and put away his clothes. Then he packed his bag, trying to envision what people wear on a cruise ship and mindful of the World of Seas online suggestions regarding appropriate dinner attire.

Then yesterday afternoon he'd locked up the peach-colored ranch-style house his parents left him along with two million dollars, drove out of his neighborhood, through the small downtown area of Marco Island, and across the short bridge to the mainland. He pointed his new loaded-to-the-grill silver Range Rover onto Route 41 away from the Gulf of Mexico and toward the Atlantic and the waiting *Sea Nymph*.

He always enjoyed the relatively peaceful two-hour drive through the Big Cypress Preserve and the Everglades; and he tried to relax and clear his mind by watching for white-tailed deer, turkey, hogs, alligators, and especially the mysterious Florida panther, which is actually a cougar.

In reality, he hardly ever saw animals along the slightly raised roadway that cut through flat wet lowlands thick with marsh grasses, scrubby bushes, and patches of eerie forbidding swampland. It was just a game he played with himself to pass the time like the ones he and his parents played during their frequent family vacations. He couldn't even recall exactly how many times they had flown down from their home in Harrisburg during winter school breaks to spend time in rented cottages on sunny beaches, and on deliciously warm drives around southern Florida.

He squinted into the climbing sun and lowered his visor. Glancing at his reflection in the small mirror, he brushed the dark bangs off his forehead. He didn't like the look of dark shadows encircling his eyes. He'd not been sleeping well for quite some time. Sighing, he adjusted the visor, and slipped into a recurring nostalgic thought process in which he tried to analyze the events that had reshaped his life during the past two years.

It always turned out the same though, and despite what he'd told Bill, he knew he'd been going a little crazy and somehow had to get back on track. Maybe this trip is a start in the right direction. *Get some closure, as they say. Or maybe I don't know what I'm getting myself into.* He understood that wanting to take responsibility in this case really didn't make sense. *Am I just getting involved with entanglements that are really none of my concern?*

The last few miles of his trip were not so pleasant or relaxing. Trying to keep his eyes straight ahead, he watched the road and traffic carefully, trying not to look too closely at the terribly run-down neighborhoods around the Miami downtown area. He finally arrived at the Marriott Hotel where he spent the night and left his car in the hotel parking garage for the duration of his travel . . . a frequent sleeper perk.

5

When Mick finally entered the terminal, he left his duffel bag with an agent who attached the label he'd printed off the cruise line's Web site. Then he found a place in the check-in line designated for last names beginning with *A* through *G*. He passed the time by watching the obviously excited passengers as they waited to complete the boarding process to start their dream vacations. Among them were many couples between forty and eighty as well as a few families with young children and teenagers.

All around him people were smiling and laughing, obviously thrilled to be starting this adventure. He guessed this really would be an exciting time if he thought of all the destinations he would get to see for the first and probably only time. Places he and Beth never even dreamed of visiting, like Barbados, Rio de Janeiro, Buenos Aires, and of course the Strait of Magellan and the Chilean fjords. Beth would be so thrilled to be embarking on this trip.

Suddenly an odd but familiar feeling of comfort enveloped him. Instinctively, he glanced to his right to enjoy the look of anticipation on Beth's face. Instead his eyes landed on the closest person to him, a middle-aged guy wearing a tan and pink Hawaiian shirt barely covering his expansive gut. Thumbing through his travel documents, the man peered impatiently over the heads of the couple directly in front of him in line. Mick's emotions crashed as they did from time to time. *How can my mind still get so confused?* At least this kind of disorientation seemed to be happening less frequently.

He shook off the disturbing mood and stepped up to the counter to present his passport and credit card. After checking his last-minute booking, the agent presented him with documents containing information about the cruise and a plastic card key, which, she explained, would allow him to board the ship, open his stateroom door, and also take the place of currency on the ship.

"You are all set, Mr. Clayton. Just go to your right and through the double doors and have a wonderful voyage." He walked away following her directions, and found himself inside the enclosed gangway where he quickly passed through security and boarded the *Sea Nymph*.

Suddenly feeling hungry, he quickly found his way to the gigantic buffet restaurant, aptly named the Whale's Tail, aft on deck 10. Sitting at an outside table he enjoyed a view of the coastline beyond the pier. Looking down at the dock, he watched members of the crew taking control of dozens of large wooden crates and hundreds of cardboard boxes. Forklift operators were busily transferring the containers from trailers to orderly stacks beside the ship while the crew systematically checked and counted all the items before hauling them onto a conveyor belt through cargo doors in the side of the ship. Mick thought for the first time about how daunting a task it must be to provision an ocean voyage of this kind.

Turning back to the inside activity, he was amazed at the amount and variety of food placed appealingly at the numerous buffet stations, all of which looked fresh and appetizing. He ate what for him was a lavish lunch consisting of several vegetable and seafood salads, cheeses, and fruits.

He even managed a little small talk with a couple seated at the table next to him. The Murrays were from New York and celebrating their twenty-fifth wedding anniversary. This was their first cruise as well, and seeing their closeness and anticipation brought back the sadness for his lost opportunities with Beth.

After lunch he considered a self-guided tour of the ship, but because he was still carrying his shoulder bag, he found himself navigating to his deck 8 stateroom instead. Cruising alone, he was paying almost the same amount as two people traveling together, but since reluctantly receiving his inheritance, he had not really splurged on anything except his car, so he'd opted for the last available stateroom with an outside balcony. He found cabin 8140 easily and was somewhat surprised at how well it was designed to accommodate passengers' belongings in such a small space. The compact room was about fourteen feet wide and twelve feet deep with the head of a king-sized bed against the right side wall. This left six feet of space between the foot of the bed and the far wall, which was almost entirely filled by a built-in light-colored wood cabinet with drawers and a desk, a small refrigerator, and a TV. The sliding glass door leading to the balcony was just beyond the bed, and beside it was a small couch and miniature coffee table.

Upon entering, he found a closet to the right and a bathroom to the left. The latter featured a small round shower with a sliding plastic door and a sink and vanity with mirrored cupboards covering the wall above. Overall, the cabin included a lot more storage space than he had expected. All that was lacking was room to move around.

He dropped his bag next to the bed, opened the glass door, and stepped out onto the narrow balcony. A patio lounge chair and a small round metal table were tucked against the wall dividing his balcony from the one next door, and a second patio chair completed the grouping. He stepped between the furniture to look over the railing. It was the side of the ship facing away from the dock. This would be the starboard side—the right side—he reminded himself as he leaned out and peered forward along the length of the ship to the bow. He stood watching as several much smaller craft navigated the waterway a short distance from where the *Sea Nymph* was moored.

A sleek and well-appointed private yacht with the not-so-imaginative name Candy Kane painted on the side was moving slowly through the water about five hundred feet away. Mick didn't know much about boats, but this one looked like a million, literally. It was at least one hundred fifty feet long with an aluminum hull painted a lush dark chocolate beneath three levels of pristine white deck.

From his high vantage point he saw the backs of two women sunbathing on lounge chairs next to a hot tub on the large sun pad. As he watched, a man appeared on deck with a tray of drinks and as the women turned over to accept the offering, Mick was treated to a view of four gorgeous naked breasts. *Jeez, this trip is getting off to a, um, titillating start.* As he stared down at the women laughing and sipping their mojitos or whatever, one of them glanced up and held up her glass seeming to toast him. He wondered whether she was Candy.

He leaned over the railing and peered each way along the length of the ship. Apparently due to the ongoing boarding process, he was virtually the only one out on a balcony. One moment he felt amused and relaxed and the next he was overtaken by a wave of mental and physical fatigue. He turned back into the room, closed the door, removed his shoes, and stretched out on the bed.

6

    Mick napped somewhat fitfully for an hour and was awakened by a knock on his door. He opened it to find an attractive dark-haired woman of about twenty-five dressed in the black slacks and blouse of the crew uniform. She introduced herself as Paulina Rosario, his stateroom attendant. She was delivering his duffel bag, and as she wheeled it in and placed it against the foot of the bed, she explained how she would take care of the cabin each day. She told him to contact her if he needed anything. This was not a sophisticated process since it amounted to simply opening the door and calling her name.

    Paulina said she was on the job in the immediate area taking care of her eight staterooms through the morning till midafternoon and again for a few hours in the evening. Her English was very good, and he was pleased that she seemed attentive and friendly since she would be in his room cleaning and fluffing several times each day for the next month. Mick noted that her name tag said "I'm from Argentina," so he politely asked if she would be able to visit her home during the cruise.

    "I will be able to leave the ship for a short time during the two days in Buenos Aires, but I won't have time to journey inland to my family's home in Cordoba. I do hope to see my sister, Flora, who works as a housekeeper for an American family in Buenos Aires."

    After Paulina left Mick alone, he decided to go exploring. He wound his way to a staircase, and climbed up four levels to the pool area at the top of the ship. He found himself far forward on deck 12 and slowly made his way aft. Amidships he found a rectangular swimming pool about thirty feet long and twenty feet wide surrounded by a large patio. In an alcove off to the side members of a steel drum band played

Caribbean music. Outfits of bright red, orange, and white floral shirts, white Bermuda shorts, and wide grins enhanced the tropical rhythms and ambiance.

Families and couples were already lounging on deck chairs arranged three rows deep along both long sides of the pool, and three couples sat in an oversized hot tub on a raised platform. Mick watched as two laughing, jostling teenage boys and a girl vied for the only two chairs left on the front row closest to the pool. No one was actually swimming.

He found himself slowly panning the crowd looking for familiar faces without success. Then he was distracted by a waiter who stopped directly in front of him with a tray of glasses filled with layers of thick yellow and pink liquid. "Would you like to try the drink of the day for the sail-away party, sir? It's a volcano made with rum, orange juice, strawberries, and guava."

"No thanks, maybe later." Checking his watch he saw it was 4:15 p.m. and then realized the ship was moving. *This is a little exciting.* At the port side railing, he watched with awe as the gigantic ship backed out of its slip then moved sideways and slowly eased away from the dock. As the ship turned to head away from shore, Mick marveled at the apparent maneuverability and wondered what it must be like to drive such an enormous conveyance.

Looking at so many couples standing at the railing happily juggling volcanoes and cameras, he thought about his own isolation. *Maybe it's time to think seriously about remedying that.* Pondering just how he could achieve a remedy, he again became lost in thought about the past and the events that led him to this trip. When he refocused on the present, he was surprised to see the Miami shoreline had become much smaller, and his view was dominated by ocean waves speeding by and lightly splashing along the side of the ship nine stories below. Looking over the side, the height combined with the moving water caused a bout of vertigo. He quickly looked up at the receding shoreline, regained his balance, then turned to leave the pool area.

Continuing aft, he soon arrived at another swimming pool covered with a retractable glass roof. This was obviously a more sedentary setting with elderly men and women lined up on padded lounge chairs. The warm, humid atmosphere under the closed canopy contained lots of hanging plants. Ornate furnishings and statues of giant shells, sea horses, and fish dominated the area—a decidedly underwater paradise theme.

No one was actually swimming in this beautiful gold-and-blue tiled pool either.

As he absorbed the ambiance and serenity, his eye fell on a middle-aged man lying beside the pool wearing swim trunks with a white towel thrown across his body. Although the man appeared to be alone, Mick quickly looked behind him and around the immediate vicinity to make sure he did not see anyone else he knew. The man did nothing but lie there with his eyes closed, but Mick experienced an odd sensation of disgust mingled with morbid curiosity. He forced himself to turn away.

As he continued aft, he found the spa and fitness center at the back of the ship. Treadmills, elliptical and spinning machines, as well as other exercise equipment dominated the large space. An open area with a wooden floor and mirrored wall could accommodate exercising, and fitness classes. Large windows allowed passengers to view the ocean as they worked off the thousands of extra calories they would likely consume. At least a dozen people were already taking advantage of the "free" exercise opportunity. Mick looked around but did not see anyone familiar. As he left the gym, he made a mental note to work out every day to counter the delicious and obviously ubiquitous food and drink.

7

I hate to spend time primping in front of a mirror, it is so girlie cliché, so I quickly dried and brushed my hair into a shoulder-length shag, gave my minimal makeup the once-over in the tiny bathroom, and stepped out to get the full effect in the mirror conveniently attached to the outside of the door. I was just standing there thinking how I looked surprisingly good and my yellow sleeveless linen dress was flattering, meaning it didn't accentuate my ass. I was going for a casual but sophisticated look with the gold strappy wedges, and I thought I had done pretty well. Actually, I was trying to distract myself from thoughts that were disturbing to say the least. Just in time, Doc stepped up behind me and interrupted my meditation.

"You look great, baby, are you ready to head out? Let's go up on deck to the sail-away party until it's time to go to the dining room."

"Sounds like a plan." I tried for a perky voice to match my outfit. The afternoon delight with Doc had been fine, but unfortunately I was now fairly sure he was not "the one" after all. Having admitted that, I was feeling kind of trapped in this month-long odyssey even though we'd only been on board a few hours. Of course I wasn't really stuck here since I could fly home from any port along the way if I had to.

It wasn't just the small cabin or confinement on the ship, but also having to go through the motions with Jason for four weeks including a total of fourteen days at sea. He did pay for the trip after all. But I just have to have my independence to say nothing of a little privacy, and those elements weren't going to be easy to come by.

Before we left the cabin, the mini-fridge provided sustenance in the form of small bags of cool ranch tortilla chips and stale M&Ms, swilled down with an orange soda. It was as if I hadn't eaten for a whole day. *Oh yeah, I haven't eaten for a whole day.*

Outside up on deck 11 we walked around the jogging track holding hands and chatting amiably. We listened to the sound of the steel drum band drifting down from the pool area above and watched the Miami skyline get smaller as we moved off into open water. After about an hour it seemed as though we were really out at sea, and then it was time for us to head to Mermaids Dining Room on deck 5 for the six o'clock dinner seating. As we made our way inside to the staircase, Doc said that during the night we would make way for Nassau and the ship would be docked by the time we got up in the morning.

When we arrived at the dining room, the maitre d' showed us to our assigned table, a six top with four people already seated. We sat down side by side and introduced ourselves to our tablemates.

I immediately focused my attention on Charlie Scott, a commercial realtor, and his partner, Don Freeburg, a freelance cartoonist from Seattle. They were very friendly guys who seemed completely at ease, and it quickly became apparent they were old hands at cruising. Charlie had thinning curly black hair that spiraled onto his forehead, intense brown eyes, and an open, pleasant face. He was a little pudgy and didn't appear to be very tall. Don on the other hand was downright gorgeous. He looked to be over six feet with shoulder-length wavy blond hair, classic symmetrical features, blue eyes, and a knockout gym-carved body. I couldn't help but think, albeit inappropriately, *what a waste*!

Their attire that first evening consisted of dark gray slacks with very hip matching tee shirts, one lime green and the other turquoise with the same rather elegant and vaguely familiar design on the front made of tiny bronze-colored studs. All through dinner I tried to figure out that logo. Finally, midway through my apple torte topped with cinnamon ice cream, I realized it was the lowercase Greek letter lambda.

Then I remembered something I hadn't thought about for nearly twenty years. A lesbian friend of mine in college wore a lambda pendant and once explained to me that since 1970 the symbol has been a way for gay people to recognize each other as well as being a sign of unity.

During the stimulating dinner conversation, Charlie and Don had unabashedly offered the news that their four-year-old daughter was the product of both their sperm having been artificially inseminated into a surrogate mother. They seemed delighted by the fact that they didn't know for certain which of them the biological father was. Obviously proud and conscientious parents, they assured us that little Penelope was safe and happy at home with her nanny while Papa and Daddy were taking a much-needed vacation.

They seemed at ease discussing their lives and appeared oblivious to the discomfort of the other obviously conservative couple at our table. Julie and Frank something or other literally squirmed in their seats and didn't say more than two words to any of us during the entire meal. She had such a look of obvious haughty distaste that I wanted to reach across the table and slap her into civility. Jason didn't seem comfortable either, which was a little surprising since he's a doctor. I found myself feeling thankful that if tonight was any indication, at least these dinners would not present much opportunity for intimacy between Doc and me.

My filet mignon with mushroom polenta was acceptable, but the two martinis were great, and those together with the dinner wine had me a little tipsy by the time we left Mermaids at seven thirty. We spent the next hour just wandering around on decks 4, 5, and 6, checking out the numerous cafes, cocktail lounges, shops, and the casino. Jason played a quarter poker machine for a few minutes but became nervous when he lost five dollars without hitting any big hands.

Then wonder of wonders, he leaned close to my face and whispered, "You know, baby, I'm really tired. I'd like to go back to the cabin and turn in. Maybe we can get up early in the morning, have coffee, and check out the gym before we go ashore."

So we returned to the cozy cabin at about nine. I fell asleep a few minutes after washing my face, undressing, and snuggling under the pure white eiderdown duvet. The bed was surprisingly comfortable except for the crack where the two single beds met in the middle. I avoided it as best I could and remember thinking I couldn't feel the ship's movement. There was, however, an almost imperceptible droning sound that was comforting in an odd way and seemed to lull me to sleep.

8

Meanwhile, up on deck 4, two men were arguing in hushed tones as they strolled around outside the ship. Suddenly one stopped and leaned menacingly toward the other with his finger jabbing the air an inch from his companion's nose. "This is getting really annoying and way too public," he hissed. "Stop this ridiculous whining! We are going to do what we have planned, and it is too late for second thoughts. Anyway, my future and everything I've ever wanted depends on this, and I always get what I want."

He was answered with a sarcastic scoff and then, "Of course it is fine for you. You will get what you want, but I'm beginning to wonder if any amount of money is worth the risk for me. When you first approached me, things were different. I didn't have the relationship I have now—too much to lose."

Instinctively he had been moving backward as he spoke and now found himself pushed up against the railing. A thin spear of pain shot down his arm, and he looked at it in bewilderment. The large meaty hand shooting from the pure white cuff and black sleeve was clenched like a vise pinching his bicep and cutting off the circulation. He looked up into the angry, hostile face now only a few inches from his and decided he had said enough.

"How would you like a firsthand demonstration of how the plan will work?" The hand tightened and slammed upward, thrusting his upper body over the railing. Then the attacker abruptly released his grip, turned, and strode away. The man left behind stood paralyzed with terror as he rubbed his arm and tried to suppress his nausea. He turned to face the railing and looked down at the ocean rushing along the side. *Things are getting way out of hand.* He swallowed the bitter taste of bile and stayed in that position for a long time before slowly making his way back inside.

* * *

Wandering about the ship, Mick found a wide staircase and descended to deck 6 where he walked forward again and checked out two cocktail lounges. The barstools were full as were most of the seats at the small tables. Once again he studied the faces of the passengers he encountered and continued his meandering. At a little before six, he realized he was supposed to go to dinner, but he had not changed clothes since boarding the ship and wasn't very hungry after his filling lunch, so he decided to skip the dining room and instead opted for an open seat at the Center Bar.

He sipped two Coronas with lime wedges pushed down inside the bottles while he had a pleasant chat with Manuel Delgado, the friendly Columbian bartender, about the features of the *Sea Nymph*. Later, Mick went back up to the Whale's Tail buffet, where he ate a light but delicious meal of freshly grilled wild salmon with mushroom polenta and asparagus. At about eight he returned to his cabin.

Kicking off his loafers he lay back on the bed. Flipping through channels, he saw that *Superman II* was just beginning. He had not seen this sequel to the 1978 *Superman: Man of Steel,* and he thought he would enjoy the distraction. But he found he didn't like it as much as the original film. Gene Hackman and Ned Beatty were pretty good, as were the outer space effects and the icy Fortress of Solitude. For some reason he didn't care for Margot Kidder as Lois. To him she didn't seem the right type to be Superman's girlfriend.

When he began to get restless around ten, he had a thought and impulsively reached for the telephone on the nightstand. He dialed the operator and asked if he could get the room number of a friend who was on board. As he feared, since the ship was just like any other good hotel, the operator said she would ring a guest's stateroom for him but could not provide a number.

"That's OK," Mick lied. "I'll be meeting with my friend later tonight." After he hung up, the room began to feel stifling despite the large open slider leading to his balcony. *I'm starting to lose it already. I have to find some patience and some ways to occupy myself until I figure things out.* He decided to start by returning to the Center Bar for another chat with Manuel. For some reason he felt comfortable there. Then an idea struck him, and he decided he would also have to check out the casino.

9

The sky is extraordinarily beautiful tonight. Captain Espen Oldervoll gazed out through the floor-to-ceiling windows spanning the forward wall of the bridge. This 130-by-20-foot room extended across the entire ship at the front of deck 10 and as such was a far cry from its namesake, the literal bridge that extended across a paddle-wheel boat in both directions from the wheel house allowing the captain to walk out to, and see beyond, the large wheels on either side.

Instead, both ends of Captain Espen's bridge had "wings," which were small glassed in rooms cantilevered over the water. From there he and his crew of navigators, three first and three second mates, could view the sides of the one-thousand-foot-long ship by normal sight or with the use of infrared cameras installed under the wings and at the rear of the vessel—something extremely important for maneuvering the large vessel in and out of ports.

The focal point of the bridge was the navigation control center, a large horseshoe-shaped console with two plush pilot chairs in the middle, facing numerous computer screens. The enormous front windows overlooking the bow and a wide swath of sea dominated this USS *Enterprise*—like space. The controls featured the very latest high-tech positioning systems, not unlike those on modern U.S. naval ships: not only the familiar Global Positioning System with its twenty-four satellites, but also the Global Navigation System, which uses a network of seventeen Russian satellites. Together, these systems provided the *Sea Nymph*'s crew with positional accuracy within a meter.

The remainder of the bridge housed additional controls and monitors for the ship's hundreds of systems including lighting, fire and watertight doors, four separate radar systems, safety monitoring, lifeboats, charting, and radio communications. Against the back wall, a comfortable couch and three chairs were nestled in the shadows.

Now that the ship was safely out of the Miami port on this clear moonlit night, the captain had placed the helm into the hands of his competent fist mate, Todd Johansen. But this helm was an automated Voyage Management System, similar to an airliner's autopilot. It would allow Johansen and the crew to maintain an accurate course and real-time positioning at all times.

The captain was more comfortable in this environment than anywhere else, and now he stood facing the window to the side of the navigation console with one hand behind his back and the other holding his coffee cup. He was contemplating the warm cheese Danish piled high on a silver tray, freshly baked in the ship's galley. A sous-chef had just delivered them to the bridge on a cart with fruit, tea, and a silver coffee service.

At age fifty, Captain Oldervoll might be considered young to be the captain of a $550-million vessel, but then, he started his maritime career at a young age. At six feet five with close-cropped blond hair, intense blue eyes, and sharp features typical of his Scandinavian heritage, he was a handsome man. He looked quite masterful in his black uniform with four gold stripes on the sleeves and epaulets. Indeed, his coworkers thought of him as a serious and intensely professional man, and that is how he saw himself.

Normally, Espen would be soothed by the steady hum of the massive diesel engines generating power far below in the bottom of the ship. Three of the six engines were currently employed to support the three propeller motors pushing them toward the Bahamas at nineteen knots. The maximum cruise speed of twenty-four knots would not be required to reach port by morning, and this would conserve at least a small portion of the two thousand seven hundred gallons of diesel fuel the hungry ship devoured each hour she ran at full speed.

This night, however, Espen was far from soothed. In fact, he was feeling an unfamiliar state of agitation. Behind him he could hear the subdued conversations among his crew as they busily worked the departure, but he was preoccupied with personal matters that he did not wish to discuss with anyone. And so he made a pretense of watching the ship's progress east toward Nassau while he thought about the things that disturbed him. *Hvordan har mitt liv fått slik ut av styring?* How did my life get so out of control? *Hva gjør kvinnen til meg?* What is the woman doing to me? These thoughts were extraordinary for this man whose life had been rock steady and on course since the age of fourteen.

He could still remember in vivid detail the trip that changed and molded his life. His father had taken him on the train from their home in Kristiansand, Norway, on a two-hundred-mile trip northeast to Oslo along a rugged coast where ten thousand years ago ice sheets carved the land into hundreds of valleys, some up to four thousand feet deep. These enormous crevices subsequently filled with seawater creating jagged fingers of rocky land separated by breathtakingly beautiful deep blue fjords.

Espen was so surprised when his normally stern and distant *Far*, a minor bureaucrat in the forestry department of Vest-Agder County, offered to take him along on a short business trip. They stayed at the historic Atrium Hotel in downtown Oslo, only a five-minute walk to the Royal Palace along Karl Johans Gate, a popular pedestrian street. He could still relive the sights, sounds, and aromas of the myriad shops and cafes along the way that astonished and delighted him.

But it was the bus ride to Bygdoy Peninsula just ten miles from the center of Oslo that inspired the sudden and lasting change in young Espen's life. He'd already learned about the Vikings in school, but his visit to the Viking Ship Museum was more thrilling than he could ever have imagined.

The ornately carved oak ships, which dated to AD 800 or 900, were unearthed in a large burial mound in Vestfold County and meticulously restored. Now they rested in an enormous sunny building alongside many other Viking artifacts, including tools and weapons, and he thought that the setting was appropriately reminiscent of a cathedral. Just looking at the ships made his blood surge and literally took his breath away.

Mesmerized, Espen stared up at the mostly charred black hull of the twenty-meter-long Oseberg with its exquisitely carved spirals atop the front and rear pillars rising vertically from the keel. He vividly imagined—with an accompanying pounding in his chest—the power of the muscular leather-clad Viking commander standing tall in the bow shouting orders to the oarsman, his long blond hair whipping in the cold breeze. Espen could easily envision the oarsmen, their bulging muscles glistening with sweat, as they strained to propel the vessel across the frigid sea. In short, the Viking ships had a profoundly spiritual effect on the boy that he would never quite be able to explain.

He reluctantly left the Vikings and boarded the bus for the short drive to the Kon-Tiki Museum. Inside the modern building, he climbed a short staircase and was once again overwhelmed at his first glimpse of Thor Heyerdahl's balsa-wood raft adrift at an angle in the middle of the room as if it were still tossing on the Pacific Ocean. The life-size diorama created almost more emotion in the boy than he could bear. From that moment, he was obsessed with the Norwegian anthropologist and particularly with his 1947 journey with five other people aboard the primitive raft sailing from Peru to the Tuamotu Archipelago.

Espen came to believe that he was directly descended from—or at least genetically linked with—the Vikings, fifty generations of Norwegian mariners, and Heyerdahl himself. From that time on he knew there was only one path for his life. He would one day be the master of a great ship. And so he studied hard, received good grades, and eventually was accepted into the Oslo Maritime College and then the Norwegian Naval Academy. He was fortunate that his family could support him through his education, and excelled in every area of study. When the time came to begin his profession, he easily passed the mandatory International Convention on Standards of Training, Certification, and Watchkeeping for Seafarers Exam.

In 1985 he began his career as a seaman on the Viking Cruise Line's new ship, the two-thousand-five-hundred-capacity *MS Mariella*, then the largest cruise ferry in the world. She ran the route between Helsinki and Stockholm and Espen could not have been happier. He secretly believed that it was a good omen that his career was beginning on a "Viking" ship.

He started working for World of Seas in 1990. Because he was well liked and respected, he had little trouble working his way up through the hierarchy from third to first mate, staff captain, and finally master captain. In 2006 he was given command of this 135,000-ton luxury cruise ship. He felt as if he had everything he could want. But then he met Suzanne.

For years Espen had taken little time for a personal life as he focused only on his professional goals. He had little experience with women, beyond a couple of short-lived shallow romances. As a result, when he met the beautiful and exotic Suzanne Moretti, the ship's hotel director, and saw her mutual attraction for him, he fell in love almost instantly.

Espen recognized right away that Suzanne was a puzzle of contradictions, but that only fueled his interest and desire. Thanks to her

South African mother and Italian father, Suzanne was a dark-skinned beauty with high cheekbones and large oval catlike eyes of an extraordinary color—dark gold with green flecks.

In addition to her exotic appearance, she was smart, multilingual, and very ambitious. At five feet eleven, she was strong and athletic. Her long sinewy muscles were deceptively powerful, but she was also endowed with sensuously curved hips and high, full breasts. She literally wore her sexuality for all to see and admire. She was also famous among those who knew her for the thick mane of black curls that cascaded around her shoulders. People could recognize her from a far distance just by her hair.

Incongruously, Espen now mused, she was also devoutly religious having been influenced by her ultraconservative, beer-guzzling, and according to Suzanne, violently controlling father. Joe Moretti had served with the U.S. Army's 101st Airborne Division in Vietnam in the early 1960s. When that was over and he was miraculously still whole, physically at least, he had decided to travel the world rather than returning home. The story is that he bummed around doing odd jobs in one location until he accumulated enough money to move to another.

In 1967 he landed in apartheid South Africa, where of all things, he met and fell in love with a Zulu tribal beauty, Ezador Jiko. Unfortunately, South African law prohibited interracial marriage. Worse still, since passage of the 1957 Immorality Amendment Act, even interracial sex was a punishable offense.

So when Ezador became pregnant in 1968 and her family rejected her out of fear, Joe realized the error of his ways. As the story goes, he begged the forgiveness of his own family for having been a rebellious maverick and moved Ezador to Topeka, Kansas, where he rejoined the family beef-processing business. He married her in a civil ceremony just two months before Suzanne's birth. Somewhere along the way he had abandoned his family's Catholicism, claiming to have been born again, which to Espen's way of thinking was just some American nonsense.

Espen met Joe only once when he and Suzanne traveled to Kansas to meet the family before their marriage. The place and the man seemed completely foreign and backward in just about every way. Joe was so overbearing Espen could not work out how Suzanne managed to overcome his insistence that she, like her obedient and downtrodden mother, adopt the traditional female role he believed God and Jesus expected of her.

And so it was clear to everyone including Espen, that he and Suzanne were completely different in appearance, personality, heritage, experience, philosophy, spirituality, and just about any other parameter one could think of with the exception of their mutual craving for uninhibited, mind-bending sex. They married in Rio four months after they met and since then, despite their inherent differences, they happily spent their lives living and working on board the ship with occasional excursions ashore for shopping and touring.

Until now, that is. He could not believe what she had done to their ordered lives—his ordered life. If the captain's position required anything, it certainly required a calm and even temperament. This was why his current state of anger, even rage, was so disconcerting. Perhaps he should have known better than to marry a member of his own crew. After all, it was impossible for twelve hundred crew members living in close quarters down on decks 1 and 2 not to hear about everything that happens among them. It didn't make any sense to him how Suzanne could expect to have a flirtation or affair or whatever the hell was going on without the news getting back to him.

Staff Captain James Early, his friend and second in command, reluctantly and with a great deal of embarrassment had explained what he had heard the crew discussing. Suzanne and the cruise director, Ronaldo Ruiz, were said to be a hot item and were spending all their free time together when Espen was on duty.

He could not imagine anything more outrageous and humiliating. He confronted Suzanne, and of course she denied everything, saying that the crew's gossiping was often way off the mark. But he knew in his heart—in his Viking warrior's soul—that there was a difference in the way she was responding to him, and most surprising and frustrating she was finding ways to avoid being intimate with him. He knew that the rumors were true, and he had to save face somehow. V*ad ska jag göra med det nu?* Now, what am I going to do about it?

10

Rachael's voice jolted me out of a sound sleep. She sounded frantic. "Mommy, Mommy, I'm scared. Where are you?" I could tell she was sobbing, but in my disorientation I wondered how she had learned to speak so well. I knew she could say words and some phrases, but now her voice sounded so impossibly grown up.

"I'm here, Rachael. Mommy will never leave you." *Oh God—there is no God—please, please let it end differently this time.* I found myself sitting upright in bed with warm tears on my face and rivulets of sweat sliding down between my breasts. With rapid breaths I gasped as if suffocating. I knew I must get to my baby before it was too late. *Wait. Something isn't right.* I tried to draw air through my nose to calm myself. I consciously checked my tongue and found that it was tight against the roof of my mouth. I moved it down behind my bottom teeth, knowing from experience this small adjustment is one of the best and immediate relaxation techniques.

The total blackness of the room was so disorienting that at first I couldn't figure out where I was. Then the all-too-familiar feelings of longing and sadness hit me, as if a boxer had given me an uppercut to the solar plexus. What little breath I had left rushed out of my lungs, and I crashed back onto the bed gulping air and feeling completely devastated. It must have been six months since I last dreamed of my Rachael. My beautiful daughter whom I last saw when she was eighteen months old.

I have learned after nearly twenty years that stress and anxiety often bring back the dream, which in turn stirs up intolerable memories. I knew I had to get up, but I couldn't remember if there was a light near the bed, or if so, where it was.

Trying not to disturb Doc who somehow slept through my ordeal, I fumbled to the foot of the bed and literally crawled out onto the floor. Standing up on wobbly legs, staring for a moment into the darkness, I tried to get my bearings. The bathroom was to the right, and I carefully negotiated my way toward it trying to avoid hitting the small glass coffee table that was somewhere between the bed and the door. It took a minute of feeling around to find the door handle, but finally, with relief, I entered the bathroom and turned on the light.

Checking my watch, I was surprised to find it was only 10:00 p.m., not the wee hours as I expected. By now my raw panic was joined by a claustrophobic feeling as well, and I knew I had to get out of the stateroom. Exiting the bathroom I quietly gathered my clothes from where I had discarded them on the couch then went back in and dressed. I applied a little mascara to my pale lashes then added some lip gloss. *No matter how dire the circumstances, you never know who you might meet.*

I left the bathroom light on and the door open a crack to create a night light for when I returned, then stepped into my sandals and quietly slipped out the door into the passageway. *Damn, which way should I go? Which is forward and which is aft? Why didn't I pay closer attention?* Finally, I started walking and soon enough arrived at the entrance to a foyer with a bank of elevators and stairs.

I climbed up two levels to deck 4 and decided to stay there because there weren't any important venues open at that spot, and therefore not many people were about. Music was playing somewhere at a distance as I walked through the automatic sliding door onto the fifteen-foot-wide outside deck. Once I hit the cool night air I was able to breathe a little easier.

I turned right toward the front of the ship and began to stroll up the deck, thinking I would keep going around next to the railing until I regained full control of myself. It would do no good to try to repress my thoughts. The past would have to play out in my mind once again so I could put things in perspective and locked back in place.

The nearly full moon was a breathtaking sight with a few elongated stratus clouds shimmering pearl gray and gold across its surface. A glistening path of golden water stretched from the horizon to the ship, keeping pace as we sliced through the cobalt Caribbean Sea. It was so lovely with the warm breeze and the gentle swishing of water against the ship that I did begin to relax. As I watched the soothing repetition of waves flying by only a couple of stories below, my thoughts floated back twenty years to my short-lived marriage to Brooks Larkin.

Brooks was unbelievably good looking. Every woman I knew at the University of New Mexico in the late 1980s would have slept with him in a heartbeat. Unfortunately, I was the one he decided to pick up after a group of us partied until closing at a dance club called the Coral Coyote in Santa Fe. At that time I only knew Brooks superficially from being in a math class with him, and I was simply taken in by his appearance and deceptive charm. In my wildest nightmares I could not conceive of having conceived the first time we had sex. But that is what happened, and without much thought or ceremony we were married when I was six months pregnant.

The following two years are honestly a blur of horrific memories. It soon became apparent that Brooks was an alcoholic who barely functioned outside of school. In school he pulled himself together to get passing grades because he was brilliant and maybe had a photographic memory. I, of course, had to drop out of school to suffer through my depressing pregnancy until giving birth to an extraordinarily beautiful and sweet daughter whom I named Rachael Elizabeth. I liked the name Rachael for no particular reason, but Elizabeth is my dad's mother's name and also my middle name. Granny Elizabeth is the only member of my sad family with whom I ever seemed to identify.

In 1955 she and my grandfather moved with their three children from Liverpool, England, to Manchester, New Hampshire, to get a piece of the good life. They were sponsored by Granny's sisters who came to the States right after World War II full of optimism about the American lifestyle and the opportunities they believed were waiting for them, based on the glowing descriptions of Yanks they met during the war. As it turned out, Grandpa George spent his entire career as a textile worker on both sides of the ocean, and Granny remained a traditional housewife all her life.

In 1966 at age nineteen, my dad married my mother, an orphaned Alabama girl he met when she traveled north with a synchronized swimming troupe, and two years later they moved out west. I was born that same year, and mercifully my parents did not produce any siblings. I never learned anything about the Swansons, my mother's family—they were never discussed, and it was as if they hadn't even existed.

Dad had high hopes for the construction foreman position he accepted at a housing project in the expanding Albuquerque area. That first job did turn out to be a good opportunity, but he had to change employers every couple of years as his deepening alcoholism caused problems with workers and customers. With each move his salary declined, and Mom picked up some of the slack with periodic secretarial jobs. In this fashion they barely managed to eke out a middle-class existence.

When Grandpa George died several years ago, Granny Elizabeth returned to her original home in Liverpool, and now in her eighties she still lives there with a niece. She is the only person I ever talked with about the pain of the events that followed Rachael's birth, which are unbearable for me to discuss even now. Though her generation is far removed from mine and we seemingly had few life experiences in common, she always listened and did not judge me.

I have done a number of positive things at her suggestion that, frankly, no one else could have convinced me to do like going back to school at the most emotionally difficult time in my life. I just hadn't been able to see how I could continue my education with a baby and without money.

Brooks was not only drunk most of the time when he was home but was increasingly resentful of having to support a family while he went to school part time. He stayed away from the apartment as much as he could, and when he did come home, he was verbally abusive and was always threatening to leave us. I knew where it was leading. It was too reminiscent of my own parents' battles, which I had heard repeated on many nights as I lay in my bed sleepless and terrified.

After our inevitable divorce, I went crazy—really and truly crazy. I just couldn't think rationally, or fathom how I would be able to raise a child, get my degree, and work enough to pay the bills. I knew that support from Brooks would be short-lived since he was spiraling more out of control all the time. If I had been able to rely on my own parents for help or if only I had talked with Granny Elizabeth about what I was planning, maybe I would not have taken the drastic and tragic step that pretty much ruined my life.

That gray morning in November 1989, I spent a lot of time with my girl and made sure she looked especially pretty in her best yellow cotton eyelet. I could not believe my luck in finding the lovely new dress with the white lace collar at the Salvation Army store. After threading narrow yellow ribbons through the sleeve caps with pretty bows tied at her chubby arms, I brushed out her long wavy blonde hair for the last time, adding a matching yellow ribbon around her head to hold back her thick bangs.

Rachael was truly the sweetest child imaginable. She had never been any trouble, and I can still feel her arms around my neck and see her big blue eyes as she cocked her head to the side and stared into mine. "Wuv oo, Mommy." She looked exactly like me, and I loved my daughter so much I thought I was giving her the greatest gift there was—to not have me for a mother.

I packed her clothes and a few toys in a little thrift shop suitcase. With tears streaming down my face and dripping onto my faded jeans, I managed somehow to drive us in a car borrowed from my best friend, Sidney, to the one-story adobe building just off the square in old downtown Albuquerque.

There weren't many parking places because so many tourists parked their cars along the side streets in order to meander around the town square, where vehicles were prohibited. Oblivious to my plight, they joyfully bustled about examining Native American jewelry and sampling fabulous Mexican food. I couldn't even imagine feeling joy. By the time I carried Rachael and her belongings a block from the car, I was beginning to panic. I kept on going, though, because my mind was made up and I had a commitment.

The dirty brown facade of the agency was set back from the street by an ancient adobe-patterned Saltillo tile terrace, and crossing it from the sidewalk to the building seemed like the longest journey of my life. A knock on the traditional old chipped blue Mexican door resulted in a warm greeting through the bars of the small eye-level grate. The big door swung wide, but I didn't step inside. Instead, I kissed Rachael several times, told her how much I loved her, and placed her into Sister Lena's open arms—and up for adoption.

The sister smiled and complimented Rachael on how clean and pretty she looked. Her already-crinkled eyes squinted over the top of rimless glasses as she waited to see if I had anything to say. I wanted desperately to add something, but guessed it had all been said on my previous visits.

I turned away, and when I looked back for the last time, Rachael smiled and waved at me. The image imprinted on my retinas at that moment became one of those mental pictures you can never erase. The bright light from the midday southwestern sun created a halo of gold around my girl's shiny hair and appeared to reflect off the yellow dress enveloping her in a golden aura. So trusting, she had no idea what was happening. And that is when my heart shattered irreparably and a part of me disappeared forever.

Two days later I knew I had made a mistake, but three weeks went by before I convinced myself I really had changed my mind and found the nerve to go back to the agency. Sister Lena was sympathetic but firm. "You have legally signed away all rights to the child, and the two-week window of opportunity to renege has passed. Besides, we already have a loving couple in the process of adopting Rachael. You must accept your original decision as being the will of God and for the best." Of course I would never be allowed to see or contact her or even know who her parents were.

The next year is missing. It's just completely gone for me. I must have been drunk almost continuously and so depressed I barely hung on from day to day. I was suicidal at one point and even went so far as thinking about how I could get a sufficient quantity of sleeping pills from the free family planning clinic down the street from my trashy apartment. I passed the clinic every day on my walk to and from Senor Miguel's where I waitressed during the day. Occasionally on my way home I stopped at a small Mexican market for minimal food and copious liquor. The job barely afforded enough income for these necessities, and I spent virtually every agonizing evening alone.

In the beginning, a few friends dropped by to comfort me, but I wouldn't let them in and they finally gave up. I even shut out my best friend, Sidney, who had been there for me through school, my awful marriage, and my pregnancy. She did everything she could to talk me out of giving up Rachael, even offering to take care of her for a year or two while I figured out my life. But no way could I let her give up her own education for me. Later she tried to convince me to fight the adoption and get Rachael back. I finally shut her out along with everyone else, and one of my biggest regrets is the loss of that friendship.

Brooks even came by a couple of times just to make things worse. Of course he had also signed away all rights to his child, but since resentment was the only emotion I ever saw him show toward her, I don't think he suffered very much.

In the end, with the help of some innate strength not inherited from my parents, I managed to overcome my depression. With Granny Elizabeth's emotional support provided during lengthy lifesaving phone conversations, I gradually began to live again, stopped the self-destructive behavior, and enrolled in school to complete my master's. I worked part time at the university, and with the help of numerous loans I was able to maintain both decent grades and a tenuous grip on my sanity. Most importantly, again with Granny's insistence, I sought counseling and stayed with it for six months.

 David Meisner, PhD and clinical psychologist, was my savior. But even twenty hours of talking with kind and understanding David could not alleviate my guilt and sadness. I just learned how to compartmentalize the memories and tried to move on. David used an analogy to explain how I had enclosed my memories of Rachael and feelings about the marriage and adoption in a prison of sorts within my mind. While I could easily break down its fragile bars, he said, I preferred to stay safe behind them rather than live with the unbearable pain and regret that came with facing my memories. I just got to the point where to the extent possible, I didn't let myself think about what I'd done.

 Still, when I have episodes like tonight, I do think of all the alternatives I could have pursued and how I could have made things work out for my girl and me. And more than anything else, I think about how I should have stood up to Sister Lena or fought back—done anything to keep my child. The worst part is that I cannot let go of the fantasy that I will see my Rachael one day, and at the same time I live in fear that she will find me, which she has every right to do. There is no excuse for what I did, so what could I ever say to her that would make any sense?

 After confronting my memories, I was able to push them back into their fragile prison once again, and I began to feel more normal. Taking in my surroundings for the first time, I looked up at the huge motorized lifeboats secured to the white underside of the deck above my head. Giant metal arms hung down from the ceiling and out over the water, ready to lift out and lower the enclosed ocean-worthy crafts if need be. Earlier in the day, Doc and I, along with all the other passengers on board, were assigned to one of these boats and shown how to muster in case of an emergency. Now I felt strangely comforted to look up and see "our" lifeboat, D16, hanging overhead.

 Against the railing large green metal barrels like fifty-gallon drums were stacked on their sides two rows high in wooden racks. A sign on each barrel indicated they contained self-inflating life rafts, and out of curiosity I stopped to read the instructions for how to unhook and roll them into the water. This was also somewhat comforting and seemed fairly straightforward, but I reckoned considerable strength would be required to dislodge the barrels from their racks.

I noticed that a two-and-a-half-foot-wide section of the railing was hinged so that when released it could swing inward. The gate was secured to cleats on the deck with thick metal rods and thumbscrews. Evidently, the opening would facilitate the process of getting the rafts over the side, and allow passengers to exit from the deck to life boats and rafts in an emergency.

Looking around, I realized I was still alone. In the dead quiet except for the sound of waves against the hull, the odd notion occurred to me that everyone had abandoned ship and I hadn't gotten the message. The railing was midriff height as I leaned over to watch the water rushing by. A disturbing involuntary shudder caused me to back away. The inherent danger was so close in an otherwise idyllic environment. A careful inspection of the back wall and ceiling did not reveal any surveillance cameras. There was no sign of any security at all. *If I were suicidal I could go right over the side here and no one would ever know what happened to me.* I wondered how many times that scenario had actually occurred.

Before coming on the cruise we saw reports in the news and on the Internet about the alarming number of people who disappeared from cruise ships never to be seen again. Some were known suicides, but others undoubtedly had been helped over the side. Stepping back from the railing, I tried to shake off the chill working its way down my spine.

Just then there was a sound something like voices, but maybe just the almost imperceptible whining sounds of the ship. I leaned over the railing again and listened. After thirty seconds, I had no doubt a conversation was taking place, and it was getting louder. Looking up, I realized people had stopped on the deck above me not too far from the railing, and for some reason this seemed alarming. I quickly pulled back into the safety of the overhang. Heavier clouds covered the moon now, and it was quite dark. Despite the few dim lights on the ceiling, I suddenly felt very ill at ease. My arms were covered with goose flesh, only partly from the chilly air.

There was no mistaking a man's accented voice raised in anger. "Don't try to change my mind. I'm going through with this. I've been on a cruise ship long enough to know how easy it is for things to happen to people." Then with a definite edge, he continued, *"Piense del resto de nosotros y piense de su propio bienestar, mi amigo."*

A second man answered, "Don't you dare threaten me as well. You are nobody! Making this arrangement was a mistake, and there is still time to back out. *Cállese y tenga inconveniente en su propio negocio."*

They were speaking Spanish, but my language skills were rusty, and I couldn't make out what they said except that one guy was angry about the other one not wanting to go through with a plan. *How can this be happening to me again?* I could not say for sure, but it made sense that these were the same men I heard earlier in the day near our stateroom.

Obviously, my part in this is just coincidence. I didn't want to succumb to the common trap of believing it was too unlikely to be chance. Still, how can I be in two places on the ship in the same day and hear men discussing a scheme of some kind? Holy shit! I had just been thinking about how easily a person could go overboard when I hear them talking about something that sounded like it might be related to that scenario.

This is really creepy, but it has to be pure chance, I told myself again. There is no connection between me being out here and these guys being up on the deck above. And I don't believe there is a cosmic plan or spiritual intent guiding individual occurrences. For me, any belief that is not supported by logic, common sense, or science must be folklore or mythology. In fact, I reminded myself that everything happens because of only three reasons: intentional or accidental actions of people, the laws of the physical world, and chance. Yet somehow, this explanation was not as comforting as it usually was.

As I stared over the railing in the dark watching the black sea race alongside, I began to wonder again why people believe that a benevolent and perfect intelligence is orchestrating an incomprehensible plan for the world when the outcomes of poverty, disease, hunger, cruelty, and war are so obviously stingy and imperfect. Wouldn't it actually be more rational for believers to acknowledge that a demon is pulling the strings and to pray to it for mercy and deliverance? Well, that would be the essence of devil worship, another faith-based religion.

I wrapped my bare arms around myself and shivered. My thought processes were clear and simple, and I didn't need or miss the bewildering and complicated layers of rationalizations and laws that people have created to bolster their belief. That is, to make the unbelievable appear believable. Maybe nonbelievers have always been a minority because most humans are too fearful to live without a scapegoat on which to blame the woes of the world or to accept that all life simply ceases to exist in the end and none of us is that special in the cosmic scheme of things.

Once again I was torn from my philosophical musings by the realization that I was freezing. I had to get inside the ship. *Should I go to security and tell them what I heard? But what could I say? I've no idea what it means or who they are.* Nonetheless, I knew without any doubt that whatever they were talking about meant something very bad for someone on the ship. I started to back up thinking I would find the nearest door into the ship, but my calf bumped noisily into a canvas and metal chair, sending it skidding across the deck. *Oh no, what a klutz!* I stopped moving and listened. After a few seconds, I heard the faint whoosh of the sliding door above, and knew the two men had just entered the ship.

Did they hear anything, and if so would they wonder if someone was listening to them? I turned quickly and jogged along the deck to the first set of doors I found and ran inside. I entered the foyer just in time to see the top of the heads of two men descending the stairs to deck 3. I couldn't get any real impression of their looks, but I was almost positive they were the guys I heard talking up on deck 5.

I couldn't help myself. I had to follow them. As I slowly and quietly descended to deck 3, careful to make sure they would not see me if they looked up, I could hear their muffled conversation but not what they were saying. When I arrived at deck 2, I realized they had continued down. The carpet ended on the middle landing and cement steps led down to deck 1. Obviously, this was not an area intended for passengers. That answered the question about whether they were crew members, didn't it? Anyway, I wasn't about to follow them into the bowels of the ship.

Instead, I slowly climbed the stairs to deck 6 and unexpectedly found the inviting Center Bar that had enchanted me as we boarded. Although it was almost eleven, I didn't think I was tired enough to sleep just yet. *Oh well. Doc is undoubtedly fast asleep, so I might as well have a nightcap.*

11

    Mick showered and changed into a pair of tan Dockers with a mauve polo shirt and light brown tasseled loafers (with socks). He'd been sitting at the Center Bar for about ten minutes working on a Corona and talking to Manuel about how the ship's crew members represented fifty-five countries. Glancing to the side, he saw a woman approaching across the star-patterned dance floor. She was five feet nine or ten with shoulder-length thick blonde hair, wearing a pale yellow dress that gently draped her obviously slender body. His first impression was that she was one of those women who seem ageless, but he guessed she was probably in her late thirties.

    As she reached the bar, he realized she was absolutely stunning with flawless skin and huge eyes as blue as any he'd ever seen. The color reminded him of the dramatic flax blossoms his mother grew in profusion in her Pennsylvania rock garden. She wore very little makeup on a finely shaped face with high cheekbones and lovely full lips that curved up slightly so it seemed she could not possibly look cross.

    Wow, she's completely unique and gorgeous. Though he could not have said why, he knew immediately she was highly intelligent and self-assured. Completing the distance to the bar in a few long strides, she plopped down on the stool next to him, and ordered what seemed a complicated martini drink. Manuel nodded knowingly, reached under the bar for a shaker and an icy glass, and began a ritualistic process. Mick turned his attention to the beautiful woman beside him. "Hi, I'm Mick Clayton," he said, extending his hand. Her handshake was firm, and her face even more beautiful when she smiled.

    "How do you do. I'm Darcy Farthing. Are you having a good time on the cruise yet?"

Mick laughed. "Well, it's a little early to say, but it looks as if I could be having some fun right now," he quipped and cringed inwardly at the triteness of his comment.

"Is Mick your real name or a nickname?"

"Actually, it's a pretty well-kept secret only a few personal friends know."

"Well, I'm obviously not in that category, but at the same time who would I tell?"

"Oh, all right, I'll reveal my biggest secret to you. My name is Michelangelo." Seeing her skeptical brow arch, Mick added, "Honest, I'm not kidding. My Catholic mom was wonderful, but she had a thing for the Sistine Chapel." Mick noticed Manuel's amused smile out of the corner of his eye.

They engaged in a little small talk, but Mick was distracted by her appearance and uncomfortable with the effect she was having on him. "I live in Colorado Springs," she was saying, and immediately he shifted uneasily in his seat. He thought his reaction had been obvious, but she did not mention it, and he quickly regained his composure as she continued, " . . . in a great patio home with a spectacular view, but I spend so much time traveling I don't get to enjoy it much."

To Mick's amazement, Darcy began to tell him about her relationship with Jason and how she already felt that letting him bring her on the cruise had been a mistake. He listened to her attentively and did not have to feign interest. At first, he was reluctant to provide personal information, but he did talk about his job with the GAO. He told her, "If you are like a lot of people, you've probably never heard of the agency."

"You're right, I haven't. Are you allowed to tell me about it?"

"Of course, and then I won't even have to kill you." Again, he groaned internally over his lack of creativity. Probably in too much detail, he went on to explain his work. "GAO is a legislative branch agency led by the comptroller general of the United States, a position parallel to a cabinet secretary in the executive branch.

"My area is criminal justice, and I'm a manager in the federal Senior Executive Service. *What the hell is wrong with me?* Even as he spoke he regretted the boring formal sounding description.

He was appalled and had no idea why he was so uncomfortable and unable to engage in light small talk. This woman was making him feel like a goofy kid. Quickly moving on, he tried to cut his explanation short, but couldn't find a place to stop. "I lead teams of analysts and auditors in investigations of programs in Department of Justice agencies. Then we report any problems we find to the Congress and wait to see if they will do anything about it."

He heard the stiffness in his own voice, and cleared his throat in an attempt to relax before continuing. "I've been looking at programs in the U.S. Marshals Service for the last few years working in partnership with the Department of Justice inspectors general. But I'm on extended leave now." Mick chuckled nervously, straining for a lighter tone. "So I'm not getting much work done."

"Well, Mick, that sounds a lot more interesting and important than my job. I'm a sales manager for Shrinden Pharmaceuticals. Actually, I lead a team of ten reps. You've undoubtedly heard of Shrinden and the miraculous male sexual performance—enhancing drugs we sell."

Mick could not help but laugh at the realization of how down to earth, straightforward, and funny she was. He told her the cruise was a spur-of-the-moment idea made easy by the fact that he was already in Florida at the house his parents left him. Then he surprised himself again by telling her he was trying to recover from his wife's and parents' deaths and the cruise was part of his therapy.

"Oh, I'm so sorry. So we are both on our first cruise and not all that content to be here."

"I guess that's so. I'm hoping once I start going ashore in the ports I'll feel as if I'm on vacation and can start to enjoy it. I've already enjoyed talking with you though, Darcy. Maybe I'll see you around the ship during the next month. That shouldn't be a stretch, but unfortunately I have to get going now." As Mick reluctantly eased off his stool, he looked into Darcy's amazing eyes one more time. Enya's haunting "Caribbean Blue" flashed into his mind. A little flustered, he said, "You take care, now." Then he walked away.

12

I took another sip of my delicious Ketel One and nodded to Manuel who was asking if I wanted another one. I munched on my last olive, delightfully stuffed with blue cheese while I thought about the friendly man I had just met. "That guy Mick was really nice, wasn't he? It's too bad he had to leave." *Yeah, it is too bad, because talking with him is the first time since I left Colorado I've felt really happy.*

"He has been here a couple of times today, and we had pleasant chats," Manuel answered. "I think he is a pretty good guy, and he seems to be alone on the cruise." He looked at me expectantly with an impudent smile so I guessed my interest was obvious.

I did like the way Mick looked, and I liked saying his name, Mick, not Michelangelo, that was just weird. I kept thinking about the Crocodile Dundee movies and the Mick character I liked, played by Paul Hogan. I loved the relationship between that Mick and his costar, Linda Kozlowski, too, and they ended up marrying in real life; I can be such a romantic sometimes.

My new acquaintance was about six two or three and built very lean like a runner. For some reason it made me happy to think that he liked to take care of himself. His dark hair was a little short for my taste, but he had cute bangs that swept across his forehead in a natural wave. His face was what had really gotten to me, though. I hadn't been able to stop looking at those warm hazel eyes with the long lashes and perfectly shaped brows. He was good looking with a strong straight nose and thin but expressive lips. There was a boyish quality too, although he seemed emotionally mature enough.

It was embarrassing in retrospect how easily I opened up to this stranger about my relationship with Doc. Somehow I just knew he was an

OK guy and I could trust him. It was comfortable chatting with him, but he seemed a little nervous or under some sort of duress. One thing I didn't share was my disturbing experiences overhearing the crew members talking. It was so bizarre he would probably think I was unbalanced or something.

Let's face it, I think he's damn sexy, and I'd better be careful I don't repeat my usual MO of getting involved too quickly, especially in this environment and being with Jason. I turned my attention back to Manuel. He was a nice guy too, and I had the feeling I'd get to know him pretty well by the time this trip was over.

13

Mick felt a little light headed as he left his new friends, Darcy and Manuel, but there was something he had to do. He checked his watch and saw it was nearly midnight. As he strolled down the promenade of stores and lounges in the middle of the ship, he glanced from side to side at the many passengers congregating in this popular spot. He thought about his reaction when Darcy mentioned Colorado, and shuddered just thinking about the state. *Wouldn't you know I'd meet someone interesting and have that connection?*

Before he could dwell on what was basically just a little coincidence and not much of one, since there are only fifty possibilities for which state a person is from, he entered the casino. Trying in vain to ignore the smoke in one of the few places on the ship where the legal addiction was still allowed, he looked around to get his bearings. He wasn't in the mood to gamble, but he put a few quarters in a machine anyway and let his gaze wander around the room as he played. He was on the higher of two levels with the slots and the casino cage. When his change ran out, he left his machine and moved to a small horseshoe-shaped bar with a few stools overlooking the gaming tables on the lower level.

He ordered a glass of sparkling water with lemon and sipped as he continued to watch the action all around him. The noise of the slot machines and passengers laughing and cheering each other on made him smile and actually seemed to lift his spirits. After hanging out for about fifteen minutes, he saw a man walk in and immediately descend the three wide steps next to where Mick was sitting.

With a small rush of adrenalin he watched as the man he had seen at the swimming pool sat down at a 21 table and pulled out a roll of dollar bills. He looked about fifty, a little stocky, with almost entirely steel gray hair and an olive complexion—very ruggedly Italian looking. He was wealthy judging by his custom-made black silk suit and gold jewelry on both wrists and several fingers.

Mick walked to the railing at the top of the steps and watched him win and lose several hands. After about twenty minutes the man left the table and headed back up to the bar. From his position at the railing Mick heard him order a double scotch. Then he turned and passed by Mick with the drink in his hand heading toward an adjacent sports bar where several TV sets loudly blared football and soccer games.

Near the entrance to the casino, Mick observed him without being seen. Shortly, a crew member walked into the bar and sat down at one of the tables close to an overhead TV. He appeared to be Latin American and wore the generic black slacks and shirt worn by most of the crew, not an officer's uniform.

To Mick's surprise, the passenger he was watching walked over and also sat down at the table. Mick could not hear any of their conversation, but it was apparent that a very intense discussion was taking place. Although he didn't know much about cruise ships, he thought this seemed unusual—for a crew member to interact with a guest in public like this. After five minutes the crew member abruptly left.

The passenger finished his scotch and also left the bar. Mick waited for him to walk about fifty feet down the wide promenade toward the center of the ship and then discreetly followed. Many passengers were milling about, and Mick had to be careful not to lose him in the crowd, but the man was in no hurry and just seemed to be passing time. He stopped twice at lounges using his ship ID card to purchase drinks, which he carried with him as he wandered through the ship. Mick noted that the man was becoming increasingly unsteady and not because of the ship's motion.

Finally, at one forty-five he headed for the elevator, and Mick followed him into the car but waited for him to push the button. As they began to rise, Mick turned away to look out the glass wall overlooking the promenade and the central dance floor below. He craned his neck to see across the floor to the bar. Manuel was chatting with a couple and Darcy was not there.

They both exited the elevator on deck 8, and as the man turned right Mick turned left and began to walk away. After a few yards he turned around and resumed his surveillance staying well behind as they wound through the passageways. When the man stopped at his door and began fumbling in his pocket for the card key, Mick walked on behind him. When he heard the door close, he went back and noted the stateroom number. Then he continued on to his cabin at the opposite end of the ship and turned in for the night.

Part Two

Dangerous Seas Ahead

14

Over the next few days as the cruise proceeded through the Caribbean ports, Doc and I settled into a sort of pattern that was not at all what we anticipated when we planned this adventure. I started spending as much time away from him as possible. As he seemed to get the hint, he started hanging out at the pool showing off his fine physique. I noticed he was engaging women who looked a little like me in conversation and drinks. *Is he really that shallow?* I wondered.

I met Mick a couple more times at the Center Bar, and we were slowly getting to know each other. Nothing yet had diminished my initial positive impression of him. I had seen him at the gym too, but other than that he seemed to be keeping a low profile and was even a little standoffish. I began to wonder why he had come on this cruise at all. He said he was here to have fun and work on his healing process, but that didn't quite make sense the way he was keeping to himself.

I have to say that on the fourth day of the cruise Doc and I had a pleasant time in Philipsburg, the capital of the Dutch-owned St. Maarten. We docked at the southern side of the thirty-seven-square-mile island situated near the top of the West Indies Archipelago. The northern side of the island is the French-owned St. Martin, and apparently it only took a couple of hundred years of wars to finally arrive at the stable division between France and Holland, which has stood peacefully now for three hundred fifty years.

It was sunny and warm with just a little breeze to cool us as we rode in a taxi to the famous Orient Beach on the French side where swimwear is optional. We enjoyed a stroll along the sand enjoying the stimulating view while fully suited ourselves. Then we spent the afternoon back in Philipsburg, a free port, looking for bargains on clothes, jewelry, and liquor along quaint cobblestoned Front Street. One street over to the south we found the boardwalk, a pedestrian street that follows Great Bay along the quiet crescent beach, and leisurely checked out the shops and restaurants along the way, enjoying the tropical climate and watching the interesting mix of tourists and locals. At Captain Hodge Wharf we stopped to photograph our ship, towering and massive in her slip across the small bay.

Along the way, we couldn't resist the allure of some inviting sand-dusted concrete steps rising gently from the boardwalk to the open lobby of the Holland House Beach Hotel. Doc was game to investigate, so we climbed to the top and were thrilled to find a beautiful terraced patio and bar where there were amazingly few people. So we spent a pleasant hour nestled there on white linen cushions set on honey-colored woven rattan couches and chairs with matching cocktail tables. Surrounded by potted palms in this chic outdoor living space, we were accompanied by a big white and brown tabby cat languorously stretched out on the couch beside us. Our companion periodically requested a chin scratch, and we didn't need an interpreter to understand him.

The warm, relaxed atmosphere or maybe the margaritas, or both, helped us have a fairly open and honest discussion about our short-lived romance. I was relieved to find that Doc had plenty of misgivings of his own and happy to realize that the remainder of the cruise would not be too awkward. We came to an agreement that we could remain friends but that the intimacy was essentially over.

On our way back to the ship, just for fun we stopped for another margarita on the deck of the famous Greenhouse Restaurant on Juancho Yrausquin Boulevard, not too far from the dock. With the tension between us largely dissipated, we relaxed and enjoyed ourselves. That night we slept together in the only bed we had on the ship, and Jason kissed the top of my head as I slipped into a calm, dreamless slumber.

The next morning when we awoke, the ship had docked at Port Zanté in Basseterre, the 380-year-old capital of St. Kitts. I walked to the front of the ship on deck 13, high above the town, to enjoy the view of coastline in both directions. My first reaction was how lush and green the island was.

I knew from the little bit of research I had managed that the West Indies were created about fifty million years ago when the Atlantic and Caribbean tectonic plates collided accompanied by violent volcanic eruptions. The string of islands formed by these forces has dense tropical foliage covering their interior hills. Specifically on St. Kitts, I was intrigued by 3,792-foot Mt. Liamuiga, which means fertile land in the native language of the Carib Indians. I wished there was time for a climbing expedition but I knew I would have to be content with the view.

The Caribs displaced the Arawakis, another of the island's original inhabitants sometime after Christopher Columbus visited the island on his second voyage to the New World. Then in 1626 the British and French massacred the Caribs and subsequently kicked out the Spanish. They warred with each other over control of the island for two hundred years.

Also during the 1600s Oliver Cromwell doomed twenty-five thousand Irish men, women, and children to indentured servitude on the island's verdant sugarcane plantations, which at one point numbered sixty-eight—one for every square mile. After the Irish were virtually exterminated by disease and overwork, they were replaced by African slaves who, until 1834, were bought and sold in the town square of Basseterre now incongruously named Independence Square.

The island's sugar producers realized early on that molasses, a by-product of the cane-refining process, could be fermented into alcohol. Thus began the island's long and famous history of rum production, which continues today with international sales of brands such as Brinley, Belmont, and St. Kitts. The British finally gained ownership of St. Kitts and its sister island, Nevis, through the Treaty of Versailles and ruled until the islands gained their independence just twenty-five years ago. Today the Federation of St. Kitts and Nevis is the smallest sovereign nation in the world with a population of about forty thousand.

I couldn't wait to go ashore and explore some of the history I read about, but I thought I would take a break from Jason. On a whim I went to look for Mick in the gym to ask if he wanted to go ashore with me. He wasn't there, and he wasn't at the Whale's Tail having breakfast either. However, as I was leaving the Tail, I ran into Charlie and Don, our dinner-table companions, and they invited me to accompany them ashore. I wasn't sure about it at first, but later I was so glad I went along with them.

The guys turned out to be great companions and were very enthusiastic about exploring the town. We hit the high spots beginning with the clothing and jewelry shops at the Pelican Shopping Mall, having passed up the even more tourist-oriented shops we saw on the dock immediately after leaving the ship. Then we checked out the national museum and the clock tower with its chipping gold and green paint, standing in the middle of "the circus," a roundabout at Fort and South Square streets. The tower is actually a memorial erected in 1883 to Thomas Berkeley Hardtman, a St. Kitts native born in 1824, who according to his plaque stayed on the island and made his mark as a "planter, politician, and citizen," living to the ripe age of fifty-six.

His longevity was considerably better than that of doomed but fertile Sarah Tyson, whose tomb we found in the front yard of the St. George Anglican Church. In 1738 at the age of forty-five, she was buried beside seven of her children. In 1867, a "Great Fire" destroyed the church and much of Basseterre. Little evidence of the fire remains except for the somewhat blackened and scarred andesite blocks. Islanders used these hand-cut volcanic stones to construct many of the town's early buildings, including the church's low turret-shaped façade.

We finally got hungry and thirsty and briefly considered the Subway sandwich shop at the corner of Fort Street and Victoria Road. We came to our senses and opted for Ballahoo, just across from the clock tower. Seated on the upstairs balcony beneath a white lattice portico, we sipped Carib beer and munched on crisps as we listened to the chatter of English, Spanish, German, French, and other languages I couldn't readily separate in the din, mingled with the delightful patois of the locals.

Then over a lunch of spicy chicken, black beans, and fried banana, I told the guys about my strange coincidental experiences on the ship. I had not shared this information with anyone, but I felt relaxed and comfortable with Charlie and Don because I didn't think they would be judgmental—that is, they wouldn't think I was crazy. "You know," I concluded, "nothing more has happened, so I think I should just forget about it since I don't really know that there was anything bad going on."

The two exchanged a look that I'm sure was full of meaning for them but indecipherable to me. Don made a quick movement with his head settling his blond waves behind his ears and looked at me speculatively. "We don't really know you that well, Darcy, but . . ."

Oh no, here it comes. They do think I'm crazy.

". . . It seems as if you are minimizing the potential seriousness of the situation. What else could they have been talking about other than hurting someone on the ship?"

"Oh. Well, at first I thought that too, but it just seemed so surreal, you know?"

Don reached across the table placing his left hand over mine. I glanced down and realized for the first time that he wore an ornately carved silver wedding band. I glanced over at Charlie's left hand, which was propping up his chin and was not surprised to see a matching band. "Look, Darcy, you should trust your instincts and go talk to someone—maybe security. Because what is the worst they can do, tell you there is no need to worry? At least it will be off your conscience."

"Maybe you're right. You know I didn't even tell Jason about what I heard. I don't really know why."

Don looked straight into and seemingly through my eyes giving me an almost queasy feeling like some sort of inner probing was taking place. "That should be fairly obvious to you based on what you've told us about what happened to that relationship. You just didn't trust him enough." A smile lit up his already-perfect face as he turned to glance at his partner, and I was struck again with how handsome he was.

In an odd gesture, Charlie dipped his chin and peered up at me through the tips of the curls hanging off his forehead. "I guess this means you trust us more, ha?"

15

That night, everyone on board was invited to meet Captain Espen at a large cocktail lounge and dance club called Triton. It was a formal affair, so I decided to really doll myself up in a skintight black sequined sheath with narrow straps and cleavage enhanced by Victoria's Secret. Black sandals with four-inch clear plastic heels made my legs look terrific and raised me to well over six feet. I have to admit I kind of liked the idea that many of the men I encountered would have to look up at me unless they were content with eye-to-breast contact. Jason looked me straight in the eye and accompanied me to the party.

We waited in line to have our picture taken with the captain. The cruise director, Ronaldo Ruiz, introduced him to each guest who wanted a photo op. Ruiz was obviously a friendly, fun-loving guy. I guess that would be a job requirement since he was the person in charge of all the entertainment on board and responsible for keeping the guests happy and occupied for the whole cruise.

The captain was tall and quite handsome in a very pale sort of way. His English was quite correct, but his Norwegian accent was pretty thick, and kind of cute. As a bonus we met the captain's wife, Suzanne Moretti, who stood beside him in the reception line greeting the guests wearing a full-length shimmering silver off-one-shoulder gown. She was also a crew member, but I didn't learn until later that she was the hotel director. I couldn't help thinking what an exciting life the two of them must have living and working on the ship together—kind of a *Love Boat* type of thing.

Also very tall and in perfect shape with a face that was both beautiful and exotic, Suzanne was simply a knockout. I had never seen hair quite like hers. It was shiny black, thick and curly, but with loose, smooth ringlets that many women would work for hours to achieve. The layers were expertly shaped so that it cascaded from her crown down her back and pooled around her well-toned shoulders in a luxurious mane that was unusual and stunning.

The large room was decorated in a sumptuous undersea motif, complete with huge stone columns and architectural elements reminiscent of ancient ruins. Every surface was covered in gold, teal, and creamy beige with carved wood and lots of the ubiquitous marble. Doc and I walked arm in arm down a short staircase and found a vacant cocktail table right alongside the dance floor. Soon we were enjoying the free champagne and hors d'oeuvres and even gamely danced to the big band sound. The ship was obviously catering to an older crowd. Doc looked great in his rented tux, and quite honestly, I thought we were the best-looking couple—and probably the youngest—on the floor.

Later, the cruise director, Ronaldo, stopped by our table to ask if we were enjoying ourselves. "You two look pretty spectacular." He grinned, showing straight white teeth. "You're a really striking couple. Do either of you have hidden talent?" It was an odd question, and I almost thought he was making a suggestive remark. Then he continued, "Because you know, we have a passenger talent contest with a final show at the end of the cruise. We work on the performances as we go along, and I'd love to see one or both of you involved."

Are we in one of those old Mickey Rooney "show must go on" movies or what? I looked at Doc and laughed out loud at his alarmed expression. "Believe it or not we don't have any talent other than standing around looking good," I quipped.

Ronaldo took a beat, then laughed and shook his head as he moved on to the next table. I watched him work the crowd and wondered what it would be like to have his job. He seemed a bit familiar, but I guess that was just because he was a normal-looking guy with dark hair and eyes. At about five feet nine, he appeared to be in good shape. I noted that he had a slight Hispanic accent. I had heard that he was a professional singer and at some point during the cruise would entertain the guests at one of the evening shows. Now having met him I was looking forward to it.

A couple of minutes later, Suzanne walked over to our table, and I wondered whether this was standard protocol or we were getting special attention. She asked if the food and drink were to our liking, and we assured her everything was fine, but instead of walking on to the next table, she looked down at me with an inquisitive look. "Do you mind if I sit for a minute?" Without waiting for a response, she followed with "Thanks, I've been on my feet all day," and plopped down in an empty chair. "The captain has returned to the bridge, and I'm off duty. I shouldn't drink with the guests, but I would so love to have a little champagne." The waiter had put two glasses in front of each of us, so I gladly pushed one of mine over to her. "Thank you, Darcy, right?"

"Yes, it's amazing you remember my name with all these guests."

Suzanne giggled, possibly from the bubbles hitting her nose. "I don't really drink very much. It wasn't hard to remember your name. You do stand out in a crowd, you know."

I probably blushed at her comment and definitely yelped when Doc kicked me under the table. What is going on here with the comments about our looks? I looked into Suzanne's startling gold and green eyes and was stunned at the impact. "Thanks, I guess. I'm a little embarrassed to be honest. Anyway, you're definitely a stand out yourself, Suzanne. Your hair alone is enough to send other women into fits of jealousy."

"Now I'm the one embarrassed. I get a lot of comments on my hair, but I got it honestly from my South African and Italian heritage. You look as if you could be related to my Espen. Are you Scandinavian?"

"Actually, I'm English, but there is a side of my family I don't know about, so maybe I'm part Swedish or something, who knows? Suzanne, I haven't met many women on board that I have much in common with—are you, um, allowed or whatever to socialize with us?"

"Well, if I was to adhere strictly to the rules, which obviously I don't, I'd say I can be friendly but not meet for drinks or anything like that. Of course, off the ship I have stretched the rules a little. Maybe we can plan to go shopping together in one of the ports."

"I'd like that. Let me know if that can work out for you."

"I surely will." She eyed me appreciatively. "You look as if you stay in shape. Sometimes I go to the passengers' gym to work out because the crew's facility is not nearly as well equipped, so if you want to, maybe we could meet there too."

"That would be great."

She downed the last of her champagne and stood up. "Thanks for letting me sit and for the conversation. It can get a little stuffy here." She nodded toward the crowd. "God bless you," she said oddly and walked away to speak with other passengers.

Doc cleared his throat as he watched her backside. "Well, you two seemed to hit it off. But, wasn't there something a little strange or inappropriate about her? I mean, she's the captain's wife as well as a crew member. Shouldn't she be a little more professional?"

"What, are you jealous of her paying attention to me or something? What is wrong with her being friendly? I like her, and we probably have a lot in common."

"Why is that, just because you are both gorgeous and around the same age?"

"Whatever, Doc, we'll see if anything even comes of it. She'll probably forget all about me."

16

The driver's ebony face was alarmingly purplish. He'd been yelling, screaming really, for several minutes. Mick was thinking the guy would be lucky if he didn't burst an aneurism on the spot. No matter where you go cabdrivers are all the same. That is, very territorial about the passengers they believe they own. Apparently, a woman from the ship had the audacity to step to the wrong cab, taking this guy's fare, and he went ballistic on the other cabby. A very tall Barbados policeman in his crisp gray uniform and equally crisp accent was trying his best to calm the fellow down and restore order.

Mick had boarded a ten-passenger van for the five-minute trip from the dock to downtown Bridgetown, the last port before a five-day cruise to Brazil. He slouched on the backseat, slightly amused as he stared out the window at the altercation. As the van moved away from the curb, he glanced forward at his mark seated behind the driver. The surveillance was getting tedious since nothing unusual had happened, and he was beginning to feel a little foolish.

Obsessing over the need to follow this guy everywhere he went was interfering with Mick's enjoyment of the cruise, but there had to be a reason why the man was on the cruise other than simple pleasure, and whatever it was, it had to benefit him personally in a big way. Knowing a little something about his personality Mick thought the benefit would mean a huge detriment to someone else.

He had also been thinking a lot about Darcy and could see potential for a closer friendship with her. But he'd been too preoccupied to give her his full attention. He was aware that she wasn't spending much time with Jason, and having seen him with other women at the pool, Mick gathered they had come to an agreement of some kind. Watching Darcy at the gym had become the highlight of his day. Her obvious strength and fitness were a complete turn on for him. He also looked forward to having more evening chats at the Center Bar and decided to step things up a little.

The van stopped at the curb and everyone climbed out. This was the main shopping district on Broad Street, and Mick assumed he and his unknowing buddy would be browsing the stores in the downtown area. Keeping a safe distance behind as they crossed the street, he was thinking about how boring the day was going to be. Suddenly he realized the pace had quickened as they turned and headed up Bay Street toward the wharf. With Mick trailing about twenty yards behind, they crossed a bridge over the Careenage inlet then turned down an alley that dead-ended at a barbed wire-topped chain-link fence.

The pace was slowing, and Mick became a little nervous as he realized the gap between them was closing rapidly. But the man quickly walked through a partially obscured gate in the fence, which he obviously knew was there. As he approached the gate himself, Mick was surprised to see that the opening led directly onto Browne's Beach, the closest one to downtown Bridgetown.

Halfway across the stretch of sand, the man stopped and removed his sandals. He was wearing khaki shorts and a thin white cotton shirt that billowed slightly in the breeze as he walked barefoot to the water's edge. Then with shoes in hand he began strolling south just at the edge of the surf as if he hadn't a care in the world.

You have to be kidding, all this just to watch him walk on the beach by himself? Maybe he's getting senile or something. Still, Mick fell in behind also carrying his shoes and thankful he too was wearing shorts, so he didn't look too much out of place. After an uneventful and not unpleasant half mile of beachcombing and watching the jet skiers fly in and out of the water, he began to feel like a fool again and decided to turn around and return to the dock.

Just then he saw an attractive tall woman walking out onto the sand from the deck of Finally Michaels Restaurant just at the edge of the beach. She was wearing a knee-length filmy white dress over a white string bikini, and Mick noted the outfit contrasted dramatically with her darkly tanned skin and dark hair. She is quite stunning, he thought, as he watched her stride directly up to the man, who also stopped to watch her approach. Halting barely a foot in front of him, she briefly clasped his right hand in both of hers.

What the hell is going on with this guy, and who is the woman? He followed as the couple continued walking down the beach. It was impossible to tell what their relationship was since they didn't touch again but seemed to be engrossed in a conversation. As they approached picturesque Needham's Point Lighthouse near the Barbados Hilton, they encountered a sea wall blocking their path. At that point they turned off the beach to a sidewalk lined on both sides with flowering shrubs.

They wound around the Barbados Yacht Club and back out to the sidewalk on Bay Street. Within a block they turned the corner at a small grocery store, little more than a shack with two rusting gas pumps sitting in front. They proceeded down a side street that curved back toward the beach. Mick soon realized they were heading toward the Hilton, which towered above the surrounding one and two-story hotels and apartment buildings up ahead.

From a discreet distance Mick watched the swaying hips of the beautiful woman with the amazing black curls cascading down her back, and thought maybe he'd seen her on the ship. Had the guy brought another woman along on the trip? That would be unbelievable. The couple crossed the narrow front parking lot and walked up the slight incline of the circular drive to the wide-open front doors of the hotel. They continued all the way through the spacious lobby past the check-in counter and the concierge.

Mick stayed close to a line of ten huge palms planted in clay pots. He didn't really need to worry about maintaining cover, though, since the two were too engrossed in each other to notice their surroundings. At the rear of the lobby they left through another set of open doors and descended a wide set of stone stairs that wound around two swimming pools, separated by a smooth water wall cascading from the higher pool into the lower one.

The tropical landscaping surrounding the pools was breathtaking, but Mick noted the couple didn't even glance at the lovely setting as they continued around to the back of the hotel facing the beach. Finally they stopped at an outdoor bar and restaurant. Obviously, at least one of them had been here before and knew exactly where they were going.

Mick entered the sunny patio behind them and sat on a barstool as the hostess seated the couple at a white metal table under a blue umbrella. They sat side by side facing the beach with their backs to him. He ordered a club soda with lime and sipped through a straw, gazing out over their heads at the beautiful ocean and cloudless sky. They ordered two Dos Equis and appeared to have resumed their conversation, although he was too far away to hear what they were saying.

Mick was baffled. Then one remotely plausible theory occurred to him. Maybe the woman works for World of Seas, and some business was being conducted possibly having to do with the ship's casino. The gambling connection could explain why the man had come on the cruise to begin with and also the encounter with the crew member in the sports bar. On the other hand, why on earth would there be all this apparent sneaking around off the ship? Mick felt his anger rising as he realized what a waste of time this whole adventure had been. *What was I thinking to get involved to this extent with something that is really none of my business? I know this guy is a world-class jerk, but whatever is going on here has nothing to do with me.*

As he was getting ready to slip off his stool, he glanced over one more time and saw that they appeared to be completing the business portion of their meeting. The man offered the woman his hand, and they sort of shook and sort of held hands for a moment. As she leaned closer to him, she reached down inside her swimsuit top and pulled out a plastic card key. As Mick mentally revised his theory, they paid their bill, left the patio, and headed up the stairs toward the lobby.

After Mick watched them enter the elevator, he walked outside and hailed a cab. On the way to the dock, he tried to make sense of what he had seen. *Is this why the guy came on the cruise, to have a liaison? But he has his wife with him. Why bring her if he was meeting a girlfriend?*

Another wave of anger rose inside his chest. Shifting uncomfortably on the back seat of the cab, he tried to calm himself. It was no use because now he would have to decide what to do with this information, and that made him wish he had never left the ship or Florida for that matter.

17

At 8:00 p.m. Captain Espen finalized his orders to the crew for their duties during the five days at sea that would take them from Barbados to Brazil. The ship could encounter storms within the next two days, and he intended to navigate around them without having to deviate too much from the course they had set for Salvador da Bahia. With the Voyage Management System automatically steering the ship and maintaining course, and with calm seas ahead for now, he was comfortable leaving command in the hands of Staff Captain James Early and First Mate Johansen.

He strode from the bridge and headed for the stairs. He rarely used the elevators, not because he wanted to avoid the passengers—this was not at all the case for he understood that they were the only reason his beloved job existed. He simply believed it was always better to walk whenever he could just for the exercise. He was thinking about changing into comfortable clothes and enjoying a relaxing evening in his suite on deck 8 with a bottle of Veuve Clicquot Brut and a rare Angus steak. *Should I go up to the Whale's Tail and have the chef grill me one to take out or just go down to the suite and call room service?*

Suzanne would be off duty tonight as well, but he had mixed feelings about spending the evening with her. He hadn't seen her all day, but that was just as well because he was still very angry and simply did not trust her any longer no matter how hard she tried to convince him she was innocent. Even if he believed her, which he did not, it was not in his nature to let go of the past. He had also been avoiding Ronaldo Ruiz as much as possible because just seeing him made Espen furious.

He thought about confronting the cruise director, who in a manner of speaking was one of his employees but such an encounter would be embarrassing and, to Espen's mind, beneath his station. And so he was keeping his distance. These thoughts were creating a lot of unwanted tension right now, and the captain tried to turn his mind to something more pleasant. As he stiffly climbed the stairs with his fists balled at his sides, he had difficulty conjuring up something pleasant in his life. So he thought about the selection of foods he would pick out for his dinner.

At that moment, Suzanne and Ronaldo were chatting quietly over the end of a light meal in the Tail. Since becoming aware of the crew's interest in their friendship, which they both considered to be outrageous meddling, they tried to keep a low profile and maintain an air of professionalism. However, to Suzanne's dismay this had not done much to alleviate Espen's suspicions, and no amount of cajoling or attempts to arrange romantic evenings for the two of them had persuaded him the rumors about Ronaldo and her were just that.

Suzanne shifted in her chair and tried to relax her expression as she looked at Ronaldo from behind a large coffee mug. She did feel a little more at ease now. She had been feeling angry and anxious about the whole situation and begun to second-guess herself—something she rarely did.

She prayed at length for guidance, but over the past few days the response she was accustomed to receiving seemed dull or garbled, as if there was a problem with reception. Without her natural God-given compass, she had been floundering—until just a few hours ago when she realized the path she should take.

Ronaldo consumed two scotches and three glasses of wine during the hour and a half since they met at the cocktail lounge and then came up for a quick meal. Now he was slurring his speech, obviously drunk. She felt her previous anxiety returning and turned her eyes away from him, trying to think about how to remedy the current situation. *I have to find a way to fix this and convince Espen that I am faithful. Darn the nosiness of the crew and lack of privacy on the ship.*

A few minutes later, the two left the Whale's Tail to return to their respective quarters. This was formal night down in the dining rooms. The second seating passengers were beginning their meal while the rest were taking their seats in the showroom excitedly anticipating the beginning of the family version of Folies Bergere. As a result very few passengers were eating up in the buffet. Likewise, no one was loitering in the area just outside the entrance next to the stairs and elevators.

Suzanne suddenly stopped. She put her hand on Ronaldo's arm and leaned forward so that her face came very close to his. She whispered discreetly, "I have to go to the ladies' room before I go downstairs. Do you want to go on ahead?"

He smiled at her, thinking about her innate sweetness. With a slightly glassy look he placed his hand on top of hers. "No, I'll wait here to ride down with you."

"OK, I'll be right back."

As Suzanne walked toward the restrooms on the starboard side, Ronaldo took a few steps forward and leaned over the railing—a glass wall with brass trim—that filled the four-foot gap between the two elevator banks. He gazed up at the huge blue and orange aluminum bird sculpture with its thirty-foot wingspan, suspended securely from thick wire cables over the open atrium. A sudden feeling of nausea and dizziness swept over him, and he quickly shifted his gaze downward to the star-patterned dance floor five decks below.

He smiled when he recognized a middle-aged couple working on their tango steps and recalled that their names were Ruth and Jack Mang from London. It was his responsibility to make sure that every passenger felt welcome and had fun while they were on the ship. He prided himself on remembering most of them, and he enjoyed the aspect of his job that allowed him to meet so many interesting people from all over the world.

The couple below looked splendid with Jack in a tuxedo—something you didn't see on the ship as often as in past years, Ronaldo thought wistfully. Ruth wore a shimmering full-length dark blue skirt slit to the knee in front to allow for tango kicks with a silver and pale blue sequined blouse. He met the distinguished pair earlier in the day when he checked on how the dance class was going and enjoyed a spirited conversation with them about Latin dances and the best places to go in Rio to see really fine professional dancers.

He leaned a little farther out, grinning as he watched the Mangs whirling around the dance floor and realized he was feeling better now—more relaxed and optimistic—partly from the alcohol but mostly because he had finally made a difficult decision, which he confided to Suzanne. He believed he'd convinced her to see things his way. *I'm so glad to have Suzanne's support.*

He was still smiling and leaning out over the glass railing when from the right out of the corner of his eye he sensed more than saw a dark flash. Before he could react and without being able to process what was happening, he heard himself yelp as gravity gave way under his feet and he sailed out over the railing. In another second Ronaldo experienced the final sensation of his life as his head shattered on the dance floor, narrowly missing the Mangs. Their frantic screams, as blood and gray matter dripped off their formal attire, were followed a short time later by another high-pitched scream from above as Suzanne peered down at the horror below.

18

The frightened woman listened intently willing her breathing to slow and smooth out, taking air in through her nose and exhaling gently through her mouth. Sure enough, the cabin door was easing open. She'd been dozing off and on for the past hour and now she desperately needed him to believe she was asleep. She could tell from the sounds of his fumbling with the door and then in the bathroom trying to undress and brush his teeth that he was drunk again. She wasn't asking much, only that he fall into bed and asleep without picking a fight.

The same scary thoughts that had plagued her during the past six weeks swirled in frightening images as she tried to feign a deep slumber. Why did he insist they come on this trip, and why did he want her with him when it was clear he wanted nothing to do with her beyond making appearances in public when necessary? He'd never before wanted to leave his business for even a few days. He'd never even mentioned wanting to go on a cruise until two months ago when he sprung the idea on her out of the blue.

It wasn't even couched in terms of a romantic vacation to help heal their relationship. In fact, he simply approached her one evening in their presidential suite on the top floor of the hotel and casino complex and announced they were going on a four-week cruise—*four weeks?* He gave her the departure date along with instructions on what she should pack for the two of them and then simply walked out leaving her alone as usual.

A wealthy and powerful man, he seemed to care for nothing but running his business with an iron hand. In fact, she had come to realize that his employees feared him almost as much as she did. For the past three years, his anger and brutality had escalated so much that now it was impossible for her to imagine how she thought she loved him so deeply when they wed on New Year's Eve ten years ago. The slow insidious behavioral changes had worn her down over time making her increasingly fearful and passive.

She'd asked herself many times how he could possibly have found out about her very short-lived affair in 2005, at a time when their marriage was already turning sour. There didn't seem to be any way he could know about it, but undeniably things got much worse after that.

Now she was only looking for a way out of her nightmare. She didn't really have a productive life and felt like a prisoner even at home in their luxury suite. Just to get free of her husband, she wondered if she could offer to void their prenuptial agreement, which as it stood would give her a sizeable piece of the business profits if they split. She was at the point of relinquishing everything, including pride, in order to gain her freedom. Her self-esteem had bottomed out and any job skills she once possessed were rusty at best and totally obsolete at worst. She had no idea what she would do without him and her marriage.

Since boarding the ship she had mostly stayed in the stateroom, which at least was a suite with a separate living room, a large bedroom and outside balcony, and a decent-sized bathroom with a tub. She read several books and watched every film offered on TV. Thank goodness she had money to spend for various treatments at the spa, which got her out of the suite for a few hours each day.

Her husband stayed away most of the time but always returned and forced her to dress and accompany him to Mermaids, where she had to endure his pretense of being a down-to-earth, friendly guy and all-around attentive husband as he chatted amiably with the other four dull and oblivious passengers at their table.

She had no idea how in the world she would be able to stand three more weeks of this, especially having to endure his obvious loathing for her not to mention his drunkenness. She knew from experience that it would be dangerous to go out about the ship on her own because just like at home, he would manage to watch her every move. She never knew what small thing she would do or conversation she might have that would ignite his anger.

He sat on the edge of the bed and reached overhead to turn off the night-light she had left on. The thick drapes at the glass doors were drawn, blocking out the moonlight, and the room was quite dark. She inched slightly toward her side of the bed as she felt him lie back against the pillow. Now she lay perfectly still breathing steadily and waiting to see what he would do. After only a few minutes she heard his familiar light rhythmic snoring and was relieved that at least for tonight there would be peace.

19

The feeling of guilt was overwhelming. Oh damn! What is wrong with me? I knew something was going to happen to someone on the ship, so why didn't I tell somebody what I heard, even after Don and Charlie encouraged me to? I'd almost decided to go to security, but waited a day too long. Now I was trying to shake the feeling that I was responsible for Ronaldo's death because I didn't report an obvious plot before it was too late. But even a day or two ago would probably have been too late for an investigation to unfold.

What happened to Ronaldo Ruiz the night before last was not what I expected at all. I don't know why I assumed a passenger rather than a member of the crew was in danger, but I would have sworn that the manner of death would be falling over the outside railing—not an inside one. It made me sick to think about how friendly and nice Ronaldo was when we talked with him at the captain's party. It was very hard to believe he was gone.

On the other hand, maybe his fall was just an unfortunate accident. Yesterday I heard talk among the passengers and crew that Ronaldo was drunk when he fell onto the Central Bar dance floor. Suzanne apparently was with Ronaldo just prior to the fall, and she reported he'd consumed quite a bit of alcohol.

Worse still, a rumor was circulating among the passengers that Suzanne and Ronaldo were having an affair. I desperately hoped this was not true, but people were saying that their relationship was common knowledge among the crew. I just couldn't get my mind around that after seeing her with the captain and thinking that she was someone I would like to get to know. That and the fact that the Central Bar, my favorite place on the ship and where I met Mick, would never be the same for me.

I'd spent most of the day in my cabin watching TV and eating snacks from the mini-fridge while I tried to decide what to do. I finally told Jason about my concerns, but he completely dismissed me, saying that I had a vivid imagination and was always looking for drama.

He was currently out and about as usual, probably playing at the pool with his latest blonde friend. So when Plato, my Haitian cabin attendant, came by to see how I was and to refresh my ice bucket, I asked him who I should contact if I had overheard someone discussing something that could be related to Ronaldo's death. "Should I talk to a security officer or someone else on the captain's staff?"

After staring at me for a few seconds as though I was demented, he looked down and contemplated the green-on-green patterned carpet as if searching for caterpillars hidden among the woven leaves. Finally, when his eyes met mine his normally open happy expression was gone. His eyes narrowed into a squint and his mouth turned down in a hard scowl. He looked a little scary in fact, as if something alien had been hidden and was now revealing itself. The deep-set eyes peering from his long narrow face were almost as black as his slicked-back hair. His expression and tone were even darker.

"Ronaldo was my friend, and I have trouble accepting that he fell over the balcony by accident, but that is what the investigation has shown. Surely, there is nothing you could tell the security authorities that they have not already considered. Why don't you enjoy the rest of your cruise and let the people who know what they are doing take care of this terrible tragedy?"

I wanted to respond in kind to Plato's patronizing tone, but something told me to let it go. He was grieving for his friend, after all, while having to continue with his day-to-day chores on the ship. After he left I decided I had to go to the main information desk and ask to speak to a security officer.

But I'm stubborn and still had some doubts. Suddenly a strong urge came over me. I had to find Mick and tell him the whole story. *I value his advice, and if he agrees with Don and Charlie and thinks I should make a report, then I will.* I checked the time and saw it was four thirty, so I headed for the shower.

20

Down in the movie theater on deck 2, the passenger Mick had been following arrived for another meeting with a member of the crew, but neither Mick nor anyone else was there to see it. The seventy-five-seat stadium-style screening room was empty except for these gentlemen, since the next showing of *National Treasure: Book of Secrets* was not scheduled to begin for an hour. Seated down in the front row the crew member looked up sullenly and watched the passenger slowly approach down the center aisle. "Why do you pull me away from my work to talk to me?"

"Are you kidding me? You had better tell me whatever you think you know about what happened to Ronaldo. Everything has spiraled out of control and I won't stand for it."

"I don't know anything. Ronaldo was not my friend. I would not even know him if you hadn't recruited me for your job, and I can't control what is happening to your plans."

"Don't be impudent with me! I don't think I believe you. You don't think his death was an accident do you?"

The crew member glared at the passenger for several moments before making a decision. "If anyone knows what happened, I would think it would be you and your friend." He spat out the last word with obvious distaste.

"I suggest you be very careful how you speak to me. I need to know what you think happened, and you also need to worry about being ready to proceed as planned. I'm still paying a lot of money for this job, and my future is at stake, but then of course so is yours, isn't that right?"

"I am still ready. You needn't threaten me and I told you I don't know what happened to Ronaldo, but maybe one of the passengers does."

"What are you talking about?"

"Oh, a woman in one of my cabins, Ms. Farthing, said she had information about his death and wanted to go to talk to security about it." He paused and gave the passenger a defiant look. "I've told my boss all about that conversation and it will be taken care of."

"I see," was all the passenger said, although he found this information to be extremely interesting.

Two decks up in the Center Bar Mick commandeered his favorite stool, and Manuel reached for his first Corona of the evening. Soon, their conversation touched on Ronaldo's death, but Manuel was very upset, having seen Ronaldo fall onto the dance floor as he stood behind his bar. "I can't get it out of my mind, and I don't really want to talk about it. There are rumors of course as always there are among the crew, but I do not like to repeat them."

They switched topics to a discussion about how much of Manuel's four-month contract with World of Seas he had yet to work before he could go home to Columbia. He explained that the money he sent to his wife in Cartagena would allow them to educate their children. "Being away from my home for months at a time is very hard, but the money I make here, it makes it worthwhile."

Just then, Mick saw Darcy approaching across the dance floor dressed casually in beige shorts and a pale blue halter top with jeweled sandals. Her skin was tanning a little, and it seemed to glow. She looked as fresh and wonderful as ever, and nothing had changed except every time he looked at that floor now he thought of how horribly the cruise director died there.

He had not met Ronaldo, but everyone was talking about what a nice guy he was. It was unbelievable that the maintenance workers immediately removed the body and cleaned and scrubbed the floor all within an hour after his fall. There could have been a crime committed, and now there would be no opportunity to gather evidence. Apparently, all the officials cared about was making the ship presentable for the guests.

Mick had learned that an accidental death at sea did not clearly fall under any country's jurisdiction, but a crime committed on a ship or a problem passenger must be reported to the FBI if the ship was passing through a U.S. port. Of course this ship was not going anywhere near a U.S. jurisdiction anytime soon. Using his investigative skills, earlier in the day he casually asked a few questions of the guest relations staff and also learned the body was taken to the ship's small morgue area, which was essentially just cold storage. After all, it was not all that unusual to have a person die while on a cruise. Often they were elderly folks who had heart attacks or strokes. Their bodies, as well as their travel companions, had to ride out the rest of the cruise or disembark at a port along the way and find transportation home.

He also wondered why a security camera did not capture Ruiz's final moments assuming cameras were ubiquitous on board the ship. He was able to get the answer by applying a little innocent flirting with the pretty French purser, Janine. She assured him there were indeed many cameras in many locations, but unfortunately the exact position of Ronaldo's fall happened to be in a blind spot between cameras. "This was most surprising and unfortunate." She arranged her features into a thoughtful pout, possibly in reaction to Mick's mock come-on. "He was such a wonderful guy, and also a very excellent cruise director. The passengers all loved him, yes?"

Darcy crossed the dance floor, looking down gingerly at the colorful inlayed boards. She smiled a little sadly as she situated herself on the stool beside Mick. "Hello, Darcy, are you well this evening?" Manuel forced a smile as he began to assemble the martini-making tools.

She waved her hand at him. "Yes, I am OK. Thanks, but I'm not drinking this afternoon, Manuel. I have to talk to Mick here about something, so I'm going to borrow him for a while." She turned to lean in close. "Is that OK with you, Mick?"

He leaned back a little and looked closely at her face. "Sure, is everything all right?"

"I'm fine, but really concerned about something, and I want to tell you about it. Let's go over to a table."

Once they were seated on a small teal love seat and Mick had set his beer down on the cocktail table, he did one of his very favorite things—he gazed into Darcy's amazing eyes. "You look beautiful as usual," he said.

"Thanks, Mick. You are very sweet and pretty cute yourself, but look, I value your opinion, and I know you have knowledge about law enforcement and crime, so I just want your professional view on something." She proceeded to explain the two conversations she'd overheard and how she now wondered if Ronaldo had been murdered and that she was feeling somehow responsible.

He listened closely watching her expressive face while she clearly and concisely laid out her story. He loved the sound of her voice although this particular subject was decidedly disturbing. "Are you certain that both times they were crew members that were talking?" he asked after she finished. Her eyes were wide with brows raised in expectation.

"Not for sure, I guess. The first time I saw their backs, and they were wearing black. I assumed they had on uniforms, but I can't be positive about the time out on the deck. It felt as if they were the same men continuing the previous conversation, and I'm pretty sure they went down to deck 1 afterward."

She looked over at the window where the sun was rapidly diving for the sea. After some apparent reflection, she turned back to him. "At least it had to be the same subject being discussed. I'm sure about that, but I'm not sure why. Otherwise, it would be too complicated, I guess. Do you know what I mean?"

"I can see where it is asking a lot to think there are two seemingly similar plots or whatever."

"But, Mick, the thing is I'm also confused because, well, I have a certain outlook on life." She looked toward the window momentarily.

Mick put his hand on her forearm and said, "Go ahead, Darcy. Whatever it is, you can tell me."

She took a deep breath. "I know a lot of people think there is no such thing as coincidence and everything is somehow meant to tie together, but I can't buy that. I think coincidences are just events that happen by chance and that there is no deeper meaning to them. But it just seems impossible, even to me, that I had these two experiences by chance out of all the passengers on the ship, you know what I mean?"

Mick's head was swimming with thoughts about his own coincidences. "Mick, did you hear me? You don't seem to be listening to me, and that's unusual."

"Oh no, Darcy, that isn't true. I am listening. I love to hear you talk. I was just thinking about what you said about coincidence. Isn't what happened to you exactly the definition you have given of a coincidence? And isn't the fact that it is hard to believe, the very reason why many people say they do not believe in them? So if *you* really believe things happen just by chance, I don't see why you should second-guess yourself now."

Darcy suddenly relaxed. "Logically, you are absolutely right and I'm normally all about logic. You are very kind and understanding. So do you believe in coincidence, Mick?"

He blushed and laughed at his own embarrassment. "Thanks. I guess I don't really know. I'm afraid I haven't thought about it much. But now that you're inviting me to, I guess my wife and parents all dying within six months is a coincidence of sorts, and certainly those events happened close together by chance even though somebody would say there is a reason I was made to suffer through all that." Mick suppressed an urge to tell Darcy about another coincidence regarding his parents.

"Thanks for your understanding, Mick. The bottom line is, do you think I should talk to somebody about what I heard?"

"Well, if it will help you feel better, I think you should. But please, Darcy, you have to understand that you had nothing to do with what happened to Ruiz. Just because you heard some things out of context and by chance you are not responsible in any way. Unless of course you believe you were meant to hear the conversations so that you could warn someone." Mick's eyes twinkled and one brow raised with this last statement.

Darcy stared at him for a moment and then laughed out loud. "Oh, Mick, that is so perfect. Of course I don't believe that. I got a little confused for a while, but you've helped me get my thinking back on track. Thank you so much. You really are a special guy." Mick's face reddened for the second time. "You know, this whole thing is so odd and disturbing. Jason and I met Ronaldo, and he seemed very together and friendly as you would expect the cruise director to be, but then I heard about the affair."

"What affair?"

"The crew is apparently saying that Ronaldo was having an affair with Suzanne Moretti, you know, the captain's wife?"

Mick felt suddenly and inexplicably anxious. "What? No, I guess I haven't been getting around much on the ship. I don't know any of the crew except Manuel and Paulina, my stateroom attendant. So the captain's wife is traveling on the ship?"

"Yes. She's the hotel director, and based on my short conversation with her, the rumor of an affair is very difficult to believe." She stopped talking and bit her bottom lip. Mick could not take his eyes from her face. "Changing the subject, Mick, I have an idea. How about if you and I go ashore tomorrow? We could have lunch and see some sites."

"Darcy, I would really love to do that. I honestly would . . ."

He's going to say but and turn me down. I can't believe this.

". . . but there are some personal things I have to take care of, and I probably won't be able to leave the ship." *Oh man, I'm lying to her. This is so wrong, but I can't tell her that I intend to shadow a guy all day.* "Please give me a rain check, will you?"

That fantastic smile lit her face. "No problem, Mick. I just remembered I'm probably going ashore with Suzanne, anyway. I have to get back to Jason now," she lied. "We're going dancing tonight." She abruptly stood up still smiling. "See you later, Mick."

Mick watched her walk away, and with a heavy sigh he returned to the bar and asked Manuel for another Corona. "I think I just blew my chance to get closer to Darcy, man."

21

After leaving Mick I went directly to the guest relations desk. I felt down about his obvious rejection and my own childish reaction to it, but I knew now that I had to tell my story to a security person right away. The fact that I'd waited this long was disconcerting and in retrospect inexplicable. After telling Raoul, the young Brazilian purser on duty, that I needed to report something related to the cruise director's death, it was only a few moments before the chief of security, Tom Smythe, came out of a door in the wall behind the counter and introduced himself.

He wore the ubiquitous black crew uniform with the addition of a badge and utility belt without a sidearm. He was a fairly nondescript man of medium height with short brown hair and pale skin ... just a plain white guy of around forty with a generic American accent. And that made him stand out among the crew like a dove at a crow convention. We shook hands, and he asked me to follow him to his office so we could speak in private.

I followed him down a short hallway and through a door into a tiny room—basically a cubicle with walls. The first thing I noticed was a surprisingly neat workspace. Maybe whatever documents and work items his job required were tucked away in the rows of built-in cabinets that lined two walls. I sat in the only chair across from his nearly bare desk and stifled a claustrophobic feeling. His personal appearance was as neat and tidy as his space and his calm demeanor and professionalism helped put me at ease, but I couldn't help but check him out as we talked and wondered how a middle-aged American guy ended up in a job like this.

He listened sympathetically to what I had to say and seemed to concentrate on my story, keeping his intelligent slightly hooded gray eyes fixed on my face. He only looked down a couple of times to jot a note as I talked. When I was finished he asked me if I now had any idea who the gentlemen I overheard were. When I told him I had no idea, he said he would put my report in the file but that there was nothing he could do at this point.

He assured me there was nothing to indicate that these out-of-context conversations in any way related to Ronaldo Ruiz. In a friendly but firm manner he made it clear that the ship's investigation showed the fall to be a tragic accident caused by too much alcohol and probably some reckless behavior. And that was the end of it. The meeting had taken about ten minutes, and all in all it was a little anticlimactic, but I had a distinct sense of being unburdened, and that was a relief.

22

Sadly, my most vivid memory of Salvador da Bahia, Brazil, is the pungent, sickly smell of alcohol-infused urine, and abject fear. There were plenty of pleasant things about the five-hundred-year-old city in the state of Bahia, but for me they became quite overshadowed by the events of the day.

The morning started out fine with the day holding a lot of promise. I contacted Suzanne through the ship's phone system the night before after talking with Officer Smythe. To obtain her number I told the operator I wanted to speak to her about a sensitive issue involving my stateroom attendant. When I got her on the line I apologized for the lie and expressed my condolences at the loss of her crewmate.

She thanked me for calling and explained how she was with Ronaldo the night he died but had been in the restroom when he fell. "Just being so close to him when it happened and then seeing him lying down there . . . so horrible. I'm having a hard time with it. Sometimes Ronaldo got a little carried away with clowning around, and I should have been watching him."

Her words were appropriate, but her emotions seemed a little flat. *There is no way there was a romance between them.* "I can't even imagine how terrible that must have been, but I hope you are not blaming yourself, Suzanne. It was not your fault at all . . . Um, I don't want to impose at this time, but I was going to ask if you would like to go ashore with me tomorrow."

She seemed to think about it for a moment. "I haven't been doing much of anything since the accident." After another pause she added, "Maybe it would be good for me to get off the ship for a few hours."

So at 10:00 a.m. we left the ship, walked the short distance to the end of the dock, and headed west to Avenue Oscar Pontes. Walking south, we continued a few blocks to Rua da Belgica where we wandered through the landmark Mercado Modelo. The market was filled to overflowing with more than two hundred vendors selling crafts, textiles, jewelry, food, and souvenirs. About halfway through the long warehouse-type building, with large sliding doors left open at both ends, we ran into Don and Charlie. It seemed as if I was always running into them . . . just by chance.

Don greeted me warmly with a hug. "Hey, Darcy, we looked for you this morning to see if you wanted to join us, but we couldn't find you."

"Thanks, guys. Have you met Suzanne, here?"

Don turned to Charlie. "I don't think we've had the pleasure, do you?"

"Nope," said Charlie, "but I know who you are, Suzanne. It's a pleasure to meet you."

"These guys are Charlie and Don, my tablemates and buddies."

"I'm glad to meet you and have you on board," Suzanne replied without much affect. "How are you enjoying the cruise, so far?"

I could not help but notice a change in her attitude, but I doubt the guys noticed anything. She seemed to be straining to appear friendly to them. Was it possible she was uncomfortable with their lifestyle? I found this odd, considering her position, but I was quite sure I wasn't imagining it.

"We couldn't be happier," Don was saying. "This is a trip of a lifetime for us, and all your crew members have been very nice and helpful."

After saying goodbye to them, we proceeded to browse through the market, chatting along the way. All she said about Charlie and Don was "I'm a little surprised you would befriend those kind of people." And that was quite enough. I didn't know what to say, but before I could respond, she began telling me about her family and how she grew up in Kansas of all places with a Zulu mom of all things and her Italian father's family.

She talked openly about her unusual history and revealed that she inherited a very conservative Christian point of view from her father. I was surprised by this revelation, which seemed incongruous with Suzanne's appearance, behavior, and career choice. I didn't comment but instead reciprocated with information about my job and all my traveling, but not about my sad family.

I never got up the nerve to ask about her relationship with Ronaldo. Given her remarks about how much she enjoyed her life with Captain Espen, not to mention her conservative bent, an affair seemed even more unlikely.

Suzanne had been to Salvador on other cruises and was quite knowledgeable about its history and features. She explained that this particularly beautiful Bahia, Portuguese for "bay," was "discovered" on November 1, 1501—All Saints' Day—by Amerigo Vespucci while sailing under the Portuguese flag. He stayed just long enough to chart it and name it Baia de Todos os Santos, meaning Bay of All Saints. Then he sailed on in search of a westward passage to India and the Orient.

Thirty-five years later, Captain Francisco Pereira Coutinho came to Bahia representing Portugal to establish one of the first New World settlements. However, Coutinho's brutal treatment of the local Tupinamba Indians ended badly for the settlers, who were killed or run off and especially for Coutinho himself who was roasted and eaten.

Despite that tragic beginning, in 1549 the first royal governor, Tomé de Souza, established Salvador da Bahia as the capital of colonial Brazil. With the help of fifty of the king's soldiers, six hundred craftsmen, and six Jesuit priests, the indigenous people were subdued and enslaved to work in sugarcane fields.

In what I thought was becoming a familiar and disturbing pattern, the Indians virtually died out from overwork, genocide, and European diseases and were replaced by African slaves. Salvador ultimately became the most important slave market in the New World, and the African influence on culture and cuisine is still obvious.

As we navigated our way through the city, my impression was that despite the myriad cars and motorcycles, Internet cafes, and cell phones, the neighborhood had a desperate feeling of poverty. Virtually all the small parks and squares we wandered through were dirty with large cracks in the pavement and were littered with bottles and trash. Many of the buildings had cracked and broken bricks or peeling or nonexistent paint.

One of Salvador's most interesting features is the difference in elevation and ambience between the lower and upper parts of the city. We were in the lower city, comprised of a narrow band of congested streets that parallel the coastline. At Cayru Square near the Mercado, we paid $.05 real (the equivalent of a few cents) to ride the Lacerda Elevator up to Thomé de Souza Square in the upper city. The impressive pale yellow rectangular concrete tower that houses the elevator rises 215 feet above the street and holds four elevator cages operating twenty-four hours a day and carrying up to 128 people at a time.

The twenty-two-second ride in the dimly lit car tightly packed with people was a little uncomfortable. At the top we quickly exited the lift and walked through a horizontal concrete span that connects the tower to the upper plateau. Spacious and well-lit with windows on both sides, the passageway afforded a spectacular view of the lower city and the ocean.

When we finally exited the building onto the expansive square, I was amazed and delighted at the difference between the lower city and this area with its beautiful colonial architecture and old cobblestoned streets. It felt as if we'd been transported to a completely different city and time.

23

Hair! Between the long flowing blonde and the thick curly black locks on the two extraordinarily beautiful statuesque women, there was no mistaking who Mick was looking at, even from this distance. After stepping out of the upper Lacerda Elevator Building, he'd wandered down the street a short block toward the colonial palace. There, he stopped to get his bearings and was chastising himself for continuing his surveillance instead of spending the day with Darcy. That is when he looked up and saw the women coming out of the building talking and laughing, oblivious to the fact that every man on the square had turned to look at them mouths agape. And little wonder!

Instantly, he felt the shock of recognition when he realized the woman with Darcy was the one he saw on the beach in Barbados. He quickly walked around the fountain to the back side and waited for them to pass by. So this must be Captain Espen's wife and the woman who was supposed to have had an affair with Ronaldo Ruiz. It seemed incredible because now Mick knew that she was also involved with a passenger.

They had all been on the ship for only twelve days. How had the man managed to lure her from both her husband and a lover? There had to be something else going on. And why was Suzanne here with Darcy, when Mick knew the man he was following was also in the city? Darcy seemed to like Suzanne and believed she was a good person, but if Suzanne was in a relationship with Ruiz, she certainly didn't appear to be very broken up about his demise.

He made a leap, and it felt right. His mark was a dangerous guy capable of eliminating any obstacle standing in the way of what he wanted. He could have killed Ruiz or possibly had him killed because he wanted Suzanne, and perhaps she was just a promiscuous woman. A death plot might make sense of the meeting he had with a crew member and also the discussions Darcy overheard. The huge problem with that logic was that Darcy's encounters took place on the first day of the cruise, presumably before the guy had a chance to meet Suzanne. It would only make sense if they already knew each other before the cruise began. Mick's mind was spinning in an attempt to create connections. *If the man plotted to eliminate Ruiz as competition for Suzanne's affection, does it mean the captain is in danger too?*

Mick plopped down on the edge of the fountain as the implications of the asshole's activities hit home. First he experienced a sudden wave of compassion for the man's wife. Mick cared about her and considered her a close friend even though she didn't know he was onboard the ship. He'd resisted contacting her so far, even though she was the primary reason he booked the cruise.

He saw her out on the deck only one time and was careful not to let her see him. *What on earth is she doing with her time on the ship? God knows she wouldn't be spending it with her husband.* He resolved to find a way to discreetly talk to her and make sure she was not in any immediate danger.

What about Darcy's involvement in this odyssey? Had she gone to security after they talked last night, he wondered? If so, and if she was taken seriously, the investigation might well be reopened. If the man was guilty of something and found out that Darcy was responsible for putting him at risk of being detected, would she also be in danger?

He thought about Darcy talking about her discomfort with coincidences that seemed too unlikely to happen only by chance, even though she firmly believed there was nothing more to them. Well, Mick did believe in coincidence after all—things just happened—it did not mean there was any fate or plan behind them. Given enough time and variables, anything is possible. He had once thought there must be a reason for the deaths of his family members within a relatively short time frame, but now he knew better. That didn't mean he couldn't appreciate Darcy's concern because they both seemed to have fallen into a tangle of circumstances with disturbing connections.

By this time, the passenger he was following was lost in the crowd, and there was no point in wandering around the city looking for him when he did not seem to be doing anything but sightseeing anyway. There was the possibility of staying and watching out for Darcy and

Suzanne, but in the end he decided it was time to return to the ship and try to contact his friend.

24

For a while Suzanne and I had a pretty good time meandering down the narrow streets, then ducking out of the blistering sun to browse boutiques and souvenir shops. We even stopped for a beer and shared a chicken and hearts of palm empanada at a cute outdoor café. Enjoying the warmth and ambiance, I slouched with my fancy beaded flip-flops dangling from the ends of my toes and tried to feel like a wealthy tourist.

Our wandering also took us past an extraordinary number of beautiful churches and religious statuary dating back to the sixteenth and seventeenth centuries. Suzanne seemed positively enthralled by them. Outside a four-hundred-year-old convent, we contemplated a marble statue of Christ, which I couldn't help noticing had been rendered with a remarkably European face. Suzanne gazed up at Jesus's stone countenance for a full minute then half whispered, "Praise the Lord." I was taken aback by her somewhat crazed expression of awe.

She immediately rearranged her features and smiled shyly. "I really am a very religious person." Then she abruptly walked on to the next church.

A little while later I'd again become lost in thought, this time about the integral relationship between Christianity and settlement of the New World and how the religious influence dramatically altered the course of history for indigenous people as well as those who subsequently inherited these lands. This naturally led me to more musings about the origins of religion and how virtually everything about human existence was and still is influenced by supernatural beliefs.

At that point we'd been staring up at the huge statue of a cross at the end of Cruzeiro de Francisco square, surrounded by old churches and the convent. I was going to say something to Suzanne about the religious influence but wondered if I should stay away from the subject all together.

I have a tendency to get lost in thought for a minute or two, but it could not have been longer than that before I looked around and realized I was alone. I assumed Suzanne stepped into one of the shops on the square, so I stayed in the immediate area for about fifteen minutes hanging out on a wood and wrought iron bench waiting for her to return.

When she didn't, I got concerned. *What happened to her?* I had one of my intuitive feelings that something was going on that I should know about but didn't. I waited another five minutes before slowly making my way back to the long two-story white stone Rio Blanco palace just down the street from the elevator building.

At the central fountain, I waited again but there was no sign of her. I just could not come up with a good reason for her disappearance other than the unlikely possibility that she lost sight of me and went through the same waiting and looking process before going on ahead.

Finally I gave up and entered the building. As I stepped into the elevator for the ride down, two Brazilian men entered and stood to either side of me. Their closeness was not altogether unexpected because the car was full of people, but something about the way they positioned themselves was unnerving.

My anxious impressions during the quick ride down were that they were about my height, slim, with dark skin and eyes. Both wore tight-fitting jeans, and the one on my right had a sleeveless white tee shirt and a bushy mustache. The other one wore a short-sleeved black shirt and sported a small goatee. Both had complex tattoos covering their lower arms, which I couldn't make out in any detail in the dim lighting. They didn't actually look at me, but my pallid unembellished arms were suddenly covered with goose flesh in the stifling car as they seemed to lean toward me in an unnecessary if not downright menacing way.

At the bottom I tried to get out of the building as quickly as possible but had to fight my way through a small crowd of people all heading for the exit at the same time. I looked over my shoulder and was relieved to see that the two men were nowhere around. Surely they had gone out another door and my imagination was just running on overtime.

Out on the plaza I had another uncomfortable moment as I gazed across the lanes of traffic to the square outside the Mercado, now filled with vendors' booths and carts and teeming with local families and tourists. *Do I remember how to get back to the ship? Shit, here I go again with my lousy sense of direction.*

I crossed the plaza to the street, thinking that I should walk with folks who appeared to be citizens since there was no traffic light and cars seemed to fly from every direction at once. At a partial break in traffic, I scooted across beside a couple pushing a stroller over to the square. We arrived safely at a coconut water stand on the corner. I stood for a minute watching the vendor deftly operate the intriguing device that punched a hole in the large green seed, while simultaneously catching the milk in a container for her customer.

After getting my bearings, I decided it was safest to retrace the route Suzanne and I had taken from the ship, which had seemed fairly straightforward. I entered the market intending to walk straight through to the other end. It was only about three and the sun was high and bright. The ship wasn't scheduled to leave the port until five, so I had plenty of time even if I did manage to make a wrong turn on my way back.

At the center point of the crowded market, I slowed down and looked from side to side at the astonishing array of merchandise then proceeded down the narrow aisle. For some reason I glanced over my shoulder and found myself almost face-to-face with white tee shirt boy. The smirk on his face told me that this, anyway, was no coincidence. *Don't panic! There are lots of people around, and I can find some help if I need it.* I remembered passing an office of the "tourist police" on our route from the ship, but wasn't sure exactly where it was.

As soon as I turned forward and picked up my pace, I saw his companion leaning with an elbow on the counter of a snack bar about twenty-five feet ahead. His eyes held mine for several seconds. Fear in the form of a melting icicle slid down the back of my tank top, but I stubbornly refused to look away. When he finally blinked and shifted his gaze to the left, I darted in the opposite direction and tried to race down a perpendicular aisle.

Actually, I was mainly running into people and not making a lot of headway. "Please, please, let me through," I cried. I was a whole lot taller, younger, and in better shape than most of the customers, and felt like a steamroller as I knocked people aside. I'd never really had a fear of men in general or of being threatened or raped, but I was making up for it now.

All around me people were yelling and gesturing angrily, but their voices slipped into the distance as I pushed frantically forward. Finally, at the end of the aisle I turned right in the direction of the front entrance. Rounding the corner I forced myself to glance back hoping I'd lost my stalkers. But there they were still moving forward through the crowd, bumping into stalls and sending textiles, carved wood statues, and pottery flying. The worst part was their eyes. They were black and intense and locked onto me with no interest at all in the havoc they were causing as they plowed through the people and stalls in their frenzy to catch me.

I ran as fast as I could, wishing I had opted for sensible tennis shoes, as I weaved around people and stalls, yelling that I needed help the whole time. Of course, no one could understand me. But they didn't need English to get the idea that I was in trouble. It didn't seem to matter, probably because they were as much afraid of my pursuers as I was. I could see the open end of the building up ahead, and if I made it that far, I could get out onto the street and surely would be safer there.

Just as I leaped out into the sunlight next to the outdoor café full of families with small children, white tee shirt boy grabbed my arm roughly just above the elbow and yanked me back into the shadow of the building. My stomach did a slow sickening roll at the feel of his dry scaly hand on my skin. People sitting and standing in the immediate area could see what was happening, but no one made a move to help me. I was panting hard, but I pulled and struggled with all my strength, even kicking at his shins.

My might and determination were apparently a little more than he expected. His partner ran up behind us to help, and just as I felt his grungy fingers grabbing at my other arm, I swiveled away and began running up the street toward the dock—I hoped.

To this day, I don't know how I avoided being run over, as I darted in a blind panic across a busy street. I just kept running and somehow found my way to the sidewalk of Avenue Oscar Pontes, which ran along the back of the port building. Gasping through my mouth and unable to cry for help, I sprinted past pedestrians, some of them tourists who stopped to see what was happening, and that is when my senses of taste and smell were suddenly assaulted by the urine.

On the side of the cement building that ran along the length of the sidewalk, dark disgusting stains marred the wall at intervals of about ten feet, and in some places the ground was still wet. Obviously, this was a popular nightspot for drunks to relieve themselves. Even in my state of terror, it was utterly revolting, and I tried to run at the outer edge of the sidewalk near the street to avoid the wetness and the stench. Coughing and gagging, I stumbled along the curb, and prayed; p*lease don't let me fall down,* to no one in particular.

I almost made it. Goatee boy caught up with me about a half block from the gate leading to the dock, and I was too tired to do much about it. He grabbed me with one arm around my waist and the other around my neck, and began pulling me into the street. He babbled something in Portuguese into my ear, and I knew instinctively that he was going to put me into a car, and that I simply could not let that happen. I glanced up and saw two other men wearing light-colored shorts, most likely ship's passengers, running up the sidewalk a couple of short blocks away waving their arms and shouting. They were too far away to save me as we moved farther away from the curb.

Sure enough, an open car door waited just a couple of feet away. I screamed like I'd never done before, and with all my strength I pulled back, twisting and kicking for what seemed like an eternity. It was no use. I was worn out and just couldn't fight any longer. The whole scene slowed to a full stop as he released his grip on my neck and grabbed at my breast to push me down onto the backseat of the car.

Suddenly I felt a sharp tug and another pair of hands on my shoulders pulling at me. *Oh no, it's white tee shirt boy too. I'm dead!* "Help, somebody help me!" I screamed over and over, as I tried to twist away from them.

"Darcy, Darcy, stop! Stop fighting. You're all right now. Calm down." Miraculously—I don't mean literally—Don had pulled me away from my captor and was holding me against his muscular chest while I continued to sob and gasp for air.

"Is she OK?" I could barely hear Charlie's voice with my face pushed into Don's shirt, but his anxiety was obvious. I felt the vibration of Don's muffled voice in my cheekbone as I tried to burrow deeper into the safety of his awesome body.

"She will be. Both guys drove off," he said. "I guess they decided not to fight since we're so close to the port entrance."

25

"Holy shit, how will I ever be able to thank you guys? I really believe you saved my life. I don't know why those guys were chasing me, but I have never been so scared in my life."

Don put his hand on mine, again. "There is no doubt they meant to kidnap you. If we had not been crossing the street right there at the port entrance and seen what was happening, they probably would have succeeded. Their car was a beat-up old Ford Fairlane, and they looked like some kind of local scum. They let go and ran as soon as we grabbed for you."

I took a sip of martini and sat back forcing myself to loosen up. I had finally stopped shaking, and that had taken a good half hour. Now I was sitting with the guys and Mick at a table in the Center Bar. Mick had somehow joined us just after we entered the ship, and he was so concerned and angry about what had happened that I realized how much he really did care about me. He looked deep into my eyes in that way that had become routine. "Why were you out there alone, Darcy? I thought you were with Suzanne."

"Oh, Suzanne! I forgot. I don't know what happened to her." I leaped out of my seat and sucked in deep breaths as I moved away from the table not knowing where I was headed. "She just disappeared when we were in the upper city. What if she was kidnapped by those guys? I have to go and make sure she is back on board. Mick, will you come with me?"

"Yes, I'll come and help you," he said calmly. "But wait a minute. Sit down and let me tell you about something else I'm concerned about. There is a passenger on board who I know. I think he is somehow involved in Ruiz's death. I know it sounds crazy, but now I have to tell you that I came on the cruise partly to keep my eye on this guy.

"I've seen him talking—actually sort of arguing—with a crew member, and I saw him with Suzanne at the Barbados Hilton." Mick gave me a hard probing look as he continued. "It looked as if they were involved romantically. Darcy, do you know anything about that? And did you tell anyone else about those conversations you overheard?"

I was so stunned at what Mick was saying about Suzanne that my mouth had gone dry and I couldn't answer for a moment. I sipped my martini, which did not help at all. "Yes, I gave a report to security, and I also sort of mentioned it to my stateroom attendant, Plato. What are you saying, Mick, that Suzanne had a relationship with this guy you know? If the rumors are true, that would mean she was having affairs with two men at once. That is crazy. And what do you mean you were keeping an eye on him? Who is he? Does it have to do with your work?"

"All I'm saying is I'm afraid there's a connection between him and the crew members you overheard, and believe me when I say he is capable of doing something to get rid of Ruiz if he saw him as competition. Now I wonder if what happened to you today is also connected, you see what I mean?"

Don had been listening intently. "You think this guy had Darcy followed to scare her or worse, because she overheard him talking to a member of the crew about getting rid of the cruise director."

Mick turned to Don. "That is quite perceptive. Yes, I think something along those lines is possible. We need to go to security to tell them about this as well as find out if Suzanne is OK."

"But I really think both of the people I heard were crew members," I said.

"I know you do. Look, let's go talk to security and then we can discuss it more."

With that, Mick and I left the bar and headed for the guest relations desk. On the way, I tried to talk to Mick about his relationship with the passenger he mentioned, but he told me to wait until later and he would explain.

Mick did most of the talking when we were finally able to speak with Officer Smythe. He introduced himself, giving his work title and explaining that he conducted investigations for the U.S. Congress in a very formal and professional tone that I hadn't heard him use before. He seemed to be trying to establish some credibility.

After we explained what happened to me on shore and provided Don's and Charlie's names as witnesses, Mick reminded Smythe about my previous report on the conversations I heard. "I have to tell you that I'm worried that the attack on Darcy and what she overheard are related to Ronaldo Ruiz's death." He described how he had seen a passenger named Paul Denezza arguing with a crew member on the ship and had also seen him on shore in Barbados with Suzanne Moretti. When I heard the name it registered with me as unusual, but also familiar. I couldn't immediately place it but figured there would be plenty of time to ask him about it later.

When Smythe heard Mick mention Suzanne, he seemed to snap to attention and emphatically raised his hand to interrupt. "Did you say that Suzanne Moretti was in Barbados with a passenger?"

"Not only was she on shore with him but there was obviously something going on between the two of them, if you know what I mean. I know this guy and I'm sure that his whole reason for being on the cruise is suspect. I realize this sounds like a stretch, but please check him out and determine where he was when Ruiz fell. I believe he is dangerous." It seemed that Mick was finessing the story in some way and I noted that he did not explain his connection to Denezza. His behavior was only adding more mystery to an already unexplainable set of events.

Then we asked if Suzanne was back on board, because I had not seen her since we lost track of each other shortly before I was accosted. Officer Smythe stepped away to the counter and checked the computer to determine who had checked back onto the ship. He returned to us and said pointedly, "Ms. Moretti is back on board, and you do not need to be concerned about the captain's wife." He was obviously uncomfortable with what we were telling him and our familiarity with her.

Then turning to Mick, he seemed to size him up in some male-to-male way I didn't completely understand. Quietly but directly he said, "Look, Mr. Clayton, having a background in law enforcement I think you can appreciate the situation we have with regard to the captain's wife. It is sensitive to say the least. There is absolutely no evidence to suggest that Ms. Moretti is involved in any illicit behavior on board the ship . . . or off. She is a highly respected member of the staff.

Mick started to speak, but Smythe raised his hand. "Now having said that, I intend to look into what you reported about Mr. Denezza, and I will keep in mind what you said about Barbados. Please understand that you simply cannot conduct an investigation of your own. You must let us determine what is going on. I appreciate the information you have provided, and I feel confident that I can trust you to be discreet and not discuss these matters with anyone else on board the ship."

He turned to me then and softened his look considerably. "I cannot tell you how sorry I am about your incident in Salvador. We understand that it can be a somewhat dangerous place, but we have never before had a serious problem like this involving a passenger."

We both graciously thanked him, and Mick asked to be notified if they found any indication that his suspicions were credible. Smythe was noncommittal, but I guessed we couldn't really expect more. Anyway, I personally could not buy what Mick was saying about Suzanne either. I hated to admit I had doubts about his credibility with respect to her. I did not, however, doubt for one second Mick's intentions toward me. I believed then that they were beyond reproach.

26

Mick was worried about what Darcy thought of his story and his secret "mission." His instincts were right. He offered a sheepish grin and a plan. "Would you like to come to my stateroom for a little while? We can sit on my balcony and talk if you like."

"That would be nice, Mick. I do have some questions for you."

The balcony was shaded, and a slight breeze off the sea cooled the ninety-degree afternoon. The ship was about to set sail, and Mick's starboard stateroom was on the side away from the dock, affording them a pleasant view of the bay.

"This is a lot different than the dark cabin I share with Jason. I guess a cabin like this provides a whole different cruise experience." Then I got straight to the point. "Look, Mick, I have the feeling there is a lot more to your story than what you told Officer Smythe. Will you please tell me what is going on with you and why you came on this cruise?"

"OK, I admit I haven't been completely open with you about why I'm here, and I hope you will forgive me. I've been a little conflicted about it and if I'm honest a little embarrassed. See, I have an old friend who is married to Paul, and recently she has felt threatened by him. He is very wealthy and powerful and also an abusive asshole—maybe worse.

"I really did come on the cruise to try and relax. I hoped to enjoy myself, but mainly I came to watch out for her because bringing her on this cruise was completely out of character for Paul, and my friend was pretty freaked out. I do think Suzanne is in a romantic relationship with him based on how I saw them behaving in Barbados, and you have to admit that with everything else going on, it is damn strange."

"I agree that a lot of things seem strange, including you stalking this guy. I still don't get that part. But, I really believe the people I heard were both members of the crew. Why would they be talking about harming someone if your guy was the one trying to get rid of Ronaldo? I don't know, something still doesn't add up for me.

"And I still can't believe what you are saying about Suzanne. I've talked with her at length, and she would have to be psychotic or something to also be that person you're describing. I need to find her and ask what happened to her today in Salvador. Maybe the attack was just local bad guys going after a tourist and not related to anything else."

"Darcy, you probably can't be certain that Paul wasn't one of the men you heard on the deck, can you?"

"No, I suppose not, but why would you think it was him?"

"I guess mainly because I saw him in that other argument with a crew member in the sports bar. It makes sense to me that it all has to be connected, you know, not a coincidence." He grinned at her and that made her smile. Maybe they were sort of on the same page, he thought optimistically.

He had told her everything he felt he could. What purpose would it serve to tell her that his relationship with Mrs. Denezza had once been more than a friendship and that when he boarded the ship he still had residual feelings for her?

He had called her stateroom that afternoon and then had gone to see her. She seemed about the same as the last time they spoke. She was still very lovely with an innocent charm he once found irresistible. When he was in Vegas, they talked about the possibility of him trying to get on the same cruise that Paul had booked, but she was sure he had subsequently changed his mind about making the trip. Mick felt better and a little vindicated after meeting with her because she was totally amazed and somewhat relieved to find that he was on the ship after all.

She told him how Paul was leaving her alone most of the time and how she had been to the spa almost every day for a steam bath or some sort of body or hair treatment, but other than that and compulsory dinners with Paul, she was staying in the suite. He felt sorry for her and was reluctant to add to her anxiety by revealing what he knew about Paul's activities and his own suspicions. Instead, he said he was keeping an eye on Paul and she should try not to worry. His biggest concern was still the complete mystery as to why Paul brought her along on the cruise at all.

Mick was well aware he was withholding information from the two women on the ship he cared about, and this wasn't sitting well with him. He turned his attention back to Darcy. He knew now how intense his feelings for her had become.

He'd been waiting on deck 3 for her to board in Salvador, and when he saw her with Don and Charlie his heart almost stopped. Her loveliness was undiminished, but the look of stark terror on her face and the uncontrollable shaking had given him a feeling he did not remember experiencing before. More than simple empathy or anger, he felt a sharp dagger of pain and fear that might have been worse than what he felt when he first heard his wife Beth's terminal diagnosis.

Having partially unburdened himself to Darcy regarding his reason for being on the cruise, he felt more relaxed with her. He reached across the small metal patio table and took her hand. She did not pull away nor did she reciprocate the gentle pressure he applied.

"Darcy, I want to tell you how much meeting you means to me. I feel closer to you than I should considering the short time I've known you, and closer by far than I have to any other woman besides Beth. I know I'm not saying this very well, but I want to get even closer." He had bared his soul and was gazing at her with an open and vulnerable expression.

"Oh, I've had a lot of similar feelings, and part of my attraction to you is that you seem so open and honest. I feel as if I can trust you. But I'm pretty jaded, and I know I can jump into relationships too quickly. Can we just keep getting to know each other and figure out what all this weirdness on the ship is about?"

"Absolutely, now would you like a glass of wine out here? I have a bottle of red from the ship's liquor store, but I'm afraid I don't know if it's any good."

"Sure, and by the way, I assume you know that Doc, I mean Jason, and I are not together except for the closeness forced by the stateroom."

"I gathered that, and I wouldn't have told you how I felt otherwise." He went inside, rustled around a little, and reappeared with the wine and two water glasses. "Sorry I don't have wine glasses," he said as he poured. He sat down on the end of the lounge chair next to her legs and looked into her eyes as he raised his glass for a toast. "Darcy, you absolutely have the most beautiful eyes I have ever seen." He shook his head and grinned. "To us getting to know each other and whatever might follow."

"To us, Mick." She leaned in and kissed his cheek then turned her face so their lips brushed as she pulled back. "Sorry, I shouldn't have done that," she whispered. "I shouldn't say this either, but everything about you is a turn-on." She giggled. "See what I mean about being impulsive?"

He was completely delighted by the kiss, and he knew by the swelling pressure he was feeling that beyond any doubt he would eventually be with her. As much as anything else, he was relieved to know that he could have these feelings again.

27

I certainly felt elated when I left Mick on his balcony last night. Could he be the one I could build a life with after all this time of floundering in and out of unsatisfactory relationships? I wanted him, wanted his hands and mouth on me, and the rest. *Just make sure you take your time and don't screw this up.*

This day we were at sea on our way to Rio, and I would be spending most of the time with Mick. I didn't have any doubts about him, but I still had some about his theories, and I had to talk to Suzanne about what happened on shore yesterday.

I didn't dare use the same telephone tactic as before to find her, so I asked Plato if he would let her know I wanted to talk to her. He seemed hesitant but then said he would be seeing her at a nine-thirty staff meeting and would let her know. Suzanne called my room at about ten, and now I was on my way to the conference center on deck 3 to meet her.

Alone in the elevator, I thought about the pretty white envelope someone pushed under my door during the night. It was embossed with a raised white logo of some sort with my name written on the outside in a calligraphic hand. Inside was an announcement saying that I had won a shore excursion. Apparently there was a drawing, and my name was picked. I never seem to win anything, so this was a little exciting. The invitation advised me to contact the head of a group to reserve my seat on their tour to a famous Buenos Aires neighborhood. At this point I had no idea what plans I would have when we reached Argentina, so I put the envelope aside for later.

When I reached the center, it appeared to be deserted. There were no meetings being held or classes in session, and while the venue was well lit, it felt cold and sort of lonely. When I entered Jamaica, the room Suzanne designated, she was already seated at the table there. In front of her was a tray with two cups, several kinds of tea bags with a carafe of hot water, and a few Danish pastries. I chuckled to myself at how you could find the same pastries in so many locations on board, yet no one ever seemed to get tired of eating them.

Suzanne looked up from a file folder she was reading from with a concerned look. "Darcy, how are you? I heard about what happened after I lost track of you yesterday. Are you all right? I was so shocked when I found out about it from security, and I had planned to contact you this morning after our staff meeting. Oh, do you want some tea and pastries?" She seemed a little breathless and anxious, and I thought that was probably from embarrassment since she had sort of abandoned me on shore.

I sat down across from her and tried to paste on a relaxed smile. "I'm fine now, but I had an awful scare, Suzanne. What happened to you? I was standing near that big cross monument, and when I looked up you were gone."

She seemed to fuss unnecessarily with the tea service, and did not exactly make eye contact. "I wish I knew what happened. I just went into a store on the square there, and when I came out I couldn't find you. Maybe I was inside longer than I realized, and there were so many people . . ."

"Well, that is just what I assumed because I couldn't come up with any other explanation, except that you had been taken by the same men who almost grabbed me. I am so thankful that is not what happened. They were very scary, and I am quite sure they intended to prevent me from returning to the ship. I don't even want to think about why. I know about human trafficking for prostitution, but I'd think I'm a little over the hill for that."

"I can't tell you how sorry I am, but the Lord always takes care of right-minded people." *What did she just say?* "But they probably would not have done anything if we had been together, so I feel partly responsible," she said, as she poured water onto a bag of green tea I had selected and placed in my cup.

Her body language was stiff, and somehow she didn't seem very remorseful. But she certainly was distressed because the hand holding the carafe was shaking almost indiscernibly, but shaking nonetheless. My powers of observation kicked in, and I noted the tight stress lines around her mouth and at the corners of her eyes, which were not normally there. *There is more to this gal than meets the eye, and maybe Doc wasn't completely wrong when he said she was a little off.*

I so badly wanted to ask her about the Barbados incident but just could not figure out a way to bring it up. I kind of felt like a wimp, but something told me it was better to wait and see what security did with the information Mick provided.

"Suzanne, I was told that nothing has ever happened to anyone on shore in Salvador before and also that no crew member has ever died on this ship before. It occurs to me that it is quite a coincidence that you and I just met and have both suffered a very unusual and traumatic event within days of each other. Don't you think that is odd?"

Her mouth tightened and her oddly speckled eyes narrowed slightly. "Oh, you mean because I was with poor Ronaldo when he fell? Well, yes, I guess it is unusual and unfortunate that we are both having a rough time on this cruise, but I'm sure these things are just coincidences, as you said. Besides, you know, Darcy, everything happens according to a plan, and everything will work out if we are patient."

According to a plan? I was incredulous that she did not seem to realize her last two statements were completely contradictory. What is she talking about? And yes, there are a few too many fucking coincidences on this cruise.

28

Espen sat in his easy chair staring out the window at the little foot-high swells and contemplating his return to the bridge for the approach to Rio de Janeiro. As required by the port authority and good sense, the Rio pilot would arrive by tug within the next half hour and would literally hop aboard as the *Sea Nymph* slowly approached the harbor. He would use his extensive knowledge of the shallow channel to help navigate into port.

Their entrance to the harbor would afford views of impressive and famous Rio sites, including a path so close to Ipanema and Copacabana beaches that passengers who were so inclined could use their telephoto lenses to view the sunbathers.

Then they would sail around the tip of the peninsula where the world-famous 1,200-foot Sugarloaf Mountain seemed to rise straight up from the sea. Clearly visible would be the dangling cars strung like toys along the thin cable stretching from the top of the mountain to its lower sister, Mount Urca. And in the distance just a little to the west they would be able to see the world-famous 2,400-foot Mount Corcovado and the massive Christ the Redeemer monument towering a hundred feet above the mountaintop.

Navigating to the dock would be tricky for the large ship and would require Espen's full attention. He would have to nudge her gently into the slip moving sideways by turning the two eighteen-foot bow thruster propellers to the side. Having responsibility for this delicate operation was not good timing since he now sat virtually paralyzed with rage and, he had to admit to himself, more than a little fear as well.

He'd been troubled enough before Staff Captain Early's latest visit. But he had known the moment he opened the door and saw his friend's strained expression that things were only going to get worse.

James was normally as calm and thoughtful as Espen himself—or as he used to be. He was a tall burly man who was nearly as dark in coloring as the captain was light, with smooth olive skin, a pleasant round face, and thick black curls. A Brit, he could easily pass for Italian or Spanish. Espen could read the rigid body language and set of his jaw as he entered the room, strode to the floor to ceiling window, and looked out onto the balcony in silence for almost a minute.

When James finally turned to face the captain, he began to present the report he'd received from Officer Smythe, while obviously trying to be as gentle and tactful as possible. The story was fantastic and unbelievable, and yet Espen knew he must accept what were clearly some very disturbing facts.

Seated in his favorite cream leather recliner, he had tried to listen attentively despite his mounting and unmanly panic, but he only became increasingly agitated. As James sensed his friend's discomfort, he crossed the room and sat down on the sofa across from him. He began speaking in a low, calming tone.

First there were the American passengers who reported incidents involving crew members. As James explained, Darcy Farthing, who came on board with an American medical doctor, told security she was concerned about two conversations she inadvertently overheard between two men she believed were crew members. These incidents occurred on the first afternoon and evening of the cruise, and she was adamant that they were plotting against someone on the ship who was going to be hurt or killed and that it involved a monetary transaction.

Then incredibly this same woman insisted that she was accosted and almost kidnapped in Salvador da Bahia. This appeared to be true, since two American gentlemen traveling together verified that they had indeed rescued her and scared off the assailants just outside the port entrance. She gave a detailed description of her two male attackers, and they appeared to be local residents. This attack was unprecedented among all the cruise ships the World of Seas Cruise Line had ever brought to Salvador.

As if that were not enough, yet another American passenger, Mr. Clayton, who works for the United States government in some capacity accompanied Ms. Farthing when she reported the incident. Mr. Clayton said he believed that another passenger, Paul Denezza, who Officer Smythe identified as a wealthy hotel and casino owner from Las Vegas, Nevada, was a dangerous man who could be involved in Ronaldo's death. Further, he suggested this passenger could have orchestrated the attack on Ms. Farthing. Clayton said he also witnessed Denezza in a personal and somewhat heated discussion with a crew member he could not identify. Finally, according to Officer Smythe, Clayton requested that security look into Denezza's whereabouts at the time of Ronaldo's fall.

As a precaution, Officer Smythe had in fact questioned several crew members and Denezza himself and also reviewed security camera footage for that night. There was no question that the man was in the casino for several hours and nowhere near The Whale's Tail that evening. Furthermore, he appeared to be a dignified businessman who was very cooperative and assured the security chief that he had no knowledge of any kind pertaining to the cruise director's death.

As he listened, Espen's emotions, some of which he was only just learning he possessed, ping-ponged in a manner that felt physically dangerous. The unfamiliar feelings of fear combined with anger were so debilitating that he was already having difficulty carrying out his normal duties and now it was getting so much worse.

As he watched James's expressions and mannerisms during this report, he sensed that something more was to come partly because none of it added up to the personal seriousness and drama his friend seemed to be implying.

"If security has ruled Ronaldo's death to be accidental, why put any credence in what these American passengers are saying?" he ventured cautiously. "There must be more to this issue."

James sat uncomfortably on the edge of the low, firm Scandinavian sofa with his long legs bent and his forearms resting on his knees. He studied his hands, which were repeatedly clenching and relaxing of their own accord. Finally he looked up at his friend's worried expression. "Oh yes, my friend. There is something more, and you will not be pleased to hear it."

Espen suddenly felt hot and sick to his stomach. His heart pounded and he felt an instantaneous sheen of sweat coat his forehead. "What are you talking about?" he asked, in as calm a voice as he could muster.

"You and I have spoken before about the rumors regarding Suzanne and Ronaldo, and you know that they were together just prior to his fall. Well, unfortunately she seems to be a common link between these other odd events as well. She went ashore with Ms. Farthing in Salvador, which of course is in violation of the crew-passenger code of ethics." Espen began to speak, but James hurriedly continued.

"The point is, Ms. Farthing said they spent several hours together, and then Suzanne disappeared, and it was just then that she was followed and attacked. We talked with Suzanne, and her story is that she simply lost track of Ms. Farthing while they were shopping, returned to the ship alone, and didn't think anything of it. She later heard about the attack, felt concerned, and has talked with Ms. Farthing about what happened."

Espen's discomfort eased a bit. "Well, of course she should not have gone ashore with a passenger, but that is not—"

"No, Sir." James cut him off. "I am afraid that is not all. Mr. Clayton swears that he also saw her at the Barbados Hilton with Mr. Denezza and that they were in a, well, a compromising encounter. This is why he thinks these events are linked. He said this man is ruthless and might have killed Ronaldo out of jealousy and possessiveness."

This was an amazing yet outrageous turn of events, and all Espen's energy was engaged in trying to behave normally and control his growing anger and indeed terror. He was truly speechless. He stared at James, trying to form some words that would defuse what he had just heard and allow him to magically return to a time when he did not know these horrible things about his wife.

"Listen to me, my friend." James could readily see the captain's distress. "We do not know for sure what relationship Suzanne might have with this passenger, but a couple of things are fairly clear to me. First, if Denezza did conspire with crew members to eliminate Ronaldo because of jealousy over Suzanne and Ms. Farthing heard them talking about it the day we sailed, then Suzanne had to have known the passenger prior to the cruise. Second, the fact that she is your wife cannot preclude her from being disciplined for her shore excursions with passengers. This is simply not allowed as you well know, and we can't ignore it and then expect the rest of the crew to adhere to the rules."

Espen found his voice enough to make a raspy reply. "Yes, I understand," he managed. "Please determine the disciplinary action you deem appropriate." He cleared his throat in a futile attempt to dislodge whatever appeared to be constricting his airway. "James, please see if we can keep this information confidential until I have a talk with Suzanne. There has to be some explanation. You know as well as I that she is a very conservative woman and not the type of person to be involved in anything truly inappropriate. Also, the least complicated explanation is usually the best, and you have already determined that Ronaldo's death was accidental."

James nodded then and told the captain he had advised security to initiate surveillance of Suzanne, Mr. Denezza, Mr. Clayton, and Ms. Farthing. On his way out he abruptly stopped and turned around. "Do you realize that if there is any truth to Suzanne having an affair with this man and he is as dangerous as Mr. Clayton believes, then you could also be in danger?"

Espen now shuddered at the memory of that earlier conversation and turned from the window. As he crossed the room heading toward the door he thought that things were happening on his ship and with his life that were unacceptable. Then an even darker thought invaded his troubled mind. On top of everything else, another person stood in the way of his happiness and threatened to humiliate him. That is when he came to terms with the full depth of the trouble that had overtaken him.

29

The next three days spent with Mick including two days in Rio were like a fantastic dream. I felt especially good about spending all my time with him because I had talked with Doc before we arrived in port, and he assured me he had no problem with me spending time with Mick. It turned out that he was a pretty understanding and cool guy after all. Of course it helped that he'd found a young single gal—leggy and fair of course—with whom he was basically hooked up.

I was apprehensive about going ashore and would never have gone alone. The trauma of what happened in Salvador da Bahia was still fresh, and I was afraid I would never completely get over it. The good news was that once on shore I felt completely safe with Mick, more secure than I had ever felt with anyone.

For some reason the stress of my ordeal had not caused me to dream about my Rachael as I would have expected. I went along with my life as usual, keeping her behind my fragile mental bars. I had not mentioned any of that part of my life to Mick, but I knew that if we continued to get closer, the time would come when I would have to open up to him as I had never done with anyone except Dr. Meisner.

Rio certainly deserves its reputation for beauty and excitement. But when Captain Andre Goncalves and the Portuguese explorer Gaspar de Lemos discovered Guanabara Bay on New Year's Day, 1502, they named it unceremoniously for the calendar month.

One story has it that Lemos mistook the bay for the mouth of a river, hence the name Rio de Janeiro. Rio served as the seat of Brazil's government for two hundred years beginning in 1763, and I was surprised to learn that it also served as the displaced capital of Portugal during the Napoleonic War when the royal family and their courtiers fled Lisbon and set up rule in exile. Knowing some of the history of Brazil, it made sense that it is the only South American country where the official language is Portuguese rather than Spanish.

On our first day in port, Mick and I took a taxi tour down Rio Blanco Avenue, the main route to downtown. Amazingly, we were traveling over an area that had once been ocean but was now a major part of the city thanks to construction over a landfill. The road wound through the arch of a stone aqueduct built in 1750 and past the 246-foot-high Saint Sebastian Cathedral, built during the 1960s and '70s to replace several former churches.

The driver's English was pretty good. He explained to us that the new version of the cathedral, which looks like a tall pyramid, is intended to suggest an Inca temple. When I suggested this seemed an odd symbol for a church in the most Catholic of all countries in the world, the driver made the situation more than clear. In 1532 Brother Cristobal de Albornoz was ordered by Spain to search for and destroy all Inca pyramid temples, called huacas. More than six hundred were burned in this area alone along with all their records and artifacts, and Catholic churches were routinely built on the ruins. The cathedral's Inca style was a nod to this horrific history.

We ended our tour of the city at Sugarloaf where we rode the cable car to the top and spent an hour just enjoying the magnificent views of the bay and city and taking photos of each other with the incredible vistas as a backdrop.

Later, we had an uneventful evening on board, enjoying drinks in our favorite bar and chatting with Manuel about our day's adventure. We opted to eat dinner by ourselves on Mick's balcony, and that truly was a perfect ending to the day's adventure.

The next day Mick asked if I wanted to visit the Cristo statue, and I told him that I was content to view it from a distance but would be happy to go there with him if he wanted. I remembered his story about his mother naming him Michelangelo because of her love for the Sistine Chapel, and I was a little surprised when he said he did not really care about visiting one of the most famous Christian landmarks in the world.

Instead we strolled through the Jardim Botanico constructed in the early 1900s by King João VI. The sprawling gardens with greenhouses, lovely fountains and ponds, and a botanical museum encompass over three hundred acres and contain eight thousand species of plants, flowers, and trees from all over the world. My botany was more than a little rusty, but I had fun stopping to read the little descriptive signs and trying to identify the plants. Mostly I just enjoyed the beauty with Mick beside me.

The last thing we did in Rio was walk hand in hand along Copacabana beach. Brazilians are understandably in love with their beaches, and there were lots of people there in the late afternoon. There were mostly families with beach umbrellas, coolers, and boom boxes, sunbathing and playing in the surf. Incongruously, we were told that the medical community advised residents to visit the beach only after work in the late afternoon, due to a hole in the ozone layer that rendered the midday sun too dangerous. Lucky for them, the light would last until about eight thirty.

And so as the sun hovered low above the horizon, we watched children play on the whitest sand I had ever seen. Teenagers built extravagant, professional-looking sand castles, while vendors walked up and down the beach with shrimp on skewers, platters of fruit, and soft drinks. In my entire life, I do not expect to have an experience as romantic and memorable—just like a honeymoon.

Our new love was by far the most intense I had ever experienced. Every sight, sound, and smell is tattooed on my mind forever. Surprisingly, to me at least, we had touched and kissed a number of times over the past two days but had restrained ourselves from going further. By the time we returned to the ship on that last day in Rio, we had somehow come to a silent agreement. We both knew we would spend the night together in Mick's cabin.

30

Others on the ship were not enjoying themselves quite as much. Around noon after the boat docked in Rio, Paul Denezza paced back and forth on the top deck deep in thought. He was unable to appreciate the extraordinary views on all sides as he angrily thought about the latest developments. He was unaccustomed to the mounting feeling that he was losing control of events and people around him. Maintaining control was the most important thing in life, after all, and fear was a tried and true method of achieving that goal. He knew he could manipulate his wife when the time came because weak and fearful as she was, she would be compliant as always.

But he could not believe that someone, apparently a passenger, had reported seeing him on shore with the captain's wife. He and Suzanne had been careful not to meet in places where they were likely to encounter passengers, but obviously not careful enough. Who could possibly even know him, and why would they care who he was with? He had to find out who was meddling in his life and put an end to it.

Thankfully, his wife had been at the spa when the security officer showed up at their stateroom to interview him. The man had been pleasant enough, but the questions he asked made it clear that somehow he was trying to link Paul to Ronaldo Ruiz's death and to Suzanne. This was completely unacceptable. He thought he'd been successful in convincing Smythe his relationship with Suzanne was simply an old friendship and nothing more. But he had to find out who saw him with Suzanne and what they knew about Ruiz.

His precious plan seemed to be spiraling out of control, and he could not let that happen. He had counted on only one outcome ever since the weekend in October when Suzanne brought Ruiz to Vegas, and Paul decided to take the World of Seas cruise.

He first met Suzanne that summer when she and her husband were vacationing in Vegas. Paul was sitting at the main casino bar at Athens Olympia when she strode in alone wearing a dazzling short metallic skintight dress. He hadn't known what to look at—her fabulous legs, her perfectly shaped breasts, her one-in-a-million face, or her astounding hair.

Ever since that first meeting he'd found it difficult to function at his normal level of efficiency, and he was completely helpless to stop the constant stream of thoughts about her that filled his head. He had never experienced anything even close to the physical and emotional attraction she held, and he was almost physically debilitated if he could not see her for even a day. She was his obsession, and nothing would stop him from carrying out his plan. He hoped to convince her to be part of his life forever because he knew only then would he be able to regain total control of his world.

He accepted her other relationships by telling himself they must be only short-term arrangements. Then the crew's rumors about a romance between Suzanne and Ruiz had threatened to destroy both his sanity and his plan. Paul's sense that events were spiraling out of control had thrown him into a near panic and desperation—an emotion he had never experienced before and did not like one bit.

On top of that, the other crew member recruited into the plan, Plato, seemed to suspect that Paul had something to do with Ruiz's death. What if Plato talked to security? That would not be wise. He had to find out just where Plato stood since he was now the most important link in carrying out the plan.

*   *   *

Meanwhile, Plato des Rameaux was entertaining disturbing thoughts of his own as he went through the mindless motions of vacuuming and making up his guest room beds, including Darcy's. He had thought he understood what was happening between Suzanne, Paul, and Ronaldo Ruiz, and his own role in the arrangement. Now, however, he was beginning to understand why Ronaldo was having second thoughts that might have gotten him killed. Plato was asking himself whether the money he was promised was worth the risks that were obviously escalating. Mr. Denezza was a very dangerous man.

Plato considered himself to be a tough guy too, having survived a poor and violent childhood in a Port-au-Prince slum. Growing up, he stayed away from his tiny depressing house, which was little more than a shack, and his constantly warring parents as much as possible and literally fought his way through his daily existence on the streets. From the age of eight he survived by stealing from small family-owned shops and picking the pockets of hapless tourists.

While he was not particularly well educated, the one thing that saved him was American music and movies. He stole a CD player when he was ten and spent untold hours listening to English song lyrics. He also routinely sneaked into the run-down and filthy movie theaters to see American films with Spanish subtitles, mostly sleazy pornography, and in this way taught himself to speak passable English. He had rightly believed this would be a ticket to escape his depressing surroundings and raise himself out of his illegitimate lifestyle.

Three years ago at the age of twenty-two he applied for a job with World of Seas without much hope of being hired, since he had no real work history and was dragging around an anchor of low self-esteem. When he recovered from the shock of actually being hired, it took many weeks before he could resign himself to his role on the ship.

He considered the cabin attendant position to be a feminine job that offended his manhood, made all the worse by having to work for a woman. Somehow he managed to keep his mouth shut because he knew there was no other way he could make the amount of money the cruise line paid him—until Ronaldo told him about Mr. Denezza's plan.

Now, however, all Plato could think about was how he was going to hold on to both his job and his life. He had already challenged Mr. Denezza about Ronaldo's death, and now he regretted having angered the man. He also believed that Darcy Farthing had gone to security with information about Ronaldo, and at the same time she had some sort of relationship with Suzanne that Plato could not fathom. Although he reported everything he knew about Farthing to Suzanne, he dared not confront her about the plan since she was his boss in every respect, and he did what she told him to do.

Worse, she was Captain Espen's wife. Nothing good could possibly come of any of this now. He knew he was foolish to allow himself to be used to make the kidnapping deal with the local thugs he'd met on previous trips to Salvador. He wondered how he let himself be dragged into this mess and how he could stop any further violence without anyone knowing of his involvement.

31

Espen sat at the desk in his suite completing routine paperwork and answering e-mail messages. He still had difficulty concentrating, and his anxiety only increased when he looked at the clock and realized that Suzanne's shift was finishing. He hadn't had an opportunity to speak with her since his conversation with James Early, and could not avoid it any longer.

He knew Suzanne was cheating on him and that somehow he had completely misjudged the type of woman he'd married. What an idiot I have been, he mused. Getting involved with her so quickly and letting my sexual desires rule my life like a teenager. *Jeg kan ikke la henne lager en tosk av meg noe lengre eller lot henne lager meg gjør ting som jeg vil beklage.* I cannot continue to let her make a fool of me and cause me to do things I regret.

As he was thinking over what he would say to her, the door opened, and she walked into the sitting room quickly flopping down on the couch. "Oh, my dear Espen, I am so exhausted. I have been on my feet all day checking the quality of all the stateroom attendants' work. I was thinking of taking a bath, and then perhaps we could have some champagne and try the Pão de Oveijo, a new cheese bread I bought in a Rio market." She looked over at him expectantly and noted his incredulous expression. "What is wrong, dear, are you feeling ill?"

His outrage bubbled over as he jumped to his feet and shouted at her. "How can you think you can walk in here and speak to me as if I am a naïve child and behave as if nothing is wrong?"

Suzanne's normally open expression immediately closed and she paled noticeably. Her already-volatile eyes flashed golden sparks up at his face as he stood over her. "Must we go over this again? It is so tedious. You must believe me when I assure you once again that I love only you."

He could readily see the effort she was making to remain calm. *If she is telling the truth, why is she so distressed?* "I don't understand what you are doing or why," he said, "but I now know with certainty you are not the woman I believed you to be. Not only did you have an inappropriate relationship with Ronaldo but now I learn that you are also intimate with the American passenger, Paul Denezza. I am not such a fool that I don't realize the connection between his hotel in Vegas and our vacation last summer."

Suzanne had been leaning on the arm of the sofa in a somewhat tense position as she stared up at him. Without warning she leaped up and charged him, her hair flaring out from her neck and shoulders and her eyes wide with rage. Before he could move out of her way, she was upon him clawing at his arms and neck like an enraged panther. She emitted a high pitched screeching sound as tears streamed down her face. Then with balled fists she continued to pummel his chest and arms.

"How dare you! You are not the man I thought you to be either. What have you done? You are ruining everything. And who has said such a thing about Paul and me?" she screamed. "I know him, of course, but it is not a sordid little affair as you think." She seemed to realize the extent of her loss of control and began to pull away at the same time that he grabbed her arms pulling her down to her knees on the floor in front of him.

He raised one hand to his neck feeling the sting of rising welts where her nails raked his skin and shook his head as he looked down at her. He was afraid of her—there was no doubt about it—but he would not let her see how badly shaken he was.

"I know that I have acted the fool since the day we met, so it is perhaps understandable that you have come to see me as one. However, Suzanne, that is all over now. Listen closely to what I am going to tell you. I will not suffer any more humiliation on my own vessel.

"You will move out of here and down to general crew quarters, and you will do your job and have nothing to do with me. Further, you will keep your mouth shut and remember that you essentially work for me and that I can easily have World of Seas fire you. And, make no mistake, my dear, I will make sure that the officers and crew know that I have separated from you and plan to divorce you."

"Oh, dear God, Espen, do not do this! You have to change your mind—I know you will when you think about it, because I understand how vulnerable you are. Do you understand me? I am so sorry for losing my temper. You must forgive me because we have to stick together." Her demeanor had changed again, and she appeared contrite and sorrowful. "You do not want to ruin everything over a misunderstanding. Please, Espen, please?" She had calmed down and was pleading with him in her normal conciliatory tone, but he knew he could not let himself be swayed. He had to finish with what he wanted to say.

"And one more thing, regarding Ronaldo's death, if you know more than you have reported to Smythe, you had better tell me now."

Suzanne felt a rush of panic as she searched her husband's face for a threat or any remnant of the love and trust she once enjoyed. When his hateful expression did not soften, she rose to her feet and turned toward the bedroom. "You are going to regret what you have done. You will see. The Lord will not allow you to ruin his plans for me," she said over her shoulder.

Espen sat down heavily in his easy chair, gripped the soft leather arms, and gazed out at the sun sparkling in darts and flashes off the white caps while he tried to gain control of himself. He could hear drawers and cabinets opening and closing in the next room, and as he waited, a cold shiver ran down the length of his back. Her last words were by far the strangest threat he'd ever heard—almost like a curse.

After about ten minutes she reappeared with her bulging duffel and wordlessly crossed to the door. He wanted to beg her to stay, and it was all he could do to stop himself. An odd mixture of sorrow and relief washed over him as he watched the door close behind her.

32

I released a heavy contented sigh and enjoyed the warmth of the waning sun on my face. My head lolled back against the lounge chair as I sipped my champagne. Mick was sitting on the end of the chair next to my legs with his hand resting lightly on my bare foot. I'd just returned from my stateroom where I showered away the Rio beach sand, quickly dried and fluffed my hair, and dressed in a simple and comfortable soft yellow shift and both types of matching thongs.

By the time I returned to Mick's cabin, he had showered too and was arranging the room service champagne and canapés out on the balcony. After kissing him hello, I crossed the room to go outside. On the way, I had an overwhelming sense of rightness that I honestly could not recall having experienced before.

I opened my eyes, and they instantly brimmed with tears at the sight of Mick's tanned face and neck above the sexy white linen shirt left open to his waist, and the backdrop of a breathtaking pink and orange sunset. This was not like me. I was completely undone by the way he was looking at me with such obvious love and tenderness.

He had already told me that he also could not believe the depth of his feelings, and admitted being a little frightened when he thought about the closeness we were developing so quickly.

He obviously could see the wetness in my eyes. "I know exactly what you're feeling," he said. "My life has completely changed in the last three days, and although I know there's a lot I have to learn about you, I've no doubt you are all I could ever want or need." He chuckled to himself as he lifted his glass to mine. "Can you believe all this is happening without us having been physically intimate?"

He leaned down and gently kissed me. What a sensation! "You are the most beautiful and wonderful woman in the world. Please let me take you inside and show you how much I already love you. I want to do everything perfectly from now on so there will be no flaw in our starting out together. You know what I mean, Darcy?"

I had to swallow tears of happiness. Touching his face, I opened up to him as best I could. "Oh, Mick, I know exactly what you mean. I ache for you, and I want it to be the best and perfect sex ever. How could it not be?" I truly wanted to just go with the flow, but it didn't happen. "I'm worried about the things you don't know about me and how you might feel when you find out what I am really like."

He kissed me again and I felt the telltale sting in the back of my nose. I didn't want to start sobbing at this romantic moment. "Nothing," he said with a quivering voice, "do you hear me? Nothing can change the woman I see here with me now. We all have things in our pasts we are not so proud of, and you and I will eventually discuss whatever we are comfortable sharing. But we can't go back, and nothing can change either the past or what is happening between us now."

I should have given in and accepted the truth of what he was saying. I didn't. "But, do you know that I am an atheist?" I blurted. "I mean an honest-to-God atheist." I was half laughing and half crying.

His face drooped. Shaking his head, he answered quietly. "No, I didn't know it was that serious." He frowned into his glass.

Damn! Why did I have to reveal information that would be a fatal flaw to many people . . . right now? He would have to either cool things down between us or try to convert me to some belief system. "Mick, I understand if this is a deal breaker for you, but it's not a whim. This is who I am and always will be. I can't help it. I don't think I have the God gene." I was panicked and needed to stop talking, but figured I might as well get it all out. A lump moved up into my throat as I tried unsuccessfully to control the tears running down my face.

Swallowing a sob, I tried to explain. "Look, my view is that there have always been people—a silent minority—who didn't believe in whatever gods, demons, or spirits were in vogue at the time. They mostly hid their skepticism so as not to invite the attention of their neighbors or the powers that controlled their lives. They stayed in the closet because they were afraid they would have to sacrifice everything, maybe even their lives, at the hands of the devout. And make no mistake, Mick, danger to nonbelievers still exists."

He wasn't looking at me but seemed to be listening. I choked back another sob but didn't wait for a reaction. "I know that religions or cults or whatever you want to call them have achieved a lot of good, but haven't they also been safe havens for God wannabes who want to control others with their supposed special knowledge? I guess the thing that bothers me the most is how so many people use God to justify their ignorance, irresponsibility, hate, and intolerance, and even to explain their own good fortune or accomplishments. Maybe it's just too scary to accept that we alone are responsible for all our setbacks and achievements as well as the advancements of our culture."

Why couldn't I stop myself? I was preaching, of all things, and these were thoughts normally kept inside my head. I guess I was trying to say something that Mick would be able to accept. He had not looked at me since I began speaking.

In desperation, I kept going. "You know, even though we understand so much about the physical world, we don't seem to have changed much since our ancestors adopted the concept of Gods to explain things like sickness, birth, death, famine, fire, earthquakes, and eclipses. Wouldn't you think we have enough information about how the world works, for people to shed the ancient superstition and fear?"

Finally I made myself stop. I sat staring at the top of his head, fully realizing what a mistake that diatribe had been. *Why can't I ever just let things be easy?*

Finally, I guess when he was sure I was finished, he looked up. "Oh, Darcy," he choked as he tried to stifle a laugh. My heart aches at the sight of your expression. You look exactly like a little girl who has disappointed her daddy, right down to the quivering lip. I'm sorry for embarrassing you, but I have to tell you again how sweet and wonderful you are."

That was not exactly what I was expecting. I tried to relax and gave him back a little laugh to show him his words had not offended me, even though they sort of did.

"I can't say that I agree with your philosophy 100 percent, but I'm open to hearing more about it eventually. I pretty much gave up on religion or belief in a grand scheme when Beth had the brain tumor and then my parents were killed so young by . . . a big rock. On the other hand, I would like to believe there is an intelligent design or plan or whatever that has brought us together like this."

My relief was obvious. I threw my arms around his neck, almost spilling the entire contents of my glass down his back. After a moment I realized what he'd said. I leaned back and inspected his face. "Wait a minute, Mick. Did you say a big rock killed your parents?"

"Yeah, it was a bizarre accident—about as unlucky as you can get by chance. The thing is it happened in your neck of the woods. They were on a ski trip in Colorado, and a boulder fell off the side of a hill on a road near I70 and Loveland Ski Area, right into the front seat of their car as they drove . . . like it was aiming for them. The police told me it has happened before, more than once, in that area." I nodded, knowing exactly how these accidents happened in the mountains, and felt more tears welling.

"Anyway, Dad was killed instantly and Mom was basically on life support for a couple of months while I got a bunch of opinions. She really was brain dead, so I let them pull the plug." He shook with the effort to control his own tears. "This is the first time I've described their deaths since just after it happened."

"Oh my god, Mick"—*there is no God*—"I don't know what to say. That is the most horrible thing imaginable." Leaning forward I encircled him in my arms and pulled him closer. I acted on pure instinct, kissing his closed eyes, his mouth, and then his chin. "I know what you mean," I whispered, "about wanting to feel like there is a reason for things. It's like the coincidences on this trip and, oh man, in our lives. I don't understand everything—no one does—but I know there is a natural and rational explanation for everything."

Mick squeezed his eyes with his thumb and forefinger and breathed deeply as he sat back and stared at me. After a few seconds, he managed a smile. "Well, now that we have that out of the way, come inside with me because I cannot stand one more minute of not seeing your gorgeous breasts naked."

Wow! I was speechless, but fortunately he didn't wait for my response. He gently pulled me up off the chair and led me by the hand in the door and to the side of the bed. All I could do was look up into his face, mesmerized. My arms remained limp at my sides while I waited to see what he would do next. I couldn't remember ever feeling so open and trusting. All I wanted was for him to touch me however he wanted and for him to let me do the same.

Still standing, we slowly undressed each other and spent the first precious moments just appreciating each other's body. With a deep thrill

I noted that the shape of him, his smooth belly and just the right amount of body hair—the dark curls whispering lightly over his groin—were perfectly to my liking just like everything about him so far.

Then we drew closer and embraced. Right away, Mick swelled and slid between my thighs. My breasts pressed against his chest, and a wave of heat and intense aching ran down my entire body. I drew in a sharp breath. I was floating and so were the words that came unbidden. "Mick, I can't wait. You are so beautiful. Everything is wonderful."

I almost shoved him down onto the bed and could not remember ever feeling this urgent and completely biological need. I had the irrational notion that I would die if he did not enter me immediately.

Mick was also beside himself with passion. He was rock hard, but he said he wanted to be patient and to take it slow with our first lovemaking. Now he rolled onto the bed, pulling me with him, and pushed with his heels to move away from the edge. I was already moving involuntarily against him with my mouth close to his ear urging him on. Later, he admitted he'd pushed an unbidden image of Beth from his mind, and then he'd understood a sweet and important part of his life was now truly over.

He forced me to lie back on the bed and began kissing my breasts. I moaned and kissed his shoulder as he moved his mouth slowly down my body. "Oh, Mick, I've never . . ." With bent knees, my body arched off the bed and I couldn't contain a yelp of pure pleasure. We kissed deeply and I tried to entice him to lie on top of me. Grasping him, I gently pulled him down.

At last he rose up and kissed me firmly. His sweet tongue pressed against mine, as he lifted his leg across me and slowly lowered himself. Looking into his eyes, I spread my legs wide while directing him inside. "Easy," he whispered. "Don't worry. I'll give you everything you need from now on."

The feeling I had then was of being completely overwhelmed with love and gratitude. No one had ever spoken to me with such tenderness and commitment. I let the waves of pleasure flow over me as he pushed, but it was impossible to contain the joy. I instinctively flexed and relaxed my muscles, desperately trying to make him a part of me.

We were locked together and in perfect unison in our increasing tempo and I heard myself yelp again. I didn't care. "More, more, please, Mick. This is unbelievable."

His breath came in short gasps and a slick layer of sweat lubricated our bodies as I tried to pull him in deeper. I will always remember the uninhibited passion we both experienced. As if to cement our belief that we would always be two bodies with the same heart, we climaxed together that first time. Little did we know then the complications that lay ahead of us.

33

I awoke to a ray of bright light dancing right in front of my eyes and the soft swish of waves against the hull. The slider leading to the balcony was open, and sunlight streamed through both the opening and the stationary glass panel projecting colorful prisms all around the room. I felt completely relaxed but for a moment didn't know where I was. My own cabin was totally dark day and night unless the lights were on.

Then Mick stirred beside me, and it all came rushing back, the incredible night of love we had just spent together. I had found my partner—the one I'd waited for so long—and everything was changed. This feeling was the real thing, and just as Mick said last night, nothing could change what we've found in each other.

I turned on my side to see him staring at me with his head lying on the crook of his arm with what can only be described as a "shit-eating grin." "Good morning, my dear," he quipped in what I interpreted to be a terrible Clark Gable impersonation. I laughed at him and rolled over so that our bodies touched, and he was immediately hard again against my belly. He said, "Oh, oh, here we go. I just don't think I can do it again until I have something to eat. Should I call room service?"

"No, Mick. We're at sea today, so there isn't any rush, but let's go out and walk in the air a little. I want everyone to see us together. I am so proud to be with you. Then we can go get something to eat, how is that?"

"Good. I'll jump in the shower. Want to join me?"

"You bet."

After we lingered over our first erotic shower together, we quickly dressed and opened the door to leave. We collided with Mick's stateroom attendant, Paulina, who had just pushed her cart to his door and wanted to see if she could make up the room. Mick put his arm around my shoulder and introduced me as his girlfriend. I knew everything was happening fast, and that is usually a bad thing, but not this time. I wouldn't have been able to explain it, but it was simply the truth.

As I was looking up basking in Mick's smile, I was aware that Paulina was looking at me in a very odd way. She kept it up even when I turned to her. She was staring, her mouth agape, and it was becoming very uncomfortable. My intuition kicked into rapid mode, and I asked myself if she could be jealous or something. Could she have developed a crush on Mick? That was certainly possible but seemed unlikely in this environment. Still, something was wrong with the way she was looking at me, and I could see that Mick was noticing it too. So in my usual direct manner I asked, "Paulina, have we met before? You seem to be looking at me in a peculiar way."

She blushed rather dramatically and cried, "Oh, I am so sorry. Please forgive me." She pulled her eyes away from me and looked up at Mick. "This is embarrassing, Mr. Mick. I am so sorry to be rude to your friend."

"It's all right, Paulina," Mick assured her. "But what is the matter?"

She peered at me again and shook her head. "It is nothing. You are just so pretty, and I am very sorry for staring at you."

I tried to put her at ease since this exchange was obviously unsettling her. "Don't worry about it. Thank you for the compliment, Paulina. It is very nice to meet you. I'm sure I will be seeing you again because I'll be spending a lot of time with Mick."

As we made our way down the passageway, I swore I could feel Paulina's eyes boring into my back. When we reached the corner I turned to look, and sure enough, she was still standing there next to her cart watching us.

34

Mick was elated over his romance with Darcy, and determined to spend as much time with her as possible. During the first of the two sea days between Rio and Montevideo, Uruguay, they spent wonderful hours lying beside the pool, working out together at the gym, and walking around the ship just behaving like lovers on vacation. But he was still worried about his other friend on board and preoccupied with thoughts about Paul's motives.

He had to do something to gain a better understanding of the situation before he could truly relax, and he'd been pondering the problem on and off all day. Finally, he decided he would watch Paul's activities at least one more night and explain to Darcy why he would not be with her this evening. Anyway, her reaction would tell him something about how their relationship was likely to develop.

Early in the evening as they sat sipping drinks at the Center Bar, he was about to talk to Darcy about his decision when she seemed to become a little pensive herself. After sitting quietly for a few minutes gazing across the room at the cloudless blue sky on the other side of the large windows, she squirmed in her seat and turned to face him.

"Mick, I wasn't going to do this yet, but now that we've become so close, I want to tell you something before we go on much farther. It is something terrible about my life that I have not shared with anyone in almost twenty years."

"Wait. Before you go on, like I said before, whatever it is it can't matter to us. I just want you to be happy, and you don't have to tell me something that will make you uncomfortable."

"Thanks. I guess it's because I know what you say is true that I want to tell you the only important secret I have and also because I think I can trust you with it. Besides, believe me, after this anything else I could ever tell you would be completely insignificant."

So Mick listened intently with growing sadness and empathy. He did not interrupt as Darcy told him the whole story of her marriage to Brooks and her daughter, Rachael. She also described her time in counseling and subsequent bouts of anxiety and nightmares.

When she finished, he put his arms around her and held her for several moments with his lips gently pressed against her neck just behind her ear, breathing in her intoxicating scent. His sadness for her was as intense as anything he'd ever felt. When he finally pulled away and looked into her glistening eyes, he told her the absolute truth.

"That is the saddest true story I have ever heard, and my heart aches for you. I would give anything if it had not happened to you, and I give you my promise that I will do whatever you want—whatever it takes to help—if you want to try and find your daughter."

She leaned against his shoulder, took a ragged breath and shuddered. "You are too good to be true, Mick. I've never experienced anything like what is happening with us. Please don't ever let it end." She looked away and out the window again as she pondered his offer. He waited patiently while she collected her thoughts.

When she turned back to him, her face was calm with obvious resolve. "As far as Rachael is concerned, I could never look for her and take the risk of her understandable rejection. And besides, if it happens that she succumbed to a childhood illness or an accident and is not even alive, I could not stand to know that. It would kill me, Mick. At least now I know you understand me and I don't have to hide my feelings. And you know something strange? It was only because I had an awful dream about Rachael that I was even out on the deck that first night when I heard the crew members talking."

"I understand what you are saying about your daughter. If you ever change your mind, I'm here for you. Do you understand that?"

She nodded and swiped her eyes. "Yes, I know you will be here."

"Since you mentioned the crew conversations, I was planning to tell you that I still want to watch Paul a little more this evening and see if I can figure out what he is up to, but if you don't want me to be away from you, I won't."

"No, you do what you think is right, and I'll see you later. I still don't see how he could be involved romantically with Suzanne."

Mick did not respond but simply smiled. "Will you meet me at my cabin at eleven?"

"I'll be there." She leaned in for a parting kiss and he gave her the penetrating gaze into her eyes that had become a delicious ritual.

35

After Mick left me at the Center Bar, I decided to pass some time before meeting up with him by doing something healthy for myself. Back in my cabin, I pulled my hair into a ponytail and changed into gym shorts, a waist-length sports bra, and running shoes. Then I literally ran back upstairs. At seven in the evening the workout facility was pretty much all mine. I especially enjoyed exercising in the relative quiet and isolation, right in front of the starboard window watching the orange sun hover over the shimmering horizon.

I rode the elliptical with the tension pushed up to level 16 until I was exhausted and my thighs burned with the accumulated lactic acid in my bloodstream. After about thirty minutes, I was done in more ways than one. After running through a few stretches, I left, intending to go back to my cabin to shower and then get something to eat at the Tail. Maybe I'd see if Don and Charlie were around and wanted to dine with me.

As I entered the dimly lit foyer and started down the stairs, I realized that someone was standing behind me on the landing above. Glancing up through the open steps, I saw the familiar black pant legs and rubber-sole shoes typical of the crew uniform starting down toward me. Oddly, whoever it was seemed to hesitate as if they were hanging back and I wondered if it was because I had entered the stairwell.

This should not have been a threat, but for some reason I felt uneasy and picked up my pace. As I approached the bottom of the first flight with my legs still feeling a little jellylike, my heel slipped off the bottom step, and I went sprawling on the landing between decks.

The sound of the person approaching from above became undeniably quicker. I thought, logically, a crew member could be concerned that a passenger was injured . . . but maybe not. The ominous prickly feeling was crawling down my spine again as I quickly picked myself up and began to jog down the steps, careful to keep my hand on the railing for balance. I had landed hard on my right knee, and it was throbbing, but I didn't let it slow me down. I didn't think I was imagining that the faster I went, the faster the person behind me came on.

I also didn't believe this was completely innocent. I was being followed silently—maybe even chased again. I quickly glanced over my shoulder trying not to lose my balance as I flew down the stairs. My pursuer, if I was correct, was just rounding the landing directly above me, and my impression without seeing a face and despite the unisex uniform and functional shoes was it could be a woman. *Is that a good thing?*

I didn't wait to find out. I ran all the way down to deck 6 and out of the foyer onto the relative safety of the crowded promenade. Jogging up the wide mall, I was attracting a lot of attention in my workout clothes. Hazarding another glance behind me, I was relieved to see that no crew member was in sight.

I ran into the empty elevator car at the forward end of the promenade, which was closest to my cabin. When I exited on deck 2, my heart was pounding and it didn't slow until well after I was inside. With the door bolted, I should have felt perfectly safe but far from it—when you are afraid of the crew on a cruise ship, there is truly no place to hide.

36

Mick casually made a circuit of all the places on the ship where he had seen Paul on other occasions including the casino and the cocktail lounges, but after about an hour without spotting him, he was ready to give up and go back to spend a pleasant evening with Darcy. First, he decided to check the upper decks. As he walked past the gym intending to descend to deck 6 to check the Center Bar one more time, he recognized the crew member who'd been talking with Paul in the sports bar starting down the stairs himself.

On a hunch, Mick dropped back a little to put one deck between them and followed him all the way down. From the landing between decks 2 and 3, Mick watched through the spaces between the carpet-wrapped steps. The crew member strolled toward the movie theater located off to the side next to the elevators. No one else was in the lobby, and Mick assumed there was no movie playing.

As he continued down the steps, the elevator tone told him that a car was arriving, and for some reason he thought to run back up to the landing. When the doors slid open, Paul stepped out and strode quickly across the lobby and into the theater.

Mick could not believe an ilicit meeting was happening again. He descended the stairs quickly and quietly, and approached the theater entrance. How many meetings like this were taking place when he was not around to witness them? Instead of a door into the theater, there was an eight-foot-long wall ending with a theater aisle at each end. He bent down on one knee and quickly peeked around the right side of the wall with his head about two feet above the floor so that he could just see over the seat backs.

The crew member was sitting on the aisle about midway to the screen, and Paul was standing beside him. They were talking, but Mick could not quite make out what they were saying. He stood up and flattened his back against the wall listening and hoping he would be able to tell when they were ready to leave.

Suddenly Paul raised his voice, and Mick had no trouble hearing his angry outburst. "Look, Plato, $100,000 is more money than you will see again at one time in your life. I suggest you do not rock the boat, so to speak. Do what you have agreed to and keep your damn mouth shut or I guarantee you'll be sorry."

Clearly, Mick thought, there really is a plot of some kind, and the crew member is apparently Darcy's room attendant, Plato? Surely there is only one crew member on board with that unusual name—the one she confided in about having information related to Ronaldo's death. Now there was no question that whatever Paul was up to had to be stopped.

He heard Plato respond to Paul but could not make out what he said. Then the conversation seemed to have stopped. Mick hurried out of the lobby and bounded up four flights of stairs. He thought briefly of confronting Paul himself but quickly realized that would only complicate matters and raise more questions than he wanted to answer. Instead he approached the guest relations desk.

Out of habit he glanced across the promenade to the Center Bar, but Darcy was not there. Janine was on duty so he turned his attention to her. Smiling broadly he asked, "Would it be possible to speak with Officer Smythe?" As he waited for her to check, he had a sense of impending doom and a stabbing fear for Darcy and also for Paul's wife. Something else bad was going to happen just as Darcy feared, and he had to convince someone on the ship to take the threat seriously.

Smythe came out of a door set into the back wall behind the counter presumably leading to offices for the administrative and security staffs. He strode out from around the counter while extending his hand. "Hello, Mr. Clayton. How are you this evening? I trust everything is going well for you."

Mick shook his hand and tried to tamp down his irritation. "No, everything is not well I'm afraid. Look, officer, I know you warned me about getting involved with your investigation, and I haven't, but odd occurrences seem to be piling up. I told you about Paul Denezza and that I did not trust him. I wish you had put one of your people tailing him so that I would not be the one telling you about this."

Smythe stiffened and his arm went up. It was obvious he was about to interrupt. Mick's anger was threatening to erupt, which did not happen very often. He ignored the gesture and hurried on.

"Anyway, I just observed him talking with the crew member again, the same one as before. Now I know he is one of your room attendants named Plato. And I clearly heard Paul talking to him about a job that Plato is supposed to do for him and something about $100,000."

No response was immediately forthcoming. Smythe was stunned by what Mick was telling him. After thinking about the best approach to take, he answered in a low and even voice, "Are you absolutely sure of this?"

"Absolutely, I heard it clearly. On top of everything else, this Plato is Darcy Farthing's cabin attendant. She told him that she overheard something that could be related to the cruise director's death and that she wanted to report it to security. Right after that, as you know, she was attacked in Salvador, and I honestly don't think it was a coincidence.

"Now I am very worried about her safety if this Plato is a bad guy. I want assurance that you will look into all of this immediately and take seriously the information we provided before. I believe you have a huge problem on this ship that you all need to face up to." Mick stopped abruptly, realizing that he was not helping his cause by challenging the security chief's competence.

Smythe tried to hide his annoyance with the insinuation that he could not handle this mysterious case. "We have not closed our investigation of Ronaldo's death, although there is no concrete evidence of anything other than an accident, and Mr. Denezza has been cleared for the time of Ronaldo's fall." He raised his hand as Mick began to protest. "But what you are saying now is quite specific, and we will go back to him and to this crew member to determine the meaning of what you heard. Thank you for the information but please refrain from following Mr. Denezza or bothering crew members and let us handle it from here."

Mick forced himself to be conciliatory and agreed to the request, but he knew he had to stay involved because there was obviously a lack of independence with respect to the investigation, probably due to involvement of the captain's wife in whatever was going on. Then he thought about the power the captain wielded on the ship, and wondered how likely it was that the staff, including security, would question him about anything involving his personal life.

After Mick left the area, Smythe returned to his office to think about how he would handle this latest development. He checked his watch and saw that it was eight thirty. A little late, but he picked up the phone anyway and dialed Suzanne's private line at Hotel Services. He left a message asking her to pull the file on her employee named Plato and bring it to his office tonight, as soon as possible. Then he dialed her new stateroom in the crew quarters and left the same message.

In his ten years working security for the cruise line, he had never encountered a situation as odd and troubling as this. He had left a cop job in LA partly for the travel opportunity but also because the cruise gig was known to be fairly benign and nonviolent. The eight years he spent on the streets serving and protecting provided enough violence to last a lifetime.

Besides, he hadn't found the right woman to spend his life with and had few family members, so he'd thought, why not take a job that afforded opportunities for some adventure and excitement?

While he believed he could still handle whatever trouble came his way, it had been a long time since he'd faced a violent offender. He bent down and pulled out the bottom drawer of his desk. He stared down at the gray steel box trying to remember the last time he had opened it. Finally he sighed and lifted it out, placing it gently on the desk in front of him. Then he retrieved a key from the top middle drawer, unlocked the box, and gently raised the lid.

As he lifted the Ruger GP100, he felt a small rush of anxiety mixed with excitement. He turned the revolver over on his palm then closed his hand around the textured grip as he gently caressed the four-inch stainless steel barrel. How many times had he been comforted and emboldened by its two-and-a-half-pound heft? The .357 was an old friend that had once been his constant companion. He sighed again and reached back into the drawer to retrieve a gun cleaning kit.

Outside in the promenade Mick walked directly to the house phone and called Darcy's room to ask her to meet him in his cabin. When she arrived he was already turning down the bed and pouring them each a glass of wine. It was only nine, but Mick was exhausted. He was worried about Darcy but knew she was safe as long as she was with him. He picked up his glass and touched it to hers. "To us, Darcy, do you mind if we drink this and go right to bed? I want to make love to you and then go to sleep."

"Of course, as long as I'm with you I'm happy. By the way, I had another little scare tonight. It seems kind of silly now, but I could have sworn a crew member was following me on the stairwell when I came back from the gym. It made me a little panicky, but now I wonder if it was in my head. I'm so jumpy about all the bizarre things that are happening."

"Your instincts seem pretty good. Tell me more about what happened, and what time it was."

A few minutes later as Darcy moved to the bathroom to undress, Mick thought about what she had described and shuddered at the possibility of another coincidence in timing. He realized he had begun to follow Plato down the stairs from the gym close to the same time as Darcy's encounter. *Where had Plato been before I saw him? Could he have been meeting with someone else up at the top of the ship? Could he have been the crew member Darcy encountered?*

He was even more worried about her now, but he made a decision to wait until morning to tell her about Plato and Paul. He hoped that security would remove Plato from his job before Darcy had to encounter him again, and it would be better if she did not have to worry about threats from the crew all night.

37

Exhausted, physically from a long day of lifting and cleaning and mentally from worry and stress, Plato moved slowly down the center of the outside deck under the lifeboats and headed toward the entrance leading to the crew stairwell. He just wanted to get to his cabin so he could lie down and think. He was depressed and confused about what to do next, and he knew he had to find a way out of the trap Mr. Denezza was holding him in like a scared and injured rabbit.

He could not live up to his commitment, but he knew that the horrible man would not stand for him trying to back out the way Ronaldo had. Then he thought again about Ronaldo's death. What really happened to him? There was simply no way he just fell over the railing. It was virtually impossible to do that unless you were trying, and Ronaldo may have been a fool in some ways, but he had too much to live for to have killed himself. He was murdered, and Plato knew the identities of the several possible killers. That knowledge was damn scary, and he had never felt so at risk, not even on the violent streets of Port-au-Prince.

Tonight he would make a decision about what to do, and tomorrow he would do whatever was necessary. He believed it was not really too late for him to extricate himself because he had not yet done anything very wrong. He was thinking about going to security to reveal Paul's plan, but he knew he was at the very bottom of the crew hierarchy and had no credibility. Plus, he did not have a clean history before being hired, and his prior illegal activities could easily be discovered by an investigation. *Either way, I will be fired. Why did I ever listen to Ronaldo Ruiz to begin with?*

He veered to the right and headed for the lacquered teak door that led down to the crew quarters. He was thinking about what a dark night it was when he realized the outside light over the doorway was burned out and made a mental note to ask maintenance to change the bulb. As he approached the darkened entrance, he was suddenly aware of someone walking quickly behind him, so he moved all the way to the wall to let whoever was in a hurry pass him by.

Immediately, he was thrown violently against the wall and felt a horrific pain move up his left side under his ribs. The breath forcefully expelled from his lungs, and he found it impossible to draw in any significant amount of air. In a panic, he tried to push himself up against the wall with one hand over the pain in his side and vaguely thought about the sticky wetness he felt there.

As he began to slide back down, completely helpless to defend himself and unable to breathe, he looked up at a shadow looming over him. In horror, he watched as the shadow darkened and spread around him like a swaddling blanket. Lost in an agony far worse than anything he could have imagined, he futilely gasped and blinked to clear his vision. He tried to speak a name but only succeeded in expelling the last of his air on a hideous wheeze. "Why?" he thought he whispered as the blanket slipped all the way over him and the darkness was complete.

The body made a soft scraping sound against the deck as it traveled across to the ocean side. Bolts holding the section of the railing designed to allow exit to those climbing into lifeboats had previously been removed, so that the gate easily swung open. Less than a minute later, Plato's body slid off the deck and splashed into the water. In another few minutes the gate had been restored to its normal nonemergency condition.

38

Mick was helping me search for the kittens. I was frantic because I had left them without food or water for almost a week, and now I couldn't find them. I could not believe I'd neglected the cute helpless creatures that I was supposed to be taking care of. How could I possibly be so stupid and insensitive? We were in the living room of a large house I had never seen before, and I was down on my knees frantically peering under the sofas and chairs. Mick was pulling books down off the shelves that lined one entire wall. As they flew to the floor, he was gently swiping each empty space with his hand. Suddenly he stopped and turned to me with the saddest expression I could ever imagine. I had a terrible feeling of dread as he began to speak to me, but my ears were suddenly filled with a loud roar. I saw his lips move, but had no idea what he was saying.

I was jolted awake by the ship's loud shrill emergency signal and then the voice—the same one I heard the night Ronaldo died—alpha, alpha, alpha followed by the location where emergency staff were to muster, in this case cabin 2401. I'd learned the meaning of the signal from other passengers, and now I knew that something had happened to someone else on the ship, and not too far from where my stateroom was located down in the ship's belly.

Mick sat up in bed and looked over at me. "What was that? Did I hear someone shouting out in the passageway?"

"It was the emergency alert. Something has happened to somebody."

"My understanding is that it's not unusual for passengers to have medical problems aboard the ship. Let's try to go back to sleep, unless there is something else you want to do?" He looked at me out of the corner of his eye and wiggled his brow. I had to laugh at him and immediately felt better. My dream was fading. It had been disturbing, and I realized it must be somehow related to my history with Rachael. If I remembered the dream in the morning, I would ask Mick what he thought of it, but now I could feel myself already drifting back to sleep with my sweet Mick's hip against mine and his hand on my thigh.

I woke up very early and decided to let Mick sleep while I went to my cabin to shower and straighten up a little before Plato came in to do his job. Mick and I had agreed we would have breakfast at the Tail, and I planned to be back before he woke up. I opened and closed the door very quietly and headed to my cabin. I was still uneasy about my encounter with the crew member last night, and found myself literally looking over my shoulder. It really pissed me off.

When I arrived Doc had already left—or maybe he'd never been there—and I was just putting laundry into a plastic bag and gathering soiled towels together when there was a knock on my door. I expected to greet Plato and was shocked to see Suzanne standing there and even more alarmed at the way she looked. She had obviously been crying and appeared to be both physically ill and distraught. "Please come in, Suzanne. What the hell has happened now?"

"Oh my god, Darcy, it is horrible. Plato is dead. They are saying he killed himself last night."

I grabbed at the edge of the desk as my legs almost gave way under me. A wave of nausea came and went, leaving me weak and almost speechless. "Why, what happened?" I managed.

"They aren't sure. He is gone though, overboard. The outside infrared camera that shoots along the side of the ship shows a person falling over at about 1:00 a.m. His roommate found a note in their cabin when he came in around two." She paused and stared at me intently. "Darcy, he said in the note that he killed Ronaldo."

"That doesn't make any sense." Then I flashed on Plato's hostile reaction the day I told him I wanted to talk to security about Ronaldo. Could he have been one of the crew members I overheard talking? *Why has that not occurred to me before? Could the other one have been Ronaldo?* Then a really sickening thought slammed me as I recalled my most recent scare in the stairwell.

"One of the reasons I came by is to tell you that you will be assigned another room attendant, and I wanted you to know why. Also, maybe the real reason I'm here is that I don't have many women I can talk with on the ship, and I am so sorry this had to happen. I just wanted to talk about it with you . . . but there is something else too." She was starting to cry and looked pitiful.

"Come sit down," I suggested. We moved to the love seat and sat next to each other. Due to our long legs, we were turned slightly inward with our knees almost touching in the narrow space in back of the coffee table. I looked at her haggard face. She did not look like herself at all, and I even wondered if she might be in shock and in need of medical attention. "What is it, Suzanne?"

Her face crumpled as she started crying again. "Everything is being ruined, and I am just trying to make it all right," she sobbed. "Oh, Darcy, Espen has left me and wants a divorce." She held her hands up to her face as her shoulders shook with grief. "It is the rumors the crew circulated about me and Ronaldo because they are jealous of my status, you know, being married to the captain. I cannot convince Espen that I love him because he has so much pride. I have prayed and prayed about this, and I don't hear God's voice telling me what I should do, this time."

I was stunned to hear she thought she heard God speaking to her at any time, but I didn't react. "Suzanne, I heard the rumor about you and Ronaldo, but I just couldn't believe it. But also, what about the passenger named Paul Denezza? Do you know him?"

She lowered her hands to her lap and looked at me oddly—glared actually—without speaking. Just as I was about to apologize for adding to her burden she wet her lips, reached behind her neck with both hands, and lifted the mass of hair out and away from her body. It fell softly around her shoulders. She began to speak in a different tone—more composed—with an almost exaggerated calm.

"Paul is a friend of mine and I have seen him a couple of times during the cruise. Someone has caused Espen to think there is something more between us." She looked at me with a dark expression similar to the one I'd seen during our meeting in the conference room. Holy crap! That would be Mick she's referring to.

"All these misunderstandings are ruining my life," she suddenly wailed. "And now another member of the crew, my employee, had to die on top of everything else. It is just too much. God will not stand for much more. I have to talk to Espen again." She abruptly stood up and left without another word.

39

After my encounter with Suzanne I dropped everything and rushed back to Mick's cabin. He was just stepping out of the shower when I arrived, but he opened the door just a crack with a towel wrapped around his waist. "I was worried about you. You should have waited for me," he said. Then, seeing my expression, he grabbed my elbow and pulled me into the room. "Darcy, what the hell?" His look of concern and tone of voice made it pretty clear how freaked out I looked . . . and felt. "Was someone following you again?"

"You won't believe this, Mick." I started to choke and tried to take a deep breath before continuing. I managed a shallow one that was a little better than nothing. I sat on the foot of the bed and tried to control my quivering body and voice. "Suzanne just left my room. She came to tell me that Plato, my cabin attendant, killed himself and left a note saying that he killed Ronaldo."

I was still breathless as the words tumbled out. "And she had nothing romantic to do with Ronaldo or Paul. They were just friendships. She is really devastated by all this, and worse, I think our having told security about seeing her with Paul has caused the captain to leave her. She said he is actually getting a divorce! Oh, Mick, I feel so responsible."

"Wait, wait, slow down." Mick sat down heavily beside me on the bed and shook his head. He ran a hand through his wet hair and stared at me as I impatiently tried to do what he had asked. "Plato is dead? You're sure?"

"That is what Suzanne said. He probably jumped overboard after he left a note confessing to the murder."

"Darcy, I didn't tell you this last night because I didn't want you to have to worry about it until this morning, but I saw Plato upstairs near the gym, probably around the time you thought you were being followed. I went down the stairs behind him and saw him meet with Paul in the movie theater, and I heard them talking about a plan and a $100,000 payoff. There is no question now that what you heard the first night is related to this, and from what you are saying it would seem that Plato killed Ronaldo, maybe for Paul, and now has killed himself." Mick hesitated while he thought about what he had just said. "But you know what, Darcy? My bet is that Plato didn't kill himself and Paul has done away with him for some reason."

"I can't believe this. Plato was in and out of my room all the time, and I told him I had information about Ronaldo's death. He could have done something to me at any time . . . maybe he tried to. Maybe he was the one following me last night and what about what happened to me in Salvador da Bahia? Now I'm completely freaked out . . . again!"

"I know, and that is why I wanted you here with me last night and why I went to security after I saw them together. Smythe promised to talk to Plato and Paul to find out what is going on. I wonder if he did talk to Plato. That could be why he decided to confess and then kill himself." Mick paused again and shook his head. "No, I just don't think that is what happened."

I got up and stood over Mick with my hand resting on his bare damp leg. "Thank you for taking care of me, Mick, but now I am really scared, and poor Suzanne. You should have seen how upset she was."

Mick looked up at me with a skeptical expression that pretty much said it all. "I don't buy that she is completely innocent. I keep telling you that I saw her with Paul, and I am absolutely sure there was something going on. I'm not that obtuse not to recognize a romantic encounter. They went up the elevator with a room key, for god's sake."

"Mick, you're jumping to a conclusion that can ruin a person's life. I told you before that based on my conversations with her she would have to have a split personality or something to be doing the things you think. She said Paul is just an old friend, and I believe her."

"Darcy, I'm not going to get into an argument with you about this. We have to stick together, and I promised Smythe I would stay hands off and let him handle the investigation. So let's just see how it goes and stay close, OK?"

"All right, but don't we have to do something?"

Mick didn't seem to be listening and I tried to wait patiently for an answer. After a few seconds he looked at me and I could tell it was something serious. "Listen, there is something else I have to tell you, and it can't wait. It's a little secret of my own, and I already know that I haven't been completely open with you, so you don't have to give me too much of a hard time about it, all right?"

"I don't know how much more revealing I can stand," I giggled despite my anxiety, as I looked at his beautiful body barely hidden by the towel. "Put some clothes on first before you catch cold."

As Mick pulled on his shorts, he began to explain that he had a short affair with Paul's wife several years ago and has never been able to get over the guilt of having betrayed Beth while she was so sick.

"The affair was over practically before it started, but when I went back to Vegas this past Thanksgiving, I couldn't help but visit Athens Olympia, Paul's hotel and casino, to see how she was doing. For a short time I thought maybe we could rekindle our relationship, but her life was a mess, and I realized I was just feeling sorry for her."

"But this is no big deal. So you had a romance with someone before. As you have said, things we've done in the past don't matter now. But I still don't get why you followed them on the cruise?"

"I know it's weird, and I want you to know everything about this now that we are all here on the cruise together and something really disturbing is going on with Paul. Anyway, Sidney was scared to death of him. She said he had become very controlling and was getting violent, and she knew he did not love her but wouldn't just leave her because of their prenuptial agreement, which would give her a huge part of his business. She couldn't understand why he was bringing her on this cruise, and I'm afraid that was the main reason I came—to make sure Sidney is all right. But, Darcy, you know that I love you and nothing will change that."

Mick stopped talking and waited. I guess he was trying to gauge my reaction. I had become completely lost in a fog of confusion, anger, and disappointment. I could feel the tears already stinging the corners of my eyes, and I knew I would be sobbing soon if I didn't get control of myself. I guess my distress was obvious.

"Please don't be mad at me. I didn't know how much I should tell you when we started getting close, and until we were in Salvador da Bahia, Sidney didn't even know I was on board."

I looked at him through the haze of tears and tried to reconcile what I was thinking now with the Mick I thought I knew and trusted. The swirl of thoughts and connections I was making was overwhelming, and

I literally felt as if I might vomit. Then I completely lost it. I jumped up and stood over him with my fists clenched tight at my sides. "Did you say that Paul's wife is named Sidney, Sidney Denezza?" I demanded.

"Yes, Darcy, but what is wrong? Your reaction seems out of proportion to—"

"Tell me what she looks like." I knew my voice was becoming higher pitched, and the volume was reverberating in the small room. I was shaking all over.

"Why?"

"Just tell me, damn it!" I yelled. I could see that Mick was startled by my outburst, but I didn't care. The room was closing in, and the sweat felt sickeningly clammy on my neck. I knew I was out of control, and I couldn't help it. *Don't faint or throw up now.*

Mick was moving away from me, obviously wary of my anger. "All right," he said sharply. "She's cute, medium height with auburn hair, and her eyes are very green—"

"Fuck! This can't be happening, not again. Not another unbelievable coincidence. No, Mick. I don't believe it. You are still not being honest with me. You have known things about me and my life all along. I don't know why, but it is the only answer that makes any sense."

"What the hell are you talking about?" Now Mick was shouting too.

"I'll tell you what. I didn't make the connection before because you never mentioned her first name. You have to know damn well that Sidney Meredith was my best friend in college back in Albuquerque. I remember getting a wedding invitation about ten years ago. It came from Vegas, and now that I hear her whole name I remember thinking how unusual the name Denezza was. We hadn't had any contact with each other since I went through that awful time with Rachael, and I didn't respond to the invitation. You already knew about me and probably Rachael, and everything, didn't you? Sidney must have told you. There is no way this is a coincidence."

I was feeling such rage at his obvious deception that I wanted to kill him. Everything was a blur, and I reached up to hit his upper arms ineffectually with both fists as the tears streamed down my face. "You have something to do with everything that is happening on this ship. What are you trying to do to me, and why?"

Mick stood up, grabbed my hands, and tried to bring them up to his lips. "Please, Darcy. I don't understand this, but I'm telling you I had no idea that Sidney was someone you knew. You have to believe me."

"I do not," I hissed and pulled my hands free. "Are you kidding me?" I was furious at him for deceiving me and at myself for being so gullible. I felt like a cat with a huge hairball stuck partway down its throat. I couldn't breathe much less speak. With one motion I turned to the door, pulled it open, and ran into the passageway.

40

Paul Denezza sat alone at the small desk in his stateroom flipping through information he had downloaded and printed from the ship's public computer system. He was studying air travel options from the ports remaining on the cruise. Sidney had not yet returned from her spa appointment, and he needed to complete this task before she did. He was, however, still completely distracted by thoughts about what was rapidly turning into a disaster for him and his well-thought-out plan. A sharp knock on the door made him jump, and when he opened it, he was shocked to see the same dowdy security officer who had visited him before, Tom Smythe.

He invited the annoying man in and sat back down in his chair at the desk trying to remain calm while he waited for whatever was to come. Smythe stood next to the desk looking down at him as he began in a friendly conversational tone. "Mr. Denezza, I am very sorry to say that there has been another death on board, and it has been called to our attention that you may have had a relationship with the deceased, so understandably, I have a few questions for you if that is all right." It was not a question.

Paul tried to match Smythe's matter-of-fact tone. "Oh, who has died?"

"Did you know a member of the crew named Plato?"

To his dismay, Paul actually heard himself suck in his breath despite his efforts to remain steady. "I don't believe I have heard that name. It is unusual, so I think I would remember. Anyway, I don't know many members of the crew other than my own stateroom attendant."

Smythe stood motionless for a few seconds. He had been holding his breath, and now he sighed and leaned down, bringing his face to within inches of Paul's shoulder. "Well, that is odd because a witness has placed you in two conversations with this person, the latest one last night in the movie theater. Are you sure you don't know who I am speaking of?"

Paul's pulse leaped upward dangerously as he became aware that the documents before him on the desk were wet from his sweating palms. He willed himself to lean back and look up into Smythe's face. "I did have a conversation with a crew member in the theater last night, but I didn't know his name. It was just a chance encounter and small talk—nothing more. Is that the person you mean?"

"That crew member, Plato des Rameaux, died not long after your talk with him, and he left a note in which he confessed to having killed Ronaldo Ruiz. I am sure you can understand why we want to talk to you about your relationship with him. Please tell me what the two of you discussed." Smythe forced himself to sound civil although he was increasingly disturbed by Denezza's obvious case of the jitters. *Maybe I should have brought along the Ruger.*

The blood had drained from Paul's face, and he quickly stood to release some tension. He walked to the window with his wet hands held against his thighs while he tried to calm down and collect his thoughts. He was fighting a panic that he feared Smythe would recognize, but he had no choice but to turn and face him.

"Of course I will tell you what I can. You say the man is dead? That is awful." As Paul tried to smile genially, he noted that Smythe had not moved from his spot beside the desk. "Last evening I was just wandering around the ship trying to find a place where it was quiet without a lot of people about. I walked into what I thought was the empty theater, but I found one man sitting there alone, and I saw that he was a member of the crew, so I said hello. I was just being friendly. That's all."

Smythe studied Paul's face, particularly his eyes, for signs of deception. "Tell me exactly what words you exchanged."

Paul could not help but notice the emphasis on the word *exactly* as he desperately tried to recall the conversation, realizing that someone must have overheard his argument with Plato. His mind was in overdrive and about to fly off a cliff as he sought a plausible explanation.

"Well, I'm not sure I remember exactly what we said. I think I mentioned how nice the theater was and commented on how much it must have cost to install these various amenities on the ship. I believe I told him the little theater alone must have required upward of $100,000 to build based on my knowledge of similar venues at my hotel and casino. The fellow didn't say very much, and frankly he appeared preoccupied, agitated actually. I thought that he wanted to be alone, so I left." The lie hadn't sounded too bad to Paul, and he began to relax a little.

"I see," Smythe said. He noted that Paul was investing a great deal of energy in trying to maintain a calm demeanor. "It seems odd that you have been interacting with crew members who appear to be involved in questionable activities that we don't quite understand." He paused for effect. "Do you still deny that your friendship with Ms. Moretti is an intimate one?"

Paul tried to sound as indignant as possible, but his hands were shaking in his pockets now, and he felt beads of sweat forming on his forehead. He was falling apart and had to get a grip on himself fast. "Absolutely! I told you before that I have known Suzanne for years. She is an old friend and part of the reason we booked this particular cruise. And after all she is married to the captain."

"Yes, she certainly is. Thank you for your cooperation, Mr. Denezza. I will let you know if we need anything further from you." Smythe's eyes wandered around the room. After glancing down at the desk one last time, he nodded at Paul and quickly left the suite.

Paul sank to his knees on the floor beside the couch and laid his forehead on the cool cotton slip cover until a wave of nausea passed. The previous night he'd gone straight from the theater to the casino where he played cards for a couple of hours, so he hoped that would suffice as an alibi. But who had followed him to the theater?

Suddenly, he recalled Smythe's words to the effect that he had been seen having two conversations with Plato. The officer had not followed up on that point. Why not? A heavy coldness had seated itself in his stomach, and it took a few seconds for him to recognize the feeling. It was fear, absolute terror. What had he been thinking to let things get this far out of hand?

Whoever saw him with Plato had to be the same person who saw him at the Hilton with Suzanne. He would find out who was following him, but he knew that no matter what, it was only a matter of time before the truth would come out. He had to speak with Suzanne in absolute secrecy, and then a huge change of plan was inevitable. He could still salvage his life if he acted quickly and carefully, didn't do anything else he would regret, and returned to the comfort and safety of his business in Las Vegas as soon as possible. He hauled himself up and returned to the desk. Another wave of anxiety and nausea hit him when he looked down at the airline documentation laid out in plain view.

41

Paul called Suzanne on her private line to arrange a meeting and was now cautiously making his way to a restricted area she had described. He found the metal door marked Crew Only outside on the starboard side of deck 4, not far from the lifeboat staging area. A small round window sat at eye level. He paused and looked up and down the deck to be sure no one saw him before approaching.

No sooner had he taken a step closer to the door than it swung inward, and Suzanne quickly grasped his arm pulling him inside. They were in a short hallway with a door on either side leading to staging areas for laundry collection and distribution of clean linens. The area was intended to reduce the number of trips the stateroom attendants had to make up and down the service elevators to the laundry facility in the bottom of the ship.

A third door at the end of the hallway obviously led further inside the ship, and Suzanne quickly stepped forward and locked it from the inside. The two of them briefly embraced, and Paul felt the rush of heat and emotion that always accompanied his physical contact with her.

She stepped back and studied his face. "What is so important that we should risk being seen together? I am already having trouble because someone reported that I went ashore with a passenger, actually two passengers."

"I know someone saw us together at the Hilton, but I don't care about that right now. What do you think, Suzanne? Plato, that's what. Security is questioning me about his death. Smythe says he killed himself and confessed to killing Ruiz. We both know that is not true, so I'm wondering what you know about what happened." Paul searched her face but saw only a general look of concern.

"I assume what security says is true," she said. "Apparently he jumped overboard because they have not found his body, and he left a note typed on his roommate's laptop. Anyway, the cameras show something going overboard around that time. Why don't you believe that Plato killed Ronaldo?"

"Come on, Suzanne. You and I discussed this before. You said Ruiz must have fallen over the railing by accident and that otherwise you would have seen someone in the area. Now you are happy to accept that Plato killed him? Why? What reason would Plato have to draw attention to our arrangement?" Before she could answer, he rushed on. "And anyway, I spoke to Plato about Ruiz's death, and he was obviously suspicious of me, for god's sake. Hell, he even insinuated that you had something to do with it. No, Suzanne, you know as well as I that Plato did not kill Ruiz." He stopped talking and searched her face trying to discern if she knew something she did not want to reveal.

Actually, her whole countenance had slowly altered while he was talking. He could readily see the dark expression form and change her appearance to something alien and frightening. When she spoke there was a menacing tone that he had never heard before. It was difficult for him to rationalize, but it made his flesh tingle, and he was again overtaken by the foreign emotion of fear.

She looked at him steadily with her sparkling golden eyes open wide. "Paul, whatever security has determined in their investigation is what happened. It does not help to question it. You and I will get through all of this as we planned. God has told me that we are doing the right thing, and so nothing will get in our way as long as you follow the plan." She literally seemed to paste on a smile that was intended to light up her face for him, but it only intensified the chill he was feeling.

He knew that she was a religious person, but this overt reference to hearing God talk to her about their plans together was beyond troubling. Her odd expression made him uneasy to say the least, and he wondered if he had been deluded about her all along. And for the first time since they met he wanted to get away from her. He began backing toward the door leading to the deck as he spoke. "I'm going now. We are taking a big chance meeting like this. I know you are right and I just have to get my mind back on track and everything will be fine."

"Oh, Paul, I am so happy to hear you say that. You must trust in our plan and know that nothing matters except for us to follow through, because you are correct that it is ordained."

Ordained? I am correct? What the hell is she talking about? He had reached the door and now turned to open it. Suzanne put her hand on his shoulder and pulled him back around, leaning her face toward his. He felt a rush of contradictory emotions—longing and repulsion. He quickly brushed a light kiss on her cheek. Then he pulled open the door and left, quite forgetting to check first to make sure no one was present on the deck outside.

As he made his way back to his stateroom, he almost welcomed the thought of seeing Sidney there, and that was truly bizarre. Then, unbidden and definitely unwanted, an idea settled itself not only in his brain but at the base of his spine like a lead weight. *Suzanne knows how Plato died.* But if that was true, why wouldn't she tell someone?

One thing had changed. It was the realization that she was more of a zealot than he realized, and it was killing his feelings for her. He now knew for certain, he would not go through with his plan in any case. He had to extricate himself from any further involvement and would have to avoid Suzanne until he could figure out how to convince her to forget about the whole terrible misguided idea.

42

Mick spent the entire morning trying to get up his nerve to talk to Darcy again and to think of a new approach for how to go about it. Twice yesterday afternoon and then again in the evening he went to her stateroom only to be ignored. She would not open the door and simply told him to go away. He also phoned her, but she did not pick up and did not return his messages pleading with her to at least talk to him. He was worried sick about her and this self-imposed isolation.

His mind and heart were in turmoil. With the recognition that Darcy and Sidney had a history, his state of mind had been one of incredulity and wonder. Darcy said all along that the coincidences on this cruise were not credible. She didn't understand how the connections could be attributed only to chance, and now he was inclined to agree. Darcy and Sidney being reunited on this sailing along with his involvement went far beyond a "small world" story. That is why he went to Sidney's stateroom late last evening, assuming correctly that Paul would be in the casino as usual.

Sidney was surprised to see him there unannounced, but she was obviously happy that he was—or maybe she was just grateful to see any friendly face. He entered the suite and sat down across from her in the living room. When he asked how things were going, she told him that Paul had become even more agitated and unpredictable over the past few days. She said he actually threatened to hit her when she did not want to go to dinner with him. Then he became enraged again when she resisted his uncharacteristic suggestion that they go out and walk around the deck "to get some exercise." "I really want to get out of this stateroom and away from him," she finally revealed, "but I'm afraid of what he might do."

"Frankly, I am afraid for you as well, Sidney. I have some things to tell you, and then we can talk seriously about getting you out of here." He didn't waste any time in laying out his version of the events that had transpired on and off the ship and the apparent connections between Paul, Ronaldo Ruiz, Suzanne, and Plato. He also took pains to make it clear to her that he had developed a serious relationship with a woman on the cruise, being careful not to mention Darcy's name. Then he told her, "regardless of that, I want to make sure you are all right, and that Paul is brought to justice for what is surely some involvement in the crew members' deaths.

Sidney was obviously doubtful about what he was saying. "Mick, I am afraid of Paul, and I have to get away from him somehow, but I absolutely cannot accept that he would put his whole life and business at risk by committing murder. Besides, I just don't believe Paul knew any of these people before the cruise." She looked around the suite as if seeing it for the first time and then back at Mick. "None of this makes any sense to me."

Then Mick drew in a deep breath and forged on with the most important reason he had come to see her. "There is something I have to tell you that might be more shocking than what I have already said." He didn't wait for her response. "This woman I told you about who I met on the ship? Her name is Darcy Farthing." Mick watched Sidney's face closely as he spoke and clearly saw her emotions change from surprise to something akin to sadness in the silence that followed.

"Darcy Farthing?" she finally asked. "Do you mean the Darcy Farthing I knew in Albuquerque years ago? I don't understand. That seems impossible."

"That is what Darcy thinks too. When I mentioned your name, she assumed I have been lying to her all along and that I must have known about you two from the beginning. She can't accept the coincidence, and quite frankly I am inclined to agree that it is a little hard to believe on top of everything else that has happened. So I ask you, Sidney, how did you both come to be on this cruise?" Mick purposely put Sidney on the spot because at this point he could not assume innocence on the part of anyone. He had to get to the truth.

"What do you mean? I haven't heard from Darcy in twenty years, and back then she shut me out of her life when she was going through, well, a very difficult time. She and I were best friends until then. I have been worried about her in the back of my mind ever since, but I've never heard from her. I'm shocked to learn she is here on the ship. It's just a coincidence. What else could it be?"

"Does Paul know Darcy or anything about her?"

"No, he knows nothing about her! I sent her a wedding invitation but Paul didn't pay any attention to the guest list, and anyway I never got a reply. I'm sure I never mentioned her to Paul. He isn't interested in hearing about my previous life."

"OK, Sidney, I just want to make sure there isn't an explanation for this. To be honest, Darcy is so upset she is locked in her cabin and won't even answer the phone. She doesn't trust me now because she can't believe I didn't know about the two of you. I guess it was the last straw after the other odd things on this trip. This is really tearing me up. I just want to talk to her, and I also want to make sure you're safe.

"I know this is radical, but I think you should come to my room and stay. If you want I can find another place to bunk myself. I have an intuition that you're in real danger with Paul. I don't know what all this has to do with you, but there is a reason why Paul made you come on this trip, and it wasn't because he wanted a romantic getaway, was it?"

After she agreed to pack up her belongings for the move to his cabin, he said he would be back to get her later and they would work out the logistics of the move. Then he left and went directly to guest relations to find Officer Smythe. He knew he had to make one more attempt at convincing him that Paul was a danger that needed to be dealt with. As he rounded the corner from the stairs and moved to the center of the ship, he saw Smythe approaching the counter from the opposite direction. He was scowling, and Mick almost decided not to bother him. But as they approached each other in front of the desk, they made eye contact, and Smythe veered from his path to greet Mick.

"Hello, Mr. Clayton. Were you coming to see me again?" he asked with an annoyed but resigned expression.

"Well, as a matter of fact I wanted to discuss the additional tragedy that has occurred, but I imagine you are pretty busy with yet another death investigation."

"I assure you, every member of the security team and every member of the crew for that matter is extremely upset and stressed by the unprecedented events on this sailing. We have never experienced anything like the deaths and particularly the accusations and suspicions surrounding both guests and crew. I believe you are part of whatever is going on, and I hope I don't find out that you have more knowledge or involvement than you are revealing. What do you know about the latest tragedy, and how do you even know about it?"

First Darcy, and now Smythe? Mick was put off by the officer's hostile tone, and suspected no matter what he said, he would not get any help with regard to eliminating Paul as a threat. He tried to frame his words carefully so as not to alienate the officer even more.

"I completely understand how distressing this must be for you and the whole crew. With my limited experience studying criminal investigations, I have only been trying to help throughout this whole ordeal and to protect my friends. I just can't explain why Darcy Farthing and possibly Denezza's wife, Sidney, appear to be caught up in the events, but one thing I know for sure is that neither of them nor I knew Ronaldo Ruiz, Suzanne Moretti, or Plato whatever his name is before we set foot on this ship. On the other hand, it is clear that Sidney's husband, Paul, did know at least Suzanne and possibly Plato before the cruise, and somehow they were involved in something very wrong, and now two of them are dead."

Smythe began to speak, but Mick forged ahead. "Wait, I'm not finished. Mrs. Denezza is now very fearful for her own safety. Paul is becoming more unstable and has physically threatened her. It is obvious to me that somehow he is involved with if not responsible for both deaths, and I don't intend to let anything happen to my friends. Suzanne spoke with Darcy yesterday morning and told her about Plato's supposed suicide. That is how I know about it, but I also know there is more to this than a simple confession and suicide, and I will be very surprised if you tell me you feel differently."

"Look, it may come as a surprise to you, but we are also professional investigators, and we know what we're doing. I spoke at length with Mr. Denezza and checked on his whereabouts during the time the camera shows a body falling over the side. As usual, he was at the casino and not near the deck where we believe Plato went overboard.

Not that it is any of your concern, but it is true that I do not trust the man based on my conversation with him and my observations. I do not believe he had anything to do, directly, with Plato's death, but he knows something he is not revealing, and his behavior is suspicious. He had a sort of plausible explanation for the conversation you overheard in the theater, but again, something about him does not ring true."

He shook his head when Mick attempted to respond. "Also, based on an examination of the deck and the note typed on the laptop in Plato's room, there is no evidence of foul play. We have to conclude that he did kill Ronaldo and himself. As to motive, well, that is something that we are still looking into, and of course our findings are confidential."

"I hope your confidential inquiries begin with Suzanne, because she is the obvious link to both of your dead crew members. And I'll ask you once again. Will you please arrange somehow to keep Paul away from his wife and Darcy Farthing for the rest of the cruise?"

"There is absolutely no way at this time we can do anything beyond watching Mr. Denezza, and I assure you we are continuing to do that. You have to excuse me now. I must make a report to the staff captain regarding this subject. Again, I ask you to stay out of the investigation and mind your own business." He did not wait for Mick's reply before turning his back and hurrying around behind the counter.

As Smythe approached his office his thoughts swirled around the few facts that were definitely raising questions about Plato's death. While Plato des Rameaux's file was not very extensive or detailed, it was clear that the man had a questionable background and was a high risk hire for the cruise line. However, he apparently had never caused a problem while on board, and Suzanne said she believed he interacted acceptably with the guests and met his job expectations.

But Smythe had also not been completely forthright with Mick about the investigation. The examination of the deck had, in fact, revealed some traces of blood next to the wall, and it was clear the floor had recently been swabbed with deck cleaner. He had collected a sample of the blood and retained it in the security office. It wasn't much and could not be linked to Plato, at least not until the ship docked back in the U.S. and forensics experts could make a determination. Anyone could have typed the suicide note—anyone who had access to the stateroom, that is. And he had seen documents on Paul's desk that were clearly related to flights out of airports in the next couple of ports. Apparently Denezza was thinking of leaving the ship. Smythe knew he had to find out why.

In addition, over the past two days, Suzanne's behavior had become an increasing concern. When she came to the security office with Plato's file, he noticed a level of agitation he hadn't seen in her before. She seemed to be trying hard—too hard—to show surprise at the description Mick Clayton gave of the theater encounter. To his trained eye it was obvious she was trying to cover an emotion, most likely anger or annoyance that seemed out of place under the circumstances. After all, he was simply making an inquiry about one of her employees. On the other hand, everyone on the crew knew that Suzanne was under enormous pressure and was depressed over the captain's public rejection of her.

He had to admit to a very uncomfortable feeling developing in his gut regarding Suzanne and her relationship with Denezza. Much more disturbing even, he was beginning to wonder about the captain's involvement as well, particularly if Espen believed his wife was having an affair with a passenger.

What is the connection with Plato, though? There was obviously a major piece of this puzzle he did not have, and that was unacceptable. He thought about how he would proceed with his interrogation of Denezza regarding the first time Clayton saw him talking to Plato in the sports bar. He had let that one slide during their interview because the man had already brought suspicion upon himself when he denied knowing Plato. That was an obvious lie.

43

I'd been self-imprisoned in my cabin for nearly two days, and was about to go crazy. I ordered food from room service and even refused to let the new stateroom attendant in to clean. Now the room was a mess, but I didn't want anything to do with any crew members. This whole cruise had become one of the worst experiences I'd ever had, and I just wanted it to be over.

Doc came by only once to get some clothes, and since he was paying for the room, I let him in. He could see I was upset, but I told him it was nothing, and he just shrugged and left.

At least Mick seemed to have given up trying to get me to talk to him, and this whole scenario was reminding me way too much of the way I reacted twenty years ago after I lost Rachael—minus the drunkenness. At one point I dozed off lying across the bed and awoke in a cold sweat with my lovely girl right there in front of me again. When I was with Mick, I honestly believed I might never have one of those panicky dreams again. That was the closest I came to leaving the cabin, but instead I washed my face with cool water and turned on the TV to distract myself.

I just could not get my mind to accept the obvious. Mick deceived me by not telling me about Sidney and played me so cruelly by pretending he did not know anything about me. But why did he do it? What possible motive did he have for pretending to be in love with me when he had a relationship with Sidney? I couldn't figure it out. Could Sidney have convinced him to hurt me like this to get back at me for ending our friendship? That just wasn't plausible after all these years.

I even asked myself if Mick was trying to get Paul out of the picture so he could be with Sidney by blaming him for Ronaldo's fall and Plato's suicide. One really disgusting aspect of this mess was that Mick seemed to be trying to ruin Suzanne's reputation for his own gain. But by far the worst of my thinking centered on the deaths themselves and how they seemed connected in some way to Mick and to me. This really had become the vacation from hell, and my head hurt from trying to figure out the convoluted possibilities when none of it made sense.

My confused mind was literally spinning without gaining clarity. I was devastated by Mick's betrayal, and worse, I knew I would continue to love him for a long time. The coincidence thing had become a huge problem for me. I could not accept that this many things could happen in such a short time frame just by chance. Of course, I was not ready to believe they were happening according to some plan or even, if I were really honest with myself, that Mick had orchestrated everything. So what other explanation could there be? *OK, go to your comfort level and think about this rationally. What would the application of Occam's razor predict?*

Franciscan friar William of Ockham who lived in fourteenth-century England developed the simple principle that when you have two competing theories that make exactly the same predictions, the simpler one is the better. For example, the razor was used to bolster Einstein's theory of special relativity—that space itself is transformed—over the previous notion that rulers contract and clocks slow down while traveling in space. I like the razor because it tends to eliminate metaphysical concepts in favor of observable results.

Around four on the second day of my confinement, while I was still pondering which answer to this mess was the simplest, there was a knock on my door. At least I asked who was there instead of completely ignoring it. Don and Charlie sounded distraught. They were worried about me, and I just did not have the heart to turn them away. I let them in and then sat down on the bed. They both looked around the room with expressions of distaste. Charlie pushed aside an empty plastic glass and a pile of clothes, and the two of them sat down side by side, filling up the little sofa.

They gazed at me with similar sad faces. Charlie was staring up at me with his chin tucked. Don said, "Darcy, why are you locked up in here like this?" He waved his arm to indicate my slovenly abode. "We ran into Mick, and he seems about to fall apart, but he wouldn't give us any details. Is it because of the crew member's death? We know he was your stateroom attendant."

I didn't want to talk about what had happened with Mick, but something about these guys always made me speak from the heart. I felt the wet warmth of tears on my face and choked back a sob.

"OK, Darcy, spill it," Charlie said. "Something is wrong way beyond your stateroom attendant having died. After all, anyone can make a bed and fold a towel into a monkey."

I couldn't help but smile at that, despite its gross lack of sensitivity. I took a deep breath and tried to explain about Sidney and Mick. I skirted around the whole issue of my daughter and just said that Sidney and I had been best friends a long time ago. "I'm going crazy trying to understand why Mick went to all this trouble to get me into a relationship when he was already in one with Sidney, who he had to know was my old friend. It was unbelievably cruel."

Don stared at my big blues with that piercing way of his while he mulled over what I had said. Then he leaned forward and reached over the little glass coffee table to put his hand on mine. "You are exactly correct, Darcy. It is not believable. Where is your self-esteem and faith in your instincts?"

I looked at him in confusion and then over at Charlie, who was still sitting with his head down looking up at me through his curly bangs, as if he was embarrassed. Was Don trying to add to my grief?

Before I could say anything, Don started talking again. "How can you give up on Mick so easily and think the worst, when you told us more than once that he is the one for you and that you know you will always be able to trust him?"

"But don't you see?" I was whining. "He had to know that Sidney and I had a history. He admitted she was the real reason he came on the cruise. What are the odds she and I would show up on the same cruise ship at the same time, and I would meet and fall in love with the guy she had an affair with? Tell me, Don, what are the odds?"

"Darcy, who cares about the odds? This is real life, not a game or a wager. Yes, it must be one of those mysteries of life, as they say." He waved his arm in a purposely exaggerated manner and rolled his eyes in a way that made me smile again.

"But we saw Mick, and he is in terrible shape because of you—because of you, Darcy, not because of this Sidney person. We pride ourselves on being good judges of character, and we've done our share of matchmaking. There is no question what you and Mick have is the real thing. Has it occurred to you to go out and find Sidney and talk to her? Just be your natural straightforward self and ask her what is going on? And for god's sake talk to Mick before he jumps overboard."

Charlie had been staring at me through his hair the entire time Don was speaking. Now he raised his chin and nodded his head in agreement. "Listen to Don," he said, looking lovingly at his partner. "I have always found that to be the best approach."

I was thinking about what they were advising when there was another soft knock on my door. "That must be Mick again," I whispered. I looked at the two of them staring at me for a few seconds and then sighed and stood up. When I opened the door I was dumbfounded to find Sidney standing there looking like a lost child. Her auburn hair was pulled back in a ponytail, and she had no makeup on her naturally pretty freckled face. She looked directly at me with her almond-shaped green eyes, and her thin lips slightly parted but did not speak. In an instant I was transported back twenty years by the familiar pixy face that seemed almost unchanged by time. Memories of our days together flashed instantaneously through my mind, and I realized right then and there how much I had missed her.

I stepped over the threshold and into her arms. We were both crying, and I realized my feelings toward her could not have been more different than they were just a few minutes before. I drew away from her embrace and pulled her into the room. Don and Charlie stood up clearly awaiting introductions.

"This is my old friend, Sidney. Sidney, these are my two new friends and all-around great guys, Charlie and Don. If you had not come to the door, they were just convincing me to find you. Can you believe that? Oh my god, another coincidence."

Sidney smiled and spoke for the first time. "I'm happy to meet you both." She plopped down on the couch and peered up at me. "Darcy, I have to say I don't quite believe any of what has happened over the past couple of days—longer than that, I guess. I don't think I have ever been as shocked as I was when Mick showed up at my door and then told me about you being on the ship. When he said you would not speak to him and I saw the pain he was in, I made him tell me your cabin number, and here I am."

"Well," Don said. "That is a straightforward move worthy of a friend of Darcy's. I can see why you two are friends." As he spoke, he moved toward the door with Charlie right behind him. Over his shoulder Charlie said, "We'll go now and let you two catch up on old times. We have a bingo game to attend."

I sat down next to her in the same position I'd shared with Suzanne just the other morning. After a few awkward minutes we began talking honestly about our experiences on the ship and her relationship with Mick. It did not take long for me to see that I was probably wrong about Mick's feelings for her. It was still impossible to understand how this reunion of sorts could be happening, but I now believed that he must love me, and that was what mattered.

I also couldn't believe the things Sidney told me about her marriage and how frightened she was. She told me she knew Paul was capable of cruelty, but she still would not believe he had killed anyone. However, she had still agreed to leave her stateroom and stay in Mick's until Paul's role in the murders was sorted out. It took us about ten more minutes of talking to arrive at the decision that Sidney would move in with me instead of with Mick. Doc had not been back to our cabin to sleep in days and had obviously found somewhere else to stay.

As we chatted, everything just sort of fell into place as if the last twenty years were a weekend hiatus. I told her how very sorry I was about rejecting her friendship back then and how difficult it had been for me to come to terms with the loss of Rachael.

"Darcy, you can't imagine how much sadness and worry I've endured over the years about the adoption and the fact that I wasn't able to help you back then."

We embraced again and both wiped away stray tears. Finally, I went with her to help bring her things back to my stateroom. After we put everything away and moved the twin beds apart with the nightstands between them, she settled herself on one of the beds with a glass of wine in her hand. She looked relaxed, and I knew she would be safe there, so I told her I had to go out to find Mick.

44

When Mick realized he could not convince Smythe to do anything actively to contain Paul, he returned to his cabin to think about what else he could do. He considered and rejected the idea of going to speak with the captain directly because of his obvious entanglement with Suzanne. For that matter, he didn't know if he could trust the captain. That was truly disheartening, given how dependent they all were on the man. That was when he acknowledged to himself that he would have to take matters into his own hands. Five minutes later he'd made a fateful decision.

Now he was sitting on the side of the bed with the ship-to-shore phone at his ear listening anxiously as it rang too many times. Finally, he was relieved to hear Senator Bill Sawyer's official greeting.

"Hi, Bill. It's me. I hope you don't mind me calling your private work line."

"Of course not, anytime, Mick. Hey, I thought you were on a cruise. Did you come to your senses and decide to come back to DC early?"

"Listen, Bill, I'm calling from the ship somewhere between Rio and Montevideo, Uruguay, where we'll be docking tomorrow. You won't believe what is going on here, and I don't know who else I can go to for help."

"What in the world . . . ?"

"Please, just listen. I have a story to tell you, so I hope you have a little time. I'm afraid I wasn't completely honest about why I came on this cruise, but let me start at the beginning and go through the whole thing before you say anything."

Ten minutes and $90 in phone charges later, Mick stopped talking and listened to the silence on the other end of the line. Just as he was beginning to think the connection had been dropped, Bill sighed and cleared his throat. "That is some story. It's a good thing I have known you so well for so long, buddy, or I would think you were nuts. I don't know a lot about cruise ships, but I think it's safe to say that two crew members dying suspiciously with the captain's wife somehow involved and all this other stuff involving your friends is a little overboard, so to speak. I guess you're going to tell me what you think I can do about it."

Mick tried to shake off the stress that had been building while he tried to lay out the story for Bill in a concise and logical fashion. Describing the entire series of events helped him gain a further appreciation for just how weird it all was. "I know this is asking way too much of our friendship, Bill, but I want to know if there is any way Denezza can be removed from the ship in Montevideo."

"Are you certain the ship's security staff won't act on the information they have from their investigation? I don't understand how they can just be continuing with the cruise as if nothing happened when they have two suspicious deaths on board and information that a guest might be violent and dangerous."

"I guess you have to be here to get it. This is not just a floating hotel. It's like a floating village. They don't seem to see a reason to disrupt several thousand people's vacations or to hurt the cruise line's reputation. And don't forget we are not "flying" under a U.S. flag. The ship is registered in the Bahamas like a lot of cruise ships, and right now we're at sea and not subject to any country's law."

"All right, Mick, let me think about this and make a couple of calls. I'm wondering what the FBI's role could be in a situation like this."

"Based on my previous working relationship, I don't think there is a role until the ship docks at a U.S. Port."

"I'll check on that too. I'll call back when I figure out if there is anything that can be done."

Several hours later Mick was just about to leave his stateroom to try to talk with Darcy again. He was unaware that Darcy and Sidney had met, much less that they had already moved Sidney into Darcy's cabin. Then two things happened simultaneously. There was a knock on his door, and the phone began to ring. Mick knew the call had to be from Bill and that he could not risk having anyone know what he was trying to do. So he ignored the knocking and grabbed the phone.

"Hello?"

"Hey, it's me, man. This has been an eye opener for me. You were correct about the government's impotency when it comes to incidents in international waters. There doesn't appear to be anything to be done officially. Unofficially, I've come up with something, but I'm not feeling entirely comfortable with it. Do you remember me mentioning my old friend Ray Alosa? He works for the State Department."

"Yeah, I remember. You guys met back when you and Julie were together and you were commuting to DC, right?"

"Right. Well, Ray happens to be posted at the U.S. Consulate in Buenos Aires. There's no way I've found to do anything in Montevideo. I have no pull there, and without evidence to hold Denezza for a crime on the ship, State Department can't officially do anything anyway."

Mick's mind was stalled on Bill's mention of yet another coincidence, but he shook it off. "And the unofficially part?"

"This is what I'm not completely comfortable with, but it's a done deal if you want to pursue it. Ray has agreed to detain him at the consulate until after the ship sails out of Buenos Aires. This will be based on a legitimate reason for him to be there and Ray will try to work it so that his missing the boat looks accidental."

"OK," Mick said slowly, then paused to think about what Bill was suggesting. "But what would be a legitimate reason for Paul to be there? How could it work?"

"Well, if he were to lose his passport, say, it appears he would have to call the consulate, and they would tell him he had to come in person with identification to get a temporary passport issued."

Mick thought about what Bill was suggesting and realized that he was being invited to commit a federal crime. "Wow, Bill. That is risky. Is there any other way?"

"Not that I have found. Look, I'm not totally familiar with the setup there, but wouldn't Mrs. Denezza have access to their stateroom, and haven't you already secured her safety? I'm just saying maybe it wouldn't be too difficult to pull off.

"I can't believe I'm doing this. I hope to God you are right about this guy and how much of a threat he is because that is how I convinced Ray to get involved. In fact, I told him that you would meet with him at 1:00 p.m. the day the ship leaves Buenos Aires to give him a firsthand account of what happened on the ship. That way he will have some assurance that what he is doing—which is not strictly legal—has some merit. Then hopefully, Denezza will have an appointment there later in the day, and Ray will make sure he is delayed until after your 5:00 p.m. departure."

Mick felt an overwhelming sense of responsibility. This whole affair was now spinning, if not already out of control, then in a very dangerous direction involving other innocent people and their careers. "Maybe we should forget it, Bill. I can't be responsible for damaging you or Ray."

"Well, Ray has agreed to do it knowing the risk, but why don't you think on it until tomorrow and then get back to me."

"I don't know how to thank you for what you tried to do. I doubt if I'll pursue this, but I'll call tomorrow. Bye for now."

Mick hung up knowing he would have to rely on the ship's security staff to handle the situation. If they did nothing to prevent Paul from carrying out whatever he was planning, he knew that he and Darcy, as well as Sidney, should abandon the cruise as soon as possible. The only problem with that plan was that since they didn't know exactly what Paul was planning and why, the rest of the passengers and crew might still be in danger.

45

I couldn't find Mick after knocking on his door and then checking the places on the ship where he was most likely to be. I looked in on Sidney and found her sleeping peacefully, so I decided to go back to the spot I loved most and the one I most associated with Mick. After all, it was the cocktail hour.

I had just ordered my favorite drink and was listening to Manuel talk about things to do on shore in Montevideo when Mick showed up, gave me a sheepish grin that melted my already-defrosted heart, and slid onto the barstool beside me as if everything was fine. A closer look at his face, though, told me otherwise.

"Mick, listen to me," I began. "I am so sorry for what I put you through over the past two days. I know now that I was wrong about you and Sidney. I don't know how many times I have said this during the cruise, but once again, I cannot believe the complicated relationships and coincidences that are happening."

"Darcy, you can't begin to understand how relieved I am." Lowering his voice to a whisper, he leaned close to my ear. "I love you so much, and now, well, there are other things in play that I need to be able to talk to you about. What changed your mind about everything?"

I enjoyed watching the changing expressions of surprise and then relief on Mick's face as I told him how Sidney and I had met and talked and how we had already moved her into my cabin. I knew him well enough to see that he was clearly relieved to hear it, but he was obviously still very troubled. "So, what is going on now?" I asked.

"First of all, it doesn't make any sense for you and Sidney to be crowded into your inside cabin. Why don't we switch rooms and you two stay in mine. It's a little bigger, and you'll have the balcony."

"Oh, Mick, that is a great idea. Thank you so much. I also have to find Jason and tell him about this, but he won't care. He has found another place to stay and seems completely involved with a new friend."

Then Mick suggested we move to a table so we could talk privately. I thought this would be a discussion about our relationship, but he had other important matters on his mind. After he filled me in on his latest discussions with Officer Smythe and his friend Bill back in DC, we just sat for a few minutes without speaking as we contemplated the setting sun spreading a bright orange glow across the waves.

I had a disquieting sensation I couldn't quite get a handle on. I guess it was what they call cognizant dissonance—when you feel opposing emotions at the same time. I knew I felt completely happy with Mick and very safe sitting there with him, and I now felt that I could trust him completely. But at the same time a very creepy feeling sitting in my gut was making me very uneasy.

I now realized that Ronaldo and Plato had most likely been murdered, and I did not understand Suzanne's involvement in any of it. I was beginning to understand that Mick was right about how dangerous Paul was, and I was suddenly even more worried about Sidney. The length Mick had gone in contacting Senator Sawyer for help pretty much said it all.

I didn't know what to say to him. I didn't think it was my place to decide whether to take Senator Sawyer up on his offer, but I could tell Mick had pretty much decided not to do it. He said he might try to talk with Officer Smythe again, but doubted it would do any good.

Then we went to talk with Sidney and to move her—and me—into Mick's stateroom. She was awake when we got there and had no problem with our idea to move again. She was understandably concerned about Paul's reaction when he realized she was not coming back to their stateroom. After thinking it over, she insisted she had to at least leave him a note saying that she was all right and was staying with a friend she had met on board. We tried, but neither of us could talk her out of it. So she wrote a note and with Mick standing guard, slipped it into their cabin.

After Sidney and I were settled in Mick's stateroom and he had moved his things down to mine, he insisted that Sidney and I stay inside for the night because he was worried about what Paul would do if he saw us on the deck or at dinner. I hated the idea of hiding out again, but I saw his point, so we ordered a lot of food: turkey sandwiches, chips, a fruit plate, and chocolate cake with layers of fudge, as well as a bottle of white wine and some orange soda—which Sidney still liked as much as I did—and settled in to watch movies on the TV. Mick stayed with us and "partied" for several hours, and somehow it was not at all awkward. Sidney seemed relieved, and maybe she was welcoming some companionship and completely relaxing for the first time in weeks.

We decided the three of us would go ashore the following morning and spend at least a few hours in Montevideo. Then Mick left us, and we got ready for bed. It was like a girl's sleepover, and we talked until 2:00 a.m. about how our lives had progressed over the past twenty years. I was overwhelmed with happiness to have my good friend back in my life, as well as Mick.

46

After Paul found Sidney's note, he reluctantly called Suzanne to ask for her help. They were meeting again in the laundry staging area. He did not want to be in her presence, but she was his only means to find out where Sidney was and what was going on with her. He was overcome with rage and confusion, and finding her note in the stateroom was just about the most shocking thing that had ever happened to him. It was quite beyond belief that he had lost control of her, and he knew she could not have done this on her own. Someone obviously had gotten to know her very well without his knowledge.

He had chastised himself over and over for leaving her alone on the ship for so many hours. What was he thinking, except that it would all be over soon and he would never have to worry about her again. In fact, the plan would already have been completed if not for the complications of Ruiz's and Plato's deaths.

Suzanne explained to Paul what she had been able to find out. "Darcy Farthing's new stateroom attendant saw a woman with red hair moving into Farthing's cabin and now there seems to be a man staying there as well. I don't believe the man is Farthing's original travel companion, Dr. Johnson, because I know he has not been staying in their cabin for much of the cruise. Anyway, I know she has a relationship with another passenger named Mick Clayton. But I don't know why your wife would be with them if that is in fact who the other woman is. I don't really know anything about Clayton, but I do know Farthing told Plato she was upset about some information she had concerning Ronaldo's death. That is all I know, but I have been very wary of her ever since and have wondered what information she could possibly have."

After Paul left Suzanne he mulled over what she had told him. Of course he remembered Plato mentioning a woman who told him she knew something about Ruiz's death, but he hadn't thought much more about it. Could it be that these people, Farthing and Clayton, were the ones who reported seeing him with Suzanne and talking to Plato? But how would they have gained knowledge about him or about Sidney? It was perfectly clear now that someone had been following him on and off the ship, and common sense told him it was probably Clayton. *Who is this guy? Surely, he would have to have known me before the cruise.*

Paul shuddered involuntarily as he thought of several individuals who would like to punish him due to his less-than-straightforward business dealings back home. Sidney would be an easy mark for someone to use to get to him, and some of these assholes were very dangerous and unpredictable. They were essentially the dregs left over from Vegas's mob-run past. Had she actually been kidnapped, perhaps by this guy Clayton, and forced to write the note? This actually made some sense to him.

At least Suzanne had given him Farthing's stateroom number, and he had convinced her to let him look inside to verify that Sidney was hiding there. Then he planned to check out the Farthing broad. He would have to track down Clayton too, but he knew that would require some stealth until he understood better who he was dealing with. He had way too much to lose if anyone learned of his now defunct plan. *At least Ronaldo and Plato are gone. And with a little planning, I won't be around here much longer either.*

47

When Mick left the girls, he went to the casino just to see if Paul was there but with no luck. Then he wandered the decks for a while, looking in the various lounges and bars. Mick figured Paul must have found Sidney's note by now and couldn't imagine what his reaction would be. He knew Sidney had spent very little time outside the stateroom during the cruise, so Paul would naturally wonder how she could have met someone and know them well enough to move in with them. This worried Mick when he thought about it, but he didn't see how Paul could connect Sidney to either Darcy or himself.

At least that is what he thought for about a minute. Then another thought slammed into him so hard he literally had to stop and lean against the wall next to the elevator. He felt completely stupid and inept. How could he have forgotten that Suzanne was in charge of housekeeping? There was, in reality, every possibility that she could find out about the switching of staterooms and figure out where Sidney was.

Mick rushed back to check on Darcy and Sidney and found them sitting happily on the bed munching and chatting like a couple of teenagers. He reminded them about the danger posed by Suzanne and Paul and asked them not to open their door for anyone, especially housekeeping. After extracting their promises on this point, he made sure their "Do Not Disturb" card was in the slot and then said good night for the second time. Then he found Paulina down the hall in the crew station filling ice buckets and approached her with a broad smile.

After his chat with Paulina, he made his way to Darcy's stateroom and tried to shake off a feeling of dread that now seemed to be settling in permanently. When he opened the door, it was quite obvious that his fears were well founded. The room was a mess. Every drawer had been emptied and the contents strewn about the floor. These were his belongings, but he was sure that whoever had done this knew it was Darcy's cabin. Whether this was another attempt to frighten Darcy or they were looking for evidence of Sidney's presence, they were probably surprised to find only a man's clothing and toiletries.

Someone had seen the women moving Sidney's things into this cabin, and it had to be either Paul or Darcy's new stateroom attendant. Despite the promise Paulina had just made to him not to say anything about the women being in Mick's cabin, he figured that Suzanne would learn about the second move soon enough, and Paul was the only other person on board who would have a reason to care.

As Mick picked up his clothes, he was grateful his ID and passport were locked in the safe. But he knew the maintenance staff had the ability to open it. In fact, he realized, everyone on board was pretty much at the mercy of the crew and staff. On this ship that was a big problem.

After assuring himself nothing was missing, he made a decision to call Bill and tell him to go ahead with the arrangements at the Buenos Aires consulate. Paul was dangerous, and they certainly couldn't hide Sidney from him for the rest of the cruise—and what about when the cruise ended? He realized it made much more sense to get rid of Paul rather than the three of them abandoning the cruise.

Suzanne's involvement in all of this was a mystery, but he felt confident that without Paul any threat from her would be neutralized. He decided to report the break-in to security, but he had no proof it had been Paul. He would have to remove Paul from the picture himself.

So, tomorrow night after they left Montevideo and were in route to Buenos Aires, he would help Sidney boost Paul's passport while he was busy in the casino. At that moment Mick had no way of knowing the extent to which his decision was to alter the course of all their lives forever.

48

Ray Alosa placed the phone on its console and leaned back in his chair. He gazed out the large open window at the thick green carpet of lawn and tropical vegetation and thought about the latest call from his old friend. He'd agreed to do something questionable, and this was already bothering him.

With late-afternoon shadows falling on the walkway outside the consulate, Ray felt the heat retracting a little as the summer sun dipped behind the beautiful purple jacaranda blossoms, magnolias, and thirty-foot rubber trees surrounding the lush grounds. It was nearly time to leave the office for the day, and he always looked forward to his short ride down the wide Avenida Libertado, then north to the lovely and quiet Avenida Alcorta near his home.

Really a mansion by U.S. standards, the house was a refurbished colonial in Palermo Chico, the most upscale of the forty-seven Buenos Aires neighborhoods. Located just behind the Museum of Latin American Art, this exclusive area was cooled even during midday by the tall Tipa trees lining both sides of the private streets with their twisty limbs and beautiful yellow blossoms forming a canopy overhead. Ray loved the vegetation, the climate, and his beautiful but temporary home.

Sometimes he felt a little guilty about the servants he and his wife Marianne hired for a pittance to make their lives comfortable, but then he reminded himself that the money was significant to the staff, and Marianne always made everyone including the domestics feel at ease and respected.

Today, Ray wasn't quite ready to leave the office for the evening. He had to think through how he would handle the technical aspects of the strange commitment he'd made.

Gazing out on the familiar and comforting scenery, he thought back to when he and Bill first met in 1990. After working his way through college at New Mexico Highlands, for a short time, Ray worked for the old U.S. Immigration and Naturalization Service in New Mexico. Before long, he applied for a transfer to the State Department and was very excited to be offered a position even though it required him to move his family to Immigration Headquarters in Washington.

He and Marianne met Bill Sawyer and his ex-wife at the townhome complex where they all lived in the Rosslyn section of Arlington, just across the Francis Scott Key Bridge from Georgetown. That is, the Alosas lived there full time, and the Sawyers stayed there when they traveled from New York, where Bill was a rising political star. Despite their inherent differences, the two couples became quite close and stayed in contact over the years.

Bill and Ray did not share a common background. No, not at all, Ray mused. Bill had led a rather privileged life with wealthy parents living in upstate New York and a Cornell education in business and law. On the other hand, Ray was the child of Italian immigrants who settled near Las Vegas, New Mexico, to raise sheep. He met Marianne when she was on vacation from New Jersey visiting Italian relatives who lived in town. He liked to joke that the moment he saw her sipping a frozen margarita on the outdoor patio at Los Lobos, his favorite restaurant, it was love at first sight and that since then he'd never looked at another woman. The thing is that was the God's truth.

Against the odds, Bill and Ray became good friends, possibly because both were starting their careers in the District and both would return home at night, invariably meeting on the terrace to discuss their separate career experiences over a couple of beers. Bill's wife also babysat for the Alosas when Marianne was out shopping or looking for part-time employment to help with expenses.

Bill ultimately became a well-respected senator, now serving his third term, but he remained a loyal friend to Ray who was working his way up the ladder at State. As a Foreign Service officer, Ray moved his family around the world carrying out assignments at various U.S. embassies and moving up the State Department hierarchy. Three years into his current four-year post as vice-consul, second in command under the consul general, Ray was happy with his job and his wonderful family. He felt blessed with his success in life, having come from such humble beginnings.

At this moment, though, he was pondering his current dilemma and two things that he knew for sure. First, he might be risking everything he had worked for to help Bill, and second, Bill would not ask for his help if it wasn't important. So not only had he arranged a peculiar meeting in three days' time with an American traveling on a cruise ship, but had agreed to carry out a dubious act with respect to another traveler.

Ray's driver interrupted his thoughts with a sharp rap on the door frame. "Are you ready to return home, Mr. Alosa?"

"Yes, Juan, let's hit the road. The family will be waiting."

49

"This is really quaint and interesting, but I just can't relax and enjoy any of it." Sidney was clearly anxious and with good reason. As she fingered the soft hand-tooled and embossed leather purses and wallets offered by the smiling street vendor, she was looking around at the mass of bustling locals mingled with tourists from the ship. I'm sure she expected at any moment to see Paul come rushing up to confront her and possibly worse.

The Montevideo harbor featured a lovely small shopping area and market within easy walking distance from the ship. Given everything that was happening, the three of us decided to spend just a few hours here rather than booking an all-day tour of the city. But after only an hour, Sidney was getting so nervous I knew we would have to return to the ship.

"I agree," I said to Mick. "We don't know how much Paul knows about where Sidney is or whether he has figured out who we are. I'm not feeling very safe either. To tell you the truth, I'm scared to death after hearing that someone came into my—your—cabin. The worst part is realizing that crew members from housekeeping or maintenance can get into any room at any time."

"Yeah, I've been thinking about that too. OK, let's go back and have lunch in my . . . I mean your cabin and lay low until tomorrow. Actually, Sidney, I want to talk to you about something very important anyway."

I knew Mick was talking about stealing Paul's passport. We had not yet told her that she should be the one to take it from their suite while Mick made sure Paul was not around. It was impossible to tell how she would react to that plan.

On our way back to the ship, we meandered through an indoor market with a colorful festive restaurant and marveled at the enormous array of meats—chicken, beef, lamb, pork, fish, shellfish—on display. The food could be prepared in virtually any fashion the customer wanted, but mostly the restaurant advertised the traditional South American barbeque. The aromas made our mouths water, but we couldn't linger too long.

Back on board, we sat out on the balcony and sipped wine while we waited for room service to bring our lunch. Mick laid out his simple plan for Sidney, and she didn't seem to react much one way or the other. I was surprised, but I think she had been through so much by then that entering the cabin and picking up her husband's passport, knowing Mick would protect her, was no big deal.

And so later that evening I went to the casino with Mick, and when we saw Paul—actually I was seeing him for the first time—all I could think of was the stereotypic mobsters from old B movies. While Mick kept oan eye on him, I ran back to Sidney and accompanied her to the scene of the crime. No one saw us arrive, and I stayed outside in the hallway to make sure no one saw us leave.

Sidney used her card key to enter the room. While I held the door open, she quickly punched in the combination to the safe, housed inside a cupboard next to the TV, and extracted the passport. She made sure that Paul's wallet and jewelry were in disarray so he could not help but notice the passport was missing. Then she quickly left the room and we headed back to our cabin.

50

After extracting additional information from her stateroom attendants, Suzanne finally gave in to her curiosity and anxiety and went to speak with Officer Smythe. He was friendly enough as she carefully explained that she wanted to alert him to some passengers who appeared to be switching staterooms, and she believed this might be a matter for security. As usual, he maintained a very conversational tone. "How do you know about this, and who are the passengers?"

"My stateroom attendant is somewhat new at the job and is very thorough. She brought it to my attention because she didn't know if it was a problem." She paused before addressing the second part of the question. "I believe the person's name is Darcy Farthing. She originally came on board with a gentleman, but he apparently has not been staying in their stateroom lately. Now she has apparently switched rooms with another passenger named Mick Clayton, and a woman is staying with Ms. Farthing in his stateroom." She paused again. "I don't know who she is."

"OK, thanks for the tip, Suzanne. We'll check it out, but it is likely these people are just playing some harmless game."

After she left, Smythe sat down and thought about the conversation. He realized that her visit only made him more suspicious of her because he reasoned, why should she care which stateroom people are sleeping in? It isn't the kind of thing she would normally be likely to make an issue of. Also, Suzanne knew Darcy Farthing very well. Further, the stateroom attendants were very discreet and probably would not bring something like this to her attention unless she pressed them. The bottom line in this case was that he already knew Mick was worried about Darcy and Mrs. Denezza, and he imagined that the switching probably had to do with those concerns. It had to be that Mrs. Denezza had left her husband and was now under Mick's protection, and he thought that was probably just as well.

Later, Smythe reported his conversation with Suzanne as well as his latest findings regarding Plato to Staff Captain Early. After completing his report, he told Early that he preferred to keep any further information between the two of them and not involve Captain Oldervoll. Early was clearly taken aback by this unprecedented disrespect for the captain's authority, but Smythe explained in no uncertain terms that he was beginning to worry that Suzanne or the captain or both, knew more about the deaths than they were saying. "Even though they are no longer living together, they are still man and wife," he said.

Early's quivering voice betrayed his attempt to remain professional, and this was not lost on Smythe. "Surely you do not suspect Espen of any wrongdoing. His private life is an entirely separate matter from the way he manages this vessel and its staff, including you, Officer."

"You know, Captain Early, there are some extremely strange and downright ominous things occurring on this cruise, and believe me that is an understatement. To my knowledge nothing like this set of extraordinary events has happened before on a cruise ship. I'll tell you one thing for sure. I am going to figure it all out regardless of who is involved. That is my job."

Smythe understood that Early and the captain were close friends and Early was not happy about keeping the captain in the dark. He also knew Early would honor his request to withhold information because the man was practical enough to realize, as did Smythe, that he might not know his friend as well as he thought . . . just as the captain apparently did not know his wife as well as he had thought either.

51

About a third of Argentina's thirty-seven million people live in Buenos Aires. It was no easy task to determine which of many possible outings we should pursue on the first of our two days in this large and colorful city. Sidney opted to stay on the ship to read and watch TV, which was a relief because as much as we wanted her to enjoy her time on the cruise, we would also feel responsible for anything that might happen to her off the ship.

So after she assured us she would not venture out of the cabin and would not let anyone in, Mick and I went to the Tail and brought back the makings for turkey and tuna sandwiches, along with chips, scones, cookies, and several bottles of water and orange soda to stock the minifridge. Then we headed out to try and enjoy some of the city's sights and meet the Portenas—the port people, as Buenos Aires citizens call themselves.

For the morning's adventure we finally decided on a three-hour bus tour that would hit the city highlights. This included a half-hour stop at the La Boca neighborhood, settled by poor Italian immigrants who created the colorful atmosphere of today's barrio, with its brightly painted red, blue, and yellow corrugated metal roofs over houses and businesses that were little more than shacks.

The famous street market was exciting and fascinating, and I felt that I had to buy something to help keep this memory alive. I settled on purchasing several very small colorful fused glass dishes from a young woman who was one of many local craftsmen selling glass, pottery, leather goods, textiles, and paintings. Then we stood hand in hand, transfixed by the sleek and elegant moves of a couple dressed in formal attire, dancing a tango in the middle of the street.

We reluctantly climbed back aboard our bus and the tour continued with a trip down Avenida de Mayo, touted as one the widest boulevards in the world. We stopped briefly at the very political heart of the city, the Plaza de Mayo, named for the start of Argentina's movement for independence on May 25, 1810. The plaza has seen countless political events since then, and it is literally surrounded by capital landmarks.

Unfortunately, we only had time for quick looks and picture taking at Casa Rosada, the presidential palace; the Cabildo, the colonial city headquarters; and the Metropolitan Cathedral with its adjacent Mausoleum of San Martin, the national independence patriot. If not for the pictures we shot at each location, we would be hard pressed to remember much about our quick visits.

For me, the best part of the morning tour was the stop at Recoleta and Eva Peron's tomb. Burial in the now-defunct cemetery was once accomplished only with presidential approval and at a steep price. We had already seen the presidential house in Plaza de Mayo Square and the balcony from which "Evita" addressed the Argentine people. There was a surreal element to this experience as I tried in vain to stop picturing Madonna up there singing to the adoring crowd below.

We stood just inside the entrance watching a crowd of tourists and a lot of skinny cats wandering through narrow aisles separating row after row of mausoleums. Gray stone pavers and concrete covered the ground, and only an occasional statue or cross interrupted the monotony of the tombs lined up like little row houses whose owners had uniquely decorated their entrances to gain some individuality.

We joined the throng, and I for one, couldn't resist the lure of the windows flanking the ornate doors on many of the tombs. It felt a little ghoulish, peering in at the tiny stone stairways leading to the burial chambers below. Above ground many of the little rooms were decorated with simple furniture or statues, but most seemed sadly neglected. Artificial and natural flowers graced some of the doors, but none came close to the display at Evita's. The front of her "little house" was completely covered with flowers, nearly obscuring the beautiful carved door and bronze plaques commemorating her life and likeness.

This got me to thinking about how people can live and die, leaving a legacy of lasting fame that is far beyond anything they could have imagined in life, like Marilyn or Van Gogh . . . or maybe the ultimate example—the man named Jesus of Nazareth or Jesus Bar-Joseph. If he had known the legacy his unorthodox teachings, cult followers, and political assassination would leave on the world, would he have done anything differently?

After completing the tour, Mick and I grabbed a light lunch of fresh fruit and cheese at another delightful outdoor café and then proceeded with our afternoon plans. A commuter train carried us from Buenos Aires' Retiro station to Tigre, a watery community about seventeen miles north of the city on the Paraná Delta. Across from the train station at the Estacion Fluvial we boarded a collective, a charming vintage mahogany commuter launch.

Mick held my hand protectively as he guided me to a wooden bench running parallel along the side of the boat and pulled me down beside him, immediately wrapping his arm around my shoulder. I remember suddenly thinking that this show of masculine dominance would have driven me crazy with anyone else, but with Mick it felt perfectly natural. We turned sideways to enjoy the view as our boat glided away from the dock and headed down the river.

It turns out that Tigre, founded in 1820 and named for the jaguars that were hunted there in the early years of settlement, is a complicated community of islands formed by the convergence of several streams and rivers into the huge Rio Plata. We soon saw the appeal of this very unusual place. Modest homes and elegant mansions alike shared the riverbanks, many with lush manicured lawns sloping to the water's edge. While the water under our craft shifted in color between shades of green and dirty brown, our guide assured us that this was only sediment from the merging rivers and that the water was clean. In fact we passed a number of beaches where adults and children were happily playing water sports and swimming.

We enjoyed the trip immensely, especially watching the residents boating around the canals on their way to visit friends and shop at floating markets. There were riverside restaurants and bars, marinas, rowing clubs, antique shops, a craft market, and even an amusement park, many accessible only from the water. Several times during our tour we were buzzed by hunky young guys on jet skis, apparently a popular mode of transportation in this watery community.

By the time we returned to the dock, I was mesmerized by the sights and sounds of the river and its people, and the feel and smell of the warm breeze across the water. My head was nestled on Mick's shoulder, and he was still holding my hand. I realized I was reveling in the smell of him too. It wasn't so much cologne or aftershave as it was just Mick, his pheromones I guess, that matched my needs and desires completely. I would have been happy if the moment had lasted forever. We hadn't talked much during the tour so as not to have to shout over the boat's engine, but the nonverbal communication had been exquisite.

52

Way beyond jumpy, Paul felt as though his flesh could not contain his anxiety much longer. Someone had stolen his passport, and he knew that only the maintenance staff or Sidney would have been able to open his safe. He had the second biggest shock of the trip two nights ago when he opened it to replace his watch and gold bracelet and saw the entire contents in disarray. He could not envision why Sidney would want his passport, and he was becoming even more convinced that his Vegas past was catching up with him here on the ship. He had come on board with a daring plan to change his life that was now being eclipsed by someone else's plans, and he was working himself into a panic over it.

He had also been trying to figure out what really happened to Ruiz and Plato and finally arrived at a sort of logic that he realized was farfetched to say the least. The captain was the one who stood to lose the most from Suzanne's relationship with Ruiz. But who would ever suspect the captain of such a crime? If the captain was guilty, it followed that Plato's demise might have been to shift blame for Ruiz's murder onto him. Then the thought occurred that the captain would be just as jealous and enraged if he knew about Paul's relationship with Suzanne.

Paul had phoned the front desk and casually asked what would happen if a guest lost their passport. He was told that this was not unusual and that the only remedy was a visit to the local U.S. consulate. So the next morning, immediately after the ship docked at Buenos Aires, he stepped out on the deck and used his satellite phone to call the number for local information.

Now as he prepared to leave for his appointment at the consulate, he wondered again why they had not been able to accommodate him earlier in the day or even yesterday afternoon. The vice-consul's secretary assured him that his 2:00 p.m. appointment should give their staff ample time to verify his identification and issue a replacement passport before he had to be back on the ship for its departure. It hardly mattered because he'd started to fantasize about taking a taxi to the Buenos Aires airport and using his new passport to catch a flight back home, leaving Sidney, Suzanne, and especially the captain behind.

53

On our second morning in Buenos Aires, we repeated the process of ensuring Sidney's safety and then headed out to have lunch in the city before Mick's 1:00 p.m. appointment at the consulate. We had not seen Paul on the ship, but we knew that without his passport he would not be able to continue the cruise. He would have to report the loss to the State Department and obtain a new one. Mick was understandably nervous about what would happen. "God, Darcy, I feel like a criminal. I don't know what kind of trouble I could be getting into, probably at least losing my job and possibly getting myself arrested, and what about Bill and his friend Ray? This is insane."

"Mick, it's not too late to call the whole thing off. Just go to the consulate and tell Mr. Alosa you changed your mind and he doesn't have to detain Paul. He'll probably be relieved. We can figure out something else."

"Let me think about it for a while. I guess I'm not happy about taking such a big risk, after all." He was quiet for a minute, then sounding a little embarrassed, he said, "I guess I usually play things pretty safe."

We took a taxi to the consulate to make sure we knew where it was, then had the driver drop us off a few blocks away at another street market. It was a fantastic neighborhood with huge blossoming trees. Their wide canopies lined every street and there were perfectly maintained flower beds everywhere. We had an hour and a half to kill before the appointment, so we strolled around for about twenty minutes checking out the local crafts and then found a quiet restaurant with yet another appealing outdoor cafe. A waiter seated us at a table next to the street with a wrought iron fence separating us from the foot traffic.

Just as we settled down to look at the menu, a familiar voice called Mick's name. We were astonished to see his stateroom attendant, Paulina, approaching the fence with another woman. It seemed strange to see her out of uniform, wearing a long colorful skirt and a sleeveless white blouse. Her long black hair, normally tied up in a bun, cascaded over her shoulders. She was very pretty.

She smiled with a much more relaxed attitude than we normally saw on the ship. After all, we were in her territory now. She was always nice enough to me, but I hadn't felt comfortable around her since the day we met when she reacted to me so strangely.

She stepped up to the railing gesturing to her companion. "Hello, Mr. Mick and Ms. Darcy, I would like you to meet my sister, Flora."

"Hola, Flora, it is a pleasure to meet you," Mick said. "Paulina, what brings you out here? It is such a big city, and I'm surprised to run into you." I knew Mick was as baffled as I was by this latest development, but what happened next completely floored both of us. I was aware that Flora was staring at me in much the same way Paulina did on the ship and Mick was obviously noticing it as well.

Paulina saw it too and quickly said, "Flora works for a family that lives very close to here." She turned to her sister, shaking her head, and spoke rapidly. "¿Usted ve lo que significo? ¿Le qué dije yo?" I knew she had asked if Flora understood her meaning about something. *"What did I tell you?"*

Obviously a little embarrassed, Paulina turned back to me and explained, "I apologize. My sister does not speak very much English. I know she wishes you could visit the home of her employer, but I know that is not appropriate. Please forgive us for interrupting your lunch, Mr. Mick."

"It is nothing, Paulina. We will see you back on the ship. Enjoy the visit with your sister."

We watched them walk away, then stared at each other. We were both thinking the same thing. I had a very peculiar feeling in my core. I cannot explain it exactly, but something had just happened that we knew was outside the realm of likelihood.

"Darcy, I know what you're thinking. It's another odd confluence of events, but so what? This is a very affluent neighborhood, and I'm sure there are plenty of Americans living here. It isn't that much of a stretch that Paulina's sister would work for a family near here."

"Who are you trying to convince, Mick? Why would she even suggest we visit her sister's employer? There is something odd going on, and I don't care what you say, I can feel it in my gut. Let's order and I want a big glass of wine please."

After finishing a delightful lunch, I looked across the table and waited for the moment of truth. He was still sipping his 2004 Trapiche Broquel Malbec, savoring the incredible deep red-black fruity taste we both enjoyed. Slowly he set his glass down next to the empty bottle and lounged back in his seat with one long leg stretched out to the side of my chair. He sat looking at me for about a minute, and I didn't interrupt. Finally he leaned forward, picked up his wine, and drained the glass.

"I guess I've decided to go talk with Ray and then decide whether to actually go through with the deception," he finally said.

"OK, let's head over there. Whatever you decide, I'm with you the whole way." I meant what I said, but I just couldn't shake the odd feeling of anticipation or dread or a combination of the two."

54

Ray Alosa glanced at the clock one more time. Mick Clayton was due to arrive within minutes, and he didn't remember ever having such mixed emotions about a meeting. Last night, at his home, he had participated in an amazing yet disturbing conversation. With little time left he still could not make up his mind what, if anything, he should say about it to Mr. Clayton. It was only a matter of minutes, however, before the decision was made for him.

His secretary called to say that his 1:00 p.m. appointment had arrived, and when Ray stepped out of his office to greet his visitor, he came very close to dropping to his knees in shock. He stared into the blue eyes of Mr. Clayton's companion and was utterly lost. He was aware of the man holding out his hand and could hear some words being spoken as if from the end of a long tunnel. He quickly caught hold of himself and shook hands with Mick and then with Darcy. "Please come in and sit down," he managed. Still struggling to recover his composure, over his shoulder, he called for coffee to be brought into his office.

As Darcy and Mick seated themselves in two comfortable black leather chairs facing Ray's big ornate antique Italian desk, Darcy watched him walk around to his chair and seat himself. He was a pleasant-looking guy, but short, maybe five six. He wore his black hair clipped on the sides and combed straight back. He gave the impression that his blue-collar looks did not fit with his high-level position, as if he was just an ordinary guy wearing an exceptionally nice suit.

Ray looked across the desk at the attractive couple, his mind racing as he tried to collect his thoughts and consider his options. Finally he spoke in a barely audible voice. "We are here to discuss Mr. Denezza, who is due here in about an hour. But I want you to know that the bottom line is that many tourists lose their passports, and there is only one procedure they can follow to have it reissued. It might seem harsh, but replacing passports for people foolish enough to lose theirs while in a foreign country is our job, but it is not our highest priority. What I mean is, it is not that unusual for a tourist to be inconvenienced or detained because of the time it takes to renew the passport. I have decided that since I have no knowledge of what happened to bring Mr. Denezza to this point . . . I mean to say, I don't know what happened to his passport, the fact that it might take a little longer than anticipated to verify his identity is fairly routine."

Mick got it. This was not going to be the terrible career-ending move he feared it would be. He was not going to have to explain why he wanted to detain Paul. "I understand, Mr. Alosa, and I appreciate anything you can do to expedite the situation. You know we have a mutual friend in Bill Sawyer, so I feel as if I already know you."

"Yes, and I feel the same, so please call me Ray," he said, as he glanced at Darcy. Just then his petite dark-eyed secretary entered with a tray holding a coffee service and a plate of unusual large round cookies, each frosted half pink and half white. She set it down on the desk and proceeded to pour very dark, wonderfully aromatic coffee from a silver carafe. She glanced at Darcy and a bemused expression disappeared as quickly as it came. Ray waited until she was finished, then asked her to leave the tray and kindly thanked her as he followed her to the door to close it behind her.

He returned to his seat and picked up his coffee. The room was very still, with just a slight breeze swaying the drapes at the open door leading to a small veranda. Darcy relaxed, picked up her cup, and sipped the exceptionally rich and delicious blend as she peered back at him. They drank and gazed at each other in silence. As if he'd reached a conclusion about something, Ray put down his coffee, leaned forward, and peered more closely at her. "I want to ask you some questions, and I hope you will bear with me on this."

Darcy realized Ray was talking directly to her, and the mixed feelings of anticipation and dread began to resolve definitively into the latter. *Why does he want to ask me questions? I'm just here to accompany Mick.* "Sure, what do you want to know?"

"For starters, where are you from?"

This is strange. She sensed Mick's bewildered reaction as he turned to look at her, but he did not say anything. "Well, I grew up in the Albuquerque area and stayed there through college . . ."

Ray had turned white. He wobbled in his seat, put his hand over his mouth, and looked as if he were going to be sick. Mick jumped out of his chair and went around the desk. "Are you all right?" he asked, as he put his hand on Ray's shoulder. Mick and Darcy were thinking heart attack or stroke or something. It was that bad. But Ray soon perked up and regained his composure, so Mick returned to his seat.

Ray took a moment to collect his thoughts, as he studied the two of them thoughtfully. "I am so sorry to alarm you. Physically, I am fine, and I don't need to ask you any more questions, Darcy, except this. Will you please agree to come to my home this afternoon to meet my wife? We don't have that many visitors from home, and I'm sure she would be delighted to see you."

Darcy and Mick exchanged an uncomfortable glance. Both were recalling the odd remark Paulina made just an hour earlier about visiting her sister's employer's home. It would be completely off-the-chart strange if they were now being invited to do just that. At this point I would hardly be surprised, Darcy said to herself. But she knew beyond any doubt that the only thing she wanted to do was return to the ship.

Just as she was about to answer Ray, Mick sealed their fate by accepting the invitation for her. "Sure, it is the least we can do after what you are doing for us." Ray seemed much more excited and happy about their acceptance of his invitation than the situation warranted. He smiled broadly at Darcy and escorted them out to the foyer where he asked them to wait while he called for his car. He returned to his office, called his driver, Juan, and then placed a second much more important call.

55

The short ride from the consulate to Ray's home was full of strange unexplained tension. Ray was sitting next to his driver in the elegantly appointed black E350 Mercedes sedan, not saying anything. I had that feeling again that something was happening that I should know about but didn't. Why had Ray asked about my background and then behaved as if my simple response was earth shattering? Something was there in the back of my mind, but I couldn't bring it forward.

I glanced over at Mick who was staring out the window and wondered if he had any clue about what was happening. I reached over and gently placed my hand on his thigh. He turned to me and smiled reassuringly as he covered my hand with his own. It was nice, but it didn't answer my questions.

We turned into a long curved gravel driveway lined with jacarandas, oleanders, and plenty of other flowering trees and stopped at the front of a huge white stucco house complete with Doric columns holding up the roof of a colonial-style porch. Just as we were exiting the car, the front door opened. A short dark-haired attractive somewhat matronly woman stepped out into the shadow of the overhang. As we followed Ray up the six wide steps, he said rather formally, "Mr. Clayton and Ms. Farthing, I would like you to meet my wife, Marianne." As he gestured toward her, she continued past him with her hand extended toward me.

"Hello, I am so pleased to meet you both," she said, as she shook my hand then Mick's, and then stepped a little closer into my personal space. "You are very beautiful," she said in a matter-of-fact tone. "I absolutely love the way you look." I tried not to show how taken aback I was by her odd and slightly amused expression as she said these words with the emphasis clearly on the word *love. Is she somehow mocking me?* "Thank you," was all I could get out, but mercifully Ray was taking over the conversation anyway.

"Let's all go inside," he urged, putting his hand affectionately on his wife's waist and directing her toward the door. We entered into a wide high-ceilinged foyer with a tan marble floor and walls lined with highly polished cherrywood panels. A round black lacquer table with legs embellished in gold scrolls and acanthus leaves sat in the center of the space topped by an enormous sapphire blue glass vase of fresh flowers. It was quite beautiful and very formal. Ray led the way past the table to a set of closed double doors on the right.

Entering the Alosa's living room was like passing through to another world. The ambience changed dramatically, and my sense was that we could have been in any middle-class living room back home. A large flat-screen television was flanked by easy chairs upholstered in pretty floral chintz, and the relatively small space was dominated by a plush creamy leather sectional.

A huge long-haired white cat was curled up on one of the chairs. It opened its bright green eyes, raised its head, and watched us with the interest of a bored student studying a pinned-down bug specimen. In the center of the room was a large fringed ottoman littered with American and Argentine magazines. Before we could sit down, a handsome Jack Russell hopped out of its cozy plaid bed and flew across the worn, slightly frayed oriental carpet to greet us. The pup hopped up and down, barely restraining itself from launching onto us.

It was obvious the Alosas wanted to live a normal, simple life to the extent possible in the privacy of their home. Ray ordered the jumping, yipping pup back to its bed and asked us to sit and make ourselves comfortable. We sat down on the couch, but nothing was going to put me at ease.

Marianne apologized for the fact that their maid, Flora, was out shopping with her sister, Paulina. "I believe you know her from the ship," she said, again with that slightly amused expression. "But I can certainly make us some coffee or tea."

I had zoned out, and I was sure Mick was also reeling from the news that this was indeed the family Paulina had told us about. Marianne's voice seemed to reach me from a far distance, and the disorientation was making me dizzy. Something almost supernatural was happening, and I didn't want any part of it. Damn Mick for accepting Ray's invitation.

"Please don't go to any trouble for us," Mick was saying. "We had lunch just a little while ago in the market, and Ray served us coffee at the consulate. By the way, we saw Flora and Paulina in the market, while we were having lunch. That was quite a coincidence . . . and now we are here," Mick offered tentatively, obviously hoping for some indication of why we were in the Alosas' home. Clearly, he was as confused as I was.

Marianne seemed to register our discomfort and quickly turned to me again. "We are sorry, but we don't know exactly how to approach this because we don't know you, and there isn't much time." *What is she talking about?* Mick turned to Ray with a questioning look and I saw Ray nod to his wife. Marianne began to speak again.

"We are religious people I guess you would say, and we believe you have been sent here specifically to meet us through the unrelated issues that brought you to Ray's office."

I was starting to get a feeling beyond discomfort and rapidly approaching panic. I remember looking to Mick for help, and suddenly everything in the room was moving in slow motion. I felt drunk, but the amount of wine I drank at lunch did not account for it.

"You see," she continued, "last night, our housekeeper's sister told us about a woman on the ship who she said looked so much like our daughter that it seemed impossible they were not related in some way. When she mentioned the name of the guest whose room she was attending and who introduced her to the look-alike, Ray was shocked to realize he had an appointment with this very person—you, Mr. Clayton. He knew he would have to at least ask you about this supposed doppelganger.

"Paulina mentioned this in all innocence, but we spent a nearly sleepless night thinking and talking about what she had said. As much as anything, we struggled with the coincidence of the meeting. Finally, we decided fate might well be dealing a hand in our lives. I was so surprised when Ray called ahead to let me know our suspicions were well founded and that you, Ms. Farthing, were standing outside his office and would, in a matter of minutes, be in our home."

What? I looked at Mick again and saw his almost comical frown and wrinkled forehead. *OK, now it's official. This is beyond weird and heading right into the twilight zone.* My panic was rising, and I had an overwhelming urge to jump up and leave the house. I absolutely did not want to hear anything else Marianne Alosa had to say. I was disoriented, and something was pressing on the inside of my skull. It was cold and alien and trying to break out, but somehow I knew that if it did I would lose something critical to my existence. The room was beginning to spin faster and I sensed Mick moving closer to me. That bitch, Marianne, would not stop talking and I couldn't block her out.

"We have a daughter . . . her name is Rachael . . . she looks exactly like you, Ms. Farthing. We did not name her . . . her birth mother did . . . back in Albuquerque."

56

Darcy screamed, but it was only inside her head. She started to get up to leave but simply slid off the couch onto the floor. Mick was immediately down at her side holding her hand. "Are you all right? Darcy, here let me help you up." His voice broke as he tried to pull her up from under the small cocktail table in front but a little to the side of the sectional. He was feeling nauseous himself and could only imagine how she must feel.

She allowed herself to be hauled up, her long legs stiff as she drew them up past the table. Perched on the edge of the sofa, she lifted her head, looking around in a daze. Suddenly Ray was there in her face causing her to lean back abruptly, but he only handed her a glass of something much stronger than water. Gulping it down resulted in a fit of choking and coughing, but after a minute or two she opened her watering eyes and looked up at the three faces staring at her with matching looks of concern.

"I have to go now," she whispered as she pushed herself up into a standing position, and willed herself to stop swaying. Marianne stood up too, and Darcy towered over both Alosas. She didn't want to spend any more time in their presence, but as she stepped around the corner of the table, Mick took her elbow and whispered into her ear, "Darcy, I'm right here. It will be all right. Listen to what they are saying. Maybe the thoughts you've had about coincidences that are not really coincidences have some merit. Obviously, something is going on here that we need to understand. You have to hear these people out. Listen to what they have to say about their daughter."

"I do not have to listen!" she yelled. "This is crazy. No one knows about my Rachael except me . . . and you." Darcy glanced at Mick, and her expression told him he had lost her trust, again. *What is she thinking, that I had something to do with orchestrating this?*

She bolted toward the door causing the cat to lurch up with a screech, nearly tripping her as it flew between her legs and out the door ahead of her. She turned left and ran through the foyer, directly into the beautiful table they had passed in the entryway. Almost unconsciously, she thought she had narrowly missed it as she swung her hips around, but she heard the crash of glass behind her. She didn't care. She only knew that she had to get back to the safety of the ship and away from these crazy people, even if she had to walk all the way back to the dock.

Under no circumstances could she listen to Marianne, who was clearly threatening to destroy everything she had worked so hard to build—and to hide. She was approaching a complete mental break down as she tried desperately to block out the gist of Marianne's comments.

Just as she ran out the door and across the porch, a young woman approached up the circular drive on a bicycle. She arrived at the front steps and dismounted, dropping her bike on the grass beside the driveway. She stood where she landed, unmoving except for a lock of golden hair caressing her forehead in the gentle breeze. Peering up with an expression of awe and disbelief she began to climb the steps. Her eyes never left Darcy's face.

Darcy was unable to think let alone move at the sight of Rachael Alosa wearing short white shorts and an orange halter top, her long tanned arms and legs gleaming with perspiration and her long blonde hair so achingly familiar. Darcy was stuck motionless where she had stopped at the top of the steps as Rachael approached and looked into her eyes with Darcy's own eyes.

Both women had exactly the same sensation of looking into a time-warped mirror. Tears streamed down both their faces as they understood their connection. Rachael tried to say something, but she had not been able to adequately prepare for this moment, and she choked on her words. She knew without doubt she was looking at her birth mother, and she was completely overwhelmed.

Darcy simply collapsed again, this time into Mick's arms as he rushed up behind her. She woke up back on the couch inside the house and experienced the most intense déjà vu of her life. What she would always remember about that moment was opening her eyes to see Rachael anxiously watching her. She had known her young daughter looked very much like her, but she could never have imagined how truly similar they would be as adults. No wonder Paulina and her sister had reacted so strangely to her appearance.

57

The Alosas quickly told the story of how Ray and Marianne had decided to adopt a child just before leaving New Mexico for Ray's new job in DC, and the Catholic agency in Albuquerque was the most reputable one they could find in their area. They had taken to Rachael the first time they were introduced and quickly fell in love with the beautiful, angelic child. Rachael had known all about this from an early age. Anyway, it was completely obvious to anyone who knew the family that this long-limbed, blue-eyed blonde could not share many genes with her parents.

They were loving and confident in their parenting and had always known there was a chance their daughter's birth parents would enter the picture if the girl went looking for them. And they had accepted long ago that this could very well happen given her inherent individuality and independence. Their love was so unconditional they welcomed, and did not appear to be threatened by, the opportunity for her to expand her family ties. Their philosophy was that there is always enough love to go around.

And so this morning before Rachael left for the beach, Ray and Marianne explained what Paulina told them about a woman named Darcy Farthing whom they were going to try to contact and might be entering their lives by fate. They told her that this woman might be related to her and suggested she not return home until late afternoon when her father would have concluded his business with a man who was traveling with Ms. Farthing.

Rachael tried to relax and not get too excited just because someone was said to resemble her. And anyway, her parents tended to see spiritual connections in many aspects of life that Rachael wasn't so sure about.

Now she revealed that she'd considered taking their advice, but in the end she curtailed her rowing exercise and returned home early, curious to know what had transpired.

Then she looked over at Darcy and smiled. "The shock of seeing you on our porch was very traumatic, but I felt some sort of bond almost immediately, not just the physical resemblance, but something else."

Darcy nodded, swiping at a tear. "I know what you mean, Rachael, because I felt the same thing. I guess it was just a little too much of a shock for me."

In that moment, Rachael knew her life would be different from what she had anticipated. At nearly twenty, she was a self-assured adult, who was also smart and talented. She was majoring in business and finance at the University of Buenos Aires, but her interests were wide ranging. She had capitalized on her physical fitness and extraordinarily broad muscular shoulders to excel on the school's rowing team, but she had aspirations to join a professional sculling crew and possibly compete at the Olympics. She had already begun a class at GIC Argentina focusing on sweep-oar rowing techniques with one oar held in both hands as well as the two-oar sport.

She loved her parents and the life they provided, particularly the opportunities to live in so many different countries. The unique experiences growing up alongside other diplomats' families in foreign cultures had molded her international perspective and given her an empathetic objectivity regarding the world's problems.

Despite being an American citizen, she had thus far spent only a total of four years living in the United States. The downside, as she well knew, was that she lacked firsthand knowledge of what it is like to be part of American society. But she quickly realized that a whole new world of people and "family" could open to her through Darcy, and while she couldn't imagine what the future would bring, she knew without doubt that she would be more whole because of this encounter.

And how did this encounter ever take place? All her life, she had wished for something to happen but had not understood exactly what it was. Now a fleeting but disturbing thought occurred. *Did I cause this by my wishing and hoping?* But Rachael knew very well that thought had just come from the tendency to try to see meaning in every situation.

They all talked about the possibility of Darcy and Mick curtailing the cruise, so they could have more time to get acquainted. But in the end, it was decided they would return to the ship and would not abandon Sidney (another shocking reunion in its own right).

Darcy apologized for breaking their beautiful vase, but Ray shrugged, saying, "No problemo, we'll just go over to Walmart and get another one."

Laughs all around, and then through their mutual tears of joy and bewilderment, everyone agreed that Rachael would come to Colorado to visit as soon as Darcy returned home. And so Darcy held her daughter in her arms for the first time in almost twenty years, felt her internal prison doors shatter, and endured another tearful goodbye with the comforting knowledge that this separation would be a temporary one.

* * *

While Darcy and Mick were getting to know the Alosas, Paul arrived at the consulate for his appointment a little before two and was interviewed by an attractive young American woman regarding his travel status. After providing his Nevada driver's and gaming licenses as identification, he was left alone in a comfortable-enough room with a carafe of exceptionally strong coffee and a plate of oddly pink-frosted sugar cookies.

He asked if he could borrow a laptop computer while he waited, and when one was provided, he passed the time working on airline reservations for later that evening. After an hour and a half he realized his plight was not a high priority for the staff and that he may well legitimately miss the boat. When nothing happened by four thirty, he knew with some relief he would not be returning to the *Sea Nymph* and would not be forced to make that decision. The slow-moving consulate staff were doing it for him.

He calmed down and actually felt safe in this environment. He believed he could escape any implication in the shipboard deaths, and had decided Suzanne could very well be involved or she was covering for the captain who was still Paul's favorite suspect. The main thing was that he never wanted to speak to Officer Smythe again if he could help it. So he phoned Suzanne and left a message telling her he could not make the 5:00 p.m. sailing and would try to catch up to the ship at the next port. He did not even consider trying to contact Sidney. In reality, he was resigned to leaving her on board with all his belongings and knew he would agree to a divorce when she finally returned home.

He was more vulnerable than he had ever been and still did not understand everything that happened on the ship, although he now recognized that his own actions and weakness had allowed Suzanne to nearly ruin him. He could not wait to get back to his casino where he would regain the feeling of control and count his blessings. Due to the actions of others, he'd narrowly avoided his own murderous plans. He only hoped his suspicions about someone from his past exacting revenge on him through Sidney were nothing but paranoia.

Part Three
Hidden Currents Run Deep

58

Captain Espen replaced the telephone receiver with exaggerated gentleness in order to resist the temptation to throw it across the room. He had come to the realization he must cut his losses and end this horrible cruise before someone else had to die, and he wanted more than anything to get off the ship, which was an alien feeling for the sea-loving captain. He had just completed his third frustrating conversation in the past two days with Johnnie Gunderson, World of Seas VP for Southern Excursions, who was essentially the captain's boss.

Espen thought Gunderson should have been more sympathetic and amenable to his requests since he himself was a retired ship's captain, not the typical administrator who had only infrequently spent time in the field. But Gunderson's ten years at World of Seas headquarters in Davie, Florida, had obviously retrained him in the mold of a typical overly structured corporate executive.

Though Espen's proposal had seemed so logical, with each conversation he sensed a deepening reluctance on the part of Gunderson or World of Seas to take any action that might call more attention to the deaths on board the luxury cruise ship. Espen could sympathize with that attitude to an extent. The only important issues seemed to be assuring the passengers enjoyed their cruise with minimal disruption and World of Seas received no negative publicity.

Gunderson politely listened to Espen's plea for the cruise to be interrupted due to the extraordinary circumstances on board. Espen pointed to his extensive experience and flawless work history to stress the uniqueness of this situation and emphasized his concern about the passengers' safety in light of two crew members having died. But he also understood that because he was leaving out important pieces of the story, it didn't come across quite as dire as he needed it to. After all, it was common knowledge that people died on cruise ships, the cruises were not curtailed because of it, and many instances of suspicious deaths at sea were never solved.

Espen's problem was that his life and career were dangerously threatened because of Suzanne's involvement and his own regrettable behavior. He also recognized his staff had begun to limit their communication with him except on matters regarding navigation and general employee issues. Even James Early seemed to be avoiding him and had curtailed his briefings on the progress of Smythe's investigation.

Of course, most of the passengers already knew something was very wrong, and for the most part seemed to view it as adding fun and intrigue to their vacations rather than cause for concern. But this was no murder-mystery dinner theater and they were not idiots. As the guests shared bits of information, theories would form and rumors would circulate. When seasoned cruisers began to question their crew member buddies about what was going on, at least a partial picture of the truth would emerge. Eventually, he feared the entire story would be told, and he would be the butt of many jokes and insults at best and left without employment or any meaningful life at worst. No, he thought for the hundredth time, I can't let this go on. *I have worked too hard to get to this level, and I must end the cruise in order to save myself.*

Espen finally gave in to the fear he'd been suppressing since that horrible night when he emerged from the stairwell next to the Tail to see Suzanne and Ronaldo together near the elevators. Never before in his life had he experienced a blind rage like the one that enveloped him as he watched the scene play out from across the lobby. Now, the phrase "damage control" repeatedly looped through his mind like bad song lyrics that would not go away.

His thoughts naturally turned to the stateroom attendant's death. *What about that? Was it connected to Suzanne or Ronaldo, or both?* He had never been so afraid and could not believe that in the end, after all his hard work and self-control, he was just another out-of-control cuckolded husband.

At that moment Suzanne was sitting alone in her dreary crew cabin seething with rage. She absolutely could not believe the curt message Paul left on her voice mail. How could he have abandoned the ship without telling her beforehand? Why did he go ashore in the first place, and what happened to cause him to miss the sailing? He said he would try to pick up the ship at the next port, but she had her doubts about that. Yet Sidney was apparently still on board. How could he have left her behind, unless he believed Sidney would be taken care of?

That thought caused another wave of apprehension. She couldn't very well ask security or any crew members about what happened to Paul because the last thing she wanted to do was raise more questions about her relationship with him. The rumors and innuendo were already having a devastating impact.

But more than anything else, she was filled with an almost uncontrollable fury whenever she thought about what was happening to her plans and about how Espen had complicated everything by behaving in a way she would never have predicted. She felt as if she was unraveling, and her thoughts were becoming increasingly disjointed and confused. She still did not understand what Darcy and the passenger named Mick had to do with Paul and his wife, but she had an idea that Darcy might be the only person she could talk to about Paul without making the situation even worse for herself.

59

I knew I would need some time to process all that had happened in a few short weeks and to think about the interconnected events that led me to finding Rachael, Sidney, and of course Mick. After Mick and I talked openly with Ray and Marianne about what happened on and off the ship, I realized they were all as baffled by these events as I was and had no conscious involvement in orchestrating them. But who had? I still could not chalk everything up to chance.

I was also well aware that my philosophical underpinnings had been shaken and eventually I would have to reassess the strength of my convictions. But for now I needed to put these thoughts aside and try to enjoy the remainder of the cruise and my new relationships.

We knew Paul had not returned to the ship, and that changed everything for the rest of us. Of course, we couldn't be positive he would not join up with us at a future port, but under the circumstances, that seemed unlikely. So, we believed there was no need to be fearful anymore.

After returning to the ship from the Alosa's home, we dined with Sidney, Don, and Charlie in the Tail and tried to explain the events with Rachael and her parents. It was mind bending, and they were understandably astounded. Sidney was particularly emotional, knowing firsthand the devastating toll Rachael's adoption had taken on me. Don and Charlie just kept shaking their heads in disbelief as the story unfolded.

Sidney expressed some mixed emotions about leaving Paul behind and anxiety about what would happen when she returned to Vegas. Despite that, she said she was able to relax for the first time since boarding the ship. "I guess I'll have some peace for at least another week. Then I'll have to find a place to stay in Vegas and hire an attorney. I'm not going back to the hotel, and I'm not going to be alone with Paul if I can help it."

After dinner Mick and I left Sidney in our cabin and returned to Mick's together. We made love with renewed passion and a shared excitement about the future—together and with Rachael on whatever terms she wanted. My life was incredibly different and undeniably better. Having found my daughter and letting go of the deeply buried depression and sadness I'd been carrying around all those years, I was able to feel the first pure joy I'd known. This thought struck me once again as I leaned over Mick to check the digital numbers on the bedside clock.

It was 2:00 a.m., and as I started to lie back down, Mick turned on his side and put his arm across my shoulder. "Are you all right, Darcy?"

"I am better than all right. I just can't stop thinking about how my life changed so dramatically today. You know, I believe I'm happier by far in a very fundamental way than I have ever been in my entire life. Thank you so much. No matter what happens with us, I will always be grateful to you for somehow bringing all these events together for me." Not that I actually thought he had made it happen.

I ran my fingers down his chest, over his taut stomach, and into the sweet tuft below. He was immediately hard again, and I slipped my leg across him just to feel him against me. He just slipped inside me so naturally. I almost climaxed as soon as he touched me. It was out of my control. I squealed, and Mick moaned and rolled me over onto my back as he thrust all the way in. We came together without preamble or foreplay, and both of us were utterly lost in the extraordinary happiness we'd found together.

60

The three days we spent sailing from Buenos Aires to Cape Horn, Argentina, were just what a cruise should be. With Paul no longer a threat, Sidney and I let our guards down. We spent many hours together just talking and laughing the way we did back in college and trying to catch up on more details of the huge chunk of each other's lives we'd missed. We spent a good portion of each day together with Mick, Don, and Charlie just hanging out at the pool, alternating between sunbathing and relaxing in the shade. We listened to music, talked about unimportant trivia, or read books borrowed from the ship's library. Of course we also sipped the ubiquitous daily fruit drink specials. Every now and then we would join in one of the many shipboard activities like a scavenger hunt, ring toss, or miniature golf.

Early each morning, Mick and I worked out in the gym. Afterwards, we strolled around the upper deck several times sipping coffee and sharing the excitement of occasional sightings of dolphins and whales in the near distance, and flying fish and sea turtles right alongside the ship.

In the evenings we all enjoyed the fabulous array of fresh food at the Tail, just a group of friends having the time of our lives. We didn't go back to Mermaids because we really enjoyed the informal atmosphere at the buffet—and our own company. And best of all, Mick and I spent the nights happily ensconced in each other's arms in his stateroom.

With Paul gone, Sidney moved back into her own cabin, so I approached Jason at the pool where he was ardently and in a somewhat exhibitionist manner making out with his new honey. Her bikini was so teeny-weeny that even I was embarrassed for her. I pulled him aside and told him he could have our cabin if he wanted it—I would not need it for the rest of the cruise. He didn't seem fazed one way or the other, obviously because he was already bunking with his new girlfriend. But he thanked me and offered, "Are you OK? I'm still concerned about you, you know."

"Do you really want to know, Jason, because something miraculous, for lack of a better term, has happened?" We sat down across from each other at a poolside table under an overhang, and I tried to explain about the Alosas and Rachael. Doc didn't know much about my old life or my marriage, and certainly nothing about Rachael. Understandably, he was completely blown away by what I was telling him now.

"The fact that we were as close as we were and you never told me a thing about having a child just shows that you weren't really into me. I wish I had realized that before we came on this cruise."

"Sorry, I guess you're right, but frankly, it looks like you are making out all right." I got up to leave, and I have to admit I was a little annoyed at his comment even though I knew he was right. But nothing could really bring down my mood. Life was so good I actually wondered more than once whether it was too good to be true. Unfortunately, I didn't take those thoughts seriously.

61

"Hey, buddy, I was wondering when you would get around to calling. I already heard most of the story from Ray, and I have to say, this is one for the books."

"It sure is, Bill. But you could never write a book or movie plot like this because it would seem totally unrealistic. I guess you know about my friend, Darcy, being Ray's daughter's birth mother. I've never been involved in anything as amazing and baffling as this. Everything just seems to have fallen into place, and I've been wondering how it's possible.

"You know, a big part of the coincidences we've experienced relate to our friendship, Bill, and your friendship with Ray. It's just unbelievable. If we had not had the problem with Paul Denezza, I would never have called you and Darcy would have passed by her daughter on a parallel course, like the proverbial ships in the night. I'm starting to agree with Darcy that it is too much to accept it all happened by chance.

"And get this, my stateroom attendant's sister is the Alosa's housekeeper, and she noticed from the start how much Darcy resembled Rachael. How's that for another bizarre connection? I know how it sounds, but it's as if multiple factors were in place to ensure that Darcy reunited with her daughter."

"I get what you're saying, Mick, and I can't come up with any kind of explanation, but I'm glad all our relationships did come together to allow Darcy and Rachael to meet. I also gather that you and Darcy are still an item. Will I be meeting her anytime soon? I already know Rachael, and she's a wonderful, brilliant girl."

"I hope you'll get to meet Darcy. She's another wonderful, brilliant girl, and you won't believe how alike they are. Darcy and I haven't really worked out the logistics of how our thing will work with her living in Colorado, but Rachael is supposed to visit there in a few weeks, and maybe I can take a few days off to go there too. By the way, do you know what happened to Paul?"

"Ray said he left the consulate at around five thirty, and the staff heard him tell a taxi driver to take him to the airport, so I guess he's out of your life for now."

"That's a relief. I assume he flew home and won't be showing up at any of our future ports, so we can all relax and enjoy the rest of the cruise. Thanks again. I don't know how we can ever repay you."

"You're in my debt, ha? I'll have to think about that. Oh hell, just a round or two at Sam and Harry's should do it." He laughed. "Take care, buddy, and I'll see you soon."

After Mick hung up, he sat on the edge of the bed thinking seriously about the conversation. He had said that he and Darcy had not worked out how they would manage their long-distance relationship, but now he realized he was thinking about this subject for the first time and that they had not discussed it at all.

There was no question about his feelings for her, but what in the world would they do to maintain a relationship with her living more than halfway across the country from him and traveling all the time to boot? His travel schedule would be hectic too once he was back to work full time, which would have to happen right away. Of course Darcy would also be focused on rebuilding a relationship with her daughter.

An uneasy feeling nagged at him as he realized how little he and Darcy knew about each other and how difficult it would be to gain that intimacy if they were hardly ever together. *Too bad we can't stay on this ship forever.*

62

Imagine Charles Darwin standing at the rail of the HMS *Beagle* alongside Captain Robert Fitzroy, feeling completely overwhelmed with the beauty and starkness of *el fin de mundo*—the end of the world. They had sailed through the Strait of Magellan between the mainland tip of South America and Tierra del Fuego, the 18,500-square-mile island archipelago to the south.

Ferdinand Magellan first navigated through this passage that bears his name in 1520. That is when he discovered the islands, which he named after viewing the natives' fires burning all along the coastline. He described these aboriginal Indians as being astoundingly primitive.

Three hundred years later, on the *Beagle*'s second voyage of discovery, Darwin reported being stunned at the utterly primal state in which the Selknam and Yanganes people were still living. In fact, on board the ship with Darwin were three of these natives Captain Fitzroy was returning to their homeland. Two years earlier, on his first voyage, he had taken four of them back to England. It made me smile to imagine them trying to cope with civilization in nineteenth-century London where they had become celebrities, even meeting the king and queen.

One of them died, however, and it seemed like an old story by now that nearly all their people eventually succumbed to diseases brought by Europeans for which they had no resistance. Of course they were also methodically hunted down and slaughtered. After twelve thousand years of struggling to survive in this brutal environment, the indigenous people became extinct within one generation.

I wonder if Darwin ever saw the irony in this, in the sense that extinctions of indigenous populations in the New World basically followed his theories of survival of the fittest. They were simply no match for the advanced European "tribes" who showed up with their sophistication, technology, greater biological resilience, and conquering attitude.

In 1881 ownership of the Tierra del Fuego Archipelago was divided by treaty between Argentina to the east and Chile to the west. Our next destination was the small island of Cape Horn, Argentina, at the southern tip of the island chain. As we sailed down the coast, the weather remained fairly warm, but as we passed the mouth of the Strait of Magellan and approached Tierra del Fuego, the temperature dipped into the thirties, and at times the wind gusted to forty miles per hour. Walking on the deck in those conditions was a challenge and actually seemed a little hazardous. We were spending a lot more time inside the cozy warmth of the ship.

We knew that sailing around the Horn is a notoriously rough and cold proposition and is, in fact, a maritime legend—one of the most challenging routes on the planet. Many modern-day sailors still prefer to traverse the continent through the sheltered strait rather than brave the chaotic waters in the Drake Passage between Cape Horn and Antarctica only seven hundred fifty miles to the south. But that is where we were headed.

Mick and I were actually looking forward to experiencing the foul weather and rough seas passage around the Horn, which was by far the highlight of the cruise. We hoped to see an iceberg, although that was unlikely this time of year, and we weren't worried about any danger, since it was summer and our ship was enormous—dwarfing the *Titanic*—and eminently seaworthy. So we were a little disappointed when both the sea and air remained relatively mild as we approached the famous island, originally named for the city of Hoorn in the Netherlands.

Finally, the crew brought the *Sea Nymph* to rest just off the coast of the island. The wind had died considerably, and with the ship stationary in the water, gusting was somewhat diminished. We had learned in a shipboard presentation that high on the bluff currently looming right in front of the ship, a young Chilean naval officer lived with his family. From the comfortable modern residence it was his duty to watch over a lighthouse, chapel, and a memorial to the many sailors who died on the journey around the Horn. The adventurous family would live alone at this southernmost station for a year, isolated and completely dependent on the crews of naval vessels to haul supplies up the steep steps attached to the rocky cliff face, and on the satellites overhead to connect them with the World Wide Web and their children's online school.

Out on the deck, we looked up at the lighthouse in silence, transfixed by the notion of living in such a forbidding place while we both tried to commit this once-in-a-lifetime moment of awe to memory. Our parkas and gloves were warm, but we'd decided to let our hair blow free in the thirty-eight-degree breeze.

Shockingly, there were a number of passengers who apparently had not understood that even summer at the end of the world could be cold and had packed only tropical clothing. These poor souls now stood peering out through the glass doors, unable to fully enjoy this unique and rare experience in the brisk air.

Once we were under way again and the island was behind us, Mick and I reluctantly moved inside the ship and headed for a café to warm up with a cup of hot chocolate. We kept returning to the deck periodically through the rest of the afternoon, though, as the ship moved north up the west coast of the continent toward the Beagle Channel, a 150-mile strait that cuts through the tip of the continent.

At one point we were lucky to be outside as the ship passed very near a large Magellanic penguin rookery, really just a pile of rock, off the starboard side where land was still in sight. We rushed to the railing and watched the cute little tuxedoed birds huddled together for warmth and protection until they and their craggy island home faded into the misty distance.

I leaned against Mick and turned my face into his chest and away from the wind. He reached up and put his gloved finger under my chin to raise my face and bent to kiss me lightly with his icy lips. "Darcy, there are not words to express how happy I am and how thankful I am that I came on this cruise." He gave me a serious look. "Only one thing bothers me though. Say we were to get married someday. How could we possibly have a honeymoon that would top this trip?"

For an instant I wondered if this was a kind of offhand proposal, but then I realized Mick was just sharing his thoughts openly without worrying I would misunderstand or be offended and that this was an example of his dry humor. I laughed to the extent my frozen jaw would allow. "Maybe we could just return to the scene of the crime, so to speak."

Later that evening while I was dressing for dinner, Mick was reading some literature on the shore excursions available for the next day in

Ushuaia, Argentina. The phone rang, and Mick stretched across the bed to reach for it. Rolling onto his back, he cheerfully said hello, expecting to hear Sidney's voice. At the sound of the reply, he shot up into a sitting position and clenched the phone. His extreme discomfort at what he was hearing was obvious and alarming. *Now what?* Then he abruptly handed me the phone.

"Hi, Darcy, this is Suzanne Moretti." This was the first time I'd talked with her since before all the excitement in Buenos Aires. A few minutes later I replaced the receiver and turned to face Mick. I could see immediately that he was unhappy and knew I was going to upset him even more. "I guess you gathered she was asking me to meet her for dinner."

"Yeah, I got that and you said you would. I was really taken aback when I realized she was calling you here in my stateroom, evidently knowing we have moved in together. I guess I shouldn't be surprised since she is in charge of housekeeping, and this confirms my assumption that she would have access to information about who is staying where. I still don't trust her, and I believe she is deliberately keeping track of us."

"Look, Mick, I know we don't entirely agree about Suzanne, but I have to follow my instincts. I think the drama on the ship is over now, and I'm still giving Suzanne some benefit of the doubt. But I'm not stupid. I do know something is a little off about her, but I feel sorry for her in a way, and there is no harm in talking a little. Anyway, maybe I'll find out something more about her relationship with Paul." I smiled up at him and winked.

He laughed in spite of his annoyance. "Fine, you do what you have to. I'll miss you at dinner and can't wait to hook up with you later. But, Darcy, I can't help my belief that she was way involved in whatever Paul was doing. Please promise you'll be careful what you tell her."

"Yes, I understand what you're saying. Actually, I'm very curious to see if she says anything about Paul being gone from the ship. I'll find you right after I get through with her."

With that, I left Mick and went to meet Suzanne. I felt a little guilty about not telling him where I was meeting her. *Why increase his anxiety?*

63

I stood in front of Captain Espen's suite with my hand raised but hesitating to knock. This did not seem right, but I was there at Suzanne's behest. Finally I tapped lightly, and Suzanne quickly opened the door and ushered me inside. She was wearing her uniform, so I assumed she was supposed to be on duty. A small dining table with a white cloth was set for two, and a bottle of wine was cooling in a clay holder with a beautiful green, blue, and bronze glaze. I recognized the relief pattern as an Inca goddess I'd seen on pots in a Buenos Aires market.

As she poured two glasses of wine, she explained that she had ordered dinner, and it should arrive momentarily. She said, "Espen is on duty on the bridge until later this evening." Then she paused to take a breath and eyed me appreciatively. "Darcy, you look fabulous as usual. That turquoise dress is perfect with your hair and eyes, and I absolutely love the belt."

So a little girl talk. I looked down at the tan tooled leather with large silver Conchos and turquoise nuggets hanging on my hips. "Thanks, Suzanne, it's a favorite of mine too. I bought it in Old Colorado City, a quaint neighborhood in Colorado Springs. But, Suzanne, I don't understand this. I thought you and the captain were living apart. You told me he wanted a divorce."

"Oh, Darcy, it is so wonderful! Espen and I are back together. He now realizes that his jealousy was unwarranted and that nothing was going on between my friend Paul and me. It was all a misunderstanding, and the past few days have been just like they used to be."

I watched Suzanne's face closely to see if she was being straight with me, and saw what appeared to be genuine happiness. "I am so glad to hear that, Suzanne. I think the two of you are a lovely couple, and it's good that you are back together."

There was a soft tap on the door, and Suzanne moved quickly to open it. She greeted the steward and moved aside to let him roll a room service cart inside. He gawked in obvious surprise at Suzanne and then at me. I guessed he was not used to seeing passengers in their stateroom. It struck me, finally, that this was highly unusual and probably very inappropriate. Before I could think any more about it, he had placed the food on the table, and was out the door.

Suzanne turned to me and gestured toward the food smiling pleasantly. "Sit down, Darcy, I thought we could just have a chat and catch up a little. I have been so busy since we left Buenos Aires, and well, of course I have been spending a lot of time with Espen."

From across the table I watched her facial expressions carefully. I could not help recalling the odd conversation down in the conference center and how she seemed to morph into someone else. Now she was smiling broadly, and her beautiful face lit up as she glanced up expectantly while removing the aluminum covers from our plates. I was a little surprised to see lamb chops with new red potatoes quartered and apparently sautéed in butter with parsley, and fresh peas. This simple (rather British) meal was topped off with bread pudding and custard sauce, sort of like an English sticky toffee pudding. I was impressed by the understated elegance. Even the Chilean Veramonte 2005 pinot noir she served seemed to go perfectly with the meal.

While we ate we chatted about benign events on the ship and in the ports, and then as we savored our dessert, Suzanne made her first personal reference. "By the way," she began, "I understand you have a gentleman friend on board—not the one you came on the cruise with. How are you and Mick doing?"

I tried not to let my surprise show at this blatant attempt to demonstrate her knowledge about our relationship and simply smiled back at her. "Everything is going great, Suzanne. Thanks for asking, and once again, I am very happy to hear you and the captain are back together."

She shrugged, tossed her hair back from her shoulders as I had seen her do before—a nervous gesture perhaps—and softly replied, "As I said, Espen now realizes I don't have a romantic relationship with Paul Denezza. We are both so bewildered about the deaths on board this sailing. Nothing like it has happened before. It has been a nightmare, and it has affected us all in a bad way. By the way, I haven't seen Paul around the ship, but I have seen his wife, Sidney, with you. Is everything all right with them too?"

Her segue was interesting to say the least. "According to Sidney, Paul missed the sailing out of Buenos Aires because he was delayed at the

U.S. consulate when he went to obtain a new passport." Although I answered readily enough, I was very much aware that she was fishing for information about Sidney and Paul. I also couldn't help but notice that she had no reaction to what I was saying about him. Surely she already knew he was off the ship.

"I think it is very nice that you have become friends with Sidney. Sometimes friendships made on a cruise ship become very close and can last a lifetime."

"Well, actually," I said, "I have known Sidney for many years, but we lost contact for a long time. It is a coincidence that we are renewing our friendship here." I couldn't help but notice that her shoulders relaxed and some of the tension I'd observed seemed to subside with this revelation.

"Oh"—she smiled radiantly—"that is wonderful. It is such a nice shipboard small-world story."

I remember thinking then that Mick was surely wrong about Suzanne and that she was just a little lonely for female companionship and wanted to share her happiness with someone. However, just as with other times I had been with her, I felt something a little disturbing that I could not quite put my finger on. Maybe she was a little too familiar or nosey. She seemed to take risks, like going ashore with me and now having me in the captain's suite, which I suspected would not please him when he found out about it. And he would find out because there was no way that steward was going to keep his mouth shut about such a juicy discovery.

* * *

After Darcy left the suite, Suzanne busied herself with cleaning up the remnants of their meal, taking care that no crumbs or other telltale signs remained. Then she called room service and ordered them to send someone immediately to retrieve the dishes. As she worked, she thought about what she'd learned from Darcy. She had a better understanding of what happened to make Paul miss the sailing, but she still wondered why he had needed to replace his passport. Mostly, she could not understand why he hadn't called her again or provided more details about his plans. Would he really meet the ship at their next stop? Somehow, she knew she would not see him again on this cruise.

She was surprised at the coincidence Darcy described in reuniting with Sidney, and suddenly the thought occurred to her that Paul must not have known about the relationship between the two women. She was sure he would have mentioned it if he had. *Why would Sidney have kept that secret from Paul? Could Darcy and Mick have suspected something about Paul's intent and alerted Sidney?* That would make sense of why the two women had been staying in the same stateroom together until Paul left. Maybe Darcy and Mick thought they needed to protect her. If that was so, had they shared their suspicions with anyone, specifically Tom Smythe? Suzanne was well aware he had become decidedly unfriendly toward her.

She also knew Espen was extremely agitated and seemed to be keeping to himself more and more, and that is certainly understandable, she thought. Even Captain Early did not seem to be spending much time with him. Were they suspicious of him, or of her, for that matter? *Well, if I'm successful, I'll soon be able to put all these terrible events behind me and get on with the life I am meant to live.*

64

The ship lowered anchor in the shallow harbor at Ushuaia, Argentina, and the passengers anxiously waited to board the tenders—the ship's motorized lifeboats—for the short trip to the dock. In the security office Smythe closed the door and picked up the phone. He wasn't entirely sure he was doing the right thing, taking this action on his own, but he didn't see how the contact he was about to make could hurt and maybe it would help. After several rings, a receptionist picked up and directed his call.

"Special Agent Grant Murray, FBI, Las Vegas, how may I help you?"

"Hello, my name is Thomas Smythe. I'm the chief security officer on the *Sea Nymph*, a World of Seas cruise ship. We are currently at sea on a four-week cruise, and now on the coast of Argentina. I want to report some disturbing circumstances we have on board the ship, including two deaths."

"Mr. Smythe, you are speaking with me at the FBI office in Las Vegas. I think you want to contact FBI headquarters. I can give you a phone number."

"I understand that. This is a little complicated, but if I can explain."

"Sure, go ahead, but I probably can't help you."

"An American passenger from Las Vegas has left the cruise prematurely, and I am quite certain he has information about the murders of two of our crew members. I called you because, well, if I give you the details of the crimes as I have been able to determine them and this passenger's personal information and address, can you open an investigation? As I said, the man has left the cruise prematurely and I believe he has returned home."

After completing the call, Smythe felt the agent had taken him seriously and would call Denezza even though it would be somewhat informal, since the FBI would not normally get involved in incidents occurring in international waters. He thought about how Agent Murray obviously already knew Denezza, and how surprised he was to learn he'd been on board a cruise ship. Apparently, the man was a well-known member of the Las Vegas community. Then it seemed as if Murray almost relished the opportunity to investigate him, saying he would make the contact within the next week, and would notify FBI headquarters of Smythe's concern. He emphasized he could not guarantee anything would come of it.

As Smythe contemplated his next call, he mulled over all the details about the crimes he had learned so far. What he was about to do would be far more difficult than his call to the FBI and could very well signal the end of his career with the cruise line.

He was continuing his investigation of both murders—not an accident and a suicide. He knew some of the circumstances surrounding Denezza's departure, but he was quite certain he had not killed Ronaldo or Plato himself, and whoever had was still on board.

He knew that Denezza asked the staff about the procedure for obtaining a passport replacement. Through a call to the consulate, he learned the details of Paul's delay. They also said he apparently went directly from there to the airport. Smythe knew Mick Clayton wanted to get rid of Denezza, and wondered if he'd somehow managed to orchestrate a scenario that resulted in his missing the sailing.

He also continued to watch Suzanne and Espen closely and had reached the conclusion that one or both of them knew about the murders. He recognized a nervousness or restlessness in the captain that was totally out of character. Of course, this could be related to his personal troubles with his wife and the fact that he was now being left out of the loop with regard to the investigation. However, Smythe's gut was telling him there was more to it. He concluded neither of them could be trusted.

This meant in Smythe's opinion that Captain Oldervoll could not be allowed to continue his command. The bottom line was Suzanne had been unfaithful, probably with two men on board the ship, and her husband must have been extremely jealous. The question was could he have been angry enough to commit murder? Smythe doubted that was possible and even if it was true, why was Plato killed? Could that poor guy have had incriminating information about Ronaldo's death? This was still a puzzle that Smythe was determined to solve.

For a while he thought Mick Clayton might know a lot more than he was admitting, but now it appeared he had no discernible motive to harm members of the crew, and with Denezza off the ship, he was acting as if any threat that existed left with him. In fact, Clayton, Farthing, and Sidney Denezza all appeared to be enjoying the cruise and behaving like normal passengers for the first time.

But Smythe was continuing his surveillance of Darcy and Sidney too because he now believed someone still thought they had damaging knowledge about the crimes. He now accepted that Farthing's attempted kidnapping on shore was no coincidence. He had no intention of allowing another incident on his watch.

He lifted the receiver to call cruise line headquarters in Florida to request the captain be removed of his command, but at the last moment he acquiesced to another gut feeling and decided he would wait another day.

65

Amazingly, our journey had taken us into the Antarctic Territory, and we were docked at Ushuaia, the capital of Tierra del Fuego. With a population of sixty thousand, it is famous for its claim of being the southernmost city in the world. A small settlement was first established there in the mid-1800s on the banks of the Beagle Channel under the auspices of the Anglican Church's Patagonia Missionary Society. Thomas Bridges was the first permanent missionary assigned to live among the Yanganes. I was surprised to learn that the Bridges family is still held in high esteem by the locals.

The subsequent growth and development of Ushuaia in the early 1900s was spurred by the budding penal system of the newly independent Argentina. Reminiscent of England's settlement of Australia, the Argentine government began sending their prisoners to the small missionary outpost. Then the construction of a large military-run prison along with the discovery of gold and the promise of profitable fishing, logging, and sheep and cattle ranching, lured settlers to Ushuaia and the surrounding region.

Mick and I stood holding hands on the second-level catwalk of the Ushuaia Prison Museum alternating between reading the history of the facility from large placards lining the inner wall to peering over the railing at the neat rows of tiny cells below. We'd just toured both levels of the now-defunct prison and squeezed into the cells to look at pictures of the previous occupants, many of whom were military or political prisoners, now immortalized there. There were fascinating displays of items related to prison administration as well as the belongings of prisoners, including letters, photos, dishes, watches, and clothing.

Currents Deep and Deadly

This was a complete departure from our morning tour, which had been a relaxing and delightful bus ride through the beautiful surrounding countryside. The blue sky reminded me of Colorado, but the distant treeless Martial Mountains were craggier and more pointed than the Rockies. The thick wooded landscape was primitive, but the two-lane main road passed almost directly under the chairlift of the world's southernmost ski area.

I wondered out loud if I would ever have the opportunity to return to try out the skiing, and Mick said that if I ever planned the trip, he would come back with me. Talk is cheap.

We ended the tour with a fine authentic Argentine barbeque lunch with lamb and Patagonia pie, a delicacy made with salmon and fresh vegetables with cheese sprinkled on top, and yerba mate, Argentina's national drink, which is a strong herbal tea.

After leaving the prison, we had about an hour left to spend at the port, so we simply strolled around the town. Now and then we stepped into a shop to search for just the right "end of the world" tee shirts. Downtown Ushuaia reminded me of coastal towns in Alaska I had visited many years ago—low wood buildings on narrow paved streets that quickly changed to gravel as they climbed away from the city center. Above the main street, small houses were neatly painted in bright colors, mirroring the profuse flowers in gardens planted around almost every home. Their owners were obviously proud to welcome the attention of tourists.

As we stood in a long line of passengers waiting to board the tenders for the trip back to the ship, I couldn't help but comment on the surroundings. "Oh, Mick, look how beautiful these flowers are. Isn't it amazing how no matter where you go in the world there is so much beauty all around? And so much diversity—I guess that is what struck Darwin and got him to thinking about how it all came about."

At intervals of about thirty feet down the length of the dock, huge weathered wood planter boxes were stuffed full of blooming perennials and annuals cascading over the sides in a riot of color. I saw everything from daisies to digitalis and cosmos, just like back home, but there were many plants I had never seen before, and I quickly snapped a dozen pictures. I thought I would look them up in my botany book when I got home.

Mick watched me and smiled warmly, then put his arm around my shoulder squeezing me closer to him. "I love the way you find so much joy in everything."

I had that feeling again that everything in my life would be wonderful from now on if Mick and of course Rachael were part of it. At the same time, another new and disturbing thought was pricking the back of my mind, and I knew I would eventually have to let it surface. But for now I simply took a deep breath to fill my lungs with the unbelievably fresh-smelling end-of-the-world air.

66

After leaving Ushuaia and exiting the Beagle Channel, then heading west through the Strait of Magellan, the *Sea Nymph* continued up Chile's western coastline, weaving through vast channels that surround the almost uncountable archipelagoes of the Chilean fjords. The route through this extraordinarily rugged and picturesque area extended north from Tierra del Fuego past several national parks and the spectacular Andes Mountain Range to the east.

On the coast hundreds of glaciers branch off the vast Patagonian ice field, the largest continental ice mass in the world next to Greenland and Antarctica. While many of the glaciers are now receding due to climate change, some still flow down the rugged mountains and into the sea creating spectacular views that can be observed only from the channels. Just a few towns and cattle ranches interrupt the stark, cold, and lonely splendor.

Espen's mind seemed sluggish as he thought about how this landscape with its stunning vistas made a fitting end to the journey. The ship was slowly moving toward Valparaiso midway up the Chilean coast just three days ahead. He stood ramrod straight watching the glide of a giant petrel. The tube-nosed gray bird, similar to an albatross, soared gracefully over the water as it eyed the surface for hapless fish and skimmed the sea with its down-turned wing. Then it nosed aloft on hidden currents, so completely at home in the frigid fjords, he thought wistfully. As the bird circled back with the setting sun glistening off the underside of its creamy wing, perhaps to get another look at the strange behemoth in the middle of its territory, his thoughts swept back to his earlier encounters with Suzanne.

Ever since leaving Buenos Aires, she had overtly been trying to gain back his confidence. He knew what she was doing all right and had resisted even speaking more than a few words to her, but gradually his resolve weakened. Finally today he agreed to meet with her and resigned himself to hear her out.

She appeared so sincere in her apology for causing him so much pain that his heart had softened a little. She assured him her transgressions were in the past and begged him to let her back into his life. "I love you so much, Espen," she whispered. "Please let us start over and let me show you how very sorry I am and how much I want our lives to be the way they were before all these terrible things happened."

He knew very well that he should not give in to her—that he did not know her as well as he once thought, and at least some of the "terrible things" were of her making. Besides, due to the regrettable circumstances on this sailing, it would be best if he kept to himself as much as possible. But damn it, he had to admit that deep down he still wanted her.

And so he agreed to share dinner with her in his suite, where she now stood at the counter in front of the bar sink, quietly opening the third bottle of champagne. She was so very tired of talking, but she knew that Espen was coming around to her side. She could tell that he wanted her, and she had been diligent in her attempts to arouse him while trying to put him at ease. Of course the alcohol was having the desired effect as well. They had just finished a delicious meal of sea scallops in butter and wine sauce with mushroom and leek risotto, and he had stepped out on the balcony to enjoy the crisp air.

She carried the bottle across the room to join him and refill his glass. Outside, she couldn't help but marvel at the thickly star-studded sky, which was quite exquisite. In fact, the night was extraordinarily clear and bright, and with the lack of ambient light, the galaxy stretched across the heavens in a bright, wide, white-washed swath.

Espen was not concentrating on this natural beauty, however. He was clearly upset over his declining relationship with his employer and the crew, and as he discussed his troubles, Suzanne sensed his vulnerability. This was so out of line with his normal self-assurance.

Only she knew how vulnerable he really was. In fact, he was very much off guard and oblivious to the fact that he had consumed most of two bottles of champagne while she sipped a small amount.

Despite the cold air, Espen felt warmed by their reconciliation, and was wondering how he could have had such terrible thoughts about his beautiful wife when she was obviously still in love with him. She admitted to a minor flirtation with the cruise director and sincerely apologized, and he now saw how the crew's gossip played a large role in their breakup. If only he had realized this sooner. Since he was confident that Ronaldo's fall would be ruled accidental, he assumed there would be no consequences for her or anyone onboard. He had decided to try and learn from his personal and professional mistakes beginning now with offering Suzanne his forgiveness.

He turned around and pulled her into his arms. Because of his height, the railing nestled against the small of his back, and he leaned out slightly holding her arms as he studied her face. She shivered and smiled up into his face. She put her arms around him, pushing in close to his body. She raised up onto her toes and kissed him, letting her tongue move over his until they found their familiar pattern, and she felt him harden against her stomach.

Sighing softly, she lowered herself to a squatting position while she quickly unzipped his trousers. His lungs burned with the sharp intake of cold air as she began to caress him in the way that originally sealed his fate to hers. Every ounce of his strength melted into her. He was completely overcome with the passion he'd held in and denied for so long. He thought he would lift her up and carry her into the warmth of the suite where they would have incredible sex as they had on so many occasions.

67

Mick lay behind Darcy up against her back with his arms around her and nestled his face into her thick hair as he breathed in the scent of flowers. They had been in bed but far from asleep for over two hours. Now as they began to drift off, he knew there was something he should say to her. He was having difficulty deciding how to approach the subject of their parting in Valparaiso, where they would board flights to return to their separate lives. He gently kissed the back of her neck to see if she was still awake.

"I love you, Mick." She turned her shoulders and face to look at him and smiled. "I was just thinking about how relaxed I am as I was falling asleep."

"I'm sorry I woke you. I feel great too, but I was just thinking about what will happen after the cruise, you know?"

"So many weird things have happened over the past four weeks, and now things are pretty normal, so I feel as if somehow everything is going to work out fine. I know we will be together somehow, and I know you realize I have this other whole thing with Rachael to consider as well."

"Of course I understand that. But the fact is you have a career, and so do I. And they are not in the same place not to mention where we both live. I just wondered if maybe we should talk about it a little."

Darcy was so tired and happy. She did not want to ruin the mood by having this conversation, at least not now. Like him, she was also worried about how they would sustain their relationship, but because of Rachael there were more scary issues she knew she would have to deal with eventually, and had no idea how she was going to do it.

"OK, Mick. Let's agree to talk about our future before we get to Valparaiso, all right?"

"That's fine. I'll be quiet and just hold you until you go to sleep."

He did as he promised, but she was asleep long before he was able to join her. Despite how pleasant the last few days had been, he was still uneasy because he did not understand why the murders had happened and what it had to do with Darcy and Sidney. He knew for sure that there had to be some connection, and he suspected Sidney had been in grave danger all along.

He believed Darcy inadvertently stumbled onto conversations she would have been far better off not overhearing. No one could think that she knew anything about the deaths. But Suzanne had to be involved somehow. So while outwardly he was happily enjoying the cruise with Darcy, inwardly he was still very worried. He sincerely hoped Officer Smythe shared his concerns and was still continuing his investigations.

68

All Espen's mind could grasp was that he'd been out on his balcony thinking that finally his life was getting back on track when suddenly he found himself in an alternate reality—a shocking, dark, and watery world. Stunned and badly broken by the six-story fall into the frigid sea, he looked up at the great ship—his great ship—just as her massive stern passed by gleaming in the moonlight only a few yards away. He had felt tremendous pain for a few moments, but now a comforting numbness was settling over him. He did not try to call for help or to swim. Those actions would have been futile if not impossible—and undignified.

Mercifully, the cold was quickly penetrating his entire body and mind, bringing with it a feeling of sleepy contentment. He looked up, and finally the beauty of the night sky registered with him. In the dead quiet, he gazed across the heavens and down to the horizon with a vague thought that this splendor was fitting as the last thing he would ever see.

Bobbing in the ship's wake and violently shaking from the cold, he gazed across the narrow channel to a distant glacier, wide where it sat atop the ridge but gradually descending to a narrow frothy spill into the sea. It was radiant in the bright moonlight like a crystal goblet studded with diamonds, and he thought it was the most beautiful thing he had ever seen.

Suddenly, in the distance, he was mildly surprised to see the familiar shimmering blue glaciers of his Norwegian homeland and the thick surrounding forests. Squinting toward the far shoreline, he was startled and relieved to see a ship approaching out of the light surface mist.

As he watched first in disbelief then with a sense of relief, he realized it was a Viking ship. Its smooth keel rose vertically from the water into an intricately carved dragon head, held high, complete with a freshly painted protruding red tongue and green scales carved in relief. The whole vessel shone with reflected light as it glided silently across a wide band of golden sea to where Espen was waiting.

Finally he was able to make out the commander standing near the bow with a fur cape covering his bare shoulders, his arms crossed over his chest and his loose blond hair flying to the side. He raised an arm, and Espen was quite sure the man was beckoning to him. The dragon's black eye caught a ray of moonlight then, and the monster seemed to momentarily glance down at him.

As he gathered enough strength to turn back one more time to see the retreating lights of the *Sea Nymph*, a calmness he had never before experienced enveloped him. He was thinking that the utter silence was quite extraordinary and pleasant while he tried in vain to bring some thought or memory of his life into focus.

Resignedly, he turned back and gazed up at the other oncoming ship, now almost on top of him. In another moment he was completely disoriented and devoid of feeling. As he glanced at the Viking ship for the last time, he smiled and began to slide down toward what he had always known was his true destiny.

69

Where the hell is he? Captain Early had checked Espen's suite three times since he failed to appear on the bridge at eight, and now it was two in the afternoon. He visited Suzanne in her cabin at around nine, but she said she had not seen her husband since last night. Then at ten he finally reported the absence to Officer Smythe. After the two of them checked the inside of Espen's suite and found nothing unusual, they decided to wait a little longer before sounding an alarm.

He'd certainly been under duress lately, and perhaps had decided he needed some time alone, although nothing could be more out of character than for him to ignore his command. Besides that, there were only so many places a person could hide on the ship without being seen.

Something had to happen soon because the first mates were becoming concerned, and several guests had asked why the captain hadn't given his daily address to the crew and passengers. These highly anticipated morning chats by the affable captain were a highlight of each day for many passengers. So after one more futile search of the ship, Early and Smythe were reluctantly meeting on the bridge to review camera footage from the previous night. There had been too much of this type of review effort on the cruise already, and both of them dreaded the task.

After looking at the forward and aft camera footage covering a time period of several hours during the night and early morning and finding nothing out of the ordinary, Early resignedly punched in the parameters for the cameras on the port side where Espen's suite was located for a timeframe beginning at eight the previous night. Both men knew without stating it that if something had happened to the captain, it probably began in the suite since he reportedly retired around that time and no one except Suzanne had seen him since.

They watched the footage first with foreboding and then with overwhelming alarm. At 12:02 a.m. something clearly had gone overboard, and the infrared technology left little doubt that it was a human being. Early sat with his face in his hands trying to gain control and hold back the tears he knew he was about to shed for his dear friend.

Smythe reached over and placed a hand on his shoulder. "I am so sorry, James. We can't be absolutely certain yet, but it does appear that Espen went over somewhere back in the fjords. There is no way a person would survive any appreciable time in that water. What do you want to do?"

Captain Early looked up and sniffed loudly as he ran the back of his hand across his eyes. "I just cannot imagine a strong man like Espen killing himself no matter what was going on in his life. If this is what it looks like, something else has to have happened. Not suicide." He shook his head. "No, I won't believe that."

Smythe was in an uncomfortable and sensitive position, and he did not want to make things worse until he could be certain of the facts. "James, I know how close you two were, but you also know that something was going on with Suzanne and others on board that had already aroused suspicion. Isn't it possible that Espen could not live with whatever he might have done or with something he knew?"

Early did not answer. He got up slowly and leaned on the console with both hands. "Someone has to talk to Suzanne," he said flatly. "Should I or do you want to talk to her yourself?"

"Let me talk to her and try to determine whether she knows anything more than she admitted to you earlier. I think you should brief the mates and impress on them that they are not to discuss the captain's disappearance with the rest of the crew or the passengers. With only a day left on the cruise, maybe we can get to Valparaiso without causing a panic on the ship."

Smythe left the bridge and headed down in the elevator to see if Suzanne was in her cabin. He could not help wondering how things might have been different if he'd made the call to Headquarters to ask that Espen be removed from command. There was no way to know if that would have resulted in a better or worse outcome . . . although he couldn't actually think of anything worse than this.

Suzanne answered his knock, and he watched her closely as he entered the tiny room. She smiled warmly as he turned to face her from only a couple of feet away. "Suzanne, I'm afraid I have some very bad news," he began.

She took a step backward and plopped down on the edge of her bed. The smile was gone as she looked up at him, and her bottom lip seemed to quiver. "Oh no," she cried. "There has been so much bad news on this sailing. Does this have something to do with my Espen?"

"I'm afraid so." He tried to demonstrate some compassion for her, but he wasn't feeling it. "He hasn't been seen today, and although we can't be positive yet, it looks as if he went overboard at around midnight." Suzanne slumped over onto her side, tears rolling down her face onto the puffy dark blue duvet.

"No, no," she moaned. "Espen and I were going to get back together. Did you know that? Maybe he is somewhere on the ship. Please find him for me. Please, please."

Smythe continued watching her closely and could not find any tell. She was obviously distraught or else she was an exceptional actor. "We'll keep looking, Suzanne, but the camera appears to show a person going over in the vicinity of his . . . I mean, your suite." He moved toward the door but turned back to her as he reached for the handle. "I'm sorry for this, Suzanne, but I need to know where you were last night. You told James Early you saw the captain at some point." He saw the flash of anger in her eyes although it was so fleeting he could easily have missed it.

"I understand why you have to ask," she answered calmly with tears still streaming down her face. Suddenly shuddering, she wrapped her arms around her body. "It won't do much good though since I was here alone all evening from around nine. We had dinner, and then I came straight back to the cabin." She shook her head from side to side in disbelief. "We talked about me moving back in with him and trying to make a fresh start. Why did this have to happen?" she sobbed.

70

Please tell me what I should do next. Why are you withholding direction from me when I need you more than ever now? Suzanne tossed and turned in the narrow bed in her crew cabin where she'd been since Smythe left her. Everything in her life seemed to be running off the tracks. Lonely and confused, she could not recall ever before feeling that she did not know what she was supposed to do.

Of course she had always been confident, since she had a unique and secret source of direction that enabled her to get everything she wanted from life. As a consequence, she knew without any doubt that whatever she decided she wanted was right and good. All she needed was the blessing for her actions.

But now for the first time, a new and foreign emotion had encroached upon her. She knew intellectually, if not emotionally, that this feeling was doubt. So she let her mind wander back to her childhood, thinking that if she returned to the beginning—the source of her strength—she could find her bearings.

She thought about her mother, Ezador, for the first time in many months. As a child, Suzanne recognized that the woman was exotic and totally out of place and time in 1970 Topeka. Because she was raised steeped in Zulu tribal culture and ritual, she naturally tried to teach her daughter to embrace many seemingly bizarre beliefs. But Suzanne soon recognized that these were simply natural and less formal versions of all religious doctrine, and no more or less believable.

Dreams had been important to her mother, and she described them in detail, always emphasizing the messages they conveyed. "Suzanne," she would say with passion as she stroked her daughter's thick curly hair, "Nkulunkulu, the creator, is not for you to worry about. He is far above and detached from all life on earth and not involved directly in our lives. You must embrace your ancestral spirits and listen as they speak to you through your dreams. The worst thing you can do is to offend them, lest they cause illness or death."

Suzanne was an educated woman, and she understood that this was simply a variation of the many primitive beliefs humans formed early on to explain aspects of life they did not understand. As a Zulu woman, Ezador wanted to teach Suzanne to embrace nature and to understand and accept her own physical and emotional strengths and needs. Sadly, Suzanne thought, she was unable to convey these ideas with any confidence because she herself was about as repressed as a person could be. The poor woman was isolated in her Kansas community, shunned by her new family, and terrorized by her husband.

When Suzanne was twelve her mother rather mercifully succumbed to ovarian cancer. By then, Suzanne was already being pulled in a direction very different from her mother's influence by her traditional Catholic grandparents and aunts and uncles. Their goal was to erase what they believed to be her mother's dangerous pagan teachings. They insisted she attend mass at least twice weekly and that she follow all edicts of the church. In particular, sexuality was deemed to be a bad thing and sex outside of marriage was as terrible a sin as murder.

When her father was around, which became less frequent after her mother's death, he tried to bully her into submission and terrorized her with his radical Christian views. He repeatedly told her that she must look to her mother as a perfect wife role model and would find happiness only in servitude to the men in her life who would take care of her, and to Jesus Christ, whose teachings would provide all the direction and satisfaction she needed. Otherwise, she would be damned to hell. Unfortunately for Suzanne, all the efforts to mold her faith only instilled bewilderment, fear, and guilt with respect to God, sex, and sin in general.

To counter the enormous stress of these contradictory influences, rather than reject religion altogether, Suzanne developed her own unique relationship with her own God. His voice became the loudest of all those who tried to tell her what to do and how to think. And because he was the highest authority imaginable, she did not dream of contradicting His instructions.

In fact, while outwardly rebelling against her father by attending college, receiving degrees in business and hotel management, and becoming a worldly woman and sophisticated professional, inwardly she subjugated her own free will and conscience to only one unquestionable voice that told her exactly what to do to achieve everything she wanted in life.

After several hours of prayer and meditation, Suzanne finally received the message she'd been waiting for. Her thoughts turned to Espen with emotions of longing and regret, but also with a sense of relief. She understood what she should do in order to get on with the life she was intended to live.

71

"*I learned my lesson well. You see, ya can't please everyone, so ya got to please yourself.*" It was Gunnar and Matthew Nelson presenting a tasteful and touching tribute to their father, Ricky.

Mick and I along with Don, Charlie, and Sidney were enjoying our last evening of the cruise in the Atlantis Theater located forward on deck 4. Some sort of show had played in the enormous Vegas-style three-tier theater almost every night of the cruise, but Sidney had only seen a couple of them, and tonight was special, so we all decided to go and sit together.

With Valparaiso and the end of the cruise just a few hundred miles away, the ship was moving very slowly up the coast of Chile. Due to a mix-up of some sort regarding the availability of our slip, we were killing some time before arriving at the harbor. Staff Captain Early had explained this little problem during his briefing to the passengers earlier in the day. He did not say why he was standing in for Captain Espen who normally made the daily announcements, and some of the passengers and crew were gossiping that the captain might be ill. Regardless, it didn't affect us in the least, and we were relaxing and having a great time.

Ricky's aging blond twins sang Gunnar's "Cross My Broken Heart," then transitioned into "After the Rain" from their 1990s album by that name.

I'm waiting as my heart beats just for you
Come on and take my hand and I'll pull you through
But things will never change until you want them to
After the rain washes away the tears
And all the pain

I leaned back in the plush velvety seat listening to the nostalgia with Mick beside me, lost in the moment. A memory rushed back from many years ago. I recalled how this song was once a favorite of mine. Tonight it suddenly seemed so apropos. Before I knew it, tears were welling and threatening to ruin my mascara. The emotion was still close to the surface even though the burden I carried for so many years was now lifted.

I was still overwhelmed by feelings of awe and gratitude, and it would take some time to adjust, but at least now I knew I would have a relationship with my daughter. And that was more than I had ever hoped for. I guess what they say is true. You can never know what life may bring just around the corner. So I really got the message now. Never, ever, give up on life!

Charlie and Don were enjoying the show too, but as usual their attention span lapsed, and Charlie leaned around Mick to tell me they were going for a walk on the deck. About fifteen minutes later Sidney said she was going to the restroom, and I told her I would come along.

The ladies' room had a short waiting line, and Sidney preceded me into a stall. Even so, I was just a minute behind her when I pulled open the door and stepped into the wide lobby outside the theater. I stood for a moment to see if she had waited for me. Actually, it was fortunate that I first looked in the direction of the starboard outside door because at that moment I was stunned by the sight of Suzanne pulling Sidney out onto the deck. *What in the world is happening now?*

Of course I had to follow them. I knew that Sidney didn't really know Suzanne, and I was experiencing that too-familiar prickly feeling in the base of my spine. I rushed through the door and looked to my left, the direction they had gone.

Alarm bells started bouncing around in my brain when I saw the struggle taking place about a hundred feet ahead. Sidney was yanking her arm and pulling back trying to loosen Suzanne's grip while she was being dragged along the deck. I yelled, "Hey, Suzanne, what are you doing?" She looked back at me with an expression that made my stomach flip. Even from that distance I recognized the look as pure evil, for lack of a better word.

I ran as fast as my four-inch spike heels would allow, and as soon as Suzanne saw me speed up, she punched Sidney in the stomach and pushed her down. Sidney slumped against the wall of the ship and didn't move. *Oh shit!* I sprinted and screamed for Sidney to get up, and in an instant I met Suzanne in the middle of the deck. Before I could say anything, she was scratching and clawing at my face with her long sharp nails, while she tried to inch closer to where Sidney was still crumpled on the deck.

My hands were busy trying to protect my face, and I turned my head to the side while I kicked at her legs several times. She screeched but did not let up. She seemed desperate to get rid of me and get back to Sidney. She was edging me toward the railing, and the whole time I was yelling for help knowing full well the deck was deserted except for the three of us. I could not believe how fiercely Suzanne fought . . . just like the wildcat she resembled. She was too much for me, and the last thing I remember as I tumbled backward was glancing back at the door and seeing Mick step onto the deck. Then I was gone.

72

Mick's mind struggled to register what he was seeing. He had taken a break from the show to see where the girls had gone. Not seeing them in the lobby, he stepped out for some fresh air. He was just in time to see Darcy being thrown down, her head bouncing off one of the green barrels lined up against the railing with a sickening thud.

Before he could process that scene, he realized Suzanne was pulling someone else up from beside the wall and hauling the obviously groggy woman across the deck. My god, its Sidney, he thought, as he moved rapidly toward the action.

Despite his speed everything seemed to be playing out in slow motion. With absolute horror and a debilitating helplessness, Mick watched Suzanne drag Sidney to an opening in the railing where she bent over her, placed her hands on Sidney's torso, and simply rolled her off the deck. The silvery shimmer of the tight-fitting cocktail dress flashed in the waning sunlight like the scales of a leaping fish as she disappeared into the blackness.

As he drew closer, he could see that the opening was a gate now swinging inward in the breeze. *Why the hell is there a gate there?* His mind just could not comprehend what his eyes were telling him. He was only six feet from Suzanne when he turned from the railing, and she lunged at him.

Only two minutes had elapsed since Darcy stepped out onto the deck, but the yelling and commotion had drawn the attention of the security guard outside the theater entrance. As he exited onto the deck to see what was happening, he looked to his right toward the stern just in time to see two male passengers running toward him shouting and waving their arms.

He turned to look up the deck in the opposite direction and gasped at the sight of two other passengers down on the deck. One was slumped over an inflatable life raft container. As he drew closer, he was horrified by the sight of blood running down the side of the barrel onto the deck.

The guard grabbed for his radio as he sprinted toward the bleeding passenger. Don and Charlie ran up beside him and breathlessly explained that they saw most of what happened from way down the deck: Darcy knocked unconscious, Sidney being rolled overboard, and then Mick being attacked, all by Suzanne.

"She ran through that metal door down there," Don managed as he bent over with one hand on his knee and pointed toward the bow with the other.

The guard glanced in that direction then looked back at them in disbelief. "Suzanne Moretti, the hotel manager?"

"Yes, yes!" Charlie screamed as the three of them moved to where Mick was lying over the barrel, unconscious. The guard looked over the railing and saw Sidney floating near the back of the ship. He spoke rapidly into his radio as he reached behind the barrels and lifted a lifesaving ring from its hook on one of the metal struts. He leaned over the railing and threw it as far back as he could, knowing it would not be far enough. Then he rushed back to Mick and lowered him onto the deck.

Don looked at the blood covering Mick's chest, then over at Darcy where she was still lying against another barrel. Then he looked at Charlie with an odd expression that was almost a smile before he turned and jumped through the gate.

"No, Don!" But Charlie was too late. He rushed to the opening and watched in horror as Don bobbed in the waves and then began swimming haltingly back to where Sidney was flailing her arms and screaming. He could not help the flow of tears or his blind panic as he frantically looked around the deck for something, anything that would help.

He looked again at the barrels in their rack and realized for the first time what they were. He frantically tried to pull one of them loose, but had no idea how they worked, and soon realized with a feeling of total despair that the effort was useless and a waste of precious time.

He turned to the security guard who was on his knees applying pressure to Mick's wound. His attempt to stop the blood gushing from the hole in Mick's chest looked about as futile as Charlie's own efforts. He stared at the thick stream of bright red, still dripping down the barrel and running along the sloping deck. Then he turned his attention back to Mick who surely had already lost too much blood to survive. A couple of yards away Darcy moaned and began to pull herself up.

Charlie turned back to the railing, pounded it with his palms, and screamed in frustration. He glanced once more at Mick and then Darcy who was wearing the same pretty yellow dress she wore at dinner on the night this odyssey began. She had managed to crawl onto her hands and knees and was shaking her head like a horse flicking flies as she stared at Mick with an uncomprehending expression.

"Just hold on," the guard was saying. "The deckhands are coming to lower the motor launch, and the medical team is on the way. It will only be a minute." As he spoke, he never let up the pressure he was applying with both hands against Mick's chest.

Charlie started toward Darcy but stopped after a few steps and turned back to the railing. He didn't hear what the guard was yelling at him as he dove off the deck.

Only because the ship was barely moving and due to his superb physical condition and rush of panic adrenaline, Don managed to reach Sidney despite having dislocated his shoulder when he hit the water. *How could I be so stupid?* He chastised himself for not having thought more about how he would need to land—feet or hands first—to avoid injury, even though it had only been a two-story fall.

Sidney miraculously appeared to be unhurt, but the cold was rapidly depleting both their bodies of heat as it also served to numb some of the pain in his shoulder. He was keeping both of them afloat by having Sidney hold on to his chest while he paddled with his good arm and kicked furiously. He could see the lifesaving ring floating about a hundred feet away and knew that reaching it was his best bet.

Lifting his chin to avoid swallowing seawater, he tried to ignore the searing pain as he watched the *Sea Nymph* pull further away against the darkening sky. He knew with overwhelming sadness that his efforts had probably been a lost cause. He gazed at the ship and prayed for some sort of help, Just as his thoughts turned to his daughter and Charlie, another wave of horror struck as he watched Charlie fly out over the side of the ship.

Sidney was surprisingly quiet and calm except that every thirty seconds or so she would let go of Don with one hand in order to clear her nose and eyes. She was willing herself to paddle with her legs to generate warmth and to help Don keep them both afloat as they aimed toward the ring floating up ahead. She was basically jolted awake when she hit the water, and that shock plus the cold was taking its toll. Her stomach ached from Suzanne's punch. Her limbs felt stiff and frozen and would barely move under her. It occurred to her she might have other injuries but just could not feel anything.

Several times they lost their momentum and slipped under the waves only to come up spluttering as they managed to regain their position. Thankfully, the sea was relatively calm and the waves were low with little breaking action. As long as they remained calm with their mouths closed, they could gently ride each one up and down. Despite their perilous situation, Sidney could not stop her mind from considering Suzanne's possible motives. She had absolutely no doubt that somehow it was all about Paul.

Charlie surfaced, apparently uninjured, and tried to swim back to his partner and Sidney who were now at least two hundred yards behind the ship. He was not a strong swimmer in the best of conditions, and he was regretting his hasty dive into the frigid water. But he had to do something. He would not return home to Penelope from this vacation without Don. *No fucking way!*

But the fact was there would have been no hope for him, Don, or Sidney if the ship had been cruising at its normal pace. As it was, even crawling through the water at under three knots, the massive vessel could not stop on a dime. Almost five minutes and three ship lengths were required for a full stop from the time the engines shut down.

In fact, on the bridge the standard emergency procedures were well under way. The moment the first mate answered the 911 call and sounded the man overboard alarm, the crew turned off the diesel generators powering the propeller motors and raised the ship's stabilizer flaps, which now jutted out to the sides just under the surface.

The flaps were normally deployed by the captain to reduce roll in rough seas, but only judiciously—when a significant number of passengers were seasick—because the added drag greatly reduced fuel efficiency. In this situation, the crew hoped the added friction would hasten the ship's glide to a full stop. Having accomplished these measures within two minutes, Captain Early and the bridge crew were watching in disbelief as the stern camera provided a bird's-eye view of the ghastly scene playing out behind the ship.

73

I could not understand what was causing the horrendously loud noise roaring in my head or the shocking pain radiating from the back of my head to my neck and shoulders. I could barely move, and my eyes didn't seem to be working correctly. Everything was a blur, and I kept shaking my head to clear my vision because I knew something had to be terribly wrong, and I should be doing something about it. Then I realized the ship's emergency alert system was blaring from a speaker almost directly above me. Talk about a migraine!

As my vision began to clear, I suddenly realized what I was looking at. The pain evaporated in an instant as I shot up off the deck and leaped toward Mick. "No, no, no!" I was already sobbing as I knelt beside him on the opposite side from the guard. I tried to calm myself so I could do something to help him. I leaned all the way down and lightly kissed his blue lips. That wasn't nearly enough, but there didn't seem to be anything else I could do. *This is not going to happen.* "Hold on, Mick. We still have to have our talk about our future, remember?" The words and my breath came in giant gulps and heaves.

With tears dripping onto the deck and onto Mick, I looked up into the dark sad eyes of the security guard, only inches away from mine as he leaned over Mick's chest. There was a message there I absolutely refused to acknowledge. If I thought I had already experienced the worst events of my life, I would have to reevaluate because this was beyond anything. How could I have found this man and now be losing him so quickly and violently? Mick had been so right. Why hadn't I seen how dangerously unbalanced Suzanne was? So much for the pride I took in my powers of observation and intuition.

Just then both of the ship's doctors and another member of the medical staff raced up pushing a rolling stretcher and began to handle the trauma in a surprisingly rapid and professional manner. I stood and backed away to give them room. My head and neck were throbbing again, and I turned to lean against the railing. Looking toward the stern, only then did I comprehend the fullness of the horror this evening had become.

I'm not sure what happened next, but my mind went into some sort of autopilot as I stared at the barrel sitting next to me on the rack, still covered with Mick's blood. There was the label with the life raft instructions I studied at the beginning of the trip, the night I heard the crew members talking on the deck above me.

Before I even thought about it I had moved around so that one of the barrels was directly in front of me, and I was already loosening the two thumbscrews that held it in place. Following the instruction placard, it was quite easy to detach, and it took me less than a minute.

I sensed the security guard shouting at me as he continued helping the medics, but ignored him. Before he could do anything to stop me, I pushed the barrel off the rack and rolled it through the gate. My adrenaline rush helped, but it was not nearly as heavy as imagined. Upon impact with the water, it sprung apart, and the yellow rubber raft inflated with a loud whoosh.

Charlie heard the raft hit the water and looked toward the ship. He hadn't made much progress, and he was already tired, so he decided to take his chances with the raft instead of relying on his-less-than-stellar swimming skills to reach Don and Sidney. He got to the raft without much trouble, but its sides were much higher than he realized, and he knew he did not have the strength to climb into it. He was too exhausted and cursed himself for not being in better shape. Then he looked back to where Don and Sidney were clearly losing their struggle to stay afloat.

Finally, the ship was at a dead quiet stop, and he could just barely hear Don calling his name above the loud onboard siren. "Charlie, bring the raft back here!" Charlie exhaled a roar from deep in his gut. With every ounce of his strength—more than he really had—he managed to get his arms over the side, and kicking furiously, began to haul himself up.

On the deck, Officer Smythe arrived and put his arms around Darcy as Mick was placed on the stretcher. He aimed to comfort her but also ensure she did not follow her friends over the side. What had happened here, as relayed by the guard and Darcy, was unbelievable. There was no doubt now. Suzanne's actions pulled the case together. She had to be responsible for the deaths on board, including Espen's. Nothing else made any sense now that she had shown her hand so dramatically. He still didn't understand why she had done it, but that was a very temporary condition. One thing he was sure of was that he'd played it right by calling the FBI in Vegas because Denezza was undoubtedly guilty as well. He put his hand to the holster now attached to his utility belt. He couldn't wait to find Suzanne.

The medics, one of them holding an IV bag high in the air, ran up the deck pushing Mick on the gurney and disappeared through a crew door while Darcy stared in disbelief. She knew she would likely never see him alive again.

A few yards from where she and Smythe were standing, four deckhands were working a winch apparatus to lower the motor launch from its stanchion high above the deck. The twenty-two-foot motorboat built by Alenyacht France served as shore excursion transportation for the captain but mostly as a potential emergency craft for situations that almost never occurred. This one certainly qualified. The hands had dislodged the cables from their thick metal cleats on the wall near the ceiling, and two of them rapidly turned the winch handle.

Overhead on a metal catwalk, four additional men used guide wires to control the descent of the craft as it was lowered into position over the water. Having practiced this procedure a hundred times, they implemented it quickly and smoothly. Within five minutes the launch had hit the water and flown toward the stern with four hands on board, including a paramedic.

The boat featured a custom central console with a small cabin, and that is where the three passengers were nestled after being hauled aboard. The crew concentrated on keeping them warm after checking to make sure there were no serious injuries besides Don's shoulder. Each was wrapped in a silvery thermal blanket for the short trip back to the *Sea Nymph*. Without the numbing effects of the cold water, Don was in excruciating pain. He leaned back against the hull with his eyes closed, breathing deeply and rhythmically.

Charlie sat across from him watching anxiously. He was exhausted but none the worse for his efforts, and Sidney simply sat on the bench next to Charlie in a total state of disbelief and shock. It was only a matter of minutes before the boat was being hoisted back up to the deck where the medical staff waited.

74

With his arm still around her shoulders, Smythe guided Darcy carefully through the door and to the elevator. When they arrived down in sick bay, he made sure the docs knew she'd been unconscious and probably had a concussion. Pulling one of them aside, he whispered Darcy's relationship to Mick, who had been taken into one of the two examining rooms. Then he left her in their hands and jogged back to the stairs.

He had to find Suzanne before she unleashed any more mayhem, and he anxiously thought about how to proceed. He kept moving, and his gut feeling was to start at home base. To save time, he headed for the elevator. His instincts had been right again. Quickly approaching the captain's stateroom, he slowed down and quieted his breathing when he noticed the door was open about a foot.

Cautiously, he moved closer, placing his body at a right angle to the door and just to the left of the hinge crack. Listening, with the newly resurrected Ruger drawn and pointed upward, he breathed deeply and silently from his gut. His palms were damp, and he knew he had to get a grip on his emotions before entering the suite. He could not believe he was standing here with his firearm at the ready on the cruise ship outside the captain's suite no less.

His belly fluttered when he heard Suzanne talking. As ridiculous as it seemed under the circumstances, she was inside having a conversation with someone. Who was in there with her, and why would they be there after what had just happened? Curious about the conversation, he drew a very shallow breath and leaned in as far as possible with his ear only a few inches from the door.

"You have never let me down," she was saying. "What did I do wrong?" No answer. "Please, please help me understand what to do next. My whole life is about pleasing you. Help me. Help me," she sobbed.

In the perfect silence of the stateroom, Suzanne waited for an answer, but neither she nor Smythe heard one. Instead, her thoughts drifted back to when she and Paul first met last summer in Las Vegas. She knew instantly that he was the one who would change and fulfill her life. The glamour and elegance of his lifestyle appealed to her, and she immediately pictured herself living among so many other rich and beautiful people.

It had been so easy to manipulate him into formulating the plan to eliminate Sidney from his life, and he was so blinded by his lust that he truly believed the plan was his own idea. That was why he even went along with the ruse of Suzanne pretending to be in love with Ronaldo in order to gain his cooperation.

Of course, Ronaldo would also have done anything for her. Fun, friendly guy that he was, he was also greedy and lacking in scruples. This is why she selected him to help carry out the plan to begin with. He had believed she was in love with him and that it was important for them to carry out Paul's plan to kill Sidney and collect $100,000 each, which he believed they would use to start their lives over together. That is, until he lost his nerve and tried to back out. What a fool he turned out to be.

And so every single thing Suzanne thought and did during the past several months was aimed at rearranging her life to be with Paul. Because this was what she wanted, she received divine guidance on how to achieve it, and the plan would have worked perfectly if it were not for the crew's gossiping, Ronaldo's weakness, Espen's shocking behavior, and the passengers who meddled in their affairs.

She could not help but think about poor Plato and how she knew he had to die because a passenger heard him talking with Paul about their plan, and he admitted to having suspicions linking Paul and her to Ronaldo's death.

A small smile played at the corners of her mouth as she recalled how startled she was when she first realized she did not really need Plato's or Ronaldo's help. She wrongly assumed that getting rid of Sidney would require their physical strength and cunning, but God had given her the strength to do what was necessary. She was empowered by her own resourcefulness and physical strength and was pleased to learn she was so capable.

Espen's rage and stubbornness had been an obstacle. She thought it would be an easy matter to just leave him after the cruise since the marriage was doomed to failure anyway, mostly due to their vast differences. But he had turned the tables and left her. This was all the more outrageous because she knew without a doubt that he pushed Ronaldo over the railing in a fit of rage and jealousy. She was sure that neither Paul nor Plato had done it, and there really was no one else with a motive.

She could not stand the loss of control over her own plans or the humiliation sure to follow when the truth about the captain was inevitably revealed. So she was told to clean up the loose ends. With Paul off the ship, it was up to her to complete their plan. When she finally found Sidney alone, Darcy and her friends interfered and ruined everything.

She knew all that she had done was right because God had sanctioned it. Even so, she was sinking in a sea of doubt and muddled mental capacity. What would happen when Officer Smythe found out she lied about her relationship with Paul? *He will figure it out now and blame me for everything.* "What should I do?" she cried again. "I'm so confused. Please speak to me."

What is going on here? Smythe asked himself. Does she have yet another lover on the ship who somehow convinced her to commit these atrocities? But that is crazy. No one in their right mind could be made to do what she had apparently done. He could not suppress a shudder as he edged further forward. Still standing sideways, he peered between the door hinges.

Suzanne was seated on the couch with both feet on the floor, her shoulders hunched forward. She was still wearing her uniform slacks and jacket, and her hands were resting one on top of the other in her lap. From his position he could see a large blood splatter on the front of her white blouse. She began to speak again, but it was obvious she was not looking at anyone in the suite. Instead, she was gazing at the ceiling with a decidedly crazed expression.

"This is your fault. You can strike me down if you want to, but all of it is your fault. You told me to kill Plato and Espen, and I did. Please, tell me what to do now," she wailed as she began rocking back and forth in her seat.

Smythe should have known better, but his body was rigid, and he'd been standing with his knees locked. Now he wobbled on stiff legs and caught himself just before he fell against the door and into the room. That would not be a desirable entry. It had been a long time since he was involved in a confrontation like this, and he knew he had to loosen his muscles and breathing in order to complete this mission. With a shake of his head and one big quiet breath, he regained his balance and again peered into the room.

With a jolt of surprise and revulsion, he realized that she was indeed alone and appeared to be talking to herself or to an imaginary individual. There was no doubt now. Suzanne was insane. Unbelievably, it sounded as if she was talking to God and blaming him for her actions.

Schizophrenia, he thought. A rush of memory brought back the extreme caution required in encounters with homeless sufferers of that disorder on the southern California streets of his previous life. Some poor souls were completely out of touch with reality, hearing and responding only to voices in their heads. Most were benign, but some were extremely violent.

Cold sweat collected under his arms and rolled down the inside of his shirt. Breathing deeply, he carefully switched the Ruger to his left hand while he wiped his palm dry against his thigh. Then he repositioned the weapon and placed his left hand against the door.

Very slowly he pushed it aside and forced himself to step through the opening. Suzanne looked up, and recognition lit her face. "Oh, hello Tom. Espen is not here, but can I do anything for you?"

Her normally radiant smile was a stiff slash reminding him of the lurid grin on a cadaver in rigor. He spoke softly to her while slowly approaching the sofa. He came to stand in front and slightly to one side of her with his right leg resting against the compact coffee table.

"Suzanne, Espen is dead. You know that. Just like Ronaldo and Plato. Do you know what you did tonight?"

"What do you mean?"

"Come on, Suzanne. Let me help you. Please stand up and come with me now."

"I don't want to go anywhere, but if you insist . . ."

She slid forward on the slippery leather to the edge of the seat and looked up directly into his eyes. She seemed perfectly normal now, and he shivered as he thought of all the times he and others had been mesmerized by that exotic stare that now seemed so feral. He lowered his weapon only slightly, but that was enough. With a smooth agile lunge she came off the seat, and he saw the flash of the bloody six-inch kitchen blade as she drew it from between her legs.

He was almost too late, *and almost dead*, he thought, as he jumped to the left and felt the knife point rake down his right arm. He fell forward using his left hand to pin her knife hand down on the seat, while he pushed the gun barrel into the side of her head. Kicking the table out of the way, he got his legs under him and tried to regain his composure. He wrenched the knife from her grasp.

She sobbed and her body went limp. She resumed pleading with God to help her. Carefully, he put the knife in his back pocket, then pulled his radio free and called for help. He was trying to regain his composure and to remember fragments of the police training he learned and implemented so many years ago.

Placing his hand under Suzanne's elbow, he helped her onto her feet. Then he told her to turn around, all the while pressing the gun to her head. Momentarily, three members of the security staff walked into the suite with identical expressions of disbelief. These are not police officers, Smythe reminded himself, and this situation is unprecedented.

After they handcuffed her, the three guards steered her out of the stateroom and down to the ship's small lockup. She didn't say anything during the process and appeared completely docile. Smythe followed them into the corridor and watched until they entered the elevator. Then he bent forward so his head almost touched his knees and clenched his right arm. Blood was oozing through his shirtsleeve, but he knew it was only a deep scratch. Gratitude and relief washed over him that he had not had to shoot Suzanne, and those feelings were quickly usurped by tremendous guilt.

He should have taken more action in response to Mick Clayton's warnings about Suzanne and Paul. He knew now he had been somewhat blinded by her apparent normalcy prior to this cruise and of course by her relationship with the captain. He understood the depth of the complacency he had fallen into in this cushy position and the knowledge that his priority in every situation was to protect his employer from adverse publicity. Sure he had quit the cop business because he hated the violence, but he was never a coward and never avoided his duty.

The gun was still dangling from his injured arm. He slowly straightened up and pushed it into its holster. Then the thought came to him in a flash of enlightenment that in all likelihood he would be fired. No matter how unreasonable it seemed, the cruise line would make him the scapegoat because he failed to stop Suzanne before she killed the captain and attacked passengers. It happened on his watch—a familiar story. He hunched his shoulders then arched his back and drew a deep cleansing breath. He would have to think about how he felt about that.

75

He moved slowly into the elevator and punched the button for deck 1. On the ride down he tried to analyze where he had dropped the ball, but it was too soon to put everything in perspective. When he arrived at sick bay to have his wound cleaned and bandaged, he looked around in dismay at the forlorn group of passengers. The crisis was not over yet, and Suzanne would probably have even more to account for by the time it was.

He crossed the small waiting room to where Darcy was sitting beside Mick, still lying on the gurney. She squinted up at him, which was the best she could do with the hammer still pounding in her head, and gingerly touched a lime-sized lump that had arisen just behind her left ear. "What happened to your arm?" she asked.

He was shocked to see how pale Mick was as he lay there still unconscious and barely breathing. Without a doubt he was in grave condition. "Let's just say Suzanne is not going to hurt anyone else, and this is not a serious wound. How are you doing, Darcy?"

"Suzanne? Oh, that's good I guess," she sighed with little affect. "The doctor says I have a mild concussion and gave me some Tylenol. He told me I don't have to take any precautions except to rest as much as possible for a few days. Like that is likely to happen." She tried and failed to suppress a sob as she looked back at Mick. She kept her eyes fastened on his face as tears streamed down her cheeks. "Just to be sure, I'm supposed to get a scan at the hospital in Valparaiso."

"I don't know what to say," Smythe said quietly, shaking his head. "I'm feeling responsible for not realizing what was really going on with Suzanne and Denezza." He didn't wait for or expect a reply. "I'm going to get my arm bandaged and talk to the doctor about Mick's condition now."

Charlie, Don, and Sidney had changed from their wet clothes to hospital gowns and Charlie and Sidney were sitting with blankets still wrapped around them. All were suffering from the effects of hypothermia but were told they would be fine within a few days.

The doctor x-rayed Don's anterior shoulder dislocation to make sure there was no fracture to the humerus, or other tangential injuries. Then he injected muscle relaxants and a local pain killer directly into the shoulder. Don sat on the edge of an examining table with his upper arm against the side of his body, and his lower arm bent at a ninety-degree angle against his chest, while the doctor gently rotated his lower arm and shoulder out to the side. Because Don's muscles and ligaments were tight, it required three painful tries to coax the joint back into place.

Now, feeling much better, he laid on his back against several pillows with his arm secured firmly to his chest. Charlie sat next to him holding his hand, and the two gazed sadly across the room at Mick and Darcy.

Sidney was also suffering from the physical shock of her ordeal and severe emotional shock as she forced herself to accept that Suzanne, a woman she didn't even know, had tried to kill her and that it was because of Paul. Her husband had not been acting as if he loved her for a long time, but the idea that he would intentionally harm her? It was devastating in a way she could never have imagined, despite the disheveled condition of their relationship.

How could she have lived with him and put up with his withholding of affection for so long only to end up such a victim? Well, she answered her own question. What had she been thinking to have allowed herself to be so weak and to stay with him at all? She realized she was lucky to be alive.

Looking across the room at Don, she was overcome with gratitude because he undoubtedly saved her life. She couldn't envision staying above water for the seven minutes the ordeal lasted without him. He and Charlie risked everything for her, and Charlie was also a hero. He had put the life raft's small oars to good use, paddling all the way back to where she and Don were struggling, and then kept them afloat until the launch arrived a few minutes later. She would never forget his calm, quiet voice, as he knelt in the raft with his head down next to hers, urging her to hang on just a little longer while he held both her arms up over the side of the raft.

Mick was another story entirely. The doctors packed his wound to staunch the blood flow and continued giving him fluids. Other than that, there wasn't much else they could do except to tell Captain Early to get to Valparaiso as soon as possible. So with the ship flying along at its top speed of twenty-four knots their ETA was just under an hour, a slip was being cleared for them, and ambulances were supposed to be waiting at the dock.

All Darcy could do was talk to him and hold his cold, clammy hand. She appeared to be praying intermittently but actually had fallen into a trance of positive thinking as she bent over him. She willed his lungs to draw each shallow breath. The doctor measured his blood pressure every few minutes and at last reading it was 70/40—still declining. Mick was dying.

76

My exhaustion was complete and completely understandable. I stood just inside the front door and looked around the room for a while. It had been five weeks, but it seemed much longer. My cozy little home seemed foreign and much emptier than I remembered. A few steps into the living room, I set my duffel bag upright, lowered the handle, and just left it there. Crossing into the breakfast nook, I couldn't help but smile at my beloved 1950s chrome metal table with the slightly scratched sunny yellow Formica top.

I slid open the large window in the back wall to let fresh, crisp Colorado air rush into the room on the bright sunlight. I hoped it would erase some of the stuffiness and also lift my spirits. It didn't help much because I was feeling as shaken and at odds with life as I had ever been.

I hadn't eaten a proper meal since leaving Valparaiso twelve hours before, but there wasn't much in the way of food in the house because I had cleaned out the fridge before leaving on the trip. I opened a cupboard and stared at the meager pickings. Finally, I opened a can of tuna and ate it straight along with a glass of water while I stood at the kitchen counter. Not exactly the gourmet meal I had become accustomed to on the ship. I sighed and thought about unpacking, but my mind was trying to go somewhere else. Finally, I gave in.

Even when things turn out all right and everything should be straightforward, they can still be complicated. The past week was a nightmarish blur of nights in a two-star Valparaiso hotel, taxi rides between there and the hospital, and anxious days spent watching over Mick as he teetered on the edge.

The U.S. economy was tanking along with my meager savings. My finances were not in the shape they should have been, where they would have been, if I'd been a little more prudent over the past ten years. Jason's investments were dwindling too, but he came through for me by paying the fee to change my airline ticket, and six nights advance on my hotel bill, before he left me in Valparaiso and flew home.

He had also come to the hospital with us to see if he could do anything for Mick, but after talking with the emergency and intensive care staffs, he told me there was nothing he could add and that he sincerely believed they would do everything possible to save him. The injury was life threatening but not complicated. Mainly, he had lost too much blood, had a collapsed lung, and his heart had stopped twice.

Still, I wished desperately for a more sophisticated U.S. hospital. Jason and the hospital staff assured me that a trip at that time would have been Mick's last. After four days in something akin to a coma and multiple blood transfusions, he finally came around. On the fifth day he was still in bad shape but insisted on booking a flight to DC, so on day six we arranged for a stretcher and wheelchair to deliver him home to Senator Sawyer's waiting arms.

Part of my disjointed thoughts and frayed emotions stemmed from the unsatisfying way we parted at the Valparaiso airport. Of course he wasn't in any shape to discuss details of our relationship. I kept hearing his last words to me before the attendant pushed him onto the plane. He looked up into my eyes from the wheelchair and smiled weakly. "I'll call you soon." But even then the miles loomed between us.

There's no way it was just a shipboard romance, I thought. Yet everything that happened ending with Mick and Sidney nearly losing their lives had somehow tainted our beautiful experience. In a way, we both wanted to forget the whole trip . . . except for Rachael, of course.

The realization of what Suzanne had done was also raw; poor Captain Espen. None of us could believe the depth of her insanity and the senselessness of the murders she apparently committed. We knew Paul would have to be held accountable too, but it wasn't clear how, since he was back in Vegas and apparently had not physically harmed anyone.

While Sidney, Don, Charlie, and I sat in the intensive care waiting room with Officer Smythe—Tom, he laid out the story of his encounter with Suzanne and her mental breakdown. He told us he was quite certain that Paul planned to murder Sidney during the cruise. He said he didn't understand all of it but that Suzanne admitted that Ronaldo and Plato were taking part in Paul's plan.

The most amazing part of the story was his conversation with Suzanne while she was being held in the ship's brig. He stayed there with her for the rest of the trip to Valparaiso and she seemed completely lucid when she admitted to killing Plato and Espen. She insisted, though, that Espen killed Ronaldo in a jealous rage and that it took her a couple of weeks before she realized it. She said her husband's unprecedented lapse in control set everything in motion in a different direction than the one she and Paul originally planned.

He shook his head in disbelief as he told us how, at the end, she asked him earnestly, "Don't you now see why God told me to arrange everything so that I could be with Paul?" He told us it was the most bizarre conversation he ever had.

He also explained how he had already called the FBI in Vegas about Paul and Suzanne, and hearing that, Sidney looked down to where her long slender fingers were laced in her lap. My heart nearly broke for her as I watched the tears fall onto her delicate freckled hands.

Tom also apologized repeatedly for not having realized Suzanne's condition sooner, but I assured him that he was not alone. I was feeling a lot of that myself, but even her husband had not understood how sick she was.

At least it was fortuitous that the ship was in Chilean waters while at least part of the drama was playing out, he explained, so that the government could not claim they had no jurisdiction over a crime at sea. Apparently, there are some holes in international law when it comes to cruise ships. Still, it was impossible to believe that a person as deranged and dangerous as Suzanne would not be dealt with appropriately. In any case, Tom handed her over to the Valparaiso police at the dock. He told us he hoped extradition to the U.S. would be swift. "Thank God the U.S. and Chile have a treaty," he said.

I hadn't spoken to Sidney since she left for her flight to Vegas the day after we landed in Valparaiso, and I was anxious to know how she was doing and where she was staying. I knew one thing for sure—she would not be with Paul.

With a heavy sigh, I walked to the phone mounted on the kitchen wall and plucked the handset. I reached for my purse, retrieved a number, and punched it in. After six rings I was about to hang up when the familiar voice sent a jolt through my body that was shocking but also music to my ears.

"Hello, this is the Alosa residence, Rachael speaking."

"Rachael, this is, um, Darcy? I just got home and thought I would follow up with you on our tentative plans for your visit . . . unless you've changed your mind, of course."

"Oh no, I haven't changed my mind. But how is Mick? Last time we heard from you it sounded very bad, and we've all been really worried."

"Well, it was bad for a while, but he is back in Washington now, and I'm sure your dad will be hearing from him when he gets a little stronger. What happened on the cruise, all of it, is so hard to understand. You know that the captain's wife turned out to be insane and murdered a crew member and her husband, right?"

"Yes, Dad found out about all of it from the security people on the ship, and they told him about the controversy regarding the captain as well. Dad said the cruise line is trying to keep it quiet but that Tom Smythe, the chief of security, is saying the captain was also guilty of murder. Dad said the State Department will have to check on the captain's wife who was left with the police in Valparaiso."

"Well, you know as much as I do."

"I can't even imagine how you must feel about everything. I know I'm still in shock just about us meeting each other and now knowing that it was brought about by such horrible events . . . it's disturbing, I guess."

"Oh, Rachael, you just might be saying what has been bothering me, but I couldn't find the words. How could this wonderful thing have come out of such a disaster? And I've yet to call Sidney to see how she is doing now that she's back in Vegas. I want her to come to Colorado to visit me as well so she can escape that environment while she waits for the divorce to go through. Meanwhile, part of me just wants to get on a plane for DC to be with Mick while he recuperates."

"My trip to see you can wait for a while so you can go to be with Mick."

"No, Rachael. You are by far my first priority. I can't wait for us to get to know each other. Never in my wildest dreams did I think I would be able to have you in my life again. Honestly, nothing else can compare. So when can you come to Colorado?"

"I'll have a break from school at the end of February, so about two weeks from now. How would that be?"

"That would be wonderful. It might be very cold here, you can never tell, and especially for you coming from a near-tropical climate, so bring warm clothing. Hopefully, in the meantime I will get a little more grounded and will take care of some things so we can relax together."

After the call, I felt a little better. What I told Rachael was the truth. I had Sidney back in my life and hoped Mick and I would be together at some point, but my daughter was the most important thing.

I requested some family-friendly leave from Shrinden, easily granted after my bosses heard what I'd been through, so I had a few weeks to work out this anxiety and get my life back on track. If only I could get rid of the spikes of painful anxiety that kept stabbing my brain, and I don't mean from the concussion.

I knew nothing would get resolved in just a few weeks, if ever, because the core of my entire belief system had been dislodged. There was simply no way I could rationalize the number and complexity of the coincidences that resulted in all these horrible and wonderful events. I was still clinging to the knowledge, rooted deep in my nonexistent soul, that there were natural explanations for all of it. Right now, I was too tired to hold the web of convoluted relationships in my mind long enough to analyze them.

I kept thinking that a yet-to-be-identified human being had somehow arranged for Sidney and me to be on the cruise together and for me to meet Rachael in Buenos Aires. Could Paul have had something to do with it, or even Bill Sawyer? I didn't really know them, and everyone was suspect. But the combination of other links in the chain of events . . . like Paulina being Mick's stateroom attendant and knowing the Alosas, Bill being Mick's friend as well as Ray's, and especially Mick's relationship with Sidney . . . well, they were either fated or one in a couple of million events.

I plopped down on my soft buttery leather sofa and propped my feet on the round yellow and green rose patterned ottoman to think. Even if I don't understand how all of it came together, rather than try to force myself to have faith in an unknowable entity, I'm still putting my money on a natural alternative, one that given enough time is completely knowable and most importantly part of the natural world. *So if it doesn't pull strings in our individual lives, it doesn't help me understand what happened on the cruise, does it?*

No, I thought, but the natural alternative surely runs the world according to a beautiful and complex set of laws. Laws that thousands of generations of brilliant and curious scientists have only scratched the surface of understanding. It could have been called God if the name had not already been assigned to a supernatural being.

I was deep into one of my bouts of musing. Maybe someday scientists will discover the what, where, why, when, and how of everything and will be able to convey the knowledge to the rest of us. The already-known science in fields like biology, physics, chemistry, astronomy, and cosmology is a good start. Maybe eventually our acceptance of theories of electricity, magnetism, gravity, plate tectonics, weather patterns, star formation, evolution, genetics, and the like, working together, will blend with our concept of God and become one and the same. When scientific knowledge finally replaces belief in a supernatural world, it will be the culmination of the progression from belief in multiple Gods once thought to control different aspects of the world to belief in one God that is supposed to control everything.

Unfortunately everyone cannot be a scientist, and the average person doesn't fully understand how these scientific disciplines work—they seem somewhat magical, and even long-accepted scientific principles are often suspect—and so there is still great skepticism and fear of the unknown, a different unknown than the one so many people readily accept based on faith alone.

These thoughts, which for a long time had come so naturally to me, now had new meaning, and I had new questions to ponder, but not right now. Sleep would help and talking to Mick, of course. I was certain he would call as promised tonight or tomorrow at the latest to let me know how he was doing. Finally I pushed the talk button again and dialed the cell phone number Sidney had given me.

77

I stared at the empty black screen. It seems so innocuous until you push the button, and then a whole world of information smacks you with knowledge, whether you are ready for it or not. I had decided what I needed to do but was taking another moment to gather my thoughts. Finally I booted up the machine and opened my e-mail. One hundred messages awaited me. Why hadn't I thought to get online while I was on the ship and check them? Too much going on I guess, and maybe I wanted the getaway to be complete. Anyway, the majority of them were spam, and within a few minutes I whittled the list down to ten messages from work colleagues and friends. I would get to them later.

Right now something else was pressing on me. It was the question or fear that had nagged me since shortly after meeting Rachael. What obligation did I have to tell her about her birth father? Worse, would I have to tell him that she was back in my life? It wasn't just me, I realized. She had two biological parents, and I was surprised she had not asked about him already. It was only a matter of time, but I knew absolutely nothing about what had happened to the man.

Google stared back at me dispassionately as I contemplated what I was about to do. The access was right here and so easy. Why did I never think of doing this before? Now seven days after Suzanne's attack on us, the idea finally came, and it wouldn't let go. Home for only a day, my usual intensity was already returning to its pre-cruise norm. I just cannot let anything go. Finally I typed in the name and held my breath waiting to see what, if any, hits I would get.

Talk about shock. I think I expected an obituary or maybe a link to a local or federal prison. To this day I can relive that moment sitting at my home office desk late at night with the sound of early crickets wafting through the open window, with absolute clarity—more vivid than any of the emotional events that took place on the cruise.

It's as if a whole world had unfolded over the past twenty years that was intricately bound to me but of which I had no awareness. That is because I let that current flow by me without letting it become part of my life. I hadn't cared, hadn't been curious, hadn't wanted to know. And worst of all, I never even entertained the thought that Brooks Larkin would pull himself together and gain success in life. My feeling was one of being left out of a part of my own existence. And that was the least of it.

Brooks Larkin, President and CEO of American Travel Corporation, with offices in Chicago, DC, Miami, and Las Vegas, and of course on the World Wide Web. My heart was pounding, and I gasped out loud as the description jumped out at me from the screen. There was no doubt. That same handsome face smiled back at me from the top right corner of his company's home page. He was older of course, with some gray at the temples. Other than that, the asshole looked about the same.

But twenty years is a long time, and Brooks was a brilliant guy even when he was completely overtaken by alcoholism. Why couldn't he have overcome his addiction and gotten on with his life, and why had I never considered that? He was a business and finance major when we were together, and he'd obviously been able to parlay his education and considerable personal assets to build a little empire and probably a financial fortune.

His name brought up three full pages of Web site entries, most of which related to travel industry advertisements and descriptions of his company. Several were articles about charity events and silent auctions for which he donated travel packages, including World of Seas cruises. My eyes almost popped out of my head.

I jumped up and raced for my travel carry-on, which I had yet to unpack. I dumped the contents onto my bed, and my hands shaking uncontrollably as I fumbled for the packet of travel documents Jason gave me when we began our trip. After ripping open the envelope, I stood motionless and in awe looking at the booking information. In black and white . . . what I had somehow known would be there.

American Travel Corporation had arranged our cruise, and the initials of the booking agent were BL. Something shifted inside me as I stood transfixed by this latest coincidence. What had Jason told me about his choice of which cruise we would take? How had he come across the specific excursion to Valparaiso? Had he booked by phone or online?

Then I saw the formal white invitation for a free tour delivered to my stateroom weeks ago. So much was going on at the time that I forgot about it until it was too late and we had already left Buenos Aires. Of course, the visit to that port turned out to be life changing, and a free tour was the last thing on my mind.

Now I picked up the envelope and looked more closely at the embossed logo, holding it under the bedside lamp. Unbelievable, but there it was all in white: ATC. I removed the card from the envelope and looked at it again. The tour would have taken me to Chico Palermo and the consulate. I felt queasy as my mind grasped the connections. Even without the arrangement we made with the consulate because of Paul, here was another avenue that would have taken me there and possibly to meet Ray.

Suddenly, I had a thread of logic. *This* was no coincidence. Oh no. No way. The president of a national travel agency does not personally book reservations. My ex-husband somehow orchestrated at least part of the "coincidences" related to my presence on this particular cruise. Why? If he was interested in my life, why not just contact me? I would have to ask Jason for specific information about how the cruise booking came about, but I knew beyond any doubt that I was seeing one missing link, one string possibly tying me to Rachael.

It didn't take very much imagination to picture a wealthy powerful CEO in the travel industry being able to locate people from his past and manipulate customers' vacation plans. It was farfetched, but not nearly so as accepting that all the related events of the past month could have happened only by chance.

I leaned over to finish reading the Web page. Another puzzle piece fell into place with the realization that Brooks's own address was his Las Vegas branch office. Is this a connection to Sydney and Paul? Of course, it has to be.

Now what was I supposed to do? I fell over onto the yellow-and-white daisy patterned comforter. My cheek rested against the cool fabric, and a light breeze ruffled the sheers above my head. *Oh, Rachael, it turns out your daddy is rich.* What effect would this have on my young girl's life?

The future was as unknown as ever, but now I had a clue. Rachael was going to bring me face-to-face, literally, with my past and with

Brooks. There would be no problem contacting him now. It was only a matter of when and how it would happen.

I wasn't thinking clearly yet, but one spidery thought was crawling through my brain. Maybe people don't change that much. Alcoholism might not be controlling Brooks's life now, but maybe he is still a jerk, and who knows what his motives were for manipulating me and possibly Sydney, and maybe trying to bring Rachael and me together? Since I did not believe for an instant that the tour offer from American Travel was a coincidence, isn't it obvious that he knew where our daughter was and tried to orchestrate our meeting?

Once again, I felt I had overlooked an alternate current flowing alongside me for nearly twenty years, one that I probably could have recognized if I hadn't completely closed off that part of my life and my memories. I still didn't see how Brooks could have knowledge about Rachael's life, but seemingly he did. Chance creates many coincidental events, but when they seem truly unbelievable, there is always a physical explanation. What I now knew about Brooks was extremely disconcerting, but at least the world was behaving more rationally again.

78

So none of this had anything to do with my associates here. Paul stared out the window at the obscene use of electricity playing out on the strip fifteen stories below. He was only now putting together all the events of the past five weeks, and embarrassment did not begin to describe how he felt about Suzanne having taken him in so completely due to his own weaknesses.

He'd already attended a tense but enlightening meeting with Sidney and her attorney—she certainly hadn't wasted any time—to discuss their settlement, and he was now resigned to giving her pretty much anything she wanted. Mousy and meek as she was, at least she was not greedy.

She had taken the opportunity to fill him in on the details of events after he left the ship and explained her fortuitous reconnection with Darcy Farthing. Finally that part made sense to him, but the coincidences, including the presence of Mick Clayton given his previous affair with Sidney, did not. She didn't seem to have any qualms telling him about that affair now. He didn't know Clayton and had only suspected Sidney's past infidelity, but deep down he hadn't really believed she had the balls to act behind his back.

Then safely tucked behind the conference table between her attorney and his burly pock-marked colleague, a thinly disguised bodyguard in a $1,000 suit, she accused him of plotting to get rid of her. She said she was positive Suzanne's actions were all initiated by him and that in the end she and her friends narrowly escaped death indirectly at his hands. The threat was not even thinly disguised. Give her what she was asking and leave her the hell alone or else she would volunteer more details to the authorities than they were asking for.

But it was the description of Suzanne's final rampage and apparent murder of Plato and her husband that physically sickened him. For two days, since the meeting with Sidney, he'd been plagued with nausea and diarrhea and had stayed cooped up in the suite most of the time.

His suspicions about the captain apparently were correct, but the fact that Suzanne was a homicidal schizophrenic who heard God telling her it was OK to kill people was about as cliché as anything he ever heard. The fact that this mental illness existed in someone he thought he knew so well and loved was beyond frightening.

But despite his own misjudgment of Suzanne and the fact that he did hire crew members to kill his wife, he was as angry as he had ever been with Sidney as well as Darcy Farthing and Mick Clayton. They interfered with the one thing he cherished above all else—control—and even though they inadvertently saved him from Suzanne's madness, he could not let their meddling stand. He would make sure they eventually paid.

But revenge would not be coming right away. The thick glass muffled virtually all the traffic and tourist sounds creating a surreal conflict between the tumult down on the street and the silence inside the suite. Paul turned from the window to face the contemporary sharp-edged black-and-white décor and felt the coldness of the room deep in his bones. Sidney hated his decorating choice saying that she constantly felt as if she was visiting a commercial business, rather than her own home. He quickly blocked out a disturbing and contradictory emotion related to her that he did not begin to understand.

Instead, he focused on the phone call he'd recently received from Special Agent Grant Murray. Getting a call from the FBI field office was disconcerting in itself, but knowing that he had to show up for an interview at the John Lawrence Bailey Memorial Building over on Lake Mead Boulevard in two days was driving him as crazy as Suzanne apparently was. He was somewhat confident he could talk his way through everything by virtue of the fact he hadn't actually done anything except have an affair, hardly a crime, and he truly had not known how insane Suzanne was.

His role in the plot against Sidney might never be proven if Suzanne kept quiet, but he knew an exhaustive investigation would be undertaken, and eventually in her madness Suzanne would probably reveal everything. But would she be credible? Sidney said Suzanne was temporarily incarcerated in a Valparaiso jail, and Paul entertained the thought that perhaps he could go there and silence her. He almost as quickly dismissed the idea when he realized it was actually a crazy one.

On the other hand, he knew the real threat would come from that weasel, Smythe. He might already have information to put the plot against Sidney together even without Suzanne's testimony. That was where he was most vulnerable. Paul understood very clearly that hiring someone to commit murder was first-degree murder nonetheless, but he wasn't sure about the complexity of the law in this circumstance since the target of the hiring was still alive while several others were not. With that thought he rushed back into the bathroom.

79

The choice of Las Vegas rather than Chicago or Miami for his "home" office was undeniably based on the glamour and excitement of the town as it was ten years ago. But that was then, and as Brooks Larkin stared out at the lights of the strip just a couple of miles up Las Vegas Boulevard from his Main Street office complex, he realized how much the intrigue of the place had waned for him. *Too much of a good thing always ends up being a bore.*

Of course, now it didn't really matter where he physically located himself. The whole world of travel . . . his whole life and his empire were just under his fingertips. He sighed, pushed the keyboard back into its slot, and thought about going home. He almost chuckled out loud at the thought of it. It wasn't what you could call a real home—the incredibly large and luxurious penthouse in the Stratosphere Hotel.

Why the hell he had chosen that place was beyond him. There was nothing homey or relaxing about listening to the screams of roller-coaster riders just two stories above his suite on the roof of the monstrosity. Now he guessed he was just too busy to think about finding another place, especially when he spent so little time there.

The band of myriad blinking lights in every color imaginable extending south all the way to McCarran International mesmerized and oddly relaxed him. Sort of hypnotic or meditative, he thought. Sitting quietly in his modest office looking out the giant south-facing window was one of his favorite pastimes. This is where he did his best thinking—and scheming. *I wouldn't be so alone,* he mused, *if I hadn't fucked up my life so royally with drinking.* Now an AA veteran for fifteen years, he was always clearheaded and would never slip back into that fog and loss of control. He had so much to lose now. Then again, he'd lost just about everything important twenty years ago.

He let himself think about his decidedly one-sided relationship with his "family." *The only real family I'll ever have even if they don't know it.* He had so many plans for his daughter he had never been able to act upon. But now he dared to feel a rush of excitement that soon, very soon, that would all change. How strange life is, he thought, as he let old memories flow through his relaxed mind.

He hadn't been in quite his usual drunken stupor, thank God, when he had the fateful encounter with the Alosas at the Italian restaurant on Central Avenue in Albuquerque. He almost fell off his stool when he saw the couple walk through the door with Ray carrying Rachael in his arms.

Of course he kept his distance and did not allow his daughter to see him. That evening he experienced something profound that was at the root of his eventual sobriety. He watched the new little family for an hour with a growing sense of horror at what he and Darcy had done.

It was about three months since the adoption, and the beautiful little girl behaved normally and appeared to be happy. His feelings for her had been ambivalent at best, and he behaved outrageously toward her mother, but now, seeing the happy family enjoying their pasta just thirty feet away, Brooks knew he had thrown away something precious and irretrievable.

He followed them outside and watched as they piled into their vehicle. As they pulled out of the parking lot, he wrote down their license plate, and that information plus his eventual recovery and the power afforded him by his rise in the travel industry changed everything. It was a simple matter to identify Ray and discern who he was and what he did for a living. So much was a matter of public record, including his government employment.

And so Brooks spent more than fifteen years vicariously living a family life through the Alosas, following their trail around the world from one consulate to another. He watched Rachael grow into a beautiful young woman from afar, through descriptions and pictures on various state department and local Web sites and unprotected social networking sites. He even made two trips—one to Italy and another to Ecuador—where he surreptitiously watched their homes for glimpses of Rachael as she came and went, enjoying her normal if somewhat exotic life.

Then of course there was Darcy, the lost love of his life. As insane as it might be, that is how he felt. During all those years, while business-wise he was on top and flying high, personally he was simply stuck in a holding pattern.

Brooks's thoughts turned to the astounding events of the cruise, the ones he had tried to control. Just for kicks, through the reservations process and conversations with Dr. Jason Johnson, Darcy's distracted travel companion, he easily arranged for her and Sidney to be on the same ship. Since he was keeping tabs on Darcy on a regular basis, it was not surprising when he saw her name on the cruise inquiry on World of Seas' Web site. It was a simple matter to intervene to ensure she and Dr. Johnson were booked on the same cruise he was arranging for Paul Denezza. Of course, he knew that Rachael was living in Buenos Aires, and he decided that somehow she had to meet her mother.

At first he planned to book himself on the cruise to make sure his plan worked, but finally he decided to use his employees to lure Darcy into a meeting with the Alosas. Two of his people were on board the *Sea Nymph* with different American Travel Corporation tour groups, and they briefed him daily regarding the bizarre crew member deaths and rumors about the captain and his wife.

Of course, to ensure the safety of his clients who were passengers, he also called his friend, the ship's chief of security, Tom Smythe. The relationship between World of Seas and ATC went back many years and cruises, including at least ten previous tour groups on the *Sea Nymph*.

Over the years he and Tom got to know one another well and built a rapport without ever meeting in person. With Brooks's careful questioning, Tom informed him of additional details including the possible involvement of passengers Paul Denezza—who Tom pointed out was from Las Vegas—and a woman named Darcy Farthing. Brooks became alarmed and couldn't fathom how Darcy could be involved in crimes on the ship. How he wished he'd gone along on the cruise himself so he could figure out what was going on.

Paul was another story. Brooks knew him well as a fellow Las Vegas businessman. He was also aware Paul was a hard character and potentially dangerous. As a "peer" it was only natural Paul contacted Brooks personally whenever he needed travel reservations, and Brooks had routinely provided this service for years.

He was well aware that Paul was married to his old acquaintance and Darcy's friend, Sidney, and he always kept his distance from her. In fact, he declined a wedding invitation from Paul for just that reason. It would not be to his advantage for her to know he was living just down the strip. Avoiding contact with Sidney caused problems for him a number of times when they were all invited to local civic or business functions. He actually lost business opportunities by declining invitations.

From everything he knew about Paul, he had his own strong suspicions about his involvement in what happened on the ship, and these were positively cemented when Tom told him the FBI had agreed to get involved.

What he still could not get over was Darcy meeting the Alosas and Rachael without his intervention. He knew about Paul's passport problems that took him to the consulate that day, but how the reunion came about was still a mystery. Having seen many photos of Rachael over the years, he knew Ray would immediately be intrigued by the physical similarity between his daughter and Darcy. So he instructed one of his tour guides to convince Darcy she'd won a free shore excursion in a shipboard drawing. The idea was that she would accompany their tour group to the famous Palermo Chico neighborhood and the consulate, where Ray would briefly welcome the touring passengers. When Darcy did not respond to the invitation, he was disappointed and assumed his little reunion plan was not going to work.

He also had a great working relationship with several staff members at the U.S. consulates who from time to time helped his clients with trouble they got themselves into on shore, as well as routine travel issues. Over the years he learned that diplomatic communities in foreign countries were very close, almost like extended families. So whenever he called Buenos Aires, he made it a practice to politely ask about Ray and his family, establishing a guise of familiarity.

About a week after the ship left Buenos Aires he called the ship to discuss an ongoing problem with one of his passengers who had gotten himself arrested for drunkenness while he was in the city. When he asked about Ray, he did not expect to hear the story that poured forth. Everyone at the consulate was excited and amazed about a strange and wonderful coincidence that reunited Ray's daughter with her birth mother, a passenger on the *Sea Nymph*.

He was stunned to hear Darcy had gone to meet Ray on her own. It was puzzling and amazing. Now that Paul was back in Vegas and Darcy was at home in Colorado Springs, Brooks intended to find out exactly how it came about.

He stood and reached for his jacket. Shrugging into it, he allowed himself to believe his plans—at least they were partly his—were about to unfold into the life he'd been denied and both Rachael and Darcy would see he was prepared to enrich their futures in more than one way. Thank God he would soon be reunited with his family. *And maybe God really had a hand in bringing us all together. After all He helped me embrace sobriety through AA, and clearly, there is no other explanation for the way these events have come together so neatly.*

80

Rudy Tapia swaggered along the dark narrow corridor toward the woman's cell. The other prisoners were sleeping as best they could in the dingy, drafty cells, but he knew she would be waiting for him. As Chilean prisons went, this one was not too bad, and it recently became infinitely better for him. Even his love life at home with Esther had improved. She seemed to be slightly less resistant to him since he began venting his lust with the prisoner. As he drew near the heavy metal door, he was already aroused with the anticipation of his nightly conquest of the exotic beauty placed in his keeping.

He ran a grimy hand through greasy black hair pushing it off his blackhead-stippled forehead and ran his tongue over his protruding teeth. He understood he was an unattractive man and was not surprised when at first the woman resisted him.

She fought him like a tiger, scratching and clawing until he lost control and knocked her head against the wall. After several nights of repeated beatings, she stopped fighting his 250-pound bulk. For the next six nights, she laid under him docile and quiet as he raped and terrorized her.

She apparently never said a word to anyone about their relationship, and he was proud of his manly prowess. His position as the carabinero responsible for taking care of the inmates between the normally peaceful hours of 1:00 and 5:00 a.m., was turning out to be very satisfying.

Processing of drunks and other new prisoners took place in another building from that which housed resident prisoners, so Rudy rarely encountered anyone during his shift. *Surely,* he thought, *Chief Contreras must know about my activities,* and he believed that this was a sign of the leeway and privilege afforded him.

He glanced over his shoulder at the door leading out to the main lobby then continued on as he fumbled under his protruding belly to unbuckle his belt while trying to suppress his violent emotions. He knew he must restrain himself for if he inflicted much obvious damage to the woman, things would quickly get complicated for him.

In the dim light from the overhead bulb, he peered up ahead at the floor, puzzled at what appeared to be liquid running from under her cell door into the drain in the center of the corridor. *What the hell is that? Did the stupid bitch urinate on the floor?* A wave of anger coursed through him as he approached, but his mood quickly changed to alarm when he saw that the liquid was bright red.

He stepped to the barred eye-level window being careful to straddle the narrow stream and tentatively looked into the cell. *Madre de Dios! ¿Qué demonios?* What the hell? He abruptly backed up against the wall opposite the door and bent forward, trying unsuccessfully to suppress his gag reflex. After a minute passed and he had finished retching, he again approached the door. With a shaking hand, he managed to insert his key in the lock and pushed open the door.

Suzanne was lying on her back on the floor with her arms outstretched and elbows bent at right angles to her body. Blood was still leaking from a gaping jagged wound in her left wrist into the stream that still trickled down the slightly slanted floor. Blood soaked the upper half of her blue prison jump suit as well as the surrounding floor. Arterial blood had sprayed across the small cell and soaked the bed four feet from where she lay.

He stood transfixed and bewildered as his eyes systematically searched the small room for a weapon. He saw nothing because of course she had been given nothing that could possibly harm her or anyone else. He turned his attention to the mass of black curls lying across her face. The once beautiful hair looked like a dirty, matted rat's nest.

Rudy ventured a few steps closer trying not to step in the blood and circled around behind her head. He bent down, peering at her with his head to one side, and then gently moved her hair with his finger to get a better look at her extraordinary face. Instantly, shock propelled him backward once again, and he landed painfully in a sitting position against the cement wall.

Her eyes and mouth were wide open, and blood filled her mouth forming a thick cake on her teeth. In fact, the entire lower half of her face was bloody and distorted with pain. He felt his gorge and his pulse rise with the realization that the crazy woman had literally chewed through her own wrist. He quickly jumped up and stumbled from the cell to the phone at the end of the corridor.

Chief of Police Thomás Contreras was awakened from a restful sleep next to his wife, Elena, by his cell phone ringing annoyingly on the bedside table. It was only 3:00 a.m., and he was not happy to be returning to the prison at this time of night.

It was a short drive though, just long enough for him to think about how he had known there was going to be trouble of some kind the moment he saw the American prisoner. Never before in his life, much less in his jail, had he seen such a tall, exotic, and beautiful woman, even as she stood on the dock clearly distraught and disheveled. He knew his officers were men of great honesty and integrity but also of great passion and they would have difficulty handling such a prisoner. She was very different from most of the women who spent a few nights in his jail. They tended to be either homeless hags or filthy whores and were of little interest to his men.

Of course, the thirty thousand Chilean carabineros—formerly the national police—included many women, and about twenty of them served under Thomás. During the day he made sure one of them was always on hand to tend to the American female prisoner's needs.

He tried to resist even accepting her, but the cruise ship's chief of security insisted he would be risking an international incident if he did not incarcerate her until the U.S. authorities could decide what to do with her. The officer pointed out that the cruise line could not keep her on board the ship and could not just leave her on her own. She was in fact an insane murderer.

Despite her blood stained shirt, he found this hard to believe as he watched her standing on the dock, head hanging down with tears falling onto her ample chest. The officer told him to call whoever he needed to in the Valparaiso city government to get reassurance. This he had done, and the mayor agreed that she must be taken into custody. If she committed the crimes in Chilean waters, the mayor said, the city and even the country could suffer terrible publicity and ostracism if they did not appear to be good citizens of the world community.

And so Thomás told himself everything would be all right for the short time until the U.S. authorities came to take her off his hands. The first day, an American diplomat assigned to the American Citizens'

Services Unit at the embassy in Santiago, an hour's drive away, arrived to visit the prisoner. To Thomás's eye the young woman looked not more than twenty years old. She seemed extremely uncomfortable in the prison environment, and the prisoner did not appear at all receptive to her efforts. The girl left quickly, and since then no one else had come. He was starting to wonder if anyone actually cared about Ms. Moretti.

Now he was afraid he'd made a grave mistake allowing Rudy Tapia to remain in his position as night jailer. Thomás reluctantly assigned him to that post rather than fire him when he realized the man was particularly aggressive and too violent for routine street duty. When the woman arrived, he should have at least assigned a second officer to accompany Rudy on his solitary shift. What he really should have done was get rid of him. Now the idiot was obviously involved in something terrible that Thomás would have to hide from his superiors lest he lose his job as well.

He thought about how he'd noticed over the past few days that the beautiful woman was becoming less and less communicative. At first she talked and prayed annoyingly, out loud and nonstop. Several times a day she demanded to know if anyone—particularly a man named Paul—had called about her. Even in her dire situation and accommodations she tried to take care of herself—at first. Then he noticed she seemed to have stopped eating, talking, and showering.

Had he turned his back on the situation? He admitted to himself he hadn't tried to investigate her condition. Instead, he told himself the U.S. authorities would show up any day now. Driving through the quiet deserted streets, he at last gained some insight into his own behavior. Perhaps he too had not fully trusted himself with her in the forced intimacy of the prison environment.

He arrived at the jail and parked his topless green 1998 Jeep Wrangler with two dented fenders at the curb in front, rather than take the time to drive around back to the parking lot. He hopped over the car door, jogged up to the entrance, and swung the door wide. As he passed by the startled night receptionist seated behind the desk reading a romance novel, she started to rise and speak to him. He silenced her with his hand and hurried to the iron door leading to the cell block. He punched his ID code into the panel to the left of the door and pushed through the instant the lock clicked open.

Immediately, Rudy came hurrying up the corridor toward him with a look of sheer panic, which Thomás found to be extremely foreign and almost comical. He could smell the man before he arrived and was disgusted to see his uniform was disheveled with his shirt hanging out over his trousers. The tan material stretched over his gut was dripping with vomit.

Panting and sweating, Rudy rushed to within six feet of Thomás, who stretched out his arms and yelled for him to stop where he was. In his condition and with his frantic phone call, it did not take much imagination to figure out that Rudy was involved in some way with the prisoner's apparent suicide.

"OK, Rudy. Listen to this very closely. You will now tell me exactly what has happened here. If you lie to me or do not tell me everything you know, I will not protect you, and I suspect you will be out of a job. After you explain this to me you will go home and stay there until I call you. You will not speak to anyone about what has happened here, and you will spend the time pulling yourself together so you can calmly and convincingly answer questions about how you found the prisoner already dead and there was nothing you could do. *Lo Entiendes?*"

"Si, I understand, Chief Contreras. I will do exactly as you say."

Thomás listened in horror and outrage while Rudy told him exactly what took place over the past week and tonight. When he was convinced he'd heard the entire story, Thomás somehow controlled his impulse to punch the *imbécil* in the face and rudely dismissed him. *"Ve, sal de mi vista"* "Go, get out of my sight," he hissed. Then he slowly proceeded down the corridor to inspect the body.

81

Tom Smythe looked out the third-story window of his mediocre hotel room at the Miami coastline. He was viewing it from a very different angle than he was used to, and several taller buildings blocked his view of the ocean and port district in the distance. After spending two days in Florida, he finally felt as if he was recovering from the long flight back and from the stress of the last few days of his employment.

The *Sea Nymph* left Valparaiso three days after arriving, amid a flurry of denial and backpedaling in response to media coverage of the deaths and attacks on board. World of Seas flew another captain in to take over the ship, and it left on schedule to retrace its course around the horn to Rio. A number of passengers—but less than might be expected—had cancelled their reservations.

When the ship arrived at the Ushuaia harbor three days later, Tom was handed his termination notice and was unceremoniously left there to find his way home. This was standard protocol for fired employees, and he spent two days trying to book flights back to Miami. Jobless and homeless, he thought as he watched the cars jammed up on the highway behind the hotel. It seemed he should be feeling a lot worse, but in a strange way he was relieved.

Being fired from World of Seas had been expected, but he was disappointed and angry with management for discounting his report on the captain. It was just a bureaucracy after all, and they believed the cruise line would not survive if the public believed it had employed a murderous captain. He could give them a little benefit of the doubt because Espen's friends and colleagues in Davie, Florida probably could not believe the accusation.

But he knew Suzanne was sincere in her confession, and she had no reason to admit to only two of the three murders. Her psychological disorder seemed to manifest itself in truthfulness about her crimes because she still believed what she had done was right. World of Seas managers also washed their hands of her and seemed not to believe they had any responsibility for the calamity she left behind as they quite literally sailed off into the sunset.

Yesterday, nine days after Suzanne's final meltdown, he received the shocking phone call from the State Department notifying him she'd killed herself in the Valparaiso jail. After leaving her on the dock with the chief of police, he called State to report what had happened and to ask that he be notified regarding her eventual extradition. Notification of her death was not what he was expecting.

Then he phoned Chief Contreras, who explained how they simply found her early in the morning in her cell, and she had already bled out from her wrist. He said she seemed subdued for a couple of days prior, but they thought she was all right, considering her circumstances.

Then Contreras haltingly explained how she used her own teeth to open the ulnar artery, and even the medical examiner had never seen anything like it before. Contreras said the doctor observed that if anyone ever really wanted to die, this woman surely did, because it would have been a very difficult and painful process to bite through the flesh and a ligament as well. The story was sickening and unbelievable, and it required several hours for Tom to settle down after hearing it. He still had difficulty keeping himself from visualizing what Suzanne's last hours must have been like. He was also developing a very bad feeling about what might actually have happened to her.

He knew he would eventually return to Valparaiso to determine how the authorities handled Suzanne and to obtain any additional information she might have provided before her death. Everything about this case was intriguing, and he was beginning to relish his involvement in it. He was sort of a free agent. Because of the confusion and questions about jurisdiction, and his new mobility, that role would probably work out fine.

The only other thing he could do was ensure the chain of custody for the samples he had collected and retained. He visited the Miami-Dade crime lab where he signed over the original plastic bag containing blood he took from the deck where Plato probably died. He planned to transport it to Vegas along with the results when they were available.

Without Plato's body, they could not get comparison DNA, but he had foreseen the problem and removed Plato's toothbrush from his stateroom immediately following his disappearance. It would yield plenty of DNA to match with the blood.

He also lifted fingerprints from the railing and gate where Plato went over and Suzanne attacked Mick and Sidney, the railing where Ronaldo had fallen, and from Espen's balcony as well. All the crew's prints were on file with World of Seas. This may have been a futile effort since so many people touched those railings, and he hadn't even been sure why he was doing it at the time, other than the good old police training kicking in.

Beyond the investigation, he would have to decide where to go and what to do. For ten years he'd basically lived on cruise ships. He kept his tacky little one-bedroom apartment in Ventura, California, just to have a U.S. address and to store some of his belongings, but he rarely stayed there. He almost always spent vacations and downtime at resorts wherever he found himself.

It was a fun and interesting lifestyle, but it was definitely over. No cruise line would ever hire him to manage security, and he had no interest in going back to being a guard, even if he could land that job, which was doubtful. And maybe he didn't even want to go there. Maybe it was time to move on and try something different as he began the second half of his life.

So what to do next? Fortunately, he had resources although his investments were taking a hit in the current market. Still there was plenty to live on for a few months at least. Besides, for the near term he planned to spend as much time as needed to ensure Denezza got what he deserved. In fact he had already called Agent Murray again and agreed to fly to Vegas to meet with him in about a week. Meanwhile, he intended to visit Mick Clayton in DC to see how he was recovering and talk to him about the case.

He knew that more than anything else especially with Suzanne gone, they needed Paul's confession. Or they needed to find another crew member who knew about Paul's arrangement with Ronaldo and Plato, presumably a plot to kill Sidney. If he'd remained on the ship, he would now be conducting interviews, beginning with the stateroom attendants, to find that person if they existed. It was still possible if the FBI or some other government agency could somehow require World of Seas to cooperate. This is one of the issues he wanted to discuss with Agent Murray and with Mick, because of his Justice Department contacts.

So there was plenty on his plate for now, and who knows what might be waiting right around the corner. He turned from the window and found his cell phone in the bottom of his briefcase. He had a number of calls to make and the first would be to a former cruise travel colleague, a friend of sorts, Brooks Larkin, to see about making airline and hotel reservations for his trip to Vegas.

82

The stitches pulled painfully, but Mick managed to get his elbows behind him and pushed his hands into the mattress to hoist himself up to a sitting position. *What a mess,* he thought as he looked around Bill's large guest room. Not the room, which was tastefully decorated in authentic and reproduction colonial pieces set against a soothing blue background. There was only a hint of floral design on pillows and valances. The mess was everything else. Mainly what bothered him was the disturbing news about Suzanne and the information he and Bill put together about jurisdiction for the crimes she and Paul committed.

Technically, the FBI is supposed to investigate any crime on a cruise ship involving a U.S. citizen when it returns to a home port, but it was unclear when the *Sea Nymph* would return to the U.S. Without an investigation and due to the complicated circumstances, the State Department did not move quickly enough to obtain an extradition order. Without that, the Chilean government or possibly just the Valparaiso police department were responsible for conducting an investigation and prosecution. He didn't see how they could have accomplished that, but regardless, they had let her die in their custody.

He was reeling from the knowledge about Suzanne's death. Tom Smythe had located Mick's cell phone number and called with the news early this morning. Surely being held in the Valparaiso jail was a punishment in itself, but could it have been so bad she killed herself using her own body as the weapon? Or was she just more insane than any of them realized?

Apparently, problems with investigating and prosecuting crimes committed on cruise ships were not news. Bill described a set of congressional hearings in 2006 where family members told hair-raising stories about unprosecuted and uncompensated crimes committed against their loved ones while on cruises.

He explained to Mick that the U.S. maritime law, the Jones Act otherwise known as the Death on the High Seas Act, covers seamen—a loosely defined term—on a ship owned and operated by American corporations. But cruise lines were not simple ownership entities. Most were multinational by nature so it was not clear that the law would apply in this case to compensate Ronaldo's, Plato's, and Captain Oldervoll's families for their losses. In reality, it might not apply depending on a legal interpretation of the World of Seas' Bahamian registration of the *Sea Nymph*.

Mick also learned that since the ship left from a Florida port, a state law applied that probably covered him because he was a part-time resident, and the Miami police department was beginning a rudimentary investigation of the attempt on his life. What would they investigate? Eyewitness accounts of Suzanne's final rampage might suffice, but any physical evidence that might have existed in the other deaths might not have been handled correctly if it was collected at all. The number of players involved and the physical distances would definitely complicate matters.

Meanwhile, the *Sea Nymph* was already back at sea with a slightly diminished boatload of passengers minus part of its former crew. In the aftermath of outrageously negative publicity, World of Seas issued a statement that swept the world's media and the Internet. The company assured the public they had fired the employees responsible for allowing the unfortunate events to unfold and the safety of their passengers was of utmost concern. World of Seas management denied that the captain who died in an unfortunate accident at sea had done anything wrong. It figured they would do everything in their power to make sure Suzanne took the blame for all the deaths, especially now.

While Tom Smythe could have been a little more diligent, Mick did not really fault him and was sorry to hear he had lost his job. He would apparently be seeing him soon and was intrigued to hear that Smythe planned to somehow continue the investigation. And so the whole mess came down to finding a way to prosecute Paul, hopefully with the help of whatever information Smythe could provide.

Earlier, Mick talked with his boss, Ken, about the possibility of opening a GAO evaluation of crimes on cruise ships. Ken was less than enthusiastic. Mick couldn't argue with his point that the international and jurisdictional issues would hinder such a study, since GAO had a limited budget and was not an enforcement agency. But Mick knew he would have to revisit the issue when he got back to work. It might be possible for Bill, as a member of Congress, to request such an assignment and GAO would have to respond to a formal Congressional request. Mick would get back on his feet eventually, and in partnership with the Justice IG, he would be in a perfect position to lead such a study.

Ken agreed to give Mick all the time he needed to recover from the horrific knife wound an inch from his heart, a collapsed lung, blood loss, and resulting weakness. Although clearly disturbed to hear Mick was staying at Bill's home, he couldn't very well say anything negative about it without demonstrating monstrous insensitivity.

Thank God for Bill and everything he was doing to help Mick. Now he was even acting as a nursemaid in between the daily visits by an actual nurse who changed his bandage, monitored him for infection, and helped with his personal care. And so here he was, improving a little each day but with a long road ahead of him.

He also knew that coming so close to death had rearranged his priorities, and he would have ample time to think about what he was going to do. When the doctors in Valparaiso told him his heart stopped for three minutes in the ambulance and he was lucky to have been revived with all his faculties intact, he decided then and there he would put the past where it belonged and begin to live his life again. All he wanted to do was return to health, get back to work, and forget about the horror of Suzanne's attack.

Except, what about Darcy? Even with his altered perspective, the feelings for her were right there on the surface. Yet trying to figure out how they could possibly bring their lives together compounded his exhaustion every time he tried to think about it.

He'd been back in DC for a week and thought of calling her several times every day, but for reasons that eluded him, he had not done it. Now he knew his procrastination was getting to the point where not contacting her was cruel, and it did not make sense given the depth his feelings for her. Wincing, he reached over to the bedside table and retrieved the phone yet again. He stared at the numbers he had long ago committed to memory.

Thoughts of his time with her on the ship were warm and comforting like the blankets the nurses piled on top of him at the hospital when his depleted blood supply caused uncontrollable shivering. He let himself float on the feeling of well-being and completeness he experienced when they made love in his stateroom or just sat quietly at the Center Bar talking and enjoying each other's company. A small involuntary smile tugged the corners of his mouth as his fingers hovered over the buttons.

Arleen Alleman

Epilogue

Looking out over the Colorado Springs landscape to the east, Rachael slowly turned her head to the right, stunned yet again to see Pike's Peak looming so high and so close. Golden rays danced and sparkled on its snowcapped peak under the clearest, bluest sky she had ever seen. Incredibly, she was lying in the warm sun on the deck at her mother's home on the bluff. Darcy warned her about the danger from the sun in the thin atmosphere at the 6,200-foot elevation, even in winter, so she slavered herself with 30 SPF lotion. Being a new daughter, she happily did as her mother suggested.

Looking over at the house, Rachael was surprised to see Darcy watching her from inside the screen door, holding a glass of fresh-squeezed lemonade in each hand. Before she could get up to help, Darcy set one of the icy glasses down on the little vintage table with its chippy yellow paint and pushed the screen along its screechy track. As she stepped onto the redwood planks and handed the drink to her daughter, they gazed at each other with the same gorgeous smile and bright blue eyes.

Darcy reached back inside to retrieve her own drink and then began to slide the door closed, as Rachael spoke quietly to her back. "I have been wondering if you can tell me anything about my birth father." There it was. The dreaded question Darcy knew would come eventually. She'd spent several sleepless nights and anxious days wrestling with how to answer it. In fact, the past couple of weeks were extremely difficult in many ways.

Mick did not call during the first week they were back from South America, and when he finally did, it was clear to both of them that their relationship would be a challenge. The news and details of Suzanne's suicide were shocking and Darcy was surprised at her mixed emotions about it. She couldn't help feeling sorry for the insane woman despite her still intense anger over Mick's near death.

Setting her other concerns aside, though, she realized her angst over Brooks and the knowledge she had about his life was futile and silly. There is nothing she could or should do but tell Rachael the truth about her father and then let her lead a path to the future.

As she turned away from the door, her breath caught at the sight of the golden halo around Rachael's head and shoulders. Everything in her field of vision appeared sunny yellow. It came in a flash of golden perception that over the past twenty years her life was colored by the last vibrant memory of her daughter in the Albuquerque sun. Subconsciously, she surrounded herself with the sunny color, which she now understood helped keep her sane and alive through her emotional torment.

Seeing the naïve look of anticipation on her daughter's radiant face, she wondered if she was witnessing the last look of simple contentment the girl would ever have. "I wondered when you would get to that. I hate to put a damper on your visit because I'm honestly having the best time of my life. You know, honey, I never ever stopped loving you with all my heart, and I've been punishing myself all this time for not having been stronger back then for both of us."

Rachael shifted uneasily. Looking down at her lap, she nodded her understanding. "I'm so sorry you have suffered so much because of me."

"Oh, Rachael, of course none of it was your doing. You haven't asked for details of why we gave you up for adoption, but I know you deserve to know everything. At the same time I have avoided even thinking about your father until very recently. As it turns out, he has apparently done very well for himself, and there is a possibility he already knows about you and your life. I'm sorry everything is so complicated, but you will eventually have to decide for yourself what to do with the information you get from me. Honey, the story of what happened between Brooks Larkin and me is not pretty, but I will tell you all of it if that is really what you want."

Want to know what happens next?

Currents of Vengeance

Darcy Farthing Adventures Book Two

Arleen Alleman

Excerpt: *Currents of Vengeance*

Lilith Schrom unwound her long tanned legs from her new black BMW 3 Series convertible and stood up. She smoothed the lap wrinkles in her tight brown silk wrap-around skirt while slowly gazing around the parking garage. Glancing down at her car, she ran her hand lovingly over the soft top. Then she looked up and still not seeing anyone about, bent down and dragged her purple sequined duffel bag out of the back seat. She stretched her back up straight and hoisted the strap over her shoulder. After one more look around, she strode to the entrance of Players Paradise.

On the way down two levels in the elevator she tried to ignore the smudges on the walls surrounding her. Upon exiting at the main floor her nose wrinkled involuntarily. This was not the sort of hotel she was used to and it seemed small and drab compared to the glittery strip establishments she'd frequented during the past several years.

Turning right through the casino, she followed the directions given to her. *Thank God I will soon be back home and I swear I will never come to this horrible city again.* The gaming tables commanded her attention as she passed, but because of her tight schedule, she looked away and did not hesitate. She hurried along to another set of elevators at the far back corner of the casino, opening the side zipper pocket of her bag as she approached. She stepped into the open car and inserted a room key into the security slot, then quickly pressed the button for floor 8 before any other guests could enter.

Lilith was thrilled to be living and working in the United States, and for the first couple of years after her arrival, she traveled around the astonishing country whenever her schedule permitted. She loved everything about it, but her favorite spots were Atlantic City and Las Vegas, especially the latter, for a while at least. She found Vegas the more glamorous of the two and the larger city offered complete anonymity. Not having anyone know about her visits was extremely important because when she was in town she assumed a completely different persona, that of a beautiful sexy player—definitely a far cry from her normal dowdy life.

Sadly, she discovered way too late she had a more addictive personality than she ever dreamed possible. Somehow over the past year she amassed a debt of $200,000 at her favorite casino and could see no way to repay it. Worse, she could not seem to stop herself from playing blackjack and poker, even though her losing streak extended back several months.

Her job at the Wilmore Neuroscience Laboratory near Boston did not exactly pay minimum wage, but still, her salary wasn't nearly enough to cover her mounting gambling debts. Thankfully, several months ago she was offered an opportunity to wipe the slate clean by carrying out this assignment. It was so dangerous it took a month for her to agree to the scheme. During that period her debt substantially increased. In the end, the new $50,000 car sweetened the deal considerably, and she reluctantly made the decision.

She knew very well if she failed—or worse, was apprehended—she would lose her career, and everything she'd worked so hard to achieve would vaporize overnight. No, she definitely did not want to return to Israel in disgrace, and so she must be very careful with what she was about to do.

She understood how fortunate she was to land her current position at the lab shortly after publishing her doctoral thesis in biochemistry at Tel Aviv University. Her work at The Adams Super Center for Brain Studies focused on deciphering brain activity related to devastating diseases. The results of her research there relating to potential cancer treatments or cures brought her instant recognition in Israel and later in the United States.

For ten years now, she had dedicated her life to running her experiments associated with treatments for cancer and diabetes in her narrow area of study, partially funded with grants from the National

Institutes of Health. She took great pride in knowing applied research teams were already using her basic research to develop methods of treatment and diagnosis for several cancers.

After stepping out of the elevator, Lilith stood in the foyer for a few moments to get her bearings. At this time of the evening, virtually everyone would be either gambling or at dinner. Seeing no one in the immediate area, she consulted the sign for directions to the rooms. She quickly strode down the hall and stopped in front of a door.

Holding her breath, she rapped loudly and as expected received no response. She let herself in using a housekeeping key and went straight to the bed. A moment of intense anxiety came and quickly passed. Drawing in a deep breath and exhaling slowly, she gently placed her bag on the bed and carefully began to unzip it.

In less than three minutes she completed her task and headed back to the elevators. As she nervously waited for the car to arrive, she could hardly stand still. When the doors opened, a rather unremarkable middle-aged man stepped out. He nodded and smiled at her, then walked down the hall in the direction from which she had just come. She had an urge to follow him just to see which room he entered, but decided her scientist's curiosity would not serve her well in this case.

She anxiously rode down to the casino, quickly retraced her steps to the parking garage and was soon driving down the exit ramp. She knew she should continue straight to Interstate 15 and head east toward home, but before she reached the highway entrance ramp just two blocks away, she convinced herself it would not hurt to spend one more hour trying to win back some of her money. She'd just completed a scary job and felt lucky. She wasn't about to stop at one of these downtown casinos, though. Instead, she turned around, found Las Vegas Boulevard, and headed south toward the familiarity of the strip.

* * *

Tom Smythe entered his room, threw his briefcase on a chair, and immediately undressed down to his underwear. He turned down the bed covers and set the alarm so he could catch an hour's nap before meeting Brooks for dinner. Then he slid between the sheets. As he drifted off, he was thinking about his earlier meeting with Brooks and about the deposition he gave to Agent Murray earlier in the day.

Half asleep, he rolled over to achieve a more comfortable position, but instead was jolted wide-awake by an intense stinging sensation in his leg. He yelped involuntarily and jumped from the bed. Knowing something had bitten him, he threw back the covers expecting to see a spider of some sort. What he saw near the bottom of the bed boggled his mind and made his stomach flutter.

Two very strange looking scorpions, each about four inches long, were curled into fetal positions with their pointed tails wrapped loosely around their bodies. That they were scorpions was evident, but these were not the normal whitish arachnids he was used to seeing in the southwest desert. Their front claws were too thin and the tails seemed fat in comparison to their bodies. But it was their color—a sickening pale greenish yellow—that made Tom's skin crawl *No, this pair did not find their way into the hotel from the surrounding desert.*

Even as he thought about grabbing a towel from the bathroom to capture them, the pain in his right ankle and calf was fast becoming excruciating. He staggered the few feet to the bathroom and pulled a bath towel off the rack. As he returned to the bed and threw the towel over the pair, gathering it up in a ball, his vision blurred and he began to wheeze. This was an unbelievably fast reaction and Tom suddenly felt overtaken by panic.

Attempting to clear his thoughts, he examined his leg and grew even more alarmed to see rapidly growing areas of swelling around two bright red sting marks. Obviously, he was having an allergic reaction to venom and didn't have a lot of time to waste thinking about it. His leg would not support him any longer and he sprawled across the bed. Now panic did not begin to describe the feeling, as he grabbed for the phone.

He realized he was going to vomit and his throat was rapidly swelling shut. Gasping for air, he willed himself not to throw up. By the time he reached the hotel operator his chest was pounding and his airway was almost completely blocked. The room closed in around him and the last thing he remembered was the operator's voice urgently asking him what was wrong.

Printed in Great Britain
by Amazon